D1076765

Blood
Prophecy

ALSO BY ALYXANDRA HARVEY

The Drake Chronicles in reading order:

My Love Lies Bleeding

Blood Feud

Out for Blood

Bleeding Hearts

Blood Moon

♦ ♦ ♦

Haunting Violet

♦ ♦ ♦

Stolen Away

Blood
Prophecy

ALYXANDRA HARVEY

BLOOMSBURY

LONDON NEW DELHI NEW YORK SYDNEY

Bloomsbury Publishing, London, New Delhi, New York and Sydney

First published in Great Britain in February 2013 by Bloomsbury Publishing Plc
50 Bedford Square, London, WC1B 3DP

First published in the USA in January 2013 by Walker Books for
Young Readers, an imprint of Bloomsbury Publishing, Inc.
175 Fifth Avenue, New York, NY 10010

A CIP catalogue record for this book is available from the British Library

ISBN 978 1 4088 3669 9

MIX
Paper from
responsible sources
FSC® C020471

Printed and bound in Great Britain by CPI Group (UK) Ltd, Croydon CR0 4YY

1 3 5 7 9 10 8 6 4 2

www.bloomsbury.com

This one's for my wonderful, tireless agent, Marlene, and everyone at Bloomsbury/Walker & Company! To Emily, who protected and promoted my babies with such care and enthusiasm, to the many publicists, copyeditors, art directors, and anyone else who worked on the Drakes in any way. Thank you, thank you, thank you. You made a dream come true.

And as always: a big fat thank-you to my readers. You guys just rock.

THE DRAKE FAMILY TREE

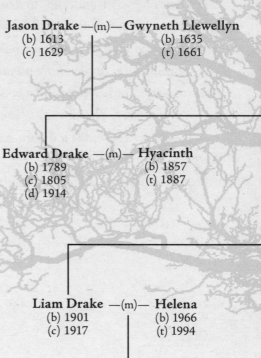

Jason Drake —(m)— **Gwyneth Llewellyn**
(b) 1613   (b) 1635
(c) 1629   (t) 1661

Edward Drake —(m)— **Hyacinth**
(b) 1789   (b) 1857
(c) 1805   (t) 1887
(d) 1914

Liam Drake —(m)— **Helena**
(b) 1901   (b) 1966
(c) 1917   (t) 1994

Sebastian   **Marcus**   **Duncan**   **Quinn**
(b) 1986   (b) 1987   (b) 1988   (b) 1990
(c) 2002   (c) 2003   (c) 2004   (c) 2006

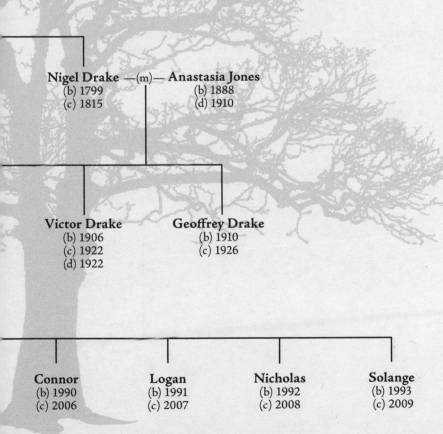

KEY

(b) ✦ Born
(d) ✦ Died
(t) ✦ Turned by another vampire
(c) ✦ Changed genetically into vampire
(m) ✦ Married

For a complete Drake family tree see
www.facebook.com/thedrakechronicles

Nigel Drake —(m)— **Anastasia Jones**
(b) 1799   (b) 1888
(c) 1815   (d) 1910

Victor Drake   **Geoffrey Drake**
(b) 1906   (b) 1910
(c) 1922   (c) 1926
(d) 1922

Connor   **Logan**   **Nicholas**   **Solange**
(b) 1990   (b) 1991   (b) 1992   (b) 1993
(c) 2006   (c) 2007   (c) 2008   (c) 2009

Prologue

Solange

Saturday night

I was a voice inside my own head.

I wasn't even sure how it had happened. I'd been hearing that strange whisper for weeks. At first I assumed it was my own subconscious. Or it was because I was losing my temper, since it seemed to happen the most when I was upset or annoyed, especially with Mom or Madame Veronique. But at some point I'd stopped recognizing the whispering voice as my own.

And by then it was too late. Frustration, bloodlust, and the need to find Nicholas after he went missing made me push too hard. It made me agree to Constantine's plan that I become queen instead of my mother, even though I never wanted to be queen. I'd watched my hands reach for the crown, plucking it from her bewildered grasp. I wasn't sure who was in control, but when the silver circlet touched my head, I definitely knew who *wasn't* in control anymore.

Me.

And again, I was too late.

Everything went red, then white. I fell through space. There was no up or down, no gravity, nothing to cling to. I clutched and grasped and found a jagged handhold here, a brittle foothold there, but it wasn't enough. I was clinging to a cliff that might as well have been made of glass. Everything was too bright. Vertigo tilted through me, and I jerked back into my body, but only for a brief moment.

Just long enough to see Lucy being dragged through the trees, to see Nicholas covered in blood, to see him bite Lucy on my command.

I struggled, but that voice came again, slamming me back to the glass cliff where I couldn't hold on for a moment longer.

I fell for a long time.

CHAPTER I

Lucy

Saturday night

The Drake farmhouse was like the chimpanzee enclosure at the zoo when feeding time was late.

You know, if all the chimpanzees were undead.

And insane.

"Um, hello?" I said, though I was pretty sure even sensitive vampire hearing wouldn't be able to pick out my voice from the chaos. "Solange and Nicholas are in trouble."

As expected, no one heard me. They didn't even notice Kieran standing right beside me.

The kitchen was crammed with dark-haired, fiercely scowling Drakes. Liam was drinking brandy, and beside him, Helena looked hollow with fury. Aunt Hyacinth had finally lifted the veil off her hat, and her scarred cheeks were pale. Uncle Geoffrey was searching through notebooks, and the brothers crowded onto the available ladder-back chairs. My cousin Christabel, newly turned, stood flattened against the wall, wide-eyed. Just a month ago she'd been human and unaware that vampires even existed. Then she'd been kidnapped and killed and turned into one—and the Drakes in this kind of a mood were still scarier than all of that had been. They were untamed, like thunder and lightning in a glass jar. You just knew, sooner or later, the jar would shatter into pieces.

Right now, exploding Drakes were actually low on my list of priorities. Not a good sign. But not exactly surprising, since I'd just been dragged into the woods by my best friend who, while wearing a crown, had ordered my boyfriend to drink my blood. Never mind that he'd been missing and we had no idea what had happened to him.

"Are they always like this?" Christabel stared at me. She was nearest to the door and was the first to notice me.

I swallowed. "No, this is something different."

"What the hell happened back there?"

"You tell me."

"Solange put on the crown," Christabel said. "And then everyone around her flew back into the air. Like . . . magic."

"Crap."

"Lucy?" Christabel asked.

"Yeah?"

"Could you not stand so close?"

I slid her a glance. "I haven't seen you in weeks, not since you got all fangy, and you still won't hang out with me?"

She flinched. "I can smell the blood under your skin."

"So?"

"So, it smells good." Her eyes widened farther, until I was actually worried they might fall right out of her head and plop on the ground. "And it's freaking me out!"

I edged away as she struggled not to throw up on her own shoes. Poor Christabel. She was so unprepared for the whole vampire thing.

"Hey!" I called out to the others.

"We can't burn the forest to the ground," Liam told Helena, his jaw clenching. "We'd never get close enough."

"A couple of fire arrows ought to keep the damned Chandramaa busy," she maintained. The Chandramaa were the secret guard who patrolled the encampment where the rare Blood Moon was being held. They basically killed any vampire who showed the slightest aggression. I assumed the only reason Helena wasn't a pile of ashes was because they were pledged to serve the queen.

But she wasn't the queen anymore. Solange was.

"We'll call that Plan B," Liam said.

"Mom's right," Quinn insisted. "We go in fast and hard now, before they have a chance to regroup."

"It's tactically sound," Sebastian agreed quietly.

"Except that we have to split our focus," Liam pointed out, draining his glass. "Nicholas is still missing. Besides which, Solange gave the order," he added bleakly. "She's not a prisoner."

"But that's not Solange," I said. They still hadn't noticed me, or even Kieran beside me, and he was a vampire hunter for crying out loud. The guards outside knew we were here since they'd let us pass, but Quinn, who was smoldering not three feet away, hadn't seen me yet.

"We have allies in the camp," Liam said over his sons' arguments. "Best start there."

Helena rubbed a hand over her face. Her hair was coming out of its severe braid. "Agreed," she said reluctantly as her frayed temper cooled. "Much as I hate to just sit here, your father's right. If we force her now, we might lose her forever."

Quinn shouted his disagreement. Connor elbowed him to shut him up. Duncan glowered.

I hopped up onto the kitchen table in my muddy boots, trying not to brain myself on the chandelier. "I said, *hey!*" I gave up and whistled shrilly around my fingers, the way Duncan had taught me when I was twelve.

Vampire silence is like no other silence in the world. It's like when the power goes out and the background noise of furnaces, water heaters, and pipes suddenly vanishes. The usual soundtrack of breathing and small unnoticed human movements was gone. It was only that throbbing silence of so many pale-eyed vampires, fangs gleaming. Even I, who was mostly immune to their pheromones, felt my stomach drop. Adrenaline flushed through me, just enough to make me feel nervous and jittery, as if I'd drunk three pots of coffee.

"Nicholas is back," I repeated, my voice suddenly small and fluttery as a moth.

Liam had his hands around my waist and was lifting me off the table before I'd blinked. "How do you know?" he asked quietly.

"He bit me."

That vampire silence again, only so much worse this time. Liam's eyes glistened, and I was suddenly terrified he was going to cry. I swung my feet, still a few inches off the ground. "Can I get down now?"

He set me down with exaggerated care. "What do you mean, Nicholas *bit* you?"

I rolled up my sleeve to show them. The puncture marks were small and had already stopped bleeding. It just looked like I'd fallen on a barbecue fork. But I'd never forget the way he'd come out of the woods, covered in bruises and blood. Something had happened to him, something horrible.

"He didn't say where he'd been or what had happened to him," I said quietly. "But he looked bad." I bit my lower lip hard to keep it from wobbling. I didn't have time to wobble. Not right now.

"But he's in one piece?" Helena asked.

I nodded. She lowered into a chair, as if she just didn't have the strength to stand anymore. We stared at her. Helena never slumped. She was a force of nature, battering at the storm windows and storm cellars of the world. Liam grabbed her hand.

"Solange made him prove his loyalty by biting me," I continued. Quinn swore viciously. "She called me his bloodslave."

"Oh, Lucy," Aunt Hyacinth said. "You know—"

"That's not Solange." I waved away the rest of her comforting speech.

"She's gone darkside, Lucy," Connor said. "She's blood-drunk."

I shook my head. "Look, I know Solange better than anyone." Even if I'd spent the last few weeks wondering what had happened to my best friend. She'd changed, there was no denying it. "That wasn't her. So we have to help her!"

"We will," Uncle Geoffrey assured me, glancing up from his notebooks. "I'm sure there's something here that I'm missing. Her bloodwork has been unique."

"What, she has the vampire flu or something?" Duncan asked. He rubbed his jaw. I remembered Nicholas telling me Solange took him out just last week. "Hell of a flu."

"I know this is difficult," Uncle Geoffrey said. "But you have to accept that Solange has changed, Lucy."

"No one changes that much, that fast." I crossed my arms stubbornly. "And I know what I know. This isn't her. I mean, I thought I caught a glimpse of the old Solange, but then she was . . . gone. She doesn't even move like herself anymore, did you notice? She was all haughty and predatory."

Logan pushed away from the wall, lace cuffs fluttering. "Isabeau said there was magic," he said. "That's what knocked us on our asses when she crowned herself."

"Language." Aunt Hyacinth clicked her tongue.

"Sorry. It's why the Hounds took off so quickly," he continued. "They were all muttering and whispering."

"Find out what you can," Liam ordered. "You're our best link to the tribe." The Hounds were decidedly reclusive and still might not help us. But Logan had been initiated as one of them, and, more importantly, Isabeau loved him. And Isabeau kicked all kinds of magic ass. "How did you find Nicholas?" he continued.

"He found me," I said. "Well, us. Solange had dragged me out into the woods." I shuddered. "I . . . it's not her," I repeated.

Logan put his arm around me comfortingly. "How did you get away?"

"Kieran found me."

They finally noticed him, all at once. Helios-Ra training had his hand hovering over the stake at his belt. "Nicholas tagged her shirt," he explained. "Probably while he was biting her. We had it worked out weeks ago so when the chip activated, I followed the coordinates."

Helena looked impressed. "That's my boy." She almost smirked. "He'll be okay." She glanced at me. "We've had our own little plan, Lucy. Nicholas knew to ally himself with Solange if it came to a choice."

"*What?*"

"We knew we might need someone to keep an eye on her," Liam elaborated. "Though I admit, I could never have imagined it would go quite like this. He's our best chance though. She'd believe he'd stay by her before anyone else."

"Except for me," I pointed out.

"Yes," he admitted gently. "But the camp isn't safe for you."

My knees felt soft with relief. "Do you really think Nicholas will be all right?"

"Of course," Helena replied. "He's a Drake."

She hadn't seen him. I wasn't so sure even the legendary Drake blood was enough to save him from whatever had happened to him while he was missing.

"We'll have to kill her," a woman said coldly. I couldn't see her over all the people between me and the door. I didn't have to see her. I could hear her just fine. "I won't have Solange undoing the honor of our name. Tomorrow night, though tonight would be better. She's become a risk to us."

"Kill her?" I exclaimed, pushing through a wall of Drake brothers. "Who the hell— Whoa."

The vampire could only be Madame Veronique, currently the oldest Drake vampire alive and the matriarch of the line. I'd never met her before, had only heard the stories the others whispered about how scary she was. I'd assumed they were exaggerating.

They totally weren't.

Despite her words, she didn't do anything outwardly aggressive. Still, all the hairs on my arms and the back of my neck stuck straight up. I felt like a threatened porcupine, every quill bristling painfully. Her brown hair was in braids that reached her hips, under an embroidered wimple. Gold glinted off her circlet and the ribbons on her long, medieval-style dress. Her eyes were such a light gray they were practically clear. Not to mention glacial.

She was pale, small, and strange. She radiated otherness in a way the Drakes didn't, not even Aunt Hyacinth—and she was almost two hundred years old. Madame Veronique was eight hundred years old, and everything about her was deadly. She was the silent poison to Helena's blade. I shivered.

"Humans?" she inquired with faint disdain. Her gaze flicked over me, dismissing me as unimportant. Quinn and Connor stood in front of me regardless, shifting casually so that I was hidden. Sebastian blocked Kieran. "Haven't we enough trouble without your unruly pets?" Madame Veronique inquired calmly, after a terrifying pause.

Logan's hand clamped on my arm, and he dragged me out the sliding glass doors, Kieran at our heels. I didn't even have a chance to say good-bye to Christabel. "Come on, before Madame Veronique sics one of her handmaidens on you."

"She has handmaidens?"

"Yes, and they look like scary undead librarians."

"She really wants to kill your sister?" I asked as we hurried through the dark gardens. They were slightly overgrown, mostly roses and fields. My parents' gardens were crowded with vegetables for canning and herbs for Mom's health tonics. Not to mention the crystals planted everywhere to help everything grow. "Can she do that?"

"Yes," Logan answered grimly.

"But . . . your mom can stop her, right?"

"I hope so," he said, his charming smile gone. "I really hope so."

"We'll stop her," Kieran said, walking silently beside us. With his Helios-Ra training he was nearly as noiseless as Logan. I was learning, but I still cracked the odd twig under my boots. "Somehow."

"I'm going to see what Isabeau knows," Logan said, leading us down the driveway to Kieran's car. "Be careful."

"You too, Logan." I hugged him tightly. "I don't want to lose any more Drakes tonight." I got into the passenger side. Logan closed the door and stood there glaring at me until I locked it. "I should call Jenna," I said, grabbing my bag from the backseat. I'd taken her and Tyson to a bonfire party with friends from my old school. A vampire snuck in and one of the girls got bitten but, luckily, she was too drunk to remember details. Tyson brought her to the school infirmary, and Jenna and I tried to track the vampire. That was when Solange's guard had grabbed me and left Jenna unconscious in the forest.

"She's fine," Kieran reminded me. "Spencer got your message and called Chloe and she got help. Jenna's back in her dorm room with a few stitches and a mild concussion."

I couldn't even argue; I was too busy yawning so hugely my cheeks tingled. Despite everything that was going on, I fell asleep on the way back to the academy. The adrenaline crash made me feel as if I were made of wet cement. When Kieran nudged me awake, I tried to punch him.

"Lucy—shit!" He ducked, smacking his head on the window.

I blinked blearily. "Sorry, Kier. Habit."

He rubbed the back of his head. "Between you and Hunter, it's a wonder I have all of my limbs still intact."

I snorted, rubbing my eyes. "You dosed me with Hypnos."

"Three months ago. Let it go, Hamilton."

I just grinned sleepily. "You have so much to learn."

CHAPTER 2

Solange

I landed on a spiraling stone stairway. I was in some kind of a castle, with dust in the air and dried flowers and hay under my bare feet. I wore a burgundy, medieval-style dress, the kind Madame Veronique favored, with a jeweled belt. She'd been turned in 1162, so my brothers and I studied the twelfth century thoroughly enough that I knew the window in front of me was actually a murder hole, through which archers shot arrows at advancing knights. Sunlight pierced through it, landing on the back of my hand. I snatched it away, as if it were an arrow being sent back at the castle.

It didn't burn.

Or make me feel weak.

I lifted my fingertips to my teeth. I still had the triple set of fangs but no desire to sink them into the nearest living thing. I wasn't thirsty for blood; and lately I was *always* thirsty. I wanted to enjoy it, but I knew I couldn't stay here. Mom would say get to high ground, or at the very least, don't let yourself get cornered. I was definitely cornered in the stairwell, but if I went up to the roof, I'd be just as confined.

I hurried down the steps, listening carefully for the sounds of the castle's inhabitants. I could hear the clang of a blacksmith's hammer from somewhere outside and the whinny of a horse, but nothing closer. The walls were whitewashed and painted with a rose in the center of each stone. Tapestries hung in the rooms that opened up out of arched doorways. I smelled smoke and roasting meat, and dried lavender under my feet.

I made it to the great hall without being discovered. I peered around one of the tapestries and saw wooden tables and benches, a fire in the center of the room, smoke rising to the rafters and staying there. Women bustled back and forth, wearing dresses similar to mine. A young boy brought in an armful of firewood. I slipped away, into the sunny courtyard.

This made no sense. I should be in the Blood Moon encampment. I felt insubstantial, as if the precious sunlight were glittering right through me. Was I invisible? Insane? Was this time travel? Or another vision like the one Kala had given me? It didn't feel the same but it was definitely some kind of magic.

It didn't matter.

I needed to get back home. I needed to make sure my family was safe and that Lucy wasn't bleeding to death in the woods. And that

Kieran didn't hate me, before he left for Scotland and I never saw him again.

I remembered the taste of his blood in my mouth. I'd bitten him long before that girl's voice started to merge with my own. I couldn't blame that on her, not entirely. She'd been there, in the background, but I'd been the one to bite him. Hadn't I? And he still hadn't turned me over to the hunters. He'd called Lucy instead of the Helios-Ra. He deserved an explanation. An apology. Everyone did.

When had I stopped being the girl with dried clay on her pants and a pathological need for solitude?

Guilt and worry would crush me if I let it. Right now, it didn't matter why or who or what. It only mattered that I get myself back home to fix the mess I'd made.

I skirted the edge of the courtyard, staying in the shadows of the rosebushes and lilac trees. I passed stables and a dovecote. There was an orchard in the distance, and a gray stone wall beyond that. I stepped on the dirt path, uneven with ruts from carts and horseshoes, toward two round towers. I ducked between them, waiting for a guard to shout out my presence. Instead, there was only the wind and a stray chicken pecking for seeds. The sun was warm and pleasant on my face. It had only been a few months since my blood-change, but I still missed the daylight.

A longer path went downhill to a lower bailey and past a huge field full of armored men practicing with swords and lances and maces. Grizzled, scarred men fought with broadswords. A cluster of younger boys, around my age, loosed arrows at a haystack painted with red and white circles. Men on horseback charged at a heavy sack on a stick, and if they didn't hit it just right, it swung back around to knock them off their saddles.

A shaft of sunlight fell on me, making my dress look like fire and my skin glow like pearls. The shadows around me darkened, as if my glowing skin were leeching the light from everything around me. I was a lantern on the longest, darkest moonless night.

Every knight stopped abruptly and turned to stare at me. And they didn't look happy.

Guess I wasn't invisible after all.

Crap.

I didn't hesitate, didn't wait to see if they were just curious, instead of outright malicious. I tore down the path toward the last two towers in the wall and the forest beyond it.

I already knew I wasn't going to be fast enough.

The wind snarled in my hair as I pushed myself on. The pounding of hoofbeats behind me got closer and closer. Stones dug into the soles of my feet, cutting through my skin. I was running fast, but not vampire-fast. An arrow sliced past me, slamming into the ground. Daggers were sharp steel rain, just close enough to pin my hem to the ground. I tripped and tore free.

Hot horse breath echoed in my ears as a destrier caught up to me on my other side. The horse was massive, muscles bunching, sweat stinging the air, and clumps of dirt hitting my ankles. Light flashed off the length of a sword. No one spoke, which made it all that much more awful. They didn't shout or laugh, only ran me to ground like a rabbit.

When I risked a glance over my shoulder, I actually stumbled to a stop, shock freezing my muscles so suddenly pain lanced through me.

It wasn't just angry knights chasing me.

It was also a dragon.

I'd never seen anything like it. It was the dark, deep indigo blue of a summer evening, with curled silver talons and leathery wings that shimmered like the northern lights. Its scales gleamed like oil, like dark rainbows. When it opened its mouth, I saw teeth the size of my arm. I couldn't help but remember the old woman in the cottage whispering the prophecy about the next Drake daughter.

Dragon by dragon defeated.

Flames hissed between giant teeth. Leaves caught fire and shriveled into ashes; grass burned around my toes. I covered my head and continued running. The knights stayed together, dispersing only when the flames got too close to them. The two knights at the end of the line turned to lift their lances at the dragon. Their horses struggled to bolt. No training in the world could make them ignore the giant-ass fire lizard in the sky.

Suddenly, being queen of the damned vampires seemed like a pretty great alternative.

The guard in the gatehouse was too busy taking cover to stop me. There was nothing between me and the forest except for a bridge over the moat ahead.

And the dead bodies.

The moat was full of bloated corpses, with bite marks all over them and bloodstains on their clothes. Blood floated in perfect ribbons in the water. I tried not to stare as I dashed down the bridge, which shook and trembled under the weight of the horses and knights still following me. The dragon followed us all, with no preference for whom he cooked to death with his breath.

Sweat clung to the back of my neck. One of the ribbons on my dress smoldered and I had to yank it off. The tip of a sword tore through my sleeve, piercing my skin. The dragon's breath was like thunder overhead, and its shadow swallowed the light when it passed over me. I smelled burned hair and scorched earth. One of the knights fell screaming into the moat, the tunic under his armor on fire.

Flames ate through the grass. I kept my eyes on the forest. I needed to find trees that were too thick to let horses pass, where the leaves would conceal me from the dragon. The flap of leathery wings created whirlwinds of dirt and pine needles. My long skirt twisted around my knees. I stumbled, heat searing my back.

And then I was finally in the woods, running over the uncomfortable ground, heedless of my bare and bloody feet. It was cool and green, like the forest at home. The dragon blew more fire, scorching through the top branches. Birds fled, squawking. Fiery leaves fell over me, burning like paper. The knights stopped at the edge of the field, suddenly losing all interest. They turned as one and stalked back to the castle, as if they'd forgotten all about me. I found a sturdy tree and clambered up into the branches to get a better view. The knights had turned away even before the dragon lost sight of me and concentrated his fiery breath on them.

I clearly wasn't a threat here in the dark green woods.

Which meant the castle was worth protecting.

Or at least something *within* it was worth protecting.

It wasn't much to go on, but it was more than I'd known before. You know, when I was actually *inside* the castle, where the knowledge would have done me some good.

And then, dragons and dragon knights weren't the only thing to worry about.

CHAPTER 3

Lucy

Sunday afternoon

I spent most of Sunday dialing Nicholas's cell phone even though I
knew he wouldn't answer. There was no reception at the camp, but
I was secretly hoping he'd gone back to the farmhouse. It was early
November and the sun had only set about an hour ago. It was too
early for him to answer regardless of where he was. I called Bruno,
just to feel as if I was accomplishing something. "Any news?" I asked.

"Afraid not, lass," he replied, sounding tired. "We'll be sending
a message in a few hours. And waiting to get information from those
still loyal to us at the camp."

"And Nicholas?" I almost ached just to say his name. Everyone
was always so worried about Solange being hurt because she was so

unique, or about me because I was human. It had never seriously occurred to me just how hurt Nicholas could be. The Drake brothers just seemed to have the kind of luck that saw them through bad places. I never imagined that their luck could run out.

I couldn't think like that. He wasn't missing, he wasn't dead. In fact, he might very well be Solange's only hope. I had to hold on to that. "Madame Veronique hasn't murdered anyone yet, has she?"

"No. You know the Drakes are harder to assassinate than that. So don't make yourself sick."

"Sheesh, one little breakdown and everyone fusses," I teased. When Nicholas first went missing, I'd climbed onto the roof of the dormitory and screamed until Theo, the school nurse, threatened to sedate me. With the kind of year I'd had, I figured I was allowed a little primal scream therapy. "I'll see you soon, Bruno."

My homework was therapeutic: kickboxing, track, and practice at the gun range. My mom would be horrified at just how relaxing it was for me to watch those targets spin. I was heading back to the dorms when I spotted Jenna in the archery field with her crossbow. I made a detour. Archery was my favorite class and Jenna's aim rivaled mine. I watched her arrows slam into the targets and itched to hold my miniature crossbow. Jenna turned when she heard my footsteps.

"Are you okay?" we asked in unison.

She lowered her crossbow. "Just a headache. I'm off classes for a few days, but I just couldn't sit around anymore." Her red hair was in its usual ponytail, a bandage on her temple. "You saved me. If you hadn't sent Spencer to find me, I probably would've ended up as a vampire's next meal."

"I didn't save you," I said, flinching. "It's my fault you were there in the first place."

She shrugged. "Who knew civilian parties could be so dangerous?"

I snorted. "Now you know." Since this was Violet Hill, that wasn't even the scariest party I'd ever been to. "And I'm sorry."

"Hey, you got me back home. We're even." She frowned. "Is it true you saw the Blood Moon camp?"

I nodded. "Yeah. Pretty cool. You know, if my best friend hadn't dragged me out back with the intention to drain me dry."

"Dude."

"Yeah."

Jenna shook her head, then winced, her hand touching her temple briefly. "I thought Solange was this delicate little thing."

"She's sick," I said steadily. I thought of the bats that followed her around. "Does rabies make people crazy?"

"I have no idea. You think Solange has rabies?"

"I guess not." I wrinkled my nose. "But the bats are new. And weird. Everything's weird."

Kieran pulled up into the student parking lot behind us, distracting me from any other theories. There were so many *Hel-Blar* roaming the area that the school was now allowing third-year students to patrol, not just fourth years like Hunter. As a third year I needed to be with a fourth year or an alumnus, and I could only go during certain classes. Since Hunter and I both wanted to keep an eye on Kieran, we alternated forcing him to patrol with us. Plus, it got me off campus, which was a bonus. I wasn't in the mood to deal with prejudice and bullies tonight. We both needed the distraction as we tried to figure out what to do about Solange and Nicholas.

Nicholas.

Nope, couldn't think about that right now.

"See you later." Jenna waved at Kieran and headed back to the dorm.

"You know that you and Hunter aren't even remotely subtle," Kieran told me through the open window.

I just grinned at him. "Wave to the top-floor corner window over there. Lia's got a crush on you."

Kieran's ears went red. "How does she even know I'm here?"

"I told her you were coming," I said, sliding into my seat. I dropped my knapsack full of weapons at my feet.

"You're a menace."

"I was twelve once." I shrugged. "A little crush in a place like this can make a difference. She's got to think about something other than vampires."

"What, like you?" he remarked drily, reversing out of the parking spot.

"Come on, drive like you're cool," I urged him, ignoring his very valid point. "Pop a wheelie or something. It'll give her something to swoon over."

He laughed despite himself. "I can't pop a wheelie in an SUV, you lunatic."

We left the school behind, exchanging the security lights for dark fields and snow-choked orchards. We startled a cat, and a coyote darted across the road, but there were no fangs or pale eyes. I tried to twirl my stake through my fingers as if it were a magic-trick coin.

"Turn left here," I said about fifteen minutes later.

"I know what you're doing," he told me, but he turned anyway. The road cut through thick bushes and red pine groves. The moon was bright enough to cast blue moonshadows over the snow. If I squinted I could just barely make out a house light through the trees, close to the mountains. We passed the familiar landmarks: the lightning-struck ash, the boulder shaped like a bull, the hill where wild daffodils grew in spring.

My phone rang the very second we crossed onto Drake land.

"Lucy Hamilton, you just keep on driving."

I gulped at Helena's stern voice. "Oops. Bye!" I wrinkled my nose at Kieran. "Busted. Keep driving."

We headed into town on the only country highway in Violet Hill. The high beams glittered on frost and ice and the wet black pavement. House lights began to pierce the gloom.

"I'm on campus duty," Kieran said as he turned in the direction of the arts college tucked in by the lake. It made sense, since he looked the part, even if he wasn't covered in tattoos or paint like most of the other local students. Violet Hill had a small arts college, mostly catering to visual arts and literature students. You got to know the look of them after a while.

"Still going to the Helios-Ra college in Scotland?" I asked.

"Let's just get through tonight," he answered.

We walked through three dorm parties and two pubs, but they were clean. I peered into all the bushes, looking for *Hel-Blar*. Wherever they were feeding tonight, it wasn't here.

It wasn't until a couple of hours later, when we were heading back to the academy, that we saw something. A concert had ended in one of the bigger pubs, and the cold streets were crowded with students and taxis. There were girls in short skirts, guys holding one another up, and couples making out as they wandered home.

And a slender girl oblivious to the cold, standing in the snow in a thin dress. No, not just standing.

Feeding.

"Stop!" I yelled. "Stop, stop, stop! That's Solange."

Kieran practically wrapped the SUV around a mailbox in his hurry to pull over. Someone cheered, thinking it was funny. I flung myself out of my seat before the wheels had stopped moving. Kieran grabbed my arm as I darted past him. Momentum swung me around so I was facing him, spitting curses. "The hell, Black."

"It's called stealth," he snapped back, jerking me down behind the cover of the SUV. The fumes from the running engine turned to fog in the cold air, obscuring us. Kieran passed me a stake but I already had one in my hand. "And clearly, neither of you have it."

He was right.

Solange stood near a circle of yellow light from a street lamp, clutching a girl in paint-splattered jeans, with short spiky hair and a nose ring. Her fangs gleamed as her red lips lifted in a delicate snarl. Seeing her wearing red lipstick and a long dress was nearly as weird as everything else. She hated dressing up.

"Shh," Solange ordered when the girl struggled briefly. The girl went silent obediently. No one noticed them, but that was through sheer dumb luck. Any minute now someone would glance their way, someone would scream. Or the girl would die.

Because Solange was still drinking.

"Anyone could see her," I whispered, horrified.

"And she doesn't care," Kieran agreed grimly. "If any other Helios-Ra saw her like this they'd shoot her on sight, no questions asked. And they'd be within treaty rights to do it."

Solange seized the girl by the neck, tilting her head to a near-breakable angle. Her fangs sank deeper through skin and flesh, blood trickling slightly as if she were biting into a ripe peach. The girl made a fist just before her arm went limp. She struggled briefly, then just dangled. There was no pretending it was two drunk room-mates holding up each other.

There was too much blood for that.

Solange looked enthralled, manic. Deadly. So I did the only thing I could think of.

I threw a snowball at her head.

It didn't hurt her, of course, but at least it made her pause. She glanced up, lips curled. I scrounged around the ground until I found a rock at the edge of the flower bed behind me. I threw it as hard as I could and it hit her on the temple. She hissed, blood me welling on her pale skin. The girl in her arms slumped to the ground unconscious, moving so gradually, she could have been water freezing into an icicle.

Solange looked right at me then, and even through the fog of exhaust fumes, her glance was cold and sharp as a needle.

And then she smiled.

"That's definitely not her," I muttered. "And I'm getting that bitch out of my best friend."

"But not tonight," Kieran said, still crouched next to me, his jaw tight as bowstring. "Tonight we have to save them both. And soon."

He was right.

"You run faster than me," I said, straightening up. "So I'll pull focus while you get her the hell out of here."

I walked around the front of the car and stood in the middle of the street. "Wooo-hoooo!" I yelled, as if I was drunk and very, very annoying. Glances flickered my way but it wasn't enough. I looked at the building in the opposite direction of Solange, reading the sign over the door. "Free keg at Kinsley Hall!" I yelled.

Not everyone detoured to take advantage, but at least they were all looking at the crazy girl in the road and not the guy in black cargos chasing down a bloodstained waif of a girl who ran like a deer.

CHAPTER 4

Solange

I knew she was a witch the moment I saw her.

She peered out of a cave set back away from the smoke-tinted woods. She wasn't old, like the woman who'd spoken the Drake prophecy, or like Kala, or like the witches I'd read about in story-books. She was only a couple of years older than me, at most. But there was something in her eye, some distant, mysterious quality that made me think of Isabeau. She had half a dozen pouches on her belt and holed stones dangling from braided yarn in her long brown hair. She smelled like mint and mud, even from here.

"You're safe for now," she said. "Once the dragon leaves, the rest of them follow. They only really care about the castle." She smiled, stepping farther out into the haze. "They don't even know I'm here."

"Where exactly is 'here,' anyway?" I asked, still trying to catch my breath. "And how the hell do I get home?"

She blinked, emerging fully from the cave to stare at me. "You're her," she murmured. Her smile wasn't remotely comforting. Neither was her laugh. "Finally." She turned back to the cave, stopping to glance over her shoulder. "Are you coming?"

I paused but ended up following her, since I didn't exactly have a lot of options.

The cave was small and damp, with water running in steady rivulets through the crevices. It wasn't like the vampire caves; it was rough and unpolished without a single tapestry or rug to cut the chill. There was only a small fire in the back, a pile of pelts, a wooden chest, and iron lanterns stuck in the crannies.

"I'm Solange. Who are you?" I asked.

"Gwyneth. I've been hiding here for centuries."

"Um. Okay. And you know who I am?" I guess I should have been used to it by now, but I just wanted to be invisible and unnoticeable. The feeling was familiar, as worn as a fleece blanket. And it was another sign that I was finally back to being myself.

"You're the one she thinks about," the girl replied. "She says your name sometimes when she sleeps. When she's not too busy moaning and weeping." She rolled her eyes, clearly unsympathetic.

"Who?" I asked, even though I was pretty sure I knew the answer.

"Viola."

"Do you know who she is?" I crept closer to the fire, trying to warm my hands. The smoke from the fire made my throat hurt.

"Daughter of a lord, isn't she?" Gwyneth answered. "Spoiled, soft, and romantic. It was that last bit that got her killed, and trapped us here. That and her vampire blood."

"How?"

"I was the one that gave her the spell. I miscalculated," she admitted, crouching by the fire. "She wanted a love spell, the girls always did. By the time they were women, they'd come for babies or poison, but she was still a girl. And I didn't know then what I know now." She sighed. "Didn't like the man her father picked out for her, preening about bloodlines and kings. So she came to me."

"Love magic," I said grimly. Montmartre had tried a love spell to control me, just after my birthday. I still remembered the alien tingle of energy inside my brain and my body. It made me itch even now, to think of it.

"My grandmother warned me not to deal with the aristocracy and matters of the heart. She preferred healing poultices and midwifery but I found it unpleasant business." She wrinkled her nose. "Babies are messy."

I stepped back warily as she stirred the contents of a stew. "Is that a spell too?" I asked. "Because if this was a story, this is where I'd ask you if you were a good witch or a bad witch."

"This is mutton stew," she said, as if I was being ridiculous. "For supper." She shrugged. "As for the rest, magic is magic. What you do with it is your own business."

"But if the spell went dark, like you said, then you bear some of the responsibility, don't you?" Just like I had to take responsibility for whatever was in me that had allowed itself to be seduced by Viola.

Assuming I ever got out of this weird-ass place.

When she smiled, it was half wild, half sad. "Love magic is always dark."

I thought of Kieran and what we'd done for each other. He'd defied the Helios-Ra, he'd saved me from the hunters even after I'd bitten him. He'd given me his own blood the night I turned sixteen so I'd survive, so I'd change into the creature he was sworn to kill.

I honestly couldn't think of anything I'd done for him that would make it all worthwhile.

The indescribable rush of warm, living human blood filling my veins made me fall back against the damp cavern wall as if I'd been shoved. The ceiling of the cave whirled above my head. Vertigo, thirst, satisfaction all prowled through me like feral cats.

I flashed back to Violet Hill, the trees dripping freezing rain on my head and blood in my mouth.

A girl I didn't recognize fell to the ground.

I slammed back into the cave, head spinning. "No!" I closed my eyes, tried to will the spinning to bring me back home. Nothing happened. "No, please!"

Gwyneth circled me slowly, pursing her lips. "Haven't you figured it out yet?"

I glared up at her through my hair. "Figured out what? That I'm time traveling?"

"No. That this place isn't real."

"I'm pretty sure if I was having a hallucination you'd be Johnny Depp, not some mouthy witch girl with burrs on her dress."

"You're inside Viola's mind," she explained impatiently.

The fact that sunlight didn't drop me like a stone made more sense. "How do you know that? And why should I trust you?"

She snorted. "I don't care either way. But she wanted a spell that was beyond my ken. I was reckless and proud. And she was far more clever than I could ever have imagined. Her spirit survived, she just needed a body. And she waited until she found one. Yours."

"Why mine?" I asked, frustrated. "Forget I asked. She's a vampire. She wanted to be queen or whatever, right?"

"No, Solange. She wants so much more than that."

"What is there left that she can take from me?" I asked dejectedly.

"Whatever it is, she'll find it. She's been waiting and waiting for this chance." Gwyneth narrowed her eyes. "You must have worked powerful magic to let her in."

"I don't even know how to do magic," I said. Except for that undoing spell Isabeau had taught me. I'd had to go out in the middle of the night and pee on Montmartre's love spell. Not pretty. And I'd totally do it again. But that was months ago. "She didn't gain full control until the crown was on my head," I said, thinking back. "Before that it was just whispers."

"Magic always finds a way in. Viola should know." Gwyneth shook her head. "Vampires and magic. They just don't mix."

I was sure Isabeau would disagree, but then the Hounds knew all sorts of things the rest of us didn't. My family hadn't even believed in magic before this year. Madame Veronique had encouraged our ignorance for her own mysterious purposes.

"So you can't use magic to set us free?" I asked.

"Won't," she corrected. "Not again. And she doesn't know I'm here. Her knights don't come into the woods."

"Ever?" Come to think of it, for knights bent on killing me, they'd given up fairly easily once I'd entered the forest. "Not even to kill me?"

"She doesn't want to kill you. She needs your connection to your body. She needs someone strong enough to survive the possession." She shook her head, stirring her cook pot again. "And if she catches you, she'll do worse than kill you."

"There's worse?"

"She needs you alive here. She doesn't need you comfortable. Believe me, you wouldn't like spending centuries in an oubliette." I knew that word. Oubliettes were dank holes in the dungeons of castles where prisoners were kept in the dark, without room to even stand up in. I shuddered. "After a while, you'd be lost. Nothing would be real, not even this place."

"What, like a ghost?"

"Worse." She laughed and it was a hollow sound.

"Why don't *you* leave? She's not possessing you."

"I don't have power here, not that kind."

"But . . ."

"Leave it, Solange. I'm not your princess in the tower to be rescued." Having uttered those very same words more times than I could count, I nearly snorted at her. But her expression was odd, tortured. Whatever it was she was feeling was physically painful. Blood oozed down her arms, soaked into the hem of her dress. The scar across her throat started to bleed as well. Her cheekbones poked through her mangled cheek.

"You're hurt!" I took a step toward her but stopped when she snarled wordlessly at me. I glanced away to give her a moment of privacy.

I forced myself to remember the training my parents had given me, the bits and pieces of strategy I'd witnessed, the long boring political intrigues that fascinated my father, the vicious fighting arts that made my mother glow.

"She's protecting something," I realized slowly. When I turned back to Gwyneth she seemed fine, and even the blood had faded from her skirt. "Viola's got something in that castle." I felt certain of it. Mom would point out that no one spent that much energy protecting something unless it was precious, unless it did one of two things: made you weak or made you strong. And at the end of the day, that was the same thing.

Which meant Viola was vulnerable.

If I could just figure out what it was she was safeguarding, I could use it to fight my way free. I stood up, finally feeling like a Drake again: determined, reckless, and just a little bit eager to kick some serious ass.

Gwyneth tilted her head. "The last girl Viola possessed spent ten years weeping in the back of my cave. It was annoying."

I paused, momentarily distracted. "There were others?"

"Some. None of them lasted. They died or went mad. Even the vampires couldn't handle it, their bodies just gave up. Viola had to retreat back here, to this warped hole between dimensions." She grinned wolfishly. "But none of them had the look you have now."

"Good." I went to the mouth of the cave. "But how do I get back in?" I wondered aloud, sorting through the weird cauldron of useless historical tidbits I knew about the twelfth century. Madame Veronique was very strict on making sure her descendants knew about the beginning of the lineage. I could be grateful for it, and still not trust her.

Twelfth-century Britain: people used spoons and knives to eat, since forks hadn't been invented yet, dresses were called kirtles, women wore wimples over their hair and hawks were kept as hunting pets.

Trebuchets, courtly love, Robin Hood.

Useless.

Wait.

Trebuchet.

They were basically giant wooden slingshots used to pelt castles with fire and stones during warfare. Nobles were always fighting one another or the king, kind of like vampire society right now. Everyone had elaborate escape routes, such as tunnels leading out of the castle.

And if they could get out, then I could get in.

A small bubble of hope nearly made me giggle. I cleared my throat. "Gwyneth?" I looked back at her. "Where's the tunnel?"

She tilted her head, impressed. "You might survive after all, girl."

I just arched an eyebrow. "The tunnel."

"Three leagues past that boulder, by the oak. Stay right."

I had no idea how far a league was, but I didn't care. I had a plan. "Thank you."

She nodded. "Oh, Solange?"

"Yes?"

"If they catch you, don't lead them back here."

It felt good to be doing something. Even if it didn't work, I felt less crazy just attempting it, less like I was suffocating under spiderwebs. The soft woods also helped to calm me, the green light and the smell of leaves and earth. It didn't take me too long to reach the oak tree, acorns crunching under my feet. I had to duck right under the branches to see the curtain of thick ivy on the other side. I wouldn't have noticed it if I hadn't been looking for it.

I pushed through the tangled ivy until my knuckles scraped against a wooden door. The boards were soft and covered in moss. The hinges were iron and they creaked loudly when I pulled at it. Centuries of dirt and water damage had warped the door. I had to brace my feet against a rock and pull until my face was sweaty and hot. It finally unstuck just enough that I could slip through the opening.

The tunnel was as narrow and dark as I'd expected and dirt crumbled down the sides as I pushed through the cobwebs. I could hear the patter of rats and the scuttling of spiders and beetles. The smell was just damp and dark enough to have me thinking of *Hel-Blar*. Instinct made the little hairs on my arms stand up.

I kept walking, following the subtle incline as the passageway led up under the outer bailey, where the knights had been training. The sound of hoofbeats overhead was muffled. Clods of dirt rained over me. I sped up.

And then the tunnel shuddered once, as if a huge fist had just come down on the earth and stones arching over me.

"You've got to be kidding me," I muttered, breaking into a lopsided run as the ground continued to move. Rocks dislodged and fell until they tripped me. "Dragons and earthquakes? I really hate this girl."

I kept running and the tunnel kept shaking until finally, just when I could see a line of light from the edge of a door, it started to cave in altogether. I couldn't go back; there were too many rocks tumbling together. I struggled to climb over the mounds of dirt gathering up to my knees. The walls collapsed inward, earth and stones and rivulets of water all rushing to fill in the spaces around me. A rock bounced off my shoulder, bruising deep. Another one smacked into my ankle.

I dug out frantically, like an animal, refusing to look away from that sliver of weak light. I could almost reach the door. The more earth I shoved away, the more took its place. I spat it out of my mouth, blinked it from my eyelashes, shook it out of my ears. My nails tore to the quick, bleeding and stinging as they finally raked against the wooden planks of the castle's tunnel entrance. I wiggled and shifted around so I could kick it with my heel until it finally groaned open.

I stumbled into the castle, bringing clods of earth and pebbles with me. I pushed my dirt-tangled hair out of my face and leaped to my feet, looking for guards. When I realized I was alone, I slumped against the wall, muscles in my arms and legs aching.

I was inside.

I indulged in a weary grin before straightening up again to get my bearings. It was dark and dusty down here, with rows of iron doors. I'd come out right by the dungeons. I thought I heard weeping but all I could see was darkness and mildew.

"Hello?" I whispered.

The weeping stopped so abruptly I reached for a weapon I didn't have.

Which was when I realized I *had* no weapons.

Crap.

Too late to turn back now, and nowhere to go besides.

I crept forward, straining to see inside the dank cells. Unlit torches lined the stone walls and soiled hay lay in heaps in the corner. A single candle flickered, stuck to the ground by melted wax. "Anyone there?"

A girl with long blond hair to her knees wearing a ragged dress crouched near the bars of a cell. She looked about seven years old and there was an iron chain clamped around her ankle. Her mouth moved as if she was trying to speak, but no sound came out. I swallowed and glanced into the next cell. A knight in tarnished armor glared at me. Next to him was an old woman cackling to herself and next to her, a woman with bite scars, a vampire so pale she was translucent. Her fangs were extended, her eyes like pale purple violets covered in frost.

"You're a fool," she said.

I didn't argue with her.

The last cell held a *Hel-Blar*, snarling and spitting through the bars. I stayed well out of reach, wrinkling my nose at the stench.

If Viola wanted them locked away in her subconscious, or wherever this was, then I wanted them free. And if I was lucky, she'd be so busy dealing with their mass exodus that I could sneak through the castle and find out what else she was hiding. Because whatever it was I was looking for, it wasn't these sad bodies. They were important enough for her to lock them away but not important enough to guard. What I needed was somewhere else entirely.

I bent to pick up one of the rocks that had tumbled out of the tunnel with me and smashed it onto one of the locks. The clang reverberated through the hall. I glanced over my shoulder at the spiral stone steps but when no one came thundering down to investigate, I smashed at the lock again. The rust eating through the iron worked in my favor.

The vampire woman was the first to leap out of her cell, then the old woman and the lady. The knight eyed me suspiciously, even as his gate swung open. The little girl's cell wasn't even locked but she wouldn't come out. I left the *Hel-Blar* where she was.

I was still holding the rock defensively, waiting to see who would move first. The vampire streaked up the stairs so quickly I barely saw her move. The knight pulled his sword from him scabbard and I stumbled back.

"I am a man of honor," he informed me coldly.

"Good, go kill a dragon or something," I suggested. "Like right now."

He nodded curtly. I released the breath I hadn't even realized I was holding. It startled me. I could breathe here, I could stand in sunlight, but I still had fangs. Viola's head made no sense.

I waited until the others had cleared out, all except the *Hel-Blar* and the little girl who was still huddled with her head under her arms, before inching up the steps. I kept close to the wall, hearing the sounds of fighting, the clang of swords, a woman's shout of warning. Through one of the narrow windows I saw the dragon fly by so close, the air from his wings ruffled my hair. His blue scales flashed like lapis lazuli.

I avoided the great hall, where the scarred woman appeared to be flinging coals from the fire at everyone. The dried lavender stalks on the ground smoldered fragrantly. A hawk resting on a wooden perch let out a piercing cry of alarm. I darted under the wooden stairs before anyone could look over and see me there. There were two knights up on the landing, standing in front of an arched oak door. Two more stood staggered on the steps. The hawk broke free and circled over the smoky hall, crying.

Under the stairs where I was hiding, there was another door. This one was smaller and unguarded. Thick dust lay on the ground in front of it. When I tested the handle, it was unlocked. I slipped inside.

Into a swarm of bats.

CHAPTER 5

Lucy

Sunday night

I slid into the driver's seat and fishtailed my way through a U-turn. Kieran and Solange were out of sight now, long since vanished into the forest bordering the campus. I cut through the field, following their footsteps. Snow and clumps of grass churned under the tires. I pulled to a stop at the edge of the trees, ducking out to stand up while still inside the car. I balanced on the edge of the seat, peering into the woods.

"Kieran!" I called out, reaching for a stake. I listened intently but I couldn't hear running or screaming or even regular night sounds. The snow muffled everything, making it too bright and too silent. My heart pounded in my ears. I was sure the teachers at the academy would tell me not to abandon the getaway car. But they wouldn't want me to abandon a fellow hunter either.

A quick glance behind me showed the empty field. Whatever the students and concert-goers were doing now, it wasn't sneaking up behind us. That would have to be good enough for now. Still torn, I jumped out.

I followed the footsteps under the tall red pine, the back of my neck prickling. It was creepy in here, far away from everything and everyone with nothing but the clouds of my frozen breath for company. The tip of my nose was numb and my fingers were cramping with cold. Ice crackled in the trees as the wind shifted. Wet snow and icy rain drifted down in veils, sliding down the back of my neck. I crept deeper into the forest, eyes straining for any movement. Moonlight slid between bare branches.

A twig snapped up ahead.

I froze, another stake clenched in my fist. "Kieran?"

"Solange, wait," I heard him say. His voice was low and urgent. I broke into a run, suddenly oblivious to the eerie silence of a forest filled with vampires. I found them past a grove of stunted birch trees. Solange wasn't alone.

"Get away from her," Kieran barked at the tall vampire at her side. He had dark hair and a quiet smirk, as if everything amused him. But there was something under the smirk, something deadly.

The elusive Constantine.

"Come back with me." Kieran took another step toward her. "We'll figure it out."

Solange smiled. There was still blood on her dress. Her eyes were so blue they looked like sapphire beads. "I'm not lost," she said sweetly. "So there's nothing to figure out." She leaned in close, as if she was about to kiss him. She stopped a breath away from his mouth. "Go away," she said instead.

Kieran flinched. He didn't say anything but the muscles in his neck strained as he fought the compulsion. He turned slowly on one foot to walk away, his back exposed. I jumped into the clearing, stake ready. Constantine shifted.

I threw the stake.

"Kieran, duck!" I hollered. He dropped to the ground just as it whistled over his head. Constantine snarled, pivoting. He knocked the stake aside, at the same time shielding Solange. Fury twisted her porcelain-doll features. If I'd had time, I would have shivered.

Constantine tugged her away, and they shot between the trees like pale stars. I'd thought for sure Constantine would have gone for my throat. Still, I didn't want to hang around for him to change his mind.

"Gotta go." I jerked Kieran to his feet. Solange's pheromones made his eyes look a little glassy, but at least the compulsion was moving him in the direction I wanted him to go.

"I lost her," he said, barely above a whisper as we ran toward the car. He was a silhouette in the piercing headlights. I couldn't see his expression. He slammed his hand onto the hood of the SUV. His breath became short gasps of white clouds in the frigid air. "I lost her," he repeated, bleakly.

"We can't stay here," I said. He just stood there, looking broken. "Kieran!" I tried to sound like a teacher back at the school. He blinked at me once. I flicked snow at him. "Snap out of it."

He shook his head suddenly, as if he was dislodging the dark thoughts that clung to him like water. "You're right." He slid into the driver's seat before I could wonder if he was in any condition to drive. He seemed okay, except for the set of his jaw and shoulders. There was blood on his sleeve. I didn't ask whose it was. I dialed Connor's cell phone as Kieran pulled back onto the road. He was the brother most likely to be connected.

"We know," Connor said right away. "Hart's on the phone with Dad."

"You know? About Solange?"

"Yeah," he said grimly. "Chloe just sent me video."

"Shit, Connor. There's *video*?"

"Security camera. I gotta go," he said, before hanging up. "Mom's going nuclear."

I rubbed the bridge of my nose. "Your uncle's on the phone with Solange's dad," I told Kieran. "There was video. How the hell did it get uploaded so fast?"

"There are Helios-Ra cameras all over town," he answered tightly, hitting the accelerator. "I've got to talk to my uncle. Now."

"I get that," I said grabbing the door when the SUV slid a few feet. "Can you not get us killed first?"

The drive was far too slow and far too fast. Snow and trees and pavement blurred into one. I kept sneaking Kieran looks. His hands were knuckle-white around the steering wheel. I couldn't process the fact that whatever happened to Solange was now happening publicly. Between the Huntsmen, the Helios-Ra, and the Blood

Moon guard, she was going to get herself killed before we could save her.

Hunter was waiting for us in the parking lot. "There's video," she said.

"We know," Kieran told her curtly, rolling down his window. "And we caught the live show."

"That's not all." She held onto the SUV before he could drive off. "They brought the vic here. If she dies . . ."

"I know what happens," Kieran said. "I have to go, Hunter."

He drove off before she could say anything else. She watched him for a long silent moment then turned away, sighing.

"He chased her into the woods," I told her. "But she was faster."

"If that student they brought in dies, the Drakes will have broken the treaty."

My breath froze, along with the rest of me. "But it's not her fault." I was more sure of that than ever before. That sweet-voiced porcelain doll with blood on her clothes wasn't Solange. No one and nothing would convince me otherwise.

Hunter looked sympathetic. "You know that won't matter to the League. Not now. Hart's already made an announcement that the treaty holds until further notice, but he won't be able to hold everyone back. Not on this."

We headed toward the dorm and went straight inside to Hunter and Chloe's room. Chloe turned in her desk chair. Her curly dark hair exploded out of a scrunchie that was slipping free and there were empty soda cans littered around her. Jenna sat on the edge of one of the beds.

"Nice misdirection with the party-girl yell," she said.

"How did you guys find the video so fast?" I asked, shrugging out of my coat.

"Hunter bugged Theo's desk in the infirmary," Chloe said.

Hunter just shrugged unrepentantly. "I think we've all spent way too much time in there. And every time, some big secret bites us in the ass. I'm sick of it."

"They're going to make action figures of her," Jenna predicted. "The Hunter doll, complete with pink cargo pants, stakes, and microchips."

"I heard him get a call about a vic outside one of the college dorms. The League has hidden cameras throughout Violet Hill, near the bars and college mostly," Chloe explained to me, while I wiped my damp palms on my jeans. "So I hacked in."

"Show me," I said quietly, even though I'd just seen it for myself.

The four of us stared at the screen as Chloe played the video clip. The light came from a streetlamp and some sort of night-vision lens. It made the shadows fluid, the light a strange acidic green. It was like watching a horror movie when you didn't want to see what would happen next but you couldn't help yourself. Chloe cut to a clip of the victim being brought in to the infirmary. There was no mistaking the spiky hair and the paint-splattered jeans. The clip cut off abruptly.

"They cut my feed," Chloe admitted, disgruntled. "I hate that."

I sank onto Hunter's bed. "Is that public access to the League?

"No."

"There's something really weird going on," I told them. "I just can't seem to figure it out. I'm not even sure where to start. So what's our next step?" I asked Hunter hopefully. She was the straight-A vampire hunter student, she had six plans going before most of us had finished breakfast. "Logan thought magic was involved that last time I talked to him."

"What about Isabeau?" Hunter asked. "What did she say?"

"He's asking her now. But she's out of range so it might take some time. Plus, you know, a Hound. Not exactly chatty."

"We need Spencer," Hunter said finally. "Magic is his speciality."

Jenna snorted. "Specialty if you pretend that spell he tried last year didn't make him smell like cheese for a month."

"Plus, he's barred from the grounds," Chloe added. "Some idiot might try to stake him."

"We'll just have to meet him off campus," I said. "Do your hacker thing and get a hold of him."

Chloe rolled her eyes. "It's called a phone. No hacking required." She blinked at me when I stood up. "What are you going to do?"

"I'm going to the library."

They all stared at me. Chloe shook her head. "Okay, that I wasn't expecting."

Jenna went with me. I let her since I was babysitting her because of her injuries, and she probably thought she was babysitting me because I now had a rep for being a little crazy. "Shouldn't you be in bed or something?" I asked her.

She rolled her eyes. "Shut up."

"You're a charming patient. I can't imagine why Theo didn't want to keep you longer for observation."

She grinned. "Please. I heard he had to physically lock you out."

"Yeah, yeah."

Campus was quiet and cold, with thousands of stars burning overhead. It was the kind of night Nicholas and I usually spent counting falling stars. I wondered what he was doing right now. Was he safe? Did he know Solange had just broken a hard-won treaty that had been in place since before we were even born? Did he care? He had to care. Because every Helios-Ra agent who wasn't on board with Hart's progressive attitude would be coming for the Drakes now. Not to mention, Huntsmen who had no affiliations to begin with.

And as a student at the Helios-Ra Academy, I was suddenly on the wrong side of the fence.

I kicked a pebble into the pond, accidentally scaring the sleepy swan. He squawked and burst into flight, scattering feathers. Jenna and I both squawked back and threw a stake at it. He dive-bombed us, insulted.

"Oops," I said as we caught our breath. "I guess we're a little tense."

"You think?" Jenna slid me a suspicious sidelong glance. "You're not going to start *ohm*-ing, are you?"

"Mom claims it helps."

"Let me guess. Your mom eats a lot of tofu, doesn't she?"

"You have no idea."

We crossed the lawn toward the buildings clustered in the center of the campus and surrounded with security lights. "You know, you don't exactly seem like the library type. Tyson would be so proud."

"I have to start somewhere," I grumbled. "Much as I'd like to just punch everyone in the face until this all makes sense, that seems like a lot of work."

The library was nearly empty. We only had a half hour until curfew and since we didn't have exams or essays due this week, everyone was pretty much anywhere else. The light was soft and the wooden study tables gleamed.

"Do you even know what you're looking for?" Jenna asked as we wandered in the back stacks.

"Not really," I admitted. I pulled out books on magic, ghosts, and vampires. It didn't take long before the pile grew to eye level. I was trying to figure out how to carry them all when Jenna checked her cell. "Chloe finally reached Spencer. He'll meet you at 2:00 a.m. tomorrow. Hunter says you know where." I knew exactly where she meant. As the only two hunter students currently dating vampires, we knew the best and most private routes to the borders of the campus. Jenna blinked at the teetering pile. "Enough books there, Hamilton?"

"I can guarantee at least half of these are wrong." I pointed to a slim volume with *Raktapa Council: Amrita, Drakes and Joiik* embossed in gold lettering. "Especially that one."

Jenna helped me cart them to the librarian, who looked briefly impressed at the sheer weight, and then out the back stairwell to the shortcut leading to the dorms. It was a better shortcut when it wasn't blocked by three idiots in dire need of anger management classes.

"Where do you think you're going?" Jody asked, the security

lights glinting off the metal clamps holding a row of stakes neatly to her belt. She reached out and shoved my arms so that my jacket and my books tumbled to the ground.

"God, could you stop being such a cliché?" I scowled, already out of my limited store of patience. "You're cranky and macho. I get it already. Now, get out of my way because I have real, actual problems that are more important than your need for therapy."

"Jenna, walk away," Jody said, ignoring me.

She narrowed her eyes. "Excuse me?"

"We're giving you a chance to redeem yourself," Ben explained, glaring at me. "To stand with us instead of the vampire lover." He was built like a truck.

Jenna looked at Jody's third friend incredulously. "Samuel, seriously? You're smarter than this."

"I thought you were too," he replied softly. He was lean and dark-haired and looked like what I imagined an assassin would: deadly and quiet. He tossed the local Violet Hill newspaper at our feet. The headlines were lurid: *Missing person cases triple* and *Dracula copycat killer on the loose*.

"Your precious Drakes broke the treaty," Jody said to me. "Just like we knew they would. Monsters don't know the meaning of honor. And you need to pay, just like them."

"She's not a Drake, asshat," Jenna pointed out.

"Yeah," I said. "So go pick on one of them if you're so tough. In fact, ask for Helena."

"Not while you're still here and able to betray all of our secrets," Jody argued. "God knows what you're telling the Drakes."

"I have the blueprints to the school," I mocked her. "Because this is a James Bond movie. Get a grip."

She shoved me in the shoulder. I hissed through my teeth.

Jenna swore and stepped between us. "Jody, let it go."

"Jenna, I'll meet you back at the dorms," I said. "You don't need this shit."

She snorted. "As if."

"You're choosing her again?" Jody snapped. "A vampire lover over your own unit? Over your duty to protect the town?"

"I'm choosing a friend over a bunch of bullies," Jenna corrected her with a sharp smile. "I don't like bullies."

Jody just smiled as Ben and Samuel shifted beside her, ready to fight. "Then it's time you realized she's not welcome here. And neither are you if you side with her. She'll only drag you down."

"Oh, right, like you'll help her be a better person," I said. "And she's recovering from a head wound, so don't be such a bitch."

"And you heard Hart," Jenna shot back, refusing to acknowledge the bandage she still wore under her ponytail. "The treaty is still in effect."

"Hart's not here."

Jenna blocked Jody's sudden swing and retaliated with an elbow to her stomach. When Ben lunged at me, I threw a book at his head.

"Leave Jenna out of this," I added, going straight for Jody while Ben clutched his head, swearing. She stumbled back instinctively, too used to people cowering away from her. I stood between her and Jenna.

So she punched me instead.

I punched her back.

Right now, my mother was reciting her nightly mala bead prayers to cleanse me of my violent tendencies.

Not enough chanting in the world, Mom.

"Jody, whatever little story you're playing out right now, I'm not interested. I have people who need my help. So take up a hobby or something and get the hell out of my face." Which hurt and already felt as if it was swelling. Pain from my aching cheek made my eyes water. Jenna and Samuel stared each other down warily.

Jody grabbed my arm suddenly, nails digging into my skin. "Are those bite marks?"

Shit.

The fight slid into an ominous pause. Everyone looked at the fang marks Nicholas had left just under the crook of my elbow. They looked redder in the fluorescent lights, or I looked paler. I could just imagine what they were thinking as I stood there with books on how to kill vampires at my feet. Even Jenna goggled. I tried to twist out of Jody's grasp. She was taller, stronger and meaner than I was.

But I was sneakier.

I yanked to the side, knowing she'd follow me. She assumed I was trying to get away but really, I was just angling her so she was facing the security camera blinking its little red light up in the corner by the door. And then I taunted her.

Luckily, I'd had lots of practice between Nicholas, Logan, and Quinn.

"Vampire boyfriend, remember?" I smirked. "And he's hot. Maybe I'll bring him to prom."

Her nostrils actually flared. I gave her my most obnoxious smile.

It was almost worth the bruises. I blocked her punch, but only barely. The force reverberated through my arm, pain flaring into my elbow.

"Careful. What if vampire tolerance is contagious?" I added, making sure my fang marks were near her hand. She snatched her arm out of the way. I rolled my eyes. "You're an idiot. Also?" I pointed to the camera. "Think of me when you're cleaning toilets for detention."

She followed my gaze, lips tightening. Ben winced. "Crap. My mom's going to kill me." He backed toward the door, letting in the frigid wind. "Let's get out of here."

Jody opened her mouth. I cut her off. "Yeah, yeah. This isn't over, I'm not welcome, I'm a blood puppet, and you're so righteous. That about cover it?" I slammed the door behind her.

"I can't believe you're walking around a vampire hunter school with bite marks," Jenna said, sounding both awed and disgusted. She crouched to help me pick up the books.

I pulled my sweater on, grimacing at the bruises already throbbing on my arm. "It's complicated."

"Not really," Jenna disagreed, standing up. "Was it willing?"

I didn't blink. "Yes," I lied. She just shook her head. "Jenna, this is who I am."

"Well, I just hope you're right about your friend Solange," she said quietly. "Because otherwise you have to know everyone here is within their rights to take her out."

"She's the victim here."

"Or she's the monster," she returned as we went outside. "And we put down monsters, Lucy, for the good of humans who don't know any better." She looked at my arm pointedly. "Even the ones who *should* know better."

We didn't speak the rest of the way to the dorms, because there was really nothing left to say. She was a new friend and I knew we had each other's backs, but we'd never agree on this particular matter. At least we wanted the same thing: to stop a war.

And Jenna wasn't wrong.

But she wasn't right either.

Bile burned in the back of my throat. We might not save Solange in time. And meanwhile she could easily bring down her entire family and decades' worth of delicate treaties that were the only thing standing between peaceful Violet Hill and a bloodbath. Everyone I loved would fight.

And everyone would die.

CHAPTER 6

Solange

Vampire princess or not, bats are just creepy when they're flying at your face.

I stumbled back, covering my head as they dipped erratically around me. There were so many of them, the sound of their wings was raspy and loud. I'd controlled more bats than these in the field with Lucy and then again at the camp when the Chandramaa guard had tried to kill Constantine for saving me from the Furies. I wondered briefly how he was doing. And then one of the bats squeaked and got tangled in my hair. Wondering about Constantine and Kieran and my entire family was going to have to wait until later, when there weren't dozens of rodents freaking out around me.

Because clearly Viola didn't want me in this room.

Which is why I knew it was exactly where I needed to be.

The bats froze, as if they'd hit an invisible wall between us. I blew hair out of my eyes, just as frozen. I couldn't stand here forever but if I moved my hand, the bats attacked me again. And the knights were bound to come along again. With my luck lately, it would be sooner rather than later.

Fine.

They could deal with the bats. I crouched slowly, keeping my arm extended, hand out. Leathery wings flapped harder. I pressed against the rough wooden doorjamb, then twisted and flung my hand out toward the hallway. As if I'd deployed a slingshot of bats, they flung past me, catching strands of my hair, careening into the wall where they crowded together. Once they were out, I pushed the heavy door shut and bolted it.

I wasn't sure what I was expecting. A room full of dragon eggs or bottles of blood or torture devices, like the dungeon.

Instead the room was full of boxes.

They ranged from small, pewter, circular boxes that could fit into the palm of my hand to a giant hope chest with iron studs. They were piled everywhere, carved from amber and bone, made of beaten gold, oak, and ivory, decorated with enamel, rubies, pearls, and silver inlay. They reached the ceiling, glinting in the light from the torches set into the stone wall. If they toppled, I could be buried forever.

"Okay, this is just not getting any less weird," I muttered.

I had no idea why they were important or what was in them. It could be blood or coins or dried rosebuds for all I knew. It could be anything.

Only one way to find out.

I was reaching for the nearest one, covered in garnet and peeling gilt paint when the alarm sounded. The clang of a giant metal bell thrummed through the castle.

"Prisoners escaped!" A knight shouted from the ramparts.

I wasn't sure if they meant the prisoners in the dungeon or me. I didn't really want to hang around to find out. I had to get out of here, but I couldn't lose the tiny advantage I'd gained by finding the hidden room full of boxes. So I'd just have to take them with me. Well, maybe not the chest nailed to the floor.

I grabbed the end of an embroidered tapestry and yanked it off the wall. I tied it over one shoulder like a sling and then stuffed as many boxes as I could into it. Men shouted on the ramparts and down in the courtyard. The bell continued to ring, shuddering the metal torch brackets, shaking my heart as if it were also made of iron.

Boxes slipped from my damp palms, bruising my shins and toes. The tapestry pouch got heavier, cutting into my skin. Faceted diamonds, jagged hinges, decorative pewter scrollwork bit into my fingertips, drawing blood. When I had as many boxes as I could possibly carry, I opened the door, peeking through a sliver of the hall that I could see. It was quiet for now, empty.

I couldn't head back down to the tunnel since the entrance had caved in. I'd have to find another way out. I hurried down the spiral staircase, stopping at every curve to listen for footsteps. There was shouting all around, so it was difficult to pinpoint exact sounds. But I could smell burning lavender from the great hall, where the lady in the fine dress and scarred skin was still flinging embers around.

The knights circled her, drawing closer with their swords unsheathed. Small fires burned, scattered everywhere. Smoke thickened the air. I crept closer, using the smoke as a shield. Her eyes flared once, like bits of broken mirror. I could have sworn she looked at me, before flinging herself right into the fire in the pit in the middle of the hall. The flames licked at the hem of her gown. She screamed as they ate higher and higher, up to her wrists and arms and throat, all scarred with bite marks. The smell of seared hair and flesh made me gag.

Everyone stopped to stare at her.

She'd sacrificed herself so that I could get free.

So I'd damn well get free.

I kept my hand to the stone wall behind me as the smoke billowed into eye-stinging curtains. I followed it to the door and eased outside, where more smoke wafted out of the windows. The horses in the nearby stables panicked, kicking their hooves through their stalls until the sounds of splintering wood and frantic neighs drowned out the screams inside.

I kept to the clutter of the stalls and dovecotes and assorted sheds along the inside of the wall. I made good time, but it wasn't enough. A glance over my shoulder showed at least five guards tearing across the courtyard after me. The boxes clanged together, slamming painfully into my elbow and hip bone with every step. If I dropped them I could run quicker, but without them I was also running blind, with no idea of what to do once I found a safe place to hide.

The back of my neck prickled. They were getting closer.

I ran until I was gasping, until my sides cramped and my legs hurt. I ran until there was nothing but the adrenaline in my veins, the slap of my boots on the ground, the rush of the air in my eyes. A box studded with rubies tumbled out of the sling, ringing against the stones. The lid popped open as it rolled away. It was empty. I kept running.

I ran until I was falling again.

1192

"Papa!" Viola hurled herself off her pony and into the arms of a tall bearded giant. Her nursemaid sniffed from where she waited for a stable boy to help her off her palfrey. The white linen of her wimple glowed in the torchlight.

"Child, you must not be so informal. You must address him as 'my lord.'"

Viola rolled her eyes at her father, who grinned back despite the fact the nursemaid had the right of it.

"Shouldn't you be asleep?" he asked her, swinging her around so that her feet dangled. It was her favorite thing in the world. It made her feel as if she were flying, but without the fear of falling, because she knew her father would always keep her safe.

"I pinched myself to stay awake," Viola answered. When he set her down she showed off the bruises on her arm with pride. "And I didn't cry once."

"My little warrior." He laughed.

She slipped her hand into his, rubbing the smoothness of his palm.

She knew other men got calluses from swinging swords and spears at their enemies, but not her father. He was invincible. Stable hands led their horses away and servants came out of the shadows to unpack the trunks from the wagon. "Why must we always travel so late at night?" she asked curiously as they crossed the bailey to the hall.

"Hush now," her nursemaid said crossly. "Don't be a pest."

Viola pouted, clinging more tightly to her father's hand so he wouldn't send her away. Golden torchlight glowed at the windows, secured with thin horn shutters. It was like sunlight and honey. It was a smaller and more ancient keep than Bornebow Hall where she lived, but it was much nicer. She preferred the smoky fire in the center of the hall and the dark wooden timbers above, the steep valleys, and the lake on the other side of the wall where fish leaped in summer.

"I miss you, Da! Couldn't I stay here with you? I'd be a good girl, I promise." When her nursemaid snorted, Viola shot her a narrowed look. "I know how."

Her father let go of her hand. "You know you can't, child. You're betrothed to Richard and they want to raise you to be a good wife to him."

She crossed her arms, suddenly feeling tired and peevish. "Why can't he live here with us and be raised to be a good husband?"

"Because that's not the way of the world," he replied, grinning down at her.

"I run faster than he does," she confided with a loud sigh. They passed a wooden post set into the courtyard behind the side door into the hall. Chains dangled from hooks set into the top. The dirt all around was packed down and sprinkled with dark spots that looked like dried blood. Viola frowned. "What's that for?"

Her father's cheerful expression flickered and died. His blue eyes went to stone and Viola shivered.

"Don't question your father," her nursemaid snapped, yanking on the back of Viola's dress.

Viola didn't know what was going on but she was suddenly aware of how little she was. Her nursemaid only snapped like that she was frightened. She stood very still. Viola's father could have been carved out of stone, unyielding and pale in the dark courtyard. He didn't speak, which was a relief, only turned on his heel and stalked toward the main hall.

Viola followed meekly. The uncharacteristic meekness lasted from one end of the hall to the other, until she lay on her pallet behind the carved wooden screen. Her nursemaid blew out the candles, leaving Viola lying in the shadows, bored and agitated.

She stayed there until her heart stopped racing, until the confusing fear had faded away and she was restless. She listened to the sounds of the servants in the hall, dragging in the wooden trestle tables and sweeping out the floor rushes to be replaced with more fragrant herbs. At Bornebow Hall they settled to sleep by the fire, but in her father's castle, they kept later hours. She could just make out her father's booming voice in the courtyard, but not his exact words.

Sleep refused to come. She counted her breaths, counted the spiders on the wall, even the embroidered leaves on the ribbon of her nightshift. When sleep still refused to be caught she pushed out of her warm nest of woolen blankets, bare toes curling over the cold stones. She'd find her mother, who always told her thrilling tales of giants and ancient kings. She'd just have to be careful not to disturb her nursemaid or her father, since they were both so cross.

She crept out of a small window, swinging easily over into the lilac hedge. It concealed her movements until she felt brave enough to dart around the back to the outside staircase leading to her mother's private solar. The oak door was locked, as usual, but Viola had long ago learned the trick of opening it. She used her hairpins and remembered the one time she'd asked her father why the door was always locked. He'd looked so sad, running a big hand over her pale hair and telling her it was so that no one would steal her mother away. Viola liked the idea of her mother always being safe, even though she herself could never have slept all locked up like that.

She pushed the door, opening it only enough to give her space to slip inside. The room was warm and lit with candles in iron lanterns. It always had a curious unused smell, like burning dust. A fire crackled in the hearth, too big and too hot for such a fine evening. But her mother was always cold, shivering when others were sweating. Viola crept closer, watching the flickering light gild Lady Venetia's face.

Lady Venetia shifted, opening her eyes. She smiled slowly, as if she'd forgotten how it was done. "Viola," she said hoarsely. "You've grown so tall."

"I can get on a horse all by myself now," Viola bragged, scrambling onto the bed. "Even though Richard still needs help." She lowered her voice as if sharing a great and mortifying secret. "I'm taller than he is."

"He'll outgrow you soon enough," Venetia murmured, touching the end of one of her daughter's braids. "Is he kind to you?"

"Sometimes. I still want to set fire to his tunic." She bounced on the bed until her mother winced. "Mama, are you ill again?"

"I'm afraid so, poppet."

"You look pale," Viola said. "But you have a sunburn on your nose."

Venetia just smiled wearily. "Tell me what you've been doing."

Viola told her about the beehive she'd found, about the baby bunnies in the gap in the orchard wall, and the way Richard thought he was better than she was. Her mother listened attentively, and when her eyelids flickered, Viola didn't take offense, though she would have shrieked herself blue in the face if her nursemaid had behaved that way. Everyone knew Lady Venetia was delicate and distracted. Viola snuggled closer when her mother shivered violently.

"I'll keep you warm," she promised, sleepily.

She pulled the blankets up, frowning at what looked like bloodstains, like tiny red beads. The firelight caught the strange scars on her mother's arms, some raw and pink, others faded and shining like silk embroidery. They were puncture marks, clustered in pairs like berries and scattered over her arms, along her collarbone and even under the laces of her neckline.

The image flickered, leaving me disoriented. I knew exactly what those marks were.

Bite marks.

CHAPTER 7

Lucy

Monday

The only reason I didn't miss my first class was because Sarita stood over me after lunch and cleared her throat annoyingly until I groaned.

"You're going to be late," she informed me disapprovingly.

"I don't care."

"Attendance is mandatory."

I rolled over, scowling at her through one eye. "Did you really just say that? Are you, like, fifty? We need to get you pierced or tattooed or something."

"Lucy." She sounded anxious. I knew being late and breaking the rules made her sweaty. We were like the worst pairing of personalities ever. She'd probably have a breakdown because of me before the Christmas holidays.

"Yeah, yeah, okay." I swung my feet over the bed. Mud crumbled off my boots onto the carpet. This time, Sarita sighed. I had to laugh. "Poor Sarita. Think Theo will diagnose you with PTSD for having to deal with me?"

"If you think it will help," she muttered.

I laughed again. More mud fell off my clothes. "I'd better hop in the shower."

"Okay, but hurry."

I grabbed my shower caddy and my bathrobe. "Don't wait for me. You'll just give yourself an ulcer." I was tempted to skip classes altogether but I couldn't afford to lose the access I had to Helios-Ra information. Not to mention that no one was going to let me stay at the Drakes' now and if I went back home, my parents would enforce their 5:00 p.m. curfew. No thanks. So I had to go to class and stick to my routine and pretend I wasn't plotting.

Sarita left, shaking her head and looking as if I'd just kicked a puppy in front of her. Honestly, the school administration was diabolical. I kind of felt bad for her. Especially when I saw how red her cheeks were when I rushed into class ten minutes late. The teacher looked unimpressed, Sarita looked downright nauseated. Jody smirked. I resisted the urge to throw a pencil at her. But only barely.

I spent most of my waking moments going through the books. I wrote in the margins on one, detention be damned. It was just so blatantly wrong. The Drakes didn't lure drunk college students out of the bars and compel them to forget being fed on. Well, maybe

Quinn used to, but I could guarantee none of those girls needed to be compelled.

At 2:00 a.m., I snuck out of my room and met Hunter and Chloe in the hall outside the ground floor guys' bathroom.

"It's the only one we can fit through," Hunter explained as we stepped into the flickering lights. White and blue tiles covered the walls, just like the girls' bathroom. "And I already shoved a pine branch over the camera outside, so we should be good." She blinked at me. "What happened to your face?"

"Jody," I said, explaining the bruises. "Apparently, I bug her as much as she bugs me."

"Why are you in your pajamas?" Chloe asked me.

I looked down at my striped flannel bottoms. "Because my room-mate is a tattletale," I replied drily. She'd gotten worse since I freaked out after Nicholas disappeared and the headmistress asked her to keep an eye on me. "This way if Sarita catches me sneaking back in, I can convince her I was just in the bathroom or watching the common room TV or something."

"Good plan," Chloe agreed. "She's a pain."

"You have no idea," I said. "She keeps trying to get me to organize my desk and iron my school cargos. Who does that?"

"Hunter does." Chloe grinned.

"I don't iron my cargos, give me a break," she returned.

"But you do organize your stakes by size and weight."

"Well, that just makes sense." She raised her eyebrows at us. "Ready?" She stepped up onto the side of the urinal and wiggled out, making it look easy and graceful.

Chloe caught my eye. "That's why we hate her just a little bit."

"If my ass gets stuck give me a push." I grinned back, trying not to slip and fall right into the urinal. The windowsill wedged uncomfortably in my belly as I wriggled out, feeling like a giant worm. Chloe followed, pushing her laptop case ahead of her.

It was snowing lightly, not enough to be really cold, just enough to make everything pretty. We darted from tree to tree, keeping to the shadows. Hunter used hand signals to warn us of cameras. We ducked into the bushes, climbed over a wooden farm fence and crossed the fields to the forest. The trail was narrow and barely noticeable, but both Hunter and I knew exactly where it led. I'd had my last date with Nicholas in the meadow at the end of the path. I didn't want to think about what Hunter and Quinn did there.

This time, it was Spencer who waited for us on the other side of the cedars, perched up in a tree. "I thought you turned into a vampire," Chloe teased, looking up at him. "Not a monkey."

"Up a tree is about the only place I can hide from school patrols and Huntsmen," he smiled, his blond dreadlocks and turquoise beads at odds with the flash of his eyes. "You guys are keeping bad company."

"Not since you left."

He climbed down, hopping nimbly from branch to branch. "Show off," Chloe muttered. But she hugged him just as fiercely as Hunter did; the same way I'd hug Logan or Quinn. He stepped back, trying to hide his fangs under his top lips. Poor guy, up until recently he'd been a student at the academy and now he was one of the "enemy."

"Use your school-issue nose plugs," I suggested. "It helps."

He blinked. "I never thought of that."

"Here." Hunter fished out a pair from the pocket of her cargos and tossed them to him. Something moved on the other side of the cedars. Everyone except Hunter froze. "It's Kieran," she explained, just before he came out of the shadows. "I called him."

"I thought vampire hunters were supposed to be stealthy." I tossed him a smile. He wore his usual black cargos and a painfully serious expression. He was going to have to learn that when you hung out with the Drakes, you had to keep your sense of humor. Sometimes it was the only shield you had.

He half smiled. "If I'm too stealthy with this bunch I'm likely to get staked."

"True," Hunter agreed, searching his face.

He nudged her shoulder. "I'm fine."

"Yeah, right." She snorted.

He turned to Spencer. "How are things at the camp?"

"Messy," he said. "I prefer the Bower. Less mind control."

I froze. "Has everyone else figured out Solange's new little gift too?"

"Hard to miss."

Kieran and I exchanged a grim glance. "And Nicholas?" I asked, even though fear made the words feel like needles in my throat. "Is he okay?"

"He's in one piece," Spencer answered carefully. I let out a shaky breath. "But he doesn't say much, so I really don't know. He sticks close to Solange or he takes off alone."

"Is she . . ." Kieran paused, clenched his jaw. "The same?"

"Worse."

"Newspapers are calling it the Dracula Killer," Spencer said.

"That's not her," Kieran and I both said in unison. I hoped I sounded more confident than he did. He just sounded desperate.

"That's why we need to talk to you," Hunter said. "Lucy has a theory."

"Can vampires be possessed?" I asked.

Spencer looked briefly intrigued. "I never really thought about it, but I guess so. I mean, I don't see why not. It would probably be pretty volatile. Vampires and magic tend to clash. It's a delicate balance at the best of times."

"Believe me, I know," I said. "But I think Solange is possessed. It's more than bloodlust that's making her like this."

"She has three sets of fangs," Spencer pointed out. "That's . . . unique. Outside of the *Hel-Blar*, anyway."

"I know I'm right about this."

Chloe bit her lip. "Don't be mad, Lucy. But don't you think you could be reading into things? Seeing things you want to see?"

I shook my head stubbornly.

"Possession could explain the change in her," Spencer agreed slowly, as he considered what I'd said. His brow furrowed. "I only met her once in the Bower with Constantine but she seemed nice. Quiet."

"She was with Constantine?" I frowned as Kieran swore under his breath. "What's with that guy, anyway? Who is he?" I added him to my list of things to research.

"I don't know," Spencer said with a ghost of a smile. "I'm new to the whole vampire thing, remember?"

"Can you find out?" Kieran asked quietly.

"I can try, but I don't go into the camp much anymore." Spencer looked thoughtful. "There was a hell of a magic punch when she put the crown on. Knocked us all off our feet."

"Did you write an essay on it yet?" Hunter asked.

Spencer grinned. "Just some rough notes."

Chloe groaned. "I hate you both."

"I didn't hang around long enough to get real data," Spencer added, serious again. "Not after Lucy told me about Jenna in the woods. And I can't get back in, not if I don't want to be brainwashed."

"Could the Hounds get in?" I asked, crossing my arms against the cold. Spencer was in a T-shirt and ripped jeans and he looked perfectly comfortable. "They must have some sort of shielding spell or something, right?"

"Maybe. But even if you got in, what could you do?"

"I could punch her in the nose," I muttered. "I owe her."

"I'll e-mail you and Kieran a list of books," Spencer promised. "There's reception in a few spots near the Bower, if you search hard enough for them. It's just far enough away from the Blood Moon signal blocks."

"Connor probably did that once they were exiled," I said.

"The magic blast could have opened the door to spirits," Spencer continued. "It's not impossible, anyway."

"It's a place to start," I said, feeling more hopeful than I had since before Nicholas went missing, since even before I'd found Solange with Kieran's blood on her lips. "Thanks."

Hunter, Spencer, and Chloe caught up for a few minutes,

referencing inside jokes and chatting about people I didn't know. Kieran just stood there, hands in his pockets, practically vibrating with suppressed frustration. Worse yet, he looked sad.

"Are you okay?" I asked him. I knew how he felt, how it was like being swallowed by winter, so that even your insides were too stark and too cold.

"Hart's good at what he does," he said bleakly. "But I don't know how long he can hold the League back, especially with Huntsmen in town. It's getting ugly, Lucy."

"Which is why the Drakes are so lucky they have us to clean up their mess."

"I hope you're right."

"I'm always right," I teased him.

"We should get back," Hunter cut in, glancing at her watch. "Chloe's got the next security patrol clocked. We have ten minutes." Spencer faded soundlessly into the forest after Hunter and Chloe both hugged him good-bye. As we headed back through the bushes, Hunter shot Kieran a speaking glance. "Call me."

Kieran nodded and hopped the fence, cutting through the lawns toward the road. We followed the path back to the dorms, mulling over the events of the night. Hunter gave the swan a wide berth as Chloe snickered. Her snickers cut off abruptly as we came around the side of the dorms, toward the guys' bathroom.

Headmistress Bellwood was waiting for us just outside the open window, her arms folded. Even her black winter coat looked stern and disapproving.

"Good evening," she said frostily. "It seems you'll be joining

Jody and her friends in bathroom duty for the rest of the month. Plus two demerits."

Chloe opened her mouth to protest, thought better of it, and snapped it shut again.

"A wise decision." The headmistress approved. "I'm not interested in your excuses. You know the rules and you must know how foolhardy it is to sneak off campus now of all times. Get to bed, all of you."

"Damn vampires," Hunter muttered crossly as we went around to the front door. "They just cost me my perfect school record."

"What are you complaining about?" I sighed. "My mom's going to make me meditate."

CHAPTER 8

Solange

I had no idea how long I'd been trapped inside Viola's memory but when I returned to myself again, I was back on the spiral stairs. I was disoriented and confused, gripping the uneven stone wall to ground me. I was back to being a spirit in Viola's subconscious parallel dimension while she was controlling my body in the real world.

Any wonder I was confused?

I wasn't sure what kind of a human-vampire spirit-thing I was in this place. I knew I didn't have to feed on blood and I couldn't feel my heartbeat but I was still panting. Psychosomatic. I was freaking out so I was hyperventilating because I'd been a human girl for a lot longer than I'd been a vampire, freaky or otherwise.

I needed more information. I'd have to open another box.

I didn't exactly relish the thought. There was something seriously disconcerting about being a faded copy of yourself in your body, never mind traipsing about someone else's memories. It would have been easier to take her on with a weapon in my hand. Instead, I was going to have to be sneakier than that.

First, I had to find a better hiding place before someone found me just standing there like an idiot. The tapestry pouch was still slung across my chest and it bumped heavily against my hip when I moved. I peered out of the murder hole. Twilight painted the sky blue and orange between the trees in the distance. Smoke rose from a small hut I assumed belonged to the blacksmith. The glow of the fire leaking out of the open door was fierce. On the right, a tall ash tree rose from cracks in the courtyard ground. Green leaves fluttered, partly obscuring the view of the stables along the wall of the inner bailey. Hay lay in piles outside and drifted between the loose wooden boards of the upper story. If I could swing into the tree and then jump onto the roof of the stable, I could hide in the hay loft.

Big if.

I crept up the stairs to the next floor, darting between torches to hide in the shadows of the corridor. The first arched oak door I came across was locked. The second opened onto a windowless room full of the sound of scurrying feet and claws. I slammed it shut again as quickly as I could. There were no tapestries on this floor, just a cold draft that snapped at the torches and the hem of my dress. It wasn't until the next room that I found a window just big enough to fit through. The chamber itself was empty except for the smell of smoke. There was nothing here to threaten me but it still just felt wrong.

I hurried to the window, pulling open the wooden shutters. There were knights above me on the ramparts but they ought to be looking beyond the walls, not directly down into the heart of the castle compound. And it was dark enough that if anyone looked up, they shouldn't be able to see me. The tree waved cheerfully from a few feet below. I swallowed. It was a lot farther than I'd thought, and the window was narrow. Almost too narrow.

I took off the tapestry bag and hung out of the window again. I swung it carefully, wincing at the light clinking of boxes as they shifted against one another. I swung it again, and again, until I had a good arc. I let go and it skimmed the outer twigs, catching on the tip of a heavier branch, and dangling precariously. I waited for a cry of alarm. When there was nothing but the steady strike of the blacksmith's hammer, I straddled the stone sill.

"If I die I'm so going to kick Viola's ass," I muttered.

And then I let go. I wasn't jumping, I was falling.

I grabbed at the tree, leaves slapping at my face, branches scratching my arms and yanking my hair. The air rushed at me. I finally got hold of a branch but it wasn't strong enough to support my weight. It broke and dropped me onto the next branch, nearly putting my eye out. I clung there, cursing.

I could smell smoke and horses and hay. I reached out, straining muscles I didn't know I had to grab the tapestry bag. When it was safely wrapped around my wrist, I crawled along the branch like an inchworm while the tree creaked warningly.

When I hit the roof of the stables, I was grinning. Aching all over and bruised, but still grinning. Mostly because no one had seen me and I wasn't lying in broken pieces on the ground. I dug through the bug-infested thatch and wiggled inside, landing on a soft mound of hay that made my nose itch. The horses below me nickered and snorted. I lay still in the darkness for a long moment.

And then I did the only thing I could do, despite the nerves firing in my belly and along my spine. I reached into the bag and pulled out a random box. It was wooden and set with colored enamel pieces in a mosaic of a lady with a dragon curled up beside her and a knight kneeling to them both.

I opened it, thinking of Kieran.

1198

Viola waited for Tristan on the hilltop, the wind blowing her woolen cloak behind her, revealing glimpses of her green surcoat. Ice glinted on every blade of grass, crunching like broken glass under her horse's hooves. A hawk circled overhead with a high-pitched shriek of warning to mice, rabbits, and all small huntable creatures below.

"You came." Viola smiled, sliding from her saddle. As always, she felt her entire body sing, just to see him.

"Of course," Tristan replied, dismounting. The indigo blue of his tunic matched his eyes. He didn't say anything else, only walked her backward until her body pressed against the trunk of the tree and the leaves sheltered them from prying eyes. Her long blond hair caught in his silver cloak clasp.

When he kissed her it felt as though there was lightning striking off her, as if she could set the whole world on fire and watch it burn with a smile just as long as they were together. There was no cold wind, no ice dripping down the back of her neck; there was nothing but him. His lips were teasing and desperate but no more so than hers. He kissed her throat and she tilted her head back, inhaling the scents of him: smoke, iron, and the rare oranges Lord Phillip had just received for Christmas. She remembered dancing with Tristan in the hall, wearing a crown of holly leaves. No one had suspected them.

He pulled back slightly but they stayed locked together, breathing as one. When she smiled, he smiled. When he leaned in, she leaned in. The last of the russet oak leaves clattered like bones around them.

When her horse shifted closer to nibble at the thawed grass, Tristan finally noticed the pack on her saddle and frowned. "Where are you going?"

"I'm going home."

"You're leaving Bornebow Hall?" He seized her arms, his eyes searing into her like ice. Her breath caught, as if she were in a runaway cart. "Without me? Why?"

"Why do you think?"

"Does Richard know?"

"Not you too." Viola made a sound of disgust. Her horse tossed her mane, recognizing the sound and impatient to run across the fields and moors. "I'm going to talk to my father. I'm fifteen years old. That's old enough to know my own mind. My own heart."

Tristan was only a few years older than she was, and had been a knight for less than a year, but he felt positively ancient at the thought of losing Viola. It was one thing to recite poetry like a troubadour, and sneak roses onto her pillow, but another thing altogether to challenge her father.

Her betrothal to Richard was made on the day she was born. But he knew the set of her jaw and what it meant. There would be no stopping her. She was like the hawk above them, hungry and wild.

"I don't want to lose you," he said softly, stepping close enough to smell the amber and lavender of her hair, to brush his mouth over her cheek.

"Nor I you," she whispered, melting into him. "So come with me. Fight for us."

"Viola, I would die for us." He touched his brow to hers. "But you know what they'll say."

"My mother might listen," she insisted stubbornly. "She wants me to be happy. She is always asking if Richard treats me well."

"And he does," Tristan felt honor-bound to remind her. He considered Richard a brother. It seemed a poor way to repay him by falling in love with his betrothed. But there was a reason they called it falling in love—you couldn't choose your landing. Fate chose for you. "He's a good man."

"But he's not you."

She jerked out of his grasp and vaulted into her saddle. "Are you afraid to prove yourself?" she asked, looking down at him, temper making her cheeks red. "Because I'm not." She kicked her horse into a gallop, churning dirt and dead leaves in her wake.

Tristan swore and leaped onto his own mount, chasing after her. They kept to the edge of the forest until it was time to follow the river, crossing the fields. They passed villages with their creaking mill wheels and goat pens. The shorn fields glittered in the fading light and it was dusk when they finally left the empty howling moors to approach Viola's father's castle. The stone walls and the keep above them were silhouetted against the pink-and-orange sky.

"Lady Viola," the guard at the gatehouse greeted her with a bow of the head. She nodded back and then they were in the outer bailey, their tired horses picking their way up the path to the inner courtyard.

Viola slid out of her sidesaddle, her legs aching from being wrapped around the pommel. Her cheeks stung from the constant onslaught of the cold wind. The courtyard was quiet, as it always was this time of day. She'd chosen her arrival carefully. She knew her father couldn't be bothered with visitors until well after supper. She might have a chance to win her mother over to her side by then.

"Mother will be in her solar," she said as Tristan handed their reins over to a stable boy. Saying the words out loud made her realize that in all her visits over the years, her mother was always buried under a pile of blankets. "She's unwell," she explained as they headed up to the old hall. Improvements had been made since she was a girl, including a new stone tower that threw the old timber hall in shadows. "She never leaves."

Until now.

Viola froze, stopping so abruptly Tristan had to take her shoulder to stop from crashing into her and knocking them both off their feet.

"I don't . . ." She trailed off, horrified.

Tristan followed her shocked gaze. A woman waited in the cold twilight of the bailey. Her long braids were bound with gold cord and her fine gown and embroidered surcoat, along with her jeweled girdle, marked her as a noblewoman. She wore a fur mantle. Anyone would have thought her the lady of the castle.

Except for the fact that she was hanging from a post by her chained wrists. There were scars on her neck that her linen wimple could not hide.

"Are you under attack, my lady?" Tristan asked, pulling his sword from its scabbard. Fury and bile burned in the back of his throat. "Who is that?" he whispered to Viola. "Do you know her?"

"That's my mother," Viola replied before bolting out into the open courtyard. Swearing, Tristan followed, searching for possible threats from the ramparts. When no arrows or hot oil poured over their heads, he risked a glance at Viola. She was clawing uselessly at the chains, her fingertips bleeding. Her mother stirred, blinked at her, confounded.

"Viola?"

"Who did this to you?" Viola asked. "Where's Father?"

"Viola, it's really you." Lady Venetia smiled as her daughter tried to slip an arm under her shoulder to support her. Her smile died, trembling with fear. "You're really here. No," she moaned. "No."

"Help me!" Viola shouted at Tristan. She glared at the servants who gathered at the doorways, watching her mutely. "What's the matter with you?"

Tristan had the same sharp, uncomfortable feeling in his belly that he'd had the time a gang of outlaws had surprised him in the woods. He'd nearly lost his head that night. He saw the flash of torchlight glinting off chain mail from along the battlements. A dog barked in the kennel.

"Viola, come away."

"No." She slapped at his hands.

Lady Venetia was as wild-eyed and desperate as her daughter, but for different reasons. "Viola, you have to leave. You have to run!" She tried to clutch at Tristan's arm, but the chains stopped her short, rattling with a cold, awful sound. "Please. They can't know she's seen me like this. It's not safe. Protect her! Run, damn your eyes!"

The clack of boot heels on the cobblestones near the tower seemed louder than the blacksmith's hammer. Lady Venetia went paler than she already was and then flung herself at the end of her chains like a wild animal. "Not my daughter!"

Viola just frowned at her grandmother who approached them, strange and pale as she always was. "And who is this you've brought with you?"

"Tristan Constantine of Bornebow Hall," he replied with a bow, though his sword was still naked in his hand.

"I see."

Viola crossed her arms. "We want to marry." She stepped closer to her mother, trying to keep her safe even though she wasn't entirely sure what the danger was.

"You're already promised to Richard Vale," Veronique replied briskly. "Return to him at once."

"No," Viola said. One of the servants gasped from where she was pressed against the dog kennel. Venetia began to weep. Tristan wondered how the hell he was supposed to fight an old woman. Viola just narrowed her eyes.

"You will do as you're told." Veronique's voice was sharp and strange. It was like nails inside their skulls.

"I won't," Viola insisted, gritting her teeth against the inexplicable pain. "I'll run away first."

"My husband is not here to mediate," she said dispassionately. "And my son has been troubled enough. But believe me when I tell you, I shan't let you further dishonor our family name by breaking a perfectly good marriage contract."

Viola could not understand how her grandfather or her father could know about this and not be filled with righteous fury. Her grandmother had always been inscrutable and cold, but Lord William had a laugh that could shake a barrel of ale out of its hinges. Her mother was baring her teeth like a bear protecting her young.

"Further dishonor?" Viola asked. "What are you talking about?"

Tristan grabbed her hand before she could get a reply, and dragged her behind him. "Run," he shouted. She turned back to stare at her mother but Tristan's hold would not break, nor his pace slacken in any way. He tossed her onto his horse and scrambled up behind her, shielding her back so she wouldn't be vulnerable in their escape. Her mare was already in the stables being rubbed down. They thundered out of the first gate-house and down the path to the main gates.

"Never mind," Veronique said to the guards waiting for her order. "This is best done away from prying eyes." Her eyes glittered as Venetia began to wail. "It's time to rid my son of this embarrassing problem."

Tristan and Viola made it out of the castle grounds and across the field before the horse stumbled. Tristan reined him in, casting a baleful glance at the sky, which was moonless and so dark he could barely see the gleam of the river in the ravine below. He could barely even see the glint of Viola's golden hair inches from his nose. He slid off the mount. "We'll have to go on foot," he said grimly. "He could break a leg over the moors."

"I don't understand," Viola said, shivering under her thick cloak.

Tristan tilted her chin up so she was looking at him. "I won't let them hurt you."

She swallowed, looking more frightened instead of comforted. Dread clawed at his spine as he turned around, expecting a dozen knights, a rabid wolf, a rain of spears.

Anything but a strange old woman.

Veronique crossed the field, quicker than anything he'd ever seen. Her hair streamed behind her under the white linen of her wimple. Her face was pale and perfect, even at a distance. And then she was suddenly standing right in front of them. Her teeth were too long and too sharp.

"Grandmother, why are you doing this?" Viola asked. "And what's wrong with your teeth?"

"Don't call me that," Veronique snapped. "You are no bloodkin of mine. But your father has a soft heart and he loves you as though you were his own."

"But . . . I am."

"Christophe cannot father children." Veronique smiled for the first time, but there was no humor in it. "For the same reason I move faster than you can imagine, for the same reason that I died over thirty years ago and yet still, here I stand."

Viola began to wonder if age had addled her grandmother's mind.

"Vampire." Tristan didn't wonder. He saw the teeth, the pale skin, and reacted as he would have reacted to any other monster. He swung his sword.

"Don't be absurd, boy." She sighed, breaking his hold with a single twist of her hand. His sword fell into the frost-tipped grass. He felt a primal ancient fear such as he'd never felt before. "Your mother tried to foist her bastard on my son," Veronique said. "And still he will not kill her. Because of you." Before Viola could blink, her grandmother had her by the throat. She forced Viola's head back even as she drove Tristan to his knees with a careless blow to the temple. Viola screamed.

And then her father was suddenly there, just as pale in his fury as his mother.

"Maman, you promised," Christophe snapped, breaking her hold. Viola couldn't say a word, though a thousand clammered to be spoken.

Veronique's fangs were fully and viciously extended. Hunger lined her gray irises with red. She snapped her attention on Tristan, who was pushing to his feet, pressing his palm to the bloody gash on his head. Blood dripped onto his tunic. Christophe's fangs lengthened as well and Viola squeaked.

"I promised I wouldn't kill your wife's bastard. I made no such promise about her lover."

Viola went cold and brittle inside. She might not have been able to save her mother but she could save Tristan. She didn't shift position, knew it would only betray her. She whipped her arm out, locking her elbow tight and catching Tristan in the throat with her fist. Already dizzy, he flew off his feet and tumbled down the ravine to the river.

Veronique turned hard gray eyes toward Viola.

Toward me.

It took me a moment to realize this wasn't the Madame

Veronique of Viola's long ago. I was back in my own body, back in the real world without castles and dragons anywhere.

I was Solange again.

But Madame Veronique was still trying to kill me.

CHAPTER 9

Christabel

Tuesday night

I hadn't had a chance to read an entire novel in weeks.

Whatever the others might say about politics, civil war, and hunters, the real evil here was lack of reading time. If they all read more they might freak out less. And if I was going to live forever I was going to have to start a reading list.

Starting with *How to Survive Your Boyfriend's Family*.

Well, not boyfriend exactly. I'd only known him a few weeks. But we *were* dating . . . when we weren't running for our lives.

Connor kept pace beside me, alert for sounds that I still couldn't quite catalogue. After all, it's not like I'd had much experience with the skittering of beetles under tree bark or an owl fluffing her wings a hundred feet over my head. It was disconcerting but at least it didn't give me splitting headaches anymore. And I kind of loved that I was only wearing a thin shirt and Aidan's wampum belt under my army jacket but I wasn't the least bit cold. I could run faster than any other creature in the forest, even in my heavy combat boots. And even when I had mixed feelings as to where I was running to.

Aidan was the one who'd turned me into a vampire. He'd saved my life by doing so, but he'd been the one to kidnap me and put me in danger in the first place. All because he thought I was Lucy and could give him leverage with the Drakes. The Drakes, who weren't too bothered with leverage at the moment, since their daughter had just had the mother of all temper tantrums. The temper tantrums I was used to didn't come with tiaras.

"Your family sure is high maintenance," I muttered, nearly tripping over a root because the sound of mole digging underneath startled me.

"Didn't used to be." Connor flashed me a very brief, slightly sad smile. "Not like this."

I was an idiot. He'd basically watched his little sister go darkside, as he put it, and it had sent the whole family into a tailspin. I stopped running. "I'm sorry," I said softly, twining my fingers through his. "Are you okay?"

He nodded, squeezing my hand. "Sure."

"Are all your brothers as bad a liar as you are?" I asked, stepping closer. I could see the widening of his pupils, and the pale blue fire of his irises. He'd told me my eyes would change too, would go lighter until they looked like amber. I couldn't imagine they'd be half as beautiful as his. He was gentle and self-deprecating and way tougher than people gave him credit for. And twin or not, he was even hotter than Quinn, in my humble opinion.

I kissed him hard but quick. Making out in the woods wouldn't make him feel better the way finding a solution to his family's dilemma would, but for now it was all I could offer.

"You'll get through this," I promised him, the same way he'd promised me I'd survive when I was fighting the bloodchange.

"I know." The dangerous edge he usually kept so hidden, the one that sent all sort of delicious shivers over the backs of my knees, flashed through his usually kind expression. He crowded me back against a tree, moving so quickly it was like a backward dance too fast for human eyes to see. His kiss was considerably darker than mine had been. It made me catch my breath, even though I didn't breathe anymore. I didn't think I'd ever get used to that. If I thought about the emptiness in my chest where there should be a heartbeat, I got sweaty and panicky.

"We're going to get Solange back," he said, against my mouth. My fangs poked into my bottom lip. "Thanks to you."

"We don't know if Aidan will even help us," I felt the need to point out. "And Saga's not exactly predictable."

"You're our best hope."

"If you call me Obi-Wan I'm going to kick you."

He grinned. "Hot. Say Obi-Wan again."

I laughed, shoving his shoulder. "Shut up."

The only reason I was their best hope was the same reason I

wore Aidan's wampum belt: he considered me his emissary. I wasn't just a regular vampire, I was Na-Foir like him. The rest of the vampire world was only just finding out about us. Apparently they'd been hiding for centuries, because the intense blue rivers of our veins made us appear faintly blue all over. As in *Hel-Blar* blue. And I'd had enough experience with the *Hel-Blar* to understand the fear. Still, I wasn't *Hel-Blar*. I wasn't that sick gangrene-blue and I didn't smell like an old swamp. According to Connor, I smelled like cinnamon. That wasn't exactly enough to convince the others; they either stared at me or went to great lengths to avoid eye contact. Except for Sky, who was more interested in convincing me to let her read one of my poems; Uncle Geoffrey, who wanted to study me; and Lucy, who didn't seem to notice the stuff other people got all worked up about.

"Where to now?" Connor asked, since I was the only one who knew the directions to their hideout.

Technically.

"Is that a cedar or a pine tree?" I asked, annoyed. "And what the hell does starboard mean?"

"I think it's pirate for 'right,'" Connor replied. He was taking a risk coming with me but he wouldn't change his mind. Aidan and Saga knew him so it would probably be all right. We kept running between the trees while I tried to remember if that boulder on the right was the one I was looking for.

And to think right now, my mother probably assumed I was home reading a book. She still had no idea what I'd become. And I wasn't going to tell her until she was out of rehab. And stable.

The fallen log beside us looked vaguely familiar.

So did the dagger that whistled through the air and slammed into the ground in front of us. Jewels glinted in the hilt. Connor leaped in front of me while I stumbled back.

Saga laughed and we both looked up to see her standing on the edge of a rock outcropping, half hidden by the top of an enormous cedar hedge. Her hands were on her hips and her red hair streamed down her back. She wore a vest over a white shirt, ripped jeans, and tall boots. "If it isn't my favorite scalawags. Fancy a cup of grog?"

"Um, no thanks." Grog was the most disgusting thing I'd ever drunk, including blood. And Connor's uncle Geoffrey still had to hook me up for blood transfusions every dusk because I just couldn't stand the idea of swallowing blood.

"Christabel," Aidan said quietly, emerging from the green boughs. I hadn't even noticed him there, watching us. Judging by Connor's violent start, he hadn't either. "What brings you here?" He glanced at Connor. "Has your sister quit playing queen and finally called council?"

"I need to ask you something," I said. "If you can help us, you might get your council faster."

"Come along then," he said, vanishing back into the cedar. We followed him to a hidden wall of rock, looking up to the caves where Saga was standing.

"Come on, lass," she grinned. "Climb up to the eagle's nest."

Climbing up wasn't easy, despite the fact that I could move faster than ever before. I still clung to thick roots and crumbling rock, muttering lines from "The Highwayman" under my breath for comfort. I didn't even realize I was doing it until Connor came up beside me.

"Don't worry," he said. He scaled the rest of the outcropping and reached down to help me up. The treetops were far below us, like pointy green spears. I felt better with sturdy ground under my boots. Behind us, the cave opening led into a scattering of smaller caves. It smelled damp and cold, even with the candles burning in the dirt along the back. Saga sat on a pile of furs, drinking from a leather wineskin. Aidan crouched beside her, the bear claw around his neck swinging like a hypnotist's pendulum.

"We need one of those copper collars," I blurted out. So much for suave political negotiation.

"Liam sends children to parley?" Saga asked.

"Liam isn't asking," I said. "I am." He didn't even know we were here. None of the brothers had suggested telling him. Though apparently, Logan was sure Sebastian would mention it so no one had told him either.

Logan's girlfriend Isabeau thought she might be able to undo some of the magic that Solange had unleashed by taking the crown from Helena. But we needed a collar to keep her powerless long enough to try. I didn't really know Solange. What little I'd seen of her, I sincerely hoped she was ill, like the Drakes thought. But in the end it didn't matter. I was doing this for Lucy and for Connor. But Aidan and Saga couldn't know about any of it. No one could. Even I knew that if word of that kind of vulnerability got out, it would be disastrous.

"And why should we help you?"

I narrowed my eyes at them both. "I seem to recall saving you from a stake to the chest. Not to mention a horde of rabid *Hel-Blar* and angry Helios-Ra hunters." And then we'd blown up the town, which Saga and Aidan had made their home base. No one was perfect.

"She has fire." Saga approved, though her eyes were silvery and cold. "I'll give you that."

"If I could have just one collar, I could bring it to Solange," I said. "We might convince her to hold the council."

"You don't care about the council," Aidan pointed out. "So why do you really want the collar, Christabel?"

"Proof," Connor interjected. We'd already decided on the proper misdirection when they started asking too many questions about Solange.

"Proof of what, boy?"

Connor's jaw clenched. I knew he hated it when they called him 'boy' like that. "Proof that you still have information to share with my uncle. You said so yourself, your scientist was eaten. What if something happens to you too?"

"Are you threatening me?" Saga's movements were silky with menace. She could have been on a ship's deck, light on her feet and quicker than wind in a sail. Connor barely had a chance to react. By the time I'd blinked, he was flat on his back in the dirt with the tip of Saga's dagger scraping his Adam's apple.

I jumped forward but Aidan held me back with an arm around my waist. It stopped me so abruptly I heard something in my neck crack. I struggled briefly but I'd have had better luck snapping steel cables in half with my bare hands when I was still human. "Stop it," I yelled.

Connor swallowed, his blue eyes not leaving hers. "I only meant, what if one of your *Hel-Blar* gets loose? You don't have the whistle to control them anymore. Anything could go wrong."

She let him up as quickly as she'd taken him down. Adrenaline spiked through me, making me tremble as Aidan released me. Connor got to his feet warily. There was a tiny drop of blood on his throat.

"It doesn't matter," Aidan said. "We don't have any to spare."

"But . . ."

"You blew up our stash, remember?" Saga pointed out. "Along with my whistle."

Oops.

"You have to have at least one. That's all I want. I mean, you had two of the *Hel-Blar* with you at the coronation." They'd strained on their leashes, held there by the collar and the threat of Saga's fury. The next day I'd dreamed it was me on that leash.

"I've no intention of making us vulnerable so you can impress your boyfriend," Saga said darkly. "We've few enough left in our army. And we still have need of them, clearly. The new queen is hardly living up to expectations."

Connor clenched his fist, struggling with his temper. I stepped partially in front of him. "There must be something."

"Max is guarding the last of our army, before you get any ideas. And he's under orders to kill anyone who tries to get past him. You included," Saga added. "But I reckon you could find a few of my escaped pets near the bogs east of here. Word has it mountain lion carcasses were found there, and a mess they'd made too. You could try your luck," she shrugged. Aidan shot her a look. She just smiled.

"Christabel, let's go," Connor murmured, nudging me back toward the opening of the cave. "They're not going to help."

The climb down the rocks was easier, since I pretty much slid down on my butt the entire way. Connor caught me before I brained myself on a boulder.

"Christabel?" Aidan said from the top of the outcropping. I glanced up through the cedar needles. "Be careful."

Connor tugged me out of the bushes onto the path before I could reply. He glanced over his shoulder a few times before feeling safe enough to pull out his phone to message his brother. "Plan B," he said.

Quinn met us at the river ten minutes later. I was already lost. Being a vampire didn't suddenly negate the fact that I'd been a city girl for eighteen years. I didn't know my way around the forest. A tree was a tree was a tree.

Quinn pushed away from a boulder he'd been leaning against, tossing his hair off his forehead. He was so much like his brother, and yet it was like looking at a stranger who'd stolen Connor's face. "So what's plan B, exactly?"

"You heard Saga." I glanced at Connor. "The bogs. Saga said there are some runaway *Hel-Blar* with collars living there. So I'll be bait. They'll chase me, thinking I'm weak. And then you'll grab one."

Quinn looked at Connor then groaned. "Oh my God, it's like talking to Lucy."

Connor jerked his hand through his hair. "Christa, you can't fight." He took a healthy step out of range while Quinn grinned. "You're not trained."

"I can run," I argued. "Look, do we need this damn collar or not?" He nodded reluctantly. "Then let's go already." I took off, assuming they'd catch up. When I couldn't hear them, I stopped, turning around with a glower. "What?"

Connor's mouth quirked. "The bogs are that way," he said, pointing in the other direction.

"Well, crap," I muttered, doubling back.

It took us just over an hour to get to the bogs. Quinn scaled one of the trees and jumped from branch to branch, keeping an eye out. Connor grabbed my hand.

"Christa, are you sure about this?"

"*I have drunken deep of joy, And I will taste no other wine tonight,*" I quoted Shelley.

"I'm not sure what that means about tonight," he returned drily. "But watch your back."

I kissed him hard. "You too."

This was way more nerve-racking than walking downtown alone in the middle of the night. At least there were streetlights there and I knew the layout of the roads and subway stations. Here it was just murky, soft mud under my boots, making a sucking sound with every step. The deeper in I went, the more it smelled like rot and mildew. I shivered.

I was trying to fight my way out of a clump of thick bulrushes when I smelled blood.

The severed remains of a cougar lay in bloody clumps a few feet away. And a few more feet beyond that, a *Hel-Blar* crouched, sniffing the air. I froze. He wasn't wearing a collar. It wouldn't do us any good if I was caught by him. I searched the cattails and bare branches for another flash of blue, or the glint of copper.

He sniffed again, with a raw snorting sound. "I smell that rotter Aidan," he said. Most of them didn't speak, but the ones that did were even more terrifying. Another *Hel-Blar* shuffled forward, hunched over as if she was walking on all fours. She wore a copper collar and was clearly beyond speech. She howled and gnashed her teeth, saliva dripping off her bloodstained chin. I didn't know if it was the collar or captivity that had made her like that, or if she'd always been savage. Two more *Hel-Blar* shuffled out of the weeds to join her. I backed up a step.

Predictably, I snapped a twig under my foot.

I'd once had to climb over a violent, passed-out drunk who hung out behind my favorite bookstore downtown and he'd never even paused in his snoring. Here in the country, I was hopeless.

And about to get eaten.

"Shit!" I yelled, abandoning any pretense at dignity or stealth. I launched into a run, the twisted reeds grabbing at my feet. I slipped and fell, my knee hitting a rock. Pain shot up my leg, water soaking into my jeans. I flailed forward out of the bog. The branches poked and bit at me and I put my arms up to shield my face so I wouldn't lose an eye.

The *Hel-Blar* closed in. The screeching and clacking of jaws behind me made me run faster, made me sweat.

The first *Hel-Blar* was the closest behind me. He snarled and spat, and was also the first to fall into dust at the end of one of Quinn's crossbow bolts. He was perched up in a tree like a particularly vicious squirrel, laughing. Connor darted out to block the next *Hel-Blar*. He flung a stake, hurling the *Hel-Blar* off his feet and pinning him to a pine tree like an insect. It didn't kill him, but at least it took him out of the fight temporarily.

The female curled her hands like claws, clacking her pointed needle teeth at me. She howled incoherently when I darted out of the way. My ankle hit the edge of a big rock and I stumbled, landing on my tailbone. The *Hel-Blar* laughed, stinking of pond scum. A crossbow bolt slammed between us, flinging mud and stones. I flung handfuls of dirt at her face until she blinked madly, covering her eyes.

Connor was fighting the other two and they circled him like hyenas with fresh meat. Their dusky blue skin and bloody teeth made them even more frightening. They widened their jaws, showing off their fangs. My own automatically extended in reaction.

Connor drove his heel into the stomach of the one nearest to him and ducked a wild swing from his howling companion. He came up, stake held against his forearm, the way he'd once taught me. The force drove the weapon into the *Hel-Blar*'s chest, sliding up under the skin, the muscles, and the ribs to pierce his heart. Ash clouded the cold air. Connor kicked the last one into the woman who was still trying to grab at my feet. They both sprawled in the dirt with the crack of bones and teeth.

But he'd forgotten about the one pinned to the tree.

We all had.

He'd pushed through the stake so that there was a ragged hole in his shoulder, bleeding sluggishly. "Connor!" I shouted, but I was too late.

Connor flew over me and hit a trunk, falling into the undergrowth. The tree shuddered, raining pine needles. Quinn dropped down off his branch, a stake in each hand. He jammed one of the stakes into the shoulder of the *Hel-Blar* who'd hurt Connor. The *Hel-Blar* shrieked, trying to yank the weapon out. Quinn shifted so he was shielding me.

Connor shook his head as if it was ringing, as he pushed himself back up. "Quinn, behind you!"

Quinn spun, his arm extended and stake out. He caught the *Hel-Blar* Connor had thrown at the woman. More ash and blood splattered and Quinn flipped out of its trajectory. Connor spun, jamming his stake into the woman's chest as she leaped at me again. She snarled and then crumpled to ash.

Connor flipped his hand over, catching the collar before it hit the ground. He smirked, just like Quinn.

"Got it."

CHAPTER 10

Lucy

I spent most of my classes reading the books Spencer recommended, which I hid under my desk. When Jody ratted me out and Ms. Kali demanded to see what I was reading, I wasn't sure which one of them was most surprised to find that it was *Ancient Magical Traditions and Secret Societies*.

"Actually, the revised edition is much better," Ms. Kali remarked with a dry smile, handing me back the book. "But you might try reading it during your free period."

I read all through my lunch period, my free period, and even in the halls walking to class. I found out all sorts of weird things.

Scatter seeds in front of a particular family of Eastern European vampires and they will be compelled to count them instead of chasing you.

Vampire hunters wear wild roses to protect themselves.

I really wanted to see if I could convince Kieran to run around wearing pink roses in his hair.

In China, the vampire is known as jiang shi.

I was on my way to the gym, with the shadows long and purple over the fields, when I read a passage that made everything click in my head. It was so loud I was surprised no one else heard it.

Hunters in a sixteenth-century banished Black Lodge drank vampire blood, believing it would make them immune to the vampire's power. This practice is merely superstition and not to be added to the modern hunter's arsenal.

I remembered a night in my backyard when Solange and I were thirteen. We camped out in a tent, telling my parents we wanted to watch a meteor shower when really we just wanted to eat the chocolate bars Solange snuck over in her sleeping bag and giggle. Giddy with sugar, we'd decided to become blood sisters. We made little cuts on our smallest fingers and pinky swore an oath to be friends forever.

Our blood had mixed.

I wasn't mostly immune to vampire pheromones *just* because I'd grown up with the Drakes.

I had Solange's blood in my system.

Which is why she couldn't compel me, even now that she was strong enough to compel other vampires, right down to members of her own family. And Nicholas was with her right now. However noble his intentions, could he stand against her compulsions?

Only if he had her blood in his veins.

But he was unreachable at the Blood Moon camp. The other

Drakes were beyond exiled, they were condemned to be shot on sight. If they were going to have the slightest chance to undo whatever had been done to Solange, they'd need this information. They'd need to know what Nicholas was doing inside the camp.

I dialed Bruno's number even as I broke into a run. I left him a message and then e-mailed Connor, just in case. Isabeau was unreachable in the caves and Christabel was far too new a vampire to be able to safely negotiate the current murky political undercurrents. Not to mention that she wasn't answering her cell phone. Even Spencer, who I considered conscripting, was off somewhere, feeding. It wasn't far past dusk, after all.

So there was no one else.

Except me.

And I couldn't wait. Every moment lost was one more second which might get Nicholas killed.

I had to find Hunter. I had to get off campus. I was so distracted I crashed right into Tyson and we both went flying. He helped me gather up my books, brushing snow off a hardcover volume that fit in the palm of my hand.

He read the title. "You're doing the homework I gave you."

"Yes, and it's the best homework ever," I shouted, letting him help me up. "And you are the best tutor in the entire world." I kissed him enthusiastically on the cheek. His dark skin flushed red. I was too busy hurtling off toward the gym to find Hunter to tease him about it. She wasn't even there. I texted her, darting back to the dorm to get my stuff. She must have texted Jenna and Chloe because all three were waiting for me by the school van, armed to the teeth.

"You look like you've been mainlining espresso," Jenna remarked. "Are your eyes supposed to be that big?"

I just grinned at her, proving her right. I felt a little manic, both thrilled and grim, as if I was going into battle. My hands shook slightly as Chloe shoved something under the back of my shirt. She climbed back into the van and started to mutter at her laptop.

Hunter checked all my weapons and the GPS Chloe had just clipped on me. "You know you're dumb, right?" Hunter asked. "And so am I for helping you out. Got your Hypnos?"

"Of course."

Chloe tapped away on the keyboard and tossed us a smug smile. "GPS is locked in. I've got your signal."

"You guys don't have to do this," I said, as Hunter slid the door shut and Jenna started to drive. There was a miniature crossbow on the dashboard in front of her.

"I think Hunter already established that we're all dumb. So yeah, we kinda do."

I caught her eye in the rearview mirror. "The last time you helped me you got knocked out."

She actually bared her teeth. "Which is why I'll wait in the damn van, instead of going in for a little payback."

I checked my stakes, hanging snugly on the strap across my chest. I knew the guards would take them away. I was counting on it. If they were focused on the obvious weapons, they might not think to check the soles of the specially rigged boots Hunter lent me. They were only a little bit too big. And the retractable stakes and metal spikes were worth the blisters.

"Got your walkie-talkie?" Hunter asked as the van rattled down the country roads.

I patted my jacket pocket. "Yes, Mom."

She ignored my sarcasm. Quinn probably inured her to all distractions. If she could resist his pretty face and his smart mouth, she could resist a nuclear bomb during exams and still pass with honors. "Got your whistle?"

"And my flare gun," I assured her. "All in my bag and none of which they'll let me keep."

"You need to show more boob," Chloe tossed over her shoulder.

"It's freezing out there," I complained, undoing another button on my blouse. "How is pneumonia sexy?" I frowned down at my cleavage. "Plus, I should have worn a push-up bra."

"Bloodslaves are supposed to show a lot of skin," Chloe insisted. "It was on the exam last year."

I sighed, twisting my hair up into a scrunchie. It was barely long enough, but Chloe was right, I needed to show more skin if I was going to be convincing. And a bare neck would do wonders toward pleading my case. I pushed up the sleeves of my blouse, under my fake-fur vest to display Nicholas's fang marks on the inside of my elbow. They were nearly healed now and barely visible. I rubbed them viciously, until they chafed and looked raw. It would have to be enough.

"Are you sure I can't talk you out of this?" Hunter asked.

"If it were Quinn, would you go?" she muttered under her breath in response. "Exactly."

"I'm a better fighter," she pointed out, but I knew it was a last-ditch attempt.

"I know," I said. "But I'm nearly immune to vampire phero-mones even without nose plugs and you're not. Which is the point. He needs more of my blood specifically."

"Shouldn't we, oh, I don't know, actually *prove* your theory before you go off all Buffy?" Jenna asked as she pulled the van into the woods and drove as far as she could, until the trees grew too close together.

"No time." I met Hunter's gaze. "We're both dating Drakes," I said. "Between us, we can handle anything." We smiled grimly at each other.

"Ready?" she asked finally, wearing what I called her "vampire hunter" face.

I nodded and she slid the door open. She traded seats with Jenna, who pulled herself up onto the roof with her crossbow. The moon was full enough to make the trees look silver and lonely. I held up the phone Chloe had given me, already set with a blue blinking dot that was me and a red blinking dot that was the Bower. Connor would be proud of all the gadgets currently stuck into every fold of clothing, including my underwear.

I ran through the woods, feeling fear in my bones despite the bravado I tended to wear like a favorite worn sweater. I knew it was monumentally stupid of me to be doing this, but I honestly had no other option. Not unless you counted letting my boyfriend be even more vulnerable than he already was—and I so didn't.

So I'd do what needed to be done.

Which would have been a more convincing pep speech if adren-aline and nerves weren't making me feel like I was going to throw up on the first vampire I saw.

I had no idea where the Blood Moon camp was. The only time I'd been close enough to spy on it was with Solange back when they were setting it up, and then briefly before she'd dragged me away to have Nicholas bite me. And being hard to find was the whole point, even to the survivalist hiker whack jobs who lived on the outskirts of Violet Hill.

But I could at least find my way to the Bower, where I'd last seen Nicholas. He'd activated the GPS tag he snuck under my collar and sent the coordinates to Kieran. Kieran, who we very specifically left out of this little adventure. He'd want to help, but throwing an ex-boyfriend at Solange right now seemed like a bad idea. Not that she'd been all that pleased to see me the last time, but at least I could punch her back.

I picked my way between the trees, frost crunching under my boots. Within half an hour I was closing in on the Bower. I slipped my phone into my pocket before coming out between two oak trees. It was as beautiful as I'd remembered, from the brief glimpse I'd had. Velvet couches and chairs with legs carved into lions and dragons sat around a long table that spanned a narrow creek. Lanterns dangled from the bare branches, glittering with candlelight and ice. Wine bottles I knew for a fact weren't filled with wine, circulated from pale hand to pale hand. Two women whispered to each other, another drank from a wooden cup. Two men argued amiably and a vampire girl who looked as if she were wearing a tutu swung her bare feet from the branch she was sitting on.

"Ah, breakfast," someone purred as I took another step closer. He was beautiful, carved from mahogany and ivory. "Who sent you, love?"

I cleared my throat as he pushed out of his chair to circle me lazily. "I'm here for Nicholas Drake," I said as firmly as I could.

"Are you now?"

The thing about joining the Helios-Ra was that I was suddenly aware of all the horrible ways I could die at the hands of a vampire. Before, I'd known the Drakes would never hurt me and it was enough. Now everything was muddled and I had to worry about hunters and Huntsmen, *Hel-Blar* and vampires I'd never even heard of. I tried to remember how Penelope had acted when we'd found her half-unconscious at Solange's feet. She'd welcomed the feeding, had acted honored. Addicted. I made my smile silly and distracted. "He sent for me," I whispered, as if I was confiding in him. He trailed his fingertip along the line of my throat and I fought my natural instinct, which was to kick him in the shin and poke him with a pink-glitter stake. Instead, I giggled and tried to look regretful and tempted.

"He doesn't like to share," I said. If I'd been able to, I would have smacked myself.

"A pity." He jerked his head to a faint trail leading west, along the creek. "That way, love."

I walked away, shoving my hands in my pockets so no one would see they were trembling. The back of my neck felt icy. Out of the frying pan, into the fire, as my grandma used to say. She also would have said to stay the hell out of the woods when they were crawling with vampires. I didn't even want to think of what my parents would say. Dad's ulcer was probably exploding even now.

The leaf-strewn trail led me to a grassy field littered with motorcycles and dirt bikes. I was about to step into the clearing when the sound of a footstep startled me.

"I wouldn't do that if I was you."

I spun, flinging a stake. The vampire bent out of the way in a fluid movement that no human could have managed. The stake slammed into a tree, spitting bark. She raised an eyebrow. "You must be Lucy."

I blinked at her. "Um."

She smiled, flashing fangs. She wore paint-splattered overalls and a pink Gerbera daisy in her Afro. "Duncan showed me a photo. He seemed certain you'd show up here at some point and need help."

I smiled back sheepishly. "Busted." I paused. "Wait. You're the girl he was kissing!"

"I usually go by Sky," she returned drily. "You'd better leave all those weapons here. Not only will they be confiscated but real bloodslaves don't arm themselves as if they're going into battle."

I let her take my stakes away and my bag of assorted weapons. I suddenly felt naked.

"You really shouldn't go in there," Sky said.

"I know," I agreed. "But I have to. I have to give Nicholas a message."

"Tell me and I'll tell—damn." She broke off as a vampire stepped into view and waved at us imperiously. "Too late."

She lowered her voice, clamping her hand around my wrist and tugging me toward the guard at the entrance. She whispered so softly I could barely hear her. "Don't fight."

I did *not* like that advice.

"I'll find Nicholas as fast as I can. I promise."

She pulled me toward the guard who watched us suspiciously. She wore the royal vampire crest on her vest. "Who's this?"

"Nicholas Drake sent for her."

"Bloodslave." The guard nodded at another vampire in the tree above us. "I'll take her."

Sky didn't let go of my wrist. "She's attached to the queen. Can't I just take her to the Drake tent?"

"You know Solange's rules. No exception." She looked at me, her pupils widening and glinting. "Come along." She was trying to use her pheromones on me. She didn't know who I was or that I was immune. It was the only weapon I had left, besides the stake in the sole of my left boot. I forced myself to follow her docilely. Sky darted away, bolting so quickly there was only a whirlwind of dust and snow where she'd been standing.

On the other side of the tree line the camp was fairly quiet. The few vampires outside turned to watch us as the guard marched me down the main path. There was the usual assortment of brocade gowns, glittering saris, medieval tunics, and ripped jeans. The vampire still clinging to the eighties with her side ponytail and teased bangs was unfortunate. There were also fangs and snarls and bloodstains in the dirt.

We passed the Drake tent, the blue-and-silver dragon pennant flapping in the cold wind under a royal banner. I didn't see Solange or Nicholas and I honestly wasn't sure if that was a good sign or not. "Where are we going?" I asked the guard. "I'm here for

Nicholas Drake. You know? The queen's brother?" Referring to Solange as the queen was just weird. "And the queen? Kind of my best friend."

"Mm-hmmm." She didn't sound convinced or even particularly impressed. Damn it. "All human visitors have to wait here for their hosts."

I balked, physically digging my heels into the dirt. It might have been midnight in the middle of a forest under a mountain, but between the full moon and the torches and camping lanterns, I could see perfectly well.

Too well.

The rows of painted canvas tents, some as large as carnival big tops, came to a natural meeting place, like a village square. In the center of the grass-flattened clearing was a tree stripped of its branches that stood at least three feet around. Hooks were set into the trunk, securing chains.

Attached to them were humans.

Some wore chains several yards long, stretching out to canvas roofs painted with vampire crests and furnished with cushions and small iron fire pits for warmth. Some were bare to the elements. While others were secured right up against the tree post with barely enough slack in their chains to sit down. Most of them were pale and wore necklaces and bracelets of dried blood.

"Oh hell, no," I said when the guard yanked me forward.

"Queen's orders," she returned drily. "You know, your best friend?"

Sarcasm is so much better as a weapon when I'm the one wielding it.

"Solange would never order something like this," I said quietly.

"That's Queen Solange to you," the guard corrected, snapping a metal cuff around my wrist and stalking away.

I pulled savagely but I already knew it wouldn't magically click open. The metal was cold on my skin and the chain was short enough that I had to lean against the tree. I couldn't help but remember the last time I'd tried to infiltrate a vampire gathering. I'd ended up in a dungeon dressed like an extra from a Marie-Antoinette movie set while another crazy "queen" ate a raw deer heart thinking it belonged to my best friend. Chained to a post with snow falling lightly, with hungry vampires pacing the perimeter, wasn't exactly an improvement.

Apparently, learning from my mistakes wasn't high on my list of priorities.

When my teeth started to chatter, I tried to ease closer to one of the fires. I managed to move about three inches. I yanked at the chain again, scowling. I'd never felt less like a vampire sympathizer or a vampire hunter in my entire life.

"You'll only hurt yourself," a guy about my age called from under the protection of a tent top and a pile of blankets. He looked comfortable and perfectly happy, watching a movie on a laptop. "They only chain the new ones or the ones being punished that close to the post."

"Great," I muttered. "And what do you mean 'being punished'? For what?"

He shrugged, the fire crackling between us casting shadows under his eyes. "Traitors, donors who can't keep a secret. The usual."

He grimaced at his own chains, glinting from the edge of one of his blankets. "Can't say I love the new system."

"Yeah," I agreed sourly. "It's kind of rude."

"Apparently the new queen is traditional."

I snorted. "Traditional whack job?"

He looked around warily. "You're new to this vampire thing, aren't you?"

I nearly laughed out loud. "Not exactly."

"Well, a little tip. Vampires have really good hearing and the queen doesn't like to hear dissension."

I had to actually bite my tongue until tears came to my eyes to stop the comment I was dying to make about the new queen and what she could do with her traditions. The pain cleared my head. "Traditional to when?" I asked instead. "Because I've never heard of this."

"The twelfth century, apparently," he replied, shrugging. "The Middle Ages or something. My host family isn't that old, so I don't know much else."

Okay, whatever had happened to Solange was somehow linked to the twelfth century. I wasn't sure why that was important, but it felt like something I might need to know. I felt a small surge of excitement that we might actually find a way to save her.

A vampire with an expression I didn't trust, circled closer to me, sniffing.

"Hey, back off." I scowled, kicking out at him. I missed, of course, but I was proving a point more than anything else. He just smiled slowly, hungrily. His fangs elongated. "Shit," I said, belatedly trying the yoga breathing my mom taught me to calm me down. *"Back off."*

"But you smell like sugar and pepper. Just a taste."

I held up my fists. "I belong to Nicholas Drake." Usually I would have rolled my eyes at a ridiculous statement like that. Right now, it seemed my best defense.

He didn't come closer, but he didn't back away either. He just kept staring at me with that creepy hungry glint in his eyes. Stay focused, I ordered myself. This is just a minor setback.

Someone rattled his chains suddenly on the other side of the post, and shouted obscenities. He jerked at his chains so frantically I heard the pop of his wrist dislocating. It didn't stop him. One of the girls nearby tried to hush him. He finally stopped fighting when a guard wearing the royal insignia punched him in the face and then walked away, looking irritated. The guy crumpled silently, dangling from his short chains.

Hell of a setback.

And then just to prove that things could always get worse, they did.

CHAPTER 11

Solange

Now I knew why Viola hated Madame Veronique.

I could still feel the visceral bite of her hatred for her, from that night in the tent when I'd challenged Veronique. I hadn't realized why I was doing it at the time. I'd been stewing in frustration for so long I'd just lashed out. But now it made sense. Madame Veronique knew Viola and tried to keep her apart from her beloved.

Constantine.

He was going by his last name now but I'd have known those eyes anywhere. Even for a human they were an odd blue. They'd have gone violet over the years, as he waited for Viola to somehow return. That must be why he'd sought me out, why'd he'd been the only one who "understood" me. He'd orchestrated my entire coup. All while staying carefully concealed from Madame Veronique.

I kind of wanted to stab him.

Mom would be so proud.

And Viola and Madame Veronique hadn't just known each other. They'd been related. They were grandmother and granddaughter.

Which made Viola Drake the first daughter born to the Drake family. The first of only two daughters, of which I was the second.

Little parts of the puzzle began to fall into place: Madame Veronique hiring an old witch woman to look into the future. She'd defined me with that damn prophecy, hundreds of years before I was even born.

And the reason the dragon had attacked Viola's knights as well as me was because it was the emblem of our family. Lucy's father would have called it our totem spirit. Viola had incorporated it into her subconscious, the same way she'd kept a piece of Gwyneth and me. She still feared Madame Veronique.

With good reason.

Memories shifted in my head until they started to make some semblance of sense. None of which I really had time to consider at the moment.

Because I'd slammed back into my body at the exact moment one of Madame Veronique's creepy handmaidens threw a stake at me. I recognized her by her medieval style dress and the heavy pendant in the shape of the Drake dragon holding ivy in its jaws.

Viola had only let me back into my own body in Violet Hill long enough to help her. I knew my body and what it could do better than she did and she knew she'd die without me. I couldn't do anything but react.

My mother's training had me flipping sideways, like a corkscrew. The cold air whistled around my ears and stung my eyes. I was already considering my options, even as I spun and spun, my hair lifting into the air as if I were underwater. Escape wasn't immediately possible. I'd have to fight. For that I needed weapons.

I was cataloguing what I could use as I landed lightly on the balls of my feet. Trees for height, branches for stakes, pheromones, speed.

They weren't going to be enough.

My left foot slipped on a bit of ice. I was still getting accustomed to being corporeal again and it made me clumsier than usual. The fact that for some reason I was wearing a white silk slip didn't help. I was practically naked.

The stake whistled past my head, showering me with splinters of wood when it landed in a nearby tree. The handmaiden snarled and advanced on me, another stake already in her hand. Three more of her sister handmaidens fanned out behind her. I ducked another stake, but only barely. It sliced through my sleeve and my upper arm, leaving a burning trail of blood to my elbow. I backed up, yanking the stake out of the tree. It was splintered but better than nothing.

Another stake whistled my way. I caught it and flung the splintered one back at the same time. It missed its target but at least the other two handmaidens had to jump out of the way. The third one leaped at me, snarling, fangs bared. She was pale and deadly as mistletoe berries. She caught me in the shoulder with the heel of her palm, hard enough that I heard the grind and pop of it dislocating. Pain seared through me and I hurled myself backward, cracking it against a tree. My shoulder popped back into place just as painfully as it had popped out.

She closed in, a dagger in one hand and a rapier in the other. The hem of her long embroidered gown flared out, like the petals of a poisonous flower.

"Viola, love, where are you at? We've barely started." Constantine sauntered into the clearing wearing nothing but leather pants and a lazy, intimate smile. It died as soon as he saw the handmaidens. There were leaves in his tousled hair and he was barefoot.

I suddenly knew exactly why I was running around the forest in my underwear.

He tackled the handmaiden who now had me by the hair. They staggered, landing several feet away in a patch of withered ferns. I whirled, preparing to meet the next two handmaidens. They moved slowly, patiently, like icebergs drifting in an arctic sea. I looked from one to the other.

"Stop," I commanded, trying to exude pheromones, gathering the power inside of me and pushing it out like wavering blasts of heat.

They paused.

Constantine and the other handmaiden were still fighting in the bushes, too far away to be affected by my compulsion.

"Drop your weapons," I ordered the other two, who were still frozen in place, glaring at me. Seven stakes, a mini crossbow, three rapiers, five daggers, and a set of silver handcuffs landed in the snow. I reached cautiously for one of the rapiers. The weight was familiar and comforting in my hand. "Now go away and leave us alone."

They turned and walked away, leaning as if they were fighting a wild wind at their back. They tried to fight the compulsion but couldn't. I had a tiny delicious moment of smug satisfaction.

And then the handmaiden fighting Constantine whistled shrilly through her teeth signaling to the others, even as she dodged a vicious jab to the jugular.

The handmaidens were bad.

Being possessed was bad.

But this was so much worse.

CHAPTER 12

Lucy

It was my experience that when vampires start bowing and looking all formal, it's best to get the hell out of the way.

Which I would have done if I wasn't chained to a post.

There was more bowing and murmurs of "My lord" and "My prince" and two of the female donors strained at the end of their chains, smiling and showing cleavage. One of them actually sighed, like she was meeting someone from a boy band. It was embarrassing. Which could only mean one thing.

A Drake brother.

And since all but one of them were exiled on pain of death, it could only mean one person specifically.

Nicholas.

My palms went damp. I wasn't sure why but I felt nervous and exposed, and it had nothing to do with the chains. The crowd parted and suddenly Nicholas was there, stalking toward me, his serious face cut in hard, uncompromising lines. His gray eyes flared silver, like jagged pieces of mirror sharp enough to slice through your skin. I half expected blood to be running down my arms.

"What is she doing here?" he asked. He sounded lethal and dark. It was hard to remember that this was the same seventeen-year-old Nicholas who'd given me a mix CD just last week. He stood like a man, not like a younger brother or a youngest son or any of the other things that defined him. They were still part of him, but the pieces now fit into a more complicated puzzle.

"She said she was here on your orders," a guard replied, glaring at me. I lifted my chin and glared back.

"I mean, what is she doing chained to the tree," Nicholas continued, so evenly the guard swallowed.

"Queen's orders," he replied quickly, defensively.

My boyfriend made a vampire guard at least twice his age nervous. I was kind of proud. Also? Really freaking nervous.

Because the truth was, I still didn't know if he was broken.

"Unchain her," Nicholas ordered while I tried to interpret his expression. He looked stronger and older.

"Beg pardon, but she hasn't been vouched for," the guard said.

Nicholas raised an eyebrow. "My sister isn't here," he said. "But I am. So Un. Chain. Her," he repeated, slowly and emphatically, his fangs lengthening to killing points.

I actually shivered. My animal self, the one who reacted to lightning and strange sounds at night, urged me to *run run run*.

My animal self was forgetting the cardinal rule with vampires: *don't run.*

The clamp of iron around my aching wrist was replaced by the clamp of Nicholas's pale fingers. It wasn't any less confining or unbending. I grabbed his arm with my free hand. "Nicholas, what—"

He spun so fast, I got dizzy.

"You will address me as 'Your Highness,'" he demanded, his voice like a whip slicing the air, or the tail of a poisonous snake. He backed me into the post, until the dangling empty chain pressed into my side. The bloodslaves parted around us. Nicholas's hand slid up my bare neck, tilting my head forcibly to the side. He dragged his lips along my jugular, pausing with his lips over my ear. I swallowed, my throat so dry I could barely form words.

"Be scared." His voice was barely a breath, tickling my ear, sending shivers over my skin.

I had to hope he was asking me to play along.

That he wasn't actually serious.

He pulled away just slightly, his pupils wide and black as a pond at night, edged with pale fog and moonlight. I could almost, almost, catch a glimpse of the real Nicholas.

And then he yanked me along behind him until I was stumbling and tripping over my own feet. One of the bloodslave girls started to weep when she realized Nicholas wasn't picking her. She made me irrationally angry. "Oh, grow a spine," I snapped at her when she tried to touch Nicholas's boot. "You're giving all girls a bad name."

Said the girl who was currently allowing her boyfriend to pull her about like a rag doll.

"I'm so going to punch you if this is a trap," I muttered.

Nicholas didn't even glance back at me and he didn't pause until we approached the Drake tent. There was a tiered table full of burning candles and flowers on a rug out front. There were wine bottles of blood, pomegranates, and baskets of silver jewelry, all at the foot of a painting of Solange. I gaped at it.

"She likes the attention." Nicholas yanked me through the opening to the tent. Except for the wooden furniture and the rugs and lanterns, it was empty.

I reached out and yanked his hair as savagely as I could. "Okay, what the bloody damn hell—"

He put his finger over my lips, silencing me. He shook his head once.

I narrowed my eyes. "It's like you think I won't bite you," I muttered, but I nodded my head to let him know I understood. He kicked a Persian rug over to reveal a wooden door leading to what I assumed was one of the tunnels. I followed him down the stairs, into the cold damp darkness, hoping I wasn't being one of those stupid girls in a horror movie.

My fists were clenched and I was getting ready to fight when Nicholas pivoted to face me. "Lucky," he said, his voice breaking.

I lowered my fists. "Are you *you*? Really you?"

He caught me up against him. His hold was just as strong as before, but it was gentle, restrained, and honest.

Nicholas.

"I missed you," he said hoarsely.

I wrapped my arms around him, not nearly as gentle. He dipped his head, slanting his mouth over mine. The kiss didn't meander or hesitate, it went straight to fire. I was a drought-dry field and Nicholas was the spark. Our tongues touched and I felt it all the way down my thighs and into my toes. He backed me up against the wall, one hand on my waist, the other flattened on the stones by my cheek. I couldn't get close enough. I finally had Nicholas back, and he wasn't lost or missing or broken. He was right here, kissing me, as desperate to touch me as I was to touch him.

I had no idea how long we'd been clinging to each other but I finally had to pull away to catch my breath. "Oh my God," I exclaimed finally, smacking him in the chest. "You scared the crap out of me, Nicholas Drake!"

"I know," he answered, his lips still hovering over mine. "I'm sorry. But bloodslaves are either obediently adoring or terrified. I needed you to be one or the other. And since a vampire can smell the difference, I chose the latter, " he added drily. "I didn't think you could pull off obediently adoring, even if your life depended on it."

I didn't bother answering, I just kissed him until he shifted against me and suddenly we were lying on one of the cots. He pressed me down into the thin mattress, hands roaming wickedly. I ran my fingers over his back, under his shirt, letting the moment take us out of the world, out of vampire politics and death threats and the heavy jagged weight I'd been carrying since he first went missing.

I touched his cheek. "I really missed you," I said, blinking when my eyes started to sting.

"Hey," he said softly, half grinning. "Are you crying?"

"Shut up," I replied, wiping my cheeks. "I don't cry over boys. Not even Drake boys." I sat up reluctantly, straightening my clothes. "We should stop. Fate of the world and all that." He groaned, still kissing my neck. I ran my fingers through his tousled hair, just because I could. "What happened to you?"

He paused, closing his eyes briefly. "It's not important."

I twisted to stare down at him. "Are you nuts?"

He scrubbed a hand over his face and pushed off the cot. "I'm okay now."

I swallowed, trying to dissolve the lump in my throat. "But you weren't okay before."

He met my gaze. "No," he replied quietly. "I wasn't. When you talk to my parents, and I know you will, tell them someone named Dawn is behind the kidnappings and at least some of the Dracula Killer crimes." He helped me to my feet, brushing his palm over the puncture marks of his fangs at the crook of my elbow. His expression stilled, went stark. "There's no excuse for what I did."

I rolled my eyes. "Oh, don't be a drama queen," I said lightly. I knew if I let him, he'd spiral into guilt and blame.

He gave a short, startled laugh. "Lucy."

"Well, come on, extenuating circumstances and all. Besides which, we have way worse to deal with, so cheer up."

"Great," he said.

"Are we secure down here?" I asked. It was a mark of how dire the situation was that he didn't tease me for sounding like I went to Vampire Hunter High.

"Not secure enough." He sighed, taking my hand. "So come on."

He led me through the tunnels, doubling back when his vampire hearing picked up sounds I couldn't hear. Torches burned sporadically and moisture seeped through the walls, staining the cement and the tiles. We passed a few doors and metal stairs leading up into the forest. He kept going until he came to a hole in the wall that I wouldn't have seen in all the thick shadows. I scraped my elbows and knees wedging myself through it. On the other side was a small circular room, just big enough for a cot and a wooden chest. A rope ladder led to a trapdoor set in the ceiling.

"Is this where you're sleeping?" I asked. For some reason, the lonely space with the twisted blanket and the candle he crouched down to light made me sad.

He shrugged unconcerned. "It's safe. And Solange keeps trying to compel me to stay closer to the family tent." He looked up at me. "For some reason, I can resist her now. Well, it's getting harder but for a while I didn't feel compelled. " He paused, the light making his eyes glitter. "Why are you smirking?"

"Because for once I actually know something," I said, dropping down onto his bed. "And it's such a nice change from not knowing anything about anything."

"So spill, Hamilton."

"I took out most of the books in the school library," I said. "And after talking to Spencer and reading several hundred very boring texts written by extremely biased asshats, I think I figured something out."

"What's that?"

"Why I'm immune to Solange."

He raised his eyebrows expectantly.

"It's partly what we've always thought," I explained, sliding off the bed to sit next to him. I wasn't sure how long we had together and I didn't want to waste a single second. "I've grown up with it so my body doesn't recognize vampire pheromones as anything out of the ordinary. But with Solange, I think it's more than that. I think that if you have her blood in your system, you can resist her."

He frowned. "I've never drunk from her."

"But you drank from me." He winced. I waved it aside.

"Wait." He paused. "That doesn't explain it. You never drank from Solange." His jaw hardened. "Right?"

"I never drank her blood," I reassured him. "Not only is that gross but . . . actually, it's just gross." I made a face. It was one thing for a vampire to drink blood, they needed it to survive. "But when Solange and I were thirteen, we swore an oath to be blood sisters. We made cuts on our little fingers and pinky swore. My theory is because we mixed blood, it's protected me."

"Actually, you might be right," he said slowly. "Solange used her blood to heal London when she was injured, on the assumption that because Solange once had minute traces of Madame Veronique's blood in her system, it might save London the way it saved Solange on her birthday. And it did." He took my hand, weaving his fingers through mine. "Have you told my parents?"

I nodded. "I e-mailed Connor before I came here. I'm pretty sure checking their e-mail isn't very high on your parents' to-do list right now, but he's always online."

He lifted our joined hands, kissing my knuckles. His mouth was soft, tempting. "Maybe you just saved us all, Lucy."

"It might not mean anything, but at least it's another possible weapon." I thought I might be blushing. "And I think you should drink from me again."

He recoiled so sharply I nearly laughed. His eyes widened as he pressed himself back against the wall, dropping my hand like it was on fire. "Are you crazy?"

"According to everything I read, this kind of blood magic can fade, sometimes more quickly than others, especially when it's not straight from the source. London would have healed faster if Madame Veronique had given her blood directly, and lots of it. You'd have better immunity if you drank from Solange directly, but you can't. And you barely drank from me. Plus, Solange's blood must be so diluted in my system only magic could detect it by now. And you said yourself, your resistance is fading."

"No."

I frowned. "Nicholas, it makes sense."

"I don't care."

I scooted closer. He skirted away, keeping out of arm's reach. I paused. "Nicky."

"No way," he returned tightly. "You just stay right there."

"Are you afraid to touch me? Seriously?"

"Just, please." He looked like he was in pain.

I shifted back against the bed. "Okay," I said gently. "Hey, it's okay."

His fangs were out and the whites of his eyes were bloodshot.

He looked worse than that time we'd made out in the tree fort so long it had taken us fifteen minutes to find my shirt snagged on a pine branch. The veins tracing his wrists and neck looked as if they burned and I could see faint scars under his shirt collar. It took a hell of a lot to scar a vampire.

"What did they do to you?" I asked, feeling a kind of bone-searing fury that made me literally see red. Nicholas licked his lips.

"Change the subject." He was practically begging, though his eyes were the eyes of a hunter.

I tried to control my temper, trying not to let the anger and sorrow turn my entire body into a grenade. "Okay, but that's not all."

"Of course it isn't."

"The Drakes are a little too good at multitasking when it comes to disasters," I agreed. I took a deep breath. "I think Solange is possessed."

That was enough to distract him from his bloodlust. "Is that even possible?" He sounded bewildered.

"Spencer says it is but I can't get a hold of Isabeau to find out for sure. Regardless, all the research I've done so far says it's possible but unpredictable. Magic and vampires are a volatile mix. There's a reason the Hounds are so . . . you know."

"Yeah," he agreed. "They are." He sat back on his heels. "If she's possessed then *she* didn't really do all the things she's done."

"Explains a lot, doesn't it?" I smiled grimly. "And if she's possessed, then it means she can be *un*possessed. Or exorcised or whatever."

"How?"

"No idea," I admitted. "But still. And it has something to do with the twelfth century."

He finally closed the distance between us. "You're kind of amazing, you know that, right?" He'd said that to me once before, the last time we'd been trying to save Solange. He kissed me again, long and deep until my breath trembled in my throat.

"Jenna thinks we're fooling ourselves," I felt compelled to add, as we sat there, foreheads touching, eyes filled with nothing but each other. "That we want Solange to be possessed because it's easier."

"Maybe," he said softly. "But I'm guessing exorcising a vampire queen with brainwashing pheromones is going to be harder than it sounds."

"Probably."

"Can't wait, can you?"

"Nope."

"Me neither."

We grinned at each other for a moment, until he got to his feet, pulling me up with him. "We have to get you out of here," he said, suddenly looking dangerous again. "*Now.*"

Chapter 13

Solange

I'd never seen anything like the vampire woman who dropped down from a branch and landed right in front of me. She wore white, from leather pants so tight they looked like wet oil paint, to the hood drawn up over her head. Her sleeves ended above her elbows and the rest of her arms were covered in leather bracers set with slim silver stakes. There were more stakes on the straps that crossed between her breasts and at her belt, and a long slender sword in a scabbard at her back.

She made my mom look like a perfectly normal member of the PTA.

The really strange part was the way everyone else froze for a heartbeat, staring at her with the kind of fear that left a coppery taste in the mouth.

"A Seki." One of the handmaidens gasped.

The animals in the forest fell back into the shadows, sensing a predator they had no hope of defeating. Viola was trembling inside my head. Seki looked directly at me, even though her irises were such a pale gray they were practically translucent, but the pupils were completely and violently red. Her fangs were out, glistening like bone needles, and she wore a pair of ornate silver-capped nose plugs.

I didn't even see her jump: there was no whisper of displaced air, just the crack of her boot on my knee and the jab of the side of her hand on my throat when I fell to the ground. I flung to the side like a rag doll in a washing machine as she kept attacking me. She knew where I was going before I'd even moved.

I fought back because I was my mother's daughter, not because I thought for one second that I could defeat her. But I was also my father's daughter, born to an ancient family. I pushed up to my knees, blood dripping from a cut under my eye. "You can't hurt me," I said, forcing pheromones so intently that I pulled a muscle in my eyelid and my teeth ground together. I could taste blood from my split lip. Bruises throbbed along the left side of my body, from neck to hip. "You *can't hurt me.*"

She didn't look convinced.

I couldn't compel her. Between the blindness and the nose plugs, she was as immune as Lucy. Constantine was on my side but we still couldn't win this. The last time we'd been this outnumbered was when he'd saved me from Lady Natasha's Furies and I'd had to save him from the Chandramaa. No sooner had the thought entered my mind than I heard the soft beat of leathery wings and the very faint squeaking of nearly a hundred bats. They flew between the red pines, filling the meadow like storm clouds with teeth. They attacked Madame Veronique, who was just now stepping out of the shadows. They bit at the handmaidens but most of all, they bit and gouged at Seki.

And I did the only thing I could do.

I ran.

Seki released silver spikes like deadly rain while the bats gnawed at her hands. Three spikes scraped me at the same time and blood stung my left elbow, right hip, and ankle. I tried to use the trees as a shield, zigzagging so I made a less predictable target. My blood sprinkled the snow and Seki paused, as if sensing my new position even through the swarm of bats. One of the handmaidens threw her own dagger. I glanced over my shoulder just as Seki grabbed her by the throat and snapped her neck. I tripped over a root. The bats flew past me in a stream of dark wings and sharp teeth.

I barely got out of the clearing before a handmaiden tackled me, despite what happened to her sister. We landed hard, branches snapping under us like gunfire. I elbowed her in the eye, struggling to get free. The handmaiden's eyes were as wild as mine were. I was bruised and scraped all over but I barely felt the pain. There was too much adrenaline sizzling through me. A bat fell next to us, wings torn by a silver spike. She kneed me in the stomach and I flailed, falling back to the icy ground. I pulled her hair because it was all I could reach. I yanked as hard as I could, overbalancing her so that she flew off me. I scrambled to my feet and kicked the dagger out of her hand.

"Where the hell are your guards?" My cousin London crashed

through the bushes, incongruous in her gelled hair and super-modern tight black pants. She still had vicious red scars under the strap of her tank top from her encounter with a Huntsman and holy water. I gaped at her. "Shit, London! Run!" I shoved her so hard she stumbled.

Behind us, Constantine emerged from his fight long enough to hurl a dagger at the back of Seki's head. She leaned casually to the side, avoiding it. The sound of so many bats made the forest shiver. Snow and cold water shook off the pine boughs.

"London, what are you doing here?" I asked, pushing her into a run again. Stakes pierced the air between us. A bat squeaked, pinned to a tree.

"I nearly got you killed last summer but you saved my life this week. I owe you." She threw me a humorless smile. "Besides, I'm a royalist, remember?" She stumbled, and then shoved me back. "Quit pushing at me, what's your problem? I can handle a few handmaidens and your weird bats."

"How about her?" I asked, still pushing her to run faster. "Can you handle that creepy-ass woman?"

London glanced back, spotted Seki between the bats and goggled. "And what the hell is *that*?"

And then there was just no time left for talking.

Seki had shaken off Constantine and the handmaidens as if they were flies. Her blind eyes were focused intently on me. She slapped bats away from her. And I'd run us into a field of frost and dead grass, with no shelter or shield to speak of. "London, get out of here," I begged her as we ducked another volley of stakes. One of them stuck in my thigh, jerking me back a step. Blood oozed instantly around the weapon.

I yanked it out just as Madame Veronique strode out of the trees with three more handmaidens, as if she were back at Queen Eleanor's courts. She was dressed in silk and furs, gold glinting at her girdle and circlet and in her braids. Viola's hatred and fear of her roiled inside me, making me nauseated, but I didn't exactly have time for her delicate sensibilities.

Madame Veronique nodded at Seki respectfully.

The bats turned even more vicious. Madame Veronique eyed them balefully. London and I turned sideways, facing away from each other. It was standard defense formation—we made a smaller target and could protect each other's back. Constantine charged to our side, vampire ashes in his hair. I threw the stake I'd pulled from my leg, still bloody, at a handmaiden. It slammed through her chest and dropped her. She turned to ash as she fell.

Madame Veronique didn't lift a finger to help, not that Seki needed her help. She was perfectly capable of killing us all on her own. Still, the other handmaidens fanned out, just in case. The bats kept everyone busy. Their sheer number made them a formidable weapon, even to Seki. But they were dying too, whirling as they dropped like punctured seed pods. London looked at me grimly. "We have to—"

A stake slid under her rib cage with such force she crumpled, screaming. I grabbed for her but she was already falling. I flung my hand out, drawing a wreath of bats to hover overhead. The rest concentrated on dive-bombing Seki.

"Son of a bitch, that hurts." London wheezed, plucking at the stake.

I tried to support her weight, even as I bit through the thin skin of my wrist so she could drink my blood. It had helped heal her before. There was a stake in the undergrowth near my knee. I reached down to grab it as London lifted my wrist to her mouth. Her eyes widened.

That was the only warning.

Suddenly she was yanking me forward and to the side, using the line of my elbow to guide me. At the same time, she swung herself around so that her back was to mine, so that she was facing whatever danger it was that she'd spotted over my shoulder. I didn't know if it was a handmaiden or Seki or Madame Veronique. I didn't know if it was spike or stake or sword.

I didn't even have time to turn around before I heard the sound.

But I knew exactly what I was listening to, knew precisely what that wet fleshy sound meant.

A silver spike pierced her chest, sliding between her ribs and right through her heart. As I turned around, feeling as though my vampire speed was suddenly slow motion, I saw my cousin crumble into ash. Her clothes fell in a heap in the dried leaves and what was left of her body drifted in the frigid air.

London was gone.

I stood slowly, rising like fog off a frozen lake. Shock made me feel hollow and brittle. My triple fangs elongated until my gums felt raw. Bats dipped around me, nipping gently, as if they were trying to comfort me. The others started to screech, like a strange high-pitched battle cry. They gathered between me and the others, blocking stakes and spikes.

"Viola." Constantine grabbed my hand, forcing me into a run. I let him drag me along until we crossed the river and headed toward the camp. The cold water slapping into my cuts, the snow falling and clinging to my eyelashes like teardrops made me stop.

Constantine turned back, gathering me into his arms. "Are you hurt?"

I shook my head mutely. London. London was hurt.

"Why did the Seki mark you?" he asked, his voice feral with anger.

"You know her?"

"I know *of* them," he said. "Seki is the name of an assassin clan. They abandon all personal ties, give up their names, and their blood lineage to become paid assassins. They're incredibly rare, and deadlier even than the Chandramaa. They all answer to the name Seki, if they bother answering at all."

I swallowed, shivering. "I've never even heard of them."

"You're safe now." He stroked my back. My cheek rested on his bare chest. "I love you, Viola," he murmured into my blood-and-snow-tangled hair. He still hadn't realized that I wasn't Viola. She responded inside my body, my heart raced, my belly tingled. Viola wanted to curl into his body and purr. She smiled at him. So I punched him in the face.

"I'm not Viola, you asshole."

His head snapped back, blood trickling from the corner of his mouth. His hands fell away from my waist. "Solange," he said.

There were so many emotions braided into his voice that I couldn't distinguish between the threads. I could hear the whole of it, pulsing with pain.

I'd show him pain.

"You helped her possess me," I said. Viola was trying to chew through my control. I shoved her back viciously. Sweat broke out on the back of my neck as I struggled to hold on. "Traitor."

"Perspective, love," he said sadly. "I'm not the villain here. I'm just a guy in love with a girl, same as anyone."

"Not quite," I returned.

"I didn't kill your little hunter, did I? When I had the chance? Or your friend when she threw a stake at me? I'd say you owe me, pet."

Ice and fire prickled through me and I was half-surprised steam didn't vent out of my pores. "What did you do to them?" I asked, just before I kicked him right between the legs.

"You're the hero of your story," he insisted, though his voice was choked and his eyes nearly crossed as he grabbed at himself. "And I'm the hero of mine."

I'd thought he was my friend. He'd kissed me. I'd felt guilty but I'd liked it too. I was every bit as much a traitor to Kieran as Constantine was to me. More.

"You're not a hero." I choked.

"Aren't I? Didn't I get myself changed into a vampire after Viola died? Didn't I search the earth for eight centuries, waiting for her to come back? Consulting witches and soothsayers?"

"That's why you became my friend," I said angrily.

"I knew she'd come back, eventually. There were rumors of magic, and a dead witch at the castle. And her voice, always her voice. Where better than the precious daughter of the Drakes?" His eyes were practically indigo. They glittered like summer storm clouds jagged with lightning. He grabbed my arm. "There was magic when she died. But she was always stronger than everyone assumed. I knew she'd find me. We swore to find each other no matter what." He smiled at me tenderly. "Can you hear me, Viola? Come back to me, love. No one can stand between us ever again."

"Until now." I jerked out of his grasp. I imagined the pheromones sizzling under my skin, felt them rise off me like steam. "Get away from me, Constantine."

He just looked at me calmly.

"Did you hear me?" I snapped. I flicked my hands as if that would increase my pheromones. "Back off!"

He didn't move. First Seki, now Constantine.

"What, are my freaking pheromones broken tonight?" I muttered.

He smiled sadly. "I'm sorry, Solange. I truly am. But I can't lose her again." He gripped my shoulders, yanking me up against him. His chest pressed against my thin, bloodstained nightgown. I tried to knee him again but he was ready for me this time. I'd wasted a good tactic by acting out of anger. My dad wouldn't approve. My mom just would have kicked Constantine so hard the first time he'd have passed out.

"You need to take control back, Viola. Now!"

His mouth covered mine in a searing kiss full of longing and desperation and the kind of heat that burned all thought away. I struggled against him but I was distracted, pulled in two directions. Because the kiss awakened Viola and she clawed at her tethers with increased violence. I fought back frantically. The kiss slid through me like a drug, teasing away the sharp edges, the weight of logic.

A kiss to tell the truth from a lie.

"Constantine." It was Viola speaking, but I was still me. The juxtaposition made me feel all bleached out inside, like the bones of the dead left in the desert. I was sunlight and brittle ash. A strong wind could blow me away entirely.

"Vi!" Constantine was still kissing me. His hands dug into my hair.

"She's . . . still fighting me," Viola said. I felt my larynx moving, felt the vibration of sound in my throat. But I wasn't the one forming the words.

He pulled back slightly. "Hang on! You need more blood." He tilted his head suddenly, nostrils flaring. "And I smell someone familiar nearby."

He tipped my head back, staring into my eyes. "Solange. I can smell your little friend Lucy," he said darkly. "If you keep fighting us, I'll have Viola drink her dry."

CHAPTER 14

Lucy

"What's going on?" I asked, following Nicholas up the rope ladder. It swung slowly, spinning me around. My stomach wobbled. He climbed up so quickly the ladder only had time to make one more slow, sick spin before he crawled out the trapdoor and was leaning down to lift me out. Frost crunched under my boots. We were in a part of the forest that was mostly red pine, tall and lonely. It was like walking under giants' legs.

"Royal guards," he said. "They're coming this way and they smell violent." Nicholas sped up and I had to concentrate on keeping up. My school training and workouts with Hunter must be helping because I didn't die after the first five minutes.

"We have to get you out of here," he said urgently. "Whoever is possessing Solange is not exactly a people person, and the royal guards obey her without question."

"We really need to find out who's doing this to her." I panted, my breath forming little white clouds in the frigid air. "So we can drag him or her the hell out of Sol."

"I'll see what I can do," Nicholas promised.

"Don't blow your cover."

He shot me a smirk over his shoulder. "Duh," he added, because it was what I usually said to him when he told me to be careful or to stay undercover while he dodged stakes and other pointy things that were bad for his health.

"I don't like leaving you here." I squeezed his hand tighter. "Madame Veronique wants to kill Solange. Did you know that?"

He stopped so suddenly I nearly broke my nose on his shoulder. There would have been a certain karmic beauty to it. "Ow." I rubbed my nose, eyes stinging. Nicholas's eyes flared like ice. He tilted his head, like a wolf hearing the soft pad of a rabbit's foot.

"No time," he snapped. "We have to go up."

"Shit," I said, my heart responding to the darkness in his gaze. Adrenaline spiked through me like crystalized honey, sweet but sharp. "I suck at climbing trees," I added, in case he'd forgotten.

"There are walkways up near the top branches," he assured me. He peered up an impossibly tall tree, frowned, then moved to the next one.

"What are you looking for?" I asked, the back of my neck prickling. I jumped at every small shift of the wind.

"One of the ropes," he replied. I darted between the trees, helping him search.

"Here," I called softly after a few minutes. He was at my side before I'd finished exhaling.

"I'm going to go up first," he told me. "And then I'll pull you up. Just hold on tight."

"Wait." I stopped him as he closed his hands around the rope, arm muscles straining. "They took all my weapons at the camp."

He pulled a stake from the back of his belt and handed it to me, before shimmying up the rope, unconcerned with little things like gravity and falling to a messy death. I wrapped the rope around my waist, then gripped it as tightly as I could. He hauled me up and I gritted my teeth and tried not to imagine what all my bones breaking when I fell would sound like. Sweat stung the rope burns on my palms. Nicholas pulled me up onto a circular platform that ran around the trunk. Narrow bridges led from tree to tree, from platform to platform. The smell of pine was thick and green.

"I never even knew this existed," I said, staring at the intricate knotwork of bridges.

"It was built for the Blood Moon," Nicholas said as we started across the first bridge. "As an escape route in case of Hunters or civil war or whatever. And I think the Chandramaa have the same setup, only closer to camp."

It was sturdier than it looked and the rope handles made me feel more secure. "This is seriously cool," I said, risking a downward glance. Bats dipped and whirled beneath us. "Terrifying, but cool."

Nicholas slipped behind me to guard my back as we hurried between the treetops. "There's this thing called gravity," I reminded him as the rope bridge swung wildly and I tried not to throw up.

"There's also this thing where I'd rather my baby sister's minions didn't eat my girlfriend." He gave me a little push.

I ran faster, blood welling on my chafed hands. The air rushed past my face, and pine needles dragged through my hair and scratched my cheeks. It was like being beaten up by Christmas. It was too dark and too high for me to see any vampires down below, but Nicholas was running as if they were right there with us.

"Shit," he said, just before Solange's voice drifted up to us, sharp and arrogant.

"Nicholas, why are we playing hide-and-seek?"

He shot me a warning glance as we stumbled to a stop. "Because I'm not in the mood to share," he called·back, sounding bored. I tried to peek through the branches at her.

"Families share," she returned as vampires moved below us, like beetles scurrying in the undergrowth. They weren't trying to be quiet or stealthy, and there were enough of them that even I could make them out from this distance.

"I'm beginning to wonder about you, big brother." Her tone changed, seemed to throb with power. Nicholas flinched. "So come down here and bring *her*."

"Lucy?" he murmured.

"Yeah?"

"We're going to need to run."

Easier said than done.

"Maybe I could talk to her?" I asked dubiously. Nicholas just shook his head. I knew he was right but it still felt wrong to run away from Solange.

"Can you exorcise her?" Nicholas asked. There was sweat on his brow and his jaw was clenched. He was holding himself as if he were in the center of a storm.

"Well, no."

"Then wait until you can."

"Well, if you're going to be all logical about it," I muttered. I reached for his hand, squeezing tightly, while he struggled against the insidious compulsion.

"Lucy," Nicholas said hoarsely. "Get out of here." Even as he said the words, he tightened his grip on me and moved toward the nearest ladder.

I yanked on the back of his shirt. "Hey!"

"She's stronger than me," he said through his teeth. The veins on his neck looked stark, blue as ink.

"But she's not stronger than *us*," I insisted.

"Go," Solange snapped at her guards. "Fetch them."

I shoved my arm under Nicholas's nose. "Drink."

"No," he said, going very still. "Lucy, get out of here."

"Nicholas, you and I both know that's not an option right now, especially since you're currently cutting off the circulation in my arm." I touched his hair, pushing a lock off his forehead. "And we don't have time for angst. So drink."

He finally lifted my arm, his touch cold and gentle. He didn't look away as he sank his fangs into me, breaking the delicate skin of my wrist. The pain was swift and sharp, like pricking myself with a needle. I couldn't help but think of Sleeping Beauty as a soft lethargy whispered through me. The need to close my eyes, to rest, to drape myself around him without resistance was seductive, tempting. Wrong.

"Nicholas, stop."

I tugged on my wrist. His fingers tightened in response. His throat muscles moved as he swallowed. His eyes glittered, his inner beast prowling dangerously near the surface. I really didn't want to stab my boyfriend. He hadn't drunk enough to do me any harm, but if he took any more, I'd be too light-headed to fight.

"*Nicky*," I snapped.

Right before I punched him in the nose.

He jerked back, with a silent snarl. His tousled hair fell back over his eye, obscuring the mist-gray glint of his irises. I arched my eyebrow at him, knuckles feeling bruised. He slowly wiped my blood off his lower lip, looking miserable but like himself again. I poked him hard in the chest before he could get all broody about it. "Don't," I whispered. "Did it work?" I mouthed. He paused, then nodded. We shared a quick, grim smile.

"I'm coming," Nicholas called down, disgruntled. "Call off your dogs." It would buy us a few minutes. The vampires paused, scattered through the trees, one of them halfway up a rope dangling from the pine behind us. I didn't think he'd spotted us yet. The wind made the branches creak ominously. It was enough to cover our sounds now but once I started running, they'd hear my footsteps.

"I'll draw them off," Nicholas whispered in my ear. It was almost a kiss. "You run like hell."

I nodded, reaching back to activate the GPS tag so Hunter and the others could find me. He sent me one last complicated glance before he hurried across the bridges leading away from me. I ran as fast as I could, the bridges swaying and creaking under me. I glanced back just long enough to see him land in a crouch, his hair falling into his gray eyes. The combination of the movement and the height made me feel queasy and light-headed, but I pushed through until I found one of the ladders. I shimmied down the length of it, the chafing on my palms leaving streaks of blood on the rope. I kept running, dodging branches and jumping over fallen trees.

I had no idea where I was or how to get back to the school van. At first that didn't matter but now that I was hopefully far enough away from Solange, I couldn't keep running blindly. Moonlight gave a blue glow to the snow that had managed to fall between the pines. It was enough to keep me from running into trees but not enough to get my bearings. People died in the Violet Hill mountains. Experienced hikers and climbers got lost and wandered for days until they succumbed to exposure. The cold air slapped at my burning lungs. I slowed to a limping jog.

I pulled the GPS tag off the hem of my shirt, squinting at the stamp-sized screen. Chloe had MacGyvered it especially for me, so that she could find me, but I could find her as well. I followed the blinking red dot, trying not to run into any trees. Branches scraped at me. Snow dislodged and fell all over me, soaking into my clothes.

And then I didn't need the GPS anymore, I just had to follow the sounds of fighting.

I reached the edge of the woods to find the van running, high beams on. Jenna was sliding out of the driver's seat, a crossbow in her hand. Chloe climbed over the seats to take over the steering wheel. Hunter was clinging to the roof, using the second crossbow. There were at least five *Hel-Blar* that I could see, snarling as they surrounded the van.

Hunter's bolt slammed into the one standing between me and the van and he erupted into a cloud of putrid-smelling ash. I leaped over the stained and tattered remains of his clothing. "I'm weaponless," I shouted at Hunter. "And I have better aim."

She slid off the roof without a word and I vaulted up to take her place. Jenna took out another *Hel-Blar* just as Hunter lured the nearest one away from Chloe's door. "Get in the damn van!" Chloe yelled. "Lucy's back. Let's get out of here!"

"We can't just leave them here," Hunter argued, dancing out of the reach of a blood-encrusted arm. The *Hel-Blar* attached to it clacked his jaws. Hunter staked him, using a roundhouse kick to shove the stake deep enough into his chest. "There are farmhouses nearby."

"Oh my God," Chloe shot back. "You're going to be the reason I'm going to get killed before I can convince one of the Drake brothers to date me."

One of the *Hel-Blar* landed on the hood, fangs flashing. The smell of slimy mushrooms made me gag. Chloe jerked back reflexively and then scrambled to slam her door shut. She honked the horn.

"Oh, like that's going to help," Jenna muttered, leaping onto the roof behind me.

I shot a crossbow bolt at him, catching him in the eye. Blood and stench splattered the windshield. Chloe shrieked. "Sorry! Sorry!" I yelled as she turned on the wipers. The next arrow caught him in the chest and went straight through his heart. Blood and ashes clumped in streaks, flung back and forth by the wipers. Jenna straightened behind me, shooting arrows at the *Hel-Blar* shambling behind us. He fell apart still gnashing his fangs.

Hunter was fighting the last one, a female who was shrieking and snarling. The sound was so high-pitched and awful it made my teeth hurt. I aimed my crossbow at her but Hunter shifted in the way. She threw one of her stakes. It went under her collarbone at a weird angle and stuck there. When she growled down at it, Hunter triggered the stake strapped to her forearm. It shot forward and she staggered, turning to dust.

Jenna and I slid into the van as Hunter raced toward us, her blond ponytail swinging cheerfully. She was barely inside when Chloe slammed the van into reverse. She slid through the icy mud, the van lilting dangerously as it careened toward the dirt road. The smell of burning rubber and exhaust replaced the reek of green water.

"What is that thing?" I glanced enviously at the stake-holder on Hunter's arm as I caught my breath. "Because I totally want one for my birthday."

CHAPTER 15

Solange

I let go.

I didn't know how else to save Lucy. I couldn't afford to call Constantine's bluff. There was no reason to think he wouldn't drink her dry, as he'd threatened.

I ended up on the stone stairs again. At least I wasn't wearing a silk slip anymore. The tapestry pouch of boxes full of Viola's memories was still slung over my shoulder. I felt disoriented and numb. Tears made my vision waver. I had to find someplace safe to hide before I fell apart completely.

I stumbled down the steps and out onto the first landing I came across. Torchlight flickered down the hall. I slipped into a room with an unlocked door. It looked relatively innocuous, full of heavy and elaborately carved medieval furniture. There was a huge cabinet on the far wall. It was big enough for me to curl up on the bottom of it and still shut the door completely. A selection of woolen dresses hung on one side, smelling strongly of cedar and smoke. Light filtered through the keyhole. I tried to take deep breaths but I couldn't stop the loud animal sobs from tearing through me.

London was dead.

She wasn't undead like the rest of us. She was well and truly gone. There wasn't even enough of her left to bury.

I cried until I felt empty and sick. The wooden slats of the cupboard were rough under my cheek and I'd lost feeling in my legs, except for the stabbing pain in my left knee. It was tempting to give up and stay here forever, hidden in an armoire where no one was currently trying to kill me or, worse, save me. I could fade away, becoming just another shadow in Viola's subconscious. Gwyneth had done it for hundreds of years.

Actually, that wasn't a comforting thought.

Gwyneth was half-crazy and alone. I could easily picture myself pale and thin, flitting between the stables and the castle, crawling over the moat filled with bloated corpses. I'd hide in the forest and eat leaves and bugs, cover myself in mud when it got cold. I'd forget this place wasn't real. I'd forget my own name, Lucy's, Kieran's. Everyone. Everything.

I didn't want that. A spark kindled in the cold pit of my stomach.

Apparently, I had some fight left in me, after all.

I'd miss my family. I'd miss the way Nicholas seemed to know what I was thinking before I thought it. The way Quinn smirked, the way Logan teased me. My mom, my dad. Eventually, I'd even miss Aunt Ruby.

I already missed Lucy. I missed how cheerful and brave she was, and her irreverence for the things that would make other people quake with fear.

And I missed Kieran. I'd been missing him before Viola possessed me completely. She'd broken us up in the end. And she'd done it so she could be with Constantine. The rat bastard. He'd fooled me right from the start. He'd made me believe I was special, that he understood me the way no one else had. I'd let him kiss me. I'd even let him drink my blood, that night in the Bower when I'd cut my hand on the wine bottle. I'd let him convince me that the only way to find Nicholas was to take the crown and control the guards.

He'd done it all for Viola.

The same way she'd stolen my very body from me, to be with him again.

They had each other now, but at what cost? I wouldn't sacrifice the world to be with Kieran. And neither would he. That was one of the things I loved most about him. He had honor and courage. He held my hand like I was just a regular girl.

London had died to keep me safe. If I stayed here and fell to pieces she'd have died in vain. I'd be selfish and weak, letting everyone suffer because I hurt inside. I'd be as bad as Viola. I don't care what happened to her in the past. She still had no right to ruin so many lives.

I forced myself to sit up and wipe the salt stains off my cheeks.

The embroidered collar of my dress was damp and my hair fell in tangles covering my face. Viola had waited over eight hundred years to steal my body. I didn't need to be told that she wouldn't give it up without a fight.

Well, she was about to get one.

Because she might be a Drake, but I was the daughter of *Helena* Drake. I'd learned how to kick ass while still in the womb.

I reached into the tapestry bag. If Constantine was Viola's strength, then he was also her weakness. I sorted through the boxes, trying to decipher what was inside by the clues provided on the outside. The last box I'd opened was decorated with a knight, a dragon, and a lady and it had shown me Viola and her own knight, Tristan Constantine. And her dragon: Madame Veronique. The Drake family.

There were seven boxes left. There was a gold one, a silver one, and one covered in brass inlay in the shape of tiny leaves. I hovered over one painted with a dragon but in the end I decided on the smallest one. It was small and sturdy and the red enamel made it look as if it was a tiny heart wet with blood.

1199

Viola thought the witch would have been older.

At the very least, older than herself. But she looked roughly the same age, with long brown hair adorned with strange beads. Viola could smell the mint on her from even a few feet away.

"Are you her?" she asked.

Viola nodded, propped up on the stone wall of the castle battlements, barely able to keep her eyes open. She'd never felt so exhausted in her entire life, and now, when she needed all of her strength, only her own willpower and love for Tristan kept her upright. "Did you bring it?"

"Of course."

Viola had tried everything else. Her father could not be convinced. He alluded to family secrets, aside from the rumors of her illegitimate birth, which the Vales already knew and were comfortable with, reminded her that Tristan was newly knighted and penniless, and in the end, lost his temper and threw his goblet at the wall, startling his favorite hunting hawk off her perch. He refused to release her mother or take down the barbaric post and chains, or even to deny Madame Veronique's claims that Viola was, in fact, a bastard. He softened long enough to remind her that he loved her as though she were truly his daughter and that she was never to speak of it again. And then he banished her to Bornebow Hall.

So it had to be tonight.

By tomorrow she'd be sixteen years old. She'd been lucky to be granted a reprieve until her sixteenth birthday. Her friend Anna was married to an old man with few teeth the day she turned fourteen. And no amount of weeping and wailing had changed her fate. Nor would it change Viola's future. But now the maidservants fretted over her pale cheeks and her lack of appetite. She slept for hours and hours, long after the sun rose, and still she felt tired.

It didn't matter. None of it mattered.

Only Tristan.

He was forbidden from being in her presence, and she was carefully guarded by soldiers and knights. Even the gatehouse keeper knew the color of her golden hair and would recognize her if she'd tried to sneak out to see him. She'd been reduced to bribing one of the kitchen maids with an enamel brooch to send word to the witch rumored to live in the woods.

"I thought witches were supposed to be old hags," Viola said.

Gwyneth shrugged. "It's naught but power and my nan taught me well." She surveyed her dispassionately. "You'd be Viola then?"

"Lady Viola Drake," Viola corrected, suddenly feeling vulnerable. Witches weren't to be meddled with, after all. Her old nursemaid's warnings prickled through her. "Can you help me?" she asked, picturing Tristan beside her to drive away her childish fears.

"That depends," Gwyneth replied.

"There's your payment." Viola motioned wearily to a pouch lying on the crenellated top of the battlements. It was filled with several of her most valuable rings and bracelets.

"It's not that," Gwyneth said. "Magic can be fickle and the price is always more than any amount of gold you can hold in your hand. Are you willing to pay it?"

"Yes," Viola said immediately. "For love, I'm willing to risk everything."

"You don't look well."

Viola waved that aside. "I was told you can make demons dance. What's a little love spell to that?"

"A great deal more." She smiled smugly. "But I can do it."

"Now? Here?"

She nodded. "Aye."

Viola fell asleep as Gwyneth puttered around her. When she woke again, she was curled on the hard stone inside a circle of salt and herbs. Gwyneth had pulled her hood up over her hair and was muttering under her breath. Viola sat up.

"Don't disturb the salt," Gwyneth said sharply.

Viola froze, adjusting the hem of her dress. She stood slowly, noticing that the salt formed more than just a circle. There were designs as well, marching round the border in complicated patterns. The world tilted dizzily for a moment but she forced herself to stay standing.

"You brought it?" Gwyneth asked. She sounded different, powerful. "As I asked?"

Viola nodded and pulled a long chain out from under her dress. Gwyneth had requested an image of Viola and her lover; a drawing or painting. Viola chose her favorite pendant. It was simple wood in a gold frame. She'd discovered one of the stable boys whittling behind the stalls one summer morning. He had impressive talent and she'd paid him with apples from the orchard and extra mutton at supper to carve a relief of her and Tristan. She'd been wearing it around her neck ever since. She'd painted it so that it looked even more like Tristan, with his dark hair and violet-blue eyes.

Gwyneth circled around Viola. "You remember what I told your serving girl? A sacrifice is required, a gift for a gift."

Viola pointed to an iron cage covered in cloth. Inside, a dove fluttered its wings as the covering slipped off and Gwyneth transferred it into the circle. "When the moon turns red," she said. "You do what must be done. Anoint the pendant with the blood and speak your wish. Are you ready?"

Viola nodded, even though she could barely keep her eyelids open. She lowered to her knees next to the cage, feeling ancient. Everything was blurring. The torchlight hurt her eyes. The sound of Gwyneth's hem dragging the ground felt like needles in her ears. Gwyneth spoke what sounded like a mixture of Saxon and Latin, throwing down handfuls of roses pierced with needles. Red thread bound them together in a garland.

Viola glanced at the moon, waiting for it to turn red. She felt as if she'd had too much mead, as if she were floating and the moon was close enough to touch. The magic must be working already. She chewed on her lip until it bled, staring at the moon. Just as she tasted the copper of her own blood on her tongue, the pale moon went faintly red, as if soaked in wine. Viola paused as she reached inside the cage. The bird flapped into the bars, panicking. Surely, this sacrifice was too small.

If she wanted to secure Tristan and her happiness, she had to be bolder. She had to be a knight on the field of battle, taking no quarter. She stood up, even though her feet were as heavy as a blacksmith's anvils.

"I will be with my love," she said. "Tristan Constantine and I will be together, nothing will keep us apart, not family, not treaties, not even death. We will always find each other, no matter the obstacle."

"No," Gwyneth snapped as Viola shuffled her feet through the salt boundary. "It's not safe. Stay in the circle."

If Viola had cared to look, she would have seen the energy whipping around the battlements, billowing under Gwyneth's cloak and blowing out the torches. The shadows seemed to form into malevolent faces, turning into kind weeping girls, into snarling beasts. But she didn't see them.

All she saw was a way to be with Tristan.

Gwyneth frowned at her. "Are you ill?" she asked over the howling of the unnatural winds.

"I'm sorry," Viola whispered, before unhooking the small dagger hanging from her belt. Ladies always carried them, mostly for embroidery floss, eating supper, or gathering herbs from the garden.

Viola had nothing ladylike in mind.

She grabbed Gwyneth by the hair, curling her fingers tightly into the tangles. She'd felt sluggish and weak before, but a sudden burst of manic energy had her jabbing up with the dagger. The blade stuck into Gwyneth's neck. She gurgled, blood welling almost instantly out of her mouth. The moon went dark. The winds died abruptly but the faint, ghostly howling remained. Viola jerked the knife across Gwyneth's throat, the witch's blood pouring out of the wound, soaking into her dress and dripping over the carved pendant of Tristan kissing Viola.

Gwyneth's body collapsed in the salt and flowers. Viola slumped over her, half-unconscious. She felt as if there were ice inside her bones, as if fire seared under her skin, as she was completely filled with power and utterly devoid of it, all at the same time. She didn't even have the energy to lift her head when she realized there was blood trickling down the side of Gwyneth's neck and over her own mouth. It tasted sharp, metallic.

Good.

She swallowed despite herself, gingerly at first, with her eyes squeezed tightly shut and then greedily as she felt indescribable vigor and strength

coursing through her. She was unstoppable. Magic fueled her. "Tristan,"
she murmured, wiping blood off her face with her sleeve.

Sated, she stood slowly, unfurling like a pale deadly flower.

She tossed Gwyneth's drained body over the side of the tower and
turned away, back to the sleeping inhabitants of Bornebow Hall.

CHAPTER 16

Lucy

Wednesday night

The next night, I went straight to the Drake farm.

"You're smiling weirdly," Kieran said, shooting me a sidelong glance as we drove away from the school. "What's up, Hamilton?"

"Nicholas is okay," I replied happily. "Well, mostly. And I'm finally allowed back at the farm."

"Yeah, to get stabbed with needles. Is that any reason to look so deranged?"

I grinned, propping my feet up on the dash of his truck. "Don't worry," I told him. "We'll save Solange soon and then you can be as deranged as me."

He snorted. "I don't think anyone can be as deranged as you."

"Ha ha. It'll work, Kieran. Don't worry."

"You can't know that."

I chose to ignore him and went back to skimming the book open across my knees. "What about the Sanguines?"

"Sisters of the Sanguine Heart?" he asked. "Twelfth-century vampire-hunter nuns? I can't see what they'd have to do with anything."

"I guess." I flipped the page. "And after all this research, what do you want to bet none of it's any use for the twenty-seven essays I still have to write for Tyson? Maybe my thesis sentence should be 'I was chained to a post because of some ass-backward twelfth-century custom.'" My cell phone interrupted me, vibrating in my bag. I answered but didn't even have a chance to say hello before my mom yelled in my ear.

"Lucky Hamilton, you're skipping school."

"Um." How did she know that? I looked at the display, half expecting her face to be staring back at me. I added a wary glance out the window to the rapidly blurring trees.

"I got a call from your headmistress," she added.

"Oh," I said, covering a sigh of relief with a cough. "Right. That. Sorry."

"You snuck off campus? *Now?* With everything that's been going on?"

"Sorry, Mom." I winced. Kieran winced back silently in solidarity. "But it's not as bad as it sounds. I was still technically on campus." She didn't need to know I'd spent last night roaming through the forest and chained to a post at the Blood Moon camp.

"Are you actively *trying* to give your father a heart attack?"

"No, Mom. Sorry, Mom." Kieran smirked. I punched his shoulder. "Yes, Mom. I know. I *know*. I won't get out of the car until I'm surrounded by Drake brothers. And Helena. I *promise*. I love you too. Bye." I didn't even look at Kieran. "Shut up."

"I thought your mom was all peace and love."

"Don't let that fool you," I said. "She can still hand you your ass, just like Helena, only she'll make you feel really guilty about it. And then she'll feed you tofu." He grimaced in response. "Exactly. Any wonder why watching my friends drink a cup of blood doesn't faze me?" I skimmed a few more pages, then paused at a drawing of a castle painted red. "What's the Bornebow massacre?"

Kieran shrugged, keeping his eyes on the road. "Wasn't on the exam so I don't remember."

"Some hotshot agent you are."

He just shook his head. "I didn't memorize medieval massacres, sorry."

I frowned. "Castle full of dead bodies drained of blood. Doesn't that scream *vampire* to you?"

"Sure."

"Do you know anything about the Vale family? Like maybe they liked to chain people to posts or something?"

"No, why?"

"It was their castle."

"Guess they pissed someone off."

"Guess so." I shut the book, frustrated. But watching the road speed by through the partially opened window wasn't any better, so

I reached for another text. I drummed my fingers on the cover, the cold air slipping under my collar.

"I thought you weren't nervous," Kieran said softly.

"Are you kidding? If I get any more wired I'll break into a thousand pieces," I said. "But the brothers need me to act calm. You know how they get."

He threw me a glance. "You're wiser than people give you credit for, Hamilton."

"About time someone realized that." I snorted as we drove down the lane to the barn. We'd decided it was the best place to meet since Madame Veronique wouldn't deign to visit it. The fields, the forest, and the Drake farmhouse and cabins secured privately in the woods felt just as much like home as my parents' house. I'd missed it here.

"Okay, now you *really* look deranged," Kieran said at my grin. I jumped out of the car and raced up to the barn.

"Lucy!" Quinn darted out of the door, followed by Connor and Logan. "Your mom will kill us." They surrounded me like bodyguards. Pale elbows poked into me. I didn't even make fun of them. Though I did roll my eyes until Helena came up behind us.

"Your mother told you to wait for me," she said.

I peeked between two well-muscled arms. "Sorry." She looked weary and sad and smaller than I remembered. All of my manic good cheer that we might finally get Solange and Nicholas back tonight fled. I didn't think I'd ever seen Helena look so . . . frail. I gulped and followed her meekly inside.

Connor went to sit by Christabel, who was curled up on one of the couches reading. Marcus puttered behind one of the lab counters, helping Uncle Geoffrey. I could smell the disinfectant from here. Duncan leaned against a wall, scowling, and Sebastian was talking to Liam and Bruno. I missed Nicholas fiercely. It was just wrong to see his brothers looking so much like him. Even so, surrounded by my favorite undead boys and Kieran, I felt better than I had in a long time.

Christabel folded the corner of her page down and sat up. "Lucy."

"Hey." I tossed her a pair of nose plugs I'd fished out of my pocket. "Put those on so you can hug me without vamping out."

She hugged me gingerly. "Hey, cuz."

I hugged her back. "Mom said to tell you to chant your mantra or some shit. Oh, and do your homework."

Christabel grinned. "I love your mom. But it's not like I'm in school anymore."

"Like that's an excuse." I looked around. "Where's London?"

"Don't know," Quinn replied, tossing his hair off his pretty face. "She doesn't exactly check in. Never has."

I glanced at Logan. He was wearing a Steampunk-esque jacket with silver buttons, lace poking through the cuffs. "Are you okay?"

"Oh yeah," he replied tightly. "My girlfriend is about to face off against my psychotic baby sister. I'm just great."

I held his hand, squeezing it tightly. "Isabeau has Magda with her and that girl is easily as psychotic as Solange's hijacker." When my phone rang, I jumped a foot in the air. It didn't help that Quinn pulled a stake on me and Logan knocked me protectively to the ground. I shoved him, catching my breath. "You weigh a ton." I reached for my phone. "Hello?" I croaked.

"Lucky, are you there yet? Are you safe?" It was my mom again. "You tell those boys I'm holding them responsible if anything happens to you."

"Mom, I'm in a barn. The only current danger is choking on Logan's lace cuff. Go have some of Dad's chamomile tea. Mom?" I blinked at my phone. "She hung up on me."

Logan helped me back up. I rubbed my elbow, which was tingling painfully.

"Lucy, if you could come and sit down over here?" Uncle Geoffrey asked. "We don't have much time."

"Nicholas told our contact he'd get Solange to the waterfalls," Liam explained as I sat in one of those chairs they had at blood donor clinics and dentists' offices. He shifted aside to let his brother by with the equipment. I shrugged out of my sweater. Liam's face went carefully blank when he saw the teeth marks on my arm.

"It's no big deal," I assured him. "Anyway, it was worth it. It gives him protection. And it will help the rest of you too." I swallowed when Marcus tied a piece of rubber above my elbow and told me to make a fist. I knew it was the right thing to do. I would give them all an advantage tonight; they wouldn't succumb to Solange's pheromones this way.

Didn't mean I had to like the pinch and slide of the needle as it went under my skin. I winced. The brothers looked politely away from my blood and I looked politely away from their fangs. Kieran just looked like his head was going to explode from whatever inner struggle he was fighting. This went against all of his training, whatever it might mean for him and Solange. He shifted between the brothers and me, even though there was no need.

"Good girl," Uncle Geoffrey murmured, taking the vials away. Marcus pressed a cotton ball on the tiny pinprick and put a Wonder Woman Band-Aid over it. I had to grin. He winked and took the medical supplies away.

"Is it enough?" Helena asked, her black leather outfit bristling with stakes and daggers. Even her braid looked like it could double as a weapon.

"There's enough for the three of us, with some for Isabeau when we see her," Uncle Geoffrey replied, carefully capping the vials. "We'll need to take them at the last minute, so it doesn't lose potency."

I frowned, sitting up. "If you need more, take more. Give it to everyone."

He shook his head. "I can't take too much at once. It's not good for you."

"I don't care!"

"We'll make do," Liam assured me gently. "You've been more than generous, Lucy."

"But I feel fine," I said, going to sit on the couch, mostly because he'd nudged me over there. I pulled books out of my knapsack, making a pile on the table in front of me. "I'm sure you can—"

"Here." Marcus cut me off, shoving a glass of orange juice and a pile of cookies at me.

Duncan snorted. "Like cookies are going to stop The Mouth." He hadn't called me that in years.

"I met your girlfriend," I said, just to bug him. It was better than giving in to the nerves and anxiety threatening to burn a hole in my stomach. "She's nicer than you."

Duncan just leaned over and shoved a cookie in my mouth. I flicked cookie crumbs at him. Christabel slid closer to the books. She never could resist them. I was pretty sure being undead wouldn't change that. "Research," I explained. "On twelfth-century vampires. And also, anything on this Dawn bitch who kidnapped Nicholas." It was hard to concentrate with Liam, Helena, Uncle Geoffrey, and Bruno sorting weapons nearby.

"That's not a grenade, is it?" Christabel whispered.

"Probably," I whispered back. "They have this awesome storage room full of cool stuff like that."

"Grenades are cool?" She looked dubious.

"Cooler than dead poets," I teased.

"Hey," both she and Logan said at the same time.

There was a pile of local newspapers on the side table beside me. Most of the headlines still screamed warnings about the Dracula Killer and blood cults. I picked one up, grimacing. "Who the hell was the genius behind Dracula Killer? And these are getting worse."

"You have no idea," Quinn agreed. "It's making the tribes bitchy." He shook his head. "It's just not safe out there with all those Huntsmen and Helios-Ra."

"It's not safe anywhere," Kieran said quietly.

"It's time," Liam confirmed finally, checking his watch. Marcus handed them the vials of blood, carefully packed in a traveling case. "You boys stay put."

They filed out of the barn. Helena paused. "Lucy?"

"Yes?"

She ran a hand over my hair and kissed my cheek, just like she kissed Solange's cheek when Solange was little. "We love you very much. But your mother and I will both lock you in a basement for the rest of your life if you try to follow us." She speared Kieran with the kind of look that made us all squirm even though it wasn't even aimed at us. "We're trusting you to take her back to school where it's safe."

He nodded. "Yes, ma'am."

"Kiss-ass," I muttered.

"Hell, yeah," he muttered back. "Like you're any braver."

Sebastian was the first to slip out the door as soon as his parents were gone. Marcus and Duncan exchanged a look, then followed immediately.

"Stay out of pheromone range," Quinn yelled after them.

"Teach Grandma to suck eggs," Duncan yelled back.

The rest of us stared at one another. There was nothing left to distract me. I deflated, feeling hollow and cold. I tried not to look as freaked out as I felt.

"Why don't they wear nose plugs too?" Christabel asked.

"It would make them vulnerable out there," Quinn answered. "Scenting an attacker before we see them gives us an advantage."

"Oh."

We stared at one another some more.

"It'll work," I blurted out, mostly because the silence was making me itchy. "Nicholas and Solange will be home by dawn."

"We should get back before campus curfew," Kieran said.

"Like I care about that," I grumbled, but I got my things together since I was already on bathroom detention duty for sneaking out.

"Okay, then I should get you back to school before Helena pulls my spleen out my nose."

"She wouldn't do that," Quinn drawled. "Too messy." He paused. "Probably."

The remaining brothers walked us back out to Kieran's car. We drove back to school in silence. I rolled down the window and watched the trees and fields fly by. "Be safe," I whispered. "Be safe." I was interrupted by the strangest sound I'd ever heard. "Was that a . . . cow?"

"Not unless . . . Crap!" Kieran swerved to avoid the person who had run out in the middle of the road, blood dripping off his jaws. When Kieran realized it was a *Hel-Blar*, he swerved back toward it, tires squealing.

"They're eating cows now? Oh man, Mom's going to be pissed," I said, trying to hold onto the dash and grab a stake at the same time. I almost put my own eye out when Kieran skidded on a patch of black ice. The front of the SUV hit the *Hel-Blar* with a thud. He flew backward, landing in the snow at an awkward angle. Kieran was out of the car and staking him before I'd unbuckled my seatbelt. By the time I slipped out, ashes clogged the snow. There was the crack of a twig behind me, and then something worse.

The clacking of jaws.

The stink of wet mushrooms hit me just as Kieran yelled, running toward me. I yelled back when another *Hel-Blar* came out of the woods behind him, skin mottled and bruised looking. She shoved Kieran so hard he flew into the air and landed on the hood. He lay there looking dazed, one of his arms twisted behind him.

I darted around the car, using it as a shield. I slid through the snow, using the momentum to shove the stake in the *Hel-Blar*'s back, feeling it bite through cotton and flesh before lodging against a rib. I swore. She screeched, jerking back. Her elbow caught me in the sternum. Pain flared through my chest and I stumbled, landing on my butt. Kieran took advantage of the distraction and added his stake to mine. He had just enough space now to stab it hard through her heart. She snarled and spat, before crumbling to ashes.

Kieran and I stared at each other, gasping. I rubbed my chest, wincing. "Ow."

"Are you hurt?" he asked immediately, hauling me to my feet.

"I'm fine. You? Your arm?"

"Not broken," he answered as we turned to face the third *Hel-Blar*.

He ignored us completely.

We paused, confused.

"That's weird, right?" I whispered. *Hel-Blar* never ignored a kill, especially not when there were two of us all sweaty and panting from a fight. Our blood probably smelled like the vampire equivalent of a candy factory.

Kieran jerked his head and I followed him gingerly, picking my way around the icy patches. The *Hel-Blar* came out of the woods entirely, passed through the undergrowth on the side of the road and kept walking.

"He's tracking," I murmured.

It wasn't long before we started to see blood in the snow. We followed the vampire who was following the blood until Kieran shook his head. "We're too far from the car. We might need it."

He was right. "I'll get it," I said, racing back down the hill to where it was still running in a pool of light and exhaust fumes. I turned it around and drove back to Kieran, who hopped into the passenger seat. He kept his door open so he could leap out. The *Hel-Blar* was clacking his jaws now, saliva dripping. The blood on the snow was getting thicker.

And now we knew why.

There were three people stumbling up the center of the road. There was a farmer in his pajamas, a woman in a business suit and heels, and a guy who looked vaguely familiar. I thought he might have been a student at my old high school, a grade behind me. They all looked drugged, walking aimlessly through the cold night. Only the woman wore a winter coat. Blood dripped from their wrists and necks as they stumbled through the snow, leaving droplets like pomegranate seeds scattered by a careless hand.

A pale, perfect hand.

They weren't aimless, after all.

"Is that . . . Solange?" I choked, slamming on the brakes. She drifted gracefully along like the undead Pied Piper. "It's the pheromones," I added, stunned. "That's why they're trailing after her like that."

Kieran looked vaguely green. "Pheromones," he agreed, tightly, fumbling for his nose plugs.

Then it hit me.

I whirled on him, eyes widening until the cold air made them tear. "Solange! She's here!"

He frowned. "Yeah, I got that, Lucy."

"If she's *here*, then she can't be *there*. At the waterfalls."

"With the others," he realized. "With Isabeau."

"And Nicholas." Who I couldn't see anywhere nearby. He could be anywhere. Anything could have happened to him. "Shit." I hit the accelerator so hard Kieran cracked his head on the windshield. I aimed for the *Hel-Blar*. He flew into the nearest tree. The three bleeding humans nearby didn't even glance back.

Solange froze, outlined in snow and light.

"Get out," I warned Kieran grimly as I backed up into the road. "Take care of that *Hel-Blar* and then call Hunter for pickup and I'll call the farm for backup. We're still pretty close."

"What are you going to do?" he asked, but he slid out obediently.

"I'm going to keep her here," I said.

"How?"

"You don't want to know."

I waited until he was out of the way before stepping hard on the accelerator. The tires hissed in protest but I didn't let up. I pulled the lever to put it into four-wheel drive. Kieran loved Solange and I knew he'd do anything to save her. But I was her best friend and I didn't have his rules about not hitting girls. So I'd do what I had to.

Including hitting her with my car.

I swerved around the humans, honking. They barely blinked. Solange snarled, her lips lifting delicately off savage fangs. I searched the tree line for Constantine but I couldn't see him anywhere. It didn't mean he wasn't there.

I was kind of looking forward to hitting *him* with the car, actually.

I dialed Connor's number, knowing he'd have his phone on. I hit the speakerphone button before tossing mine onto the seat. "Solange!" I yelled, my teeth rattling as I sped over the uneven ground. "On Highfield, by Eighth Line! Call Isabeau while I stall her!"

Solange lifted her hand to block the high beams from blinding her. Her sensitive eyes flared red. I'd just taken away one of her advantages. A glance in the rearview mirror showed Kieran fighting the *Hel-Blar*. The boy slumped to the ground beside them. I turned back to Solange, who was stumbling in the snow, snarling. The wheels spun out in the slush. I gripped the steering wheel tightly, refusing to let go. I kept my eyes on Solange. She flailed, half-blind.

"Ha!" I was practically standing on the gas pedal.

I hit her just before she could dart into the safety of the forest.

She rolled over the hood and hit the windshield. I eased off the accelerator and the car spun out madly. My stomach pressed against my spine. I slid down the hill backward, narrowly avoiding the farmer, Solange still clinging to the window. Her white dress fluttered against the glass, blocking my view. I slammed into a fence post and the sound of metal crushing in on itself made my teeth hurt. The car stopped with a violent jolt. Solange flew into the snow, rolled to the edge of the road, and lay there motionless. For a long time all I could hear was the hammer of my pulse in my ears. The seatbelt was digging into my stomach and my cheek hurt from where I'd bit it when the car hit the fence.

The driver's door flew open. Kieran grabbed my shoulder. "Shit!" he shouted in my face.

I burst out laughing. I couldn't help it. He was usually so calm and confident, like Hunter.

"I'm okay," I told him. I tried to unbuckle my seatbelt but my fingers were trembling so much he had to do it for me. Adrenaline made me light-headed. "I just hit my best friend with a car." Nausea rolled through me. "I'm going to hell."

He crouched next to Solange warily. "She's out." He reached out to brush her hair off her face but stopped himself, drawing back out of reach.

"For now." I slid off the seat. The cold air was bracing and helped clear my head. I took a few deep breaths. "Won't last long." I pulled a crossbow out of the trunk and armed it. I stood over Solange with my teeth chattering and my hands shaking, an arrow aimed at her chest. "I'm immune, I'll stay with her. You get some rope or something."

He pulled chains, ropes, bright yellow twine, and two pairs of handcuffs out of a bag in the backseat. The last time she'd lain so still, he'd had to feed her his own blood to revive her. This time, he cuffed her wrists together and then wound thick rope around her arms and torso. He used the twine on her ankles.

"Where is she?" Quinn and Connor skirted the slumped bodies sprawled in the road without a second glance. I spun around, crossbow still at the ready. They leaped out of the way. Quinn flipped into the air and right over my head. Connor landed in a tree, balancing on a lower branch. One time. I'd accidentally shot Marcus *one* time.

"Isabeau's on her way," Connor said, dropping back down to the ground. Snow drifted off his jacket. "Mom and Dad, are, of course, out of range. But Aunt Hyacinth went to find them and Christabel is going to keep calling from the barn."

The twins circled their little sister carefully. I lost feeling in my toes. It felt like hours before Hunter drove up in one of the school vans. Her friend Jason was with her.

"Sorry," Kieran said curtly. "If we called the emergency unit for the vics, they'd have to take Solange too."

"I know," Hunter said, all business. "Help me get them in the van."

The victims were all breathing normally but the boy's cheeks were white with cold. There was no way of knowing how far he'd walked or how long he'd been following Solange. Jason grabbed him under the arms and dragged him to the van without a word. Kieran helped the woman and Hunter guided the farmer as he shuffled toward the backseat. He sat down with a groan, looking confused.

I crouched in front of him, smiling gently and hiding the crossbow behind my back. "You're going to be okay," I told him. "They're going to take you to the doctor."

"Caught some hooligans in my field," he slurred. "Did something to my cows."

"Did they touch you?" Kieran asked sharply from the other side.

"High on something," he mumbled. "Smelled like they hadn't showered in weeks."

"But did they *touch* you?" Hunter repeated.

The farmer smiled. "Had my shotgun. Scared them off good and proper." We exchanged a sigh of relief. "Rather go home," he mumbled. The wrinkles on his face were like crevices.

"Too bad," she said cheerfully. "We're taking you to the doctor first."

"Smart mouth. Just like my granddaughter." He opened one eye. "How do I know you aren't after my cows too?"

I tried to buckle him in. "Do you know Cass Hamilton?" I asked. "The vegetarian animal-rights activist who hands out flyers at the farmers' market?" He scowled. I patted his hand. "She's my mom. Your cows are safe."

He was still grumbling when he passed out. Jason slid into the driver's seat as Quinn carried the woman to the back of the van. Kieran looked grimly at the neat row of bite marks on the back of her neck.

"At least it wasn't *Hel-Blar*," I told him. She'd have scars though, they all would. Apparently Solange had abandoned her delicate supper manners. Aunt Hyacinth would be horrified. I stepped back in time to see Quinn lean into the open window and kiss Hunter quickly, but fiercely. She touched his cheek. He turned and pressed another kiss into her palm before straightening up and stepping back.

The van sped away. We were left in the warped prisms of light from the broken headlight, three Drake brothers, a hunter, and my best friend tied up at our feet.

"Um, guys?" I said, staring at the edge of the woods. "We have another problem."

Chapter 17

Solange

I didn't need a memory box to know that the residents of Bornebow Hall hadn't survived Viola's first night as a vampire.

It was too easy to picture them falling out of their blood-soaked beds, littered around the fire or discarded in the hay, the horses wild with the scent of violence. Still, I wasn't actually convinced it was enough to cause Madame Veronique's fear of her. After all, she hadn't stopped her son from chaining his wife to a post on and off for years, all because they assumed Lady Venetia cheated on him. They'd had no idea yet that the Drake men could father children, even as vampires. It was horribly unfair. As was what had happened to Gwyneth. It made sense now, why she hid in the forest, with her scarred throat, bruised face, and blood on her gown. And I understood why she wanted to stay away from Viola. But I was going to need her help if I wanted my undead life back.

I left the relative safety of the cupboard, creeping out as quietly as I could. I paused long enough to rummage through the clothing hanging from the hooks, choosing a simple gray cloak and pulling its hood up to conceal my face. The hall was deserted and cold. I took the spiraling stone staircase, trying to move as if I belonged here and had a purpose. The guards would be searching for a girl who was clinging to the shadows.

I was so nervous when I passed the first knight, I was sure I was going to throw up all over him, especially when he stopped me. His arm blocked me. "Supper's late in the kitchens," he said. "Lend them a hand, would you? I'm half-famished."

I swallowed, grateful that Aunt Hyacinth had been so strict about teaching the proper curtsy. She'd made me practice for so many hours I could now curtsy perfectly even when terrified and nauseated. "Yes, my lord," I whispered.

He let me pass and I struggled not to break into a run. I followed the circular stairs, listening intently for shouts of alarm or warning. There was nothing but the murmur of voices from the hall and the cursing of the cook in the kitchen. He was red-faced and sweating through his shirt as he wrestled with a giant pig on a roasting spike. I skirted around the doorway, heading lower still to the cellars and dungeons. Another guard waited at the bottom of the steps.

"You there." He frowned. "What are you doing down here?"

I smiled, hoping it didn't look like a grimace. "The cook sent me for turnips," I said. "He's in a right bad mood."

The guard snorted. "Not turnips. Can't stand his mashed turnips."

"I'll see if I can find some leeks instead."

He smiled. "Good lass."

I went down the corridor and turned the corner out of sight. I allowed myself a brief moment to slump against the wall and catch my breath before continuing on to the fallen-in tunnel. Dust and debris leaked out from under the door. I'd been hoping I could clear just enough space to fit through, but the door was wedged shut with the pressure of the dislodged stones. I'd have to find another way out. For that I'd have to pass the second guard again. I opened all the doors until I found a cold cellar with barrels and baskets full of turnips, leeks, dried lentils, and onions. I stuffed leeks into a basket and headed back out, making sure the guard saw that I'd left the turnips behind. He winked at me.

Since everyone was currently obsessed with food, I'd use it to my advantage. I dumped the leeks out onto a table littered with carrot tops and stuffed the basket full of bread and apples. I added a wheel of cheese wrapped in cloth. "Eh, where you off to with that?" the cook barked, as he hacked off one of the pig's legs with a giant cleaver.

"To the gatehouse," I replied, keeping my eyes downcast. "They're complaining."

The cook snorted. "They're always complaining. Don't take them good cheese."

I left the cheese behind and slipped out the door before he could stop me again. The courtyard was full of knights bustling back and forth and a man in a stained coat feeding the dogs in the kennel. Fires burned in iron holders, belching smoke. The sun was setting slowly behind the trees on the other side of the lower bailey.

I wanted to sneak out before night fell completely, just in case Viola was stronger at night. She was a vampire, after all.

I went through the first gatehouse without incident. The grassy lawns were empty of knights as they returned to the hall for dinner. I hurried to the last iron gate, glad to see the portcullis was raised. One less obstacle to deal with.

I stopped at the arched doorway. "I've brought your supper," I called up the tower. My voice echoed. I took one of the torches out of its holder as the guard came down the stairs, scowling. "About time," he said.

I just smiled and whacked him in the head with the torch.

He hit the wall, his helmet ringing against the stones. He slumped on the stairs. I shoved his feet up out of the side and then put the basket next to his head. "Sorry," I whispered, before replacing the torch. And then I darted over the bridge, trying hard not to look at the moat of bobbing corpses. Sunset leaked red light through the trees, reflecting off the murky water. Bile burned the back of my throat. I ran faster.

An alarm bell started to ring from the gatehouse. My lungs and leg muscles were taking turns stabbing me by the time I reached the edge of the forest. The sun had nearly completely set. I could see the shadow of the dragon circling over the castle and the borders of the woods, silhouetted against the lilac and red sky. I ducked into the oak trees, pushing the hood off my head so I could see it better. I had no way to fight it if it saw me and decided to attack.

I followed the scorch marks from my last encounter with the dragon until I reached the caves. Warm firelight glowed from one of the openings. I climbed up, sweat soaking into my hair, which lay cold and damp over my neck. By the time I stumbled inside, I was covered in dirt and grime. Gwyneth didn't even look up from the fire she was poking with a stick. "I knew you'd be back."

"I need to talk to you," I said as politely as I could.

"Of course you do." She finally glanced at me. "You've already lasted longer than I'd thought. I'm impressed." She tilted her head, like a bird. "And you got out."

"Yes," I admitted, giving in to fatigue and sitting down next to her. "I got back to Violet Hill. But not for long." Just long enough to get London killed. I pushed back at the bleak sorrow and guilt. I could mourn and survive at the same time. They didn't have to be mutually exclusive.

"Still," Gwyneth continued. "That's an accomplishment, believe me. You should be proud."

"I just want my life back," I said wearily.

She ran her fingers over the scar on her throat. From this angle her face was young and pretty, the ruined side turned away from me. "Viola doesn't give. She takes."

"I know that," I said. "But I'm not going to let her get away with—" I whirled, hearing the scuff of footsteps behind me. A shadow moved across the uneven cave wall. I caught a glimpse of blond hair and red eyes.

"Don't mind her," Gwyneth said, unbothered.

"But . . . it's *Viola.*"

"Just an echo," she said.

"What, like a ghost?" Viola flickered. It was disconcerting. She was covered in dirt and blood, her hair matted, her dress torn. Bats flitted around her, diving in and out. I walked back and forth in front of her. Her eyes followed me. It was creepy. "Are you sure she can't see us?"

"Quite sure," Gwyneth answered.

I reached out to touch her, just to be sure. She flickered erratically and my hand passed through a cold draft. It was distinctly unpleasant. "Gross." I wiped my fingers vigorously on my dress, stepping back. The firelight caught the decorative hinges of the hope chest. The painted lid was open and I caught a glimpse of boxes, like the ones I'd stolen from the castle. "You have them too," I said.

"We have to store our memories somehow," Gwyneth explained, getting to her feet swiftly and slamming the lid back down. She secured the heavy iron lock. "Else we forget them and we forget who we are."

"Are they always kept in boxes?" I asked curiously.

"Only here in Viola's spirit. It's how she keeps them. I keep them the same way so she's less likely to notice." She looked wistful. "If I had my way, my memories would be birds."

Viola shifted behind us. I heard a dripping sound and I honestly didn't want to turn around to look. It could as easily be the blood all over her as it could be rainwater seeping into the cave. I hunched my shoulders defensively. "It's like she's staring at me. Why would you stay here?"

"She spent her first few weeks as a vampire here, after she fled what was left of Bornebow Hall. She didn't know what was happening to her. She won't come back here."

I could almost feel sorry for her. Almost. "The bloodchange made her crazy," I said.

"Oh, it wasn't just that. She let love burn her up until she scorched everything she touched. It's like that sometimes."

"She didn't understand the thirst. I'm surprised she didn't turn *Hel-Blar*." I could understand the thirst, at least. Mine was sharper than anyone else's in my family. I touched my fangs with the tip of my tongue. Something occurred to me. "That's why," I realized. "My extra fangs, my need for so much more blood. It's Viola's thirst, not just mine."

"Aye." Gwyneth nodded. "She latched on to you proper on the night of your birthday. The same night she changed."

I thought about the prophecy again. *Dragon by dragon defeated.* I'd assumed it referred to my mother and me at the coronation, or at least the dragon that had tried to roast me the first time I'd fled the castle. But now I wondered if it was actually about Viola and me, about our bloodlines, our battle.

I felt a moment of annoyance for the cryptic nature of prophecies. Then I remembered that this particular one had been spoken by a crazy old woman high on mushroom tea, and I was amazed we had even this much to work with. Madame Veronique had kept it secret all this time. She'd helped me survive so the rest of the prophecy wouldn't blow up in her face.

Unseat the dragon before her time, and increase ninefold her crimes.

I watched the logs in the fire shift, sending up sparks. It came down to love and power. Viola wanted both. So I'd have to use them to lure her out, to force her to confront me. To evict her completely. "If we work together, I think we can beat her," I said to Gwyneth. "You could be free."

She smiled humorlessly. "I don't deserve to be free."

"You made a mistake," I said. "That's not the same thing as what Viola did. She murdered an entire castle full of people! And you already paid for it with your life."

"That's not all she did," Gwyneth murmured, her braids falling forward to screen her expression. She pulled small round stones out of a pouch at her belt and rolled them in her palm. "That was just the beginning."

"Is that why Madame Veronique fears her?"

"She wasn't blameless, that one."

No kidding. Madame Veronique had kept secrets from all of us. Not to mention she'd set an assassin on me. "She hid all of this from me, from my whole family. She pretended she knew nothing about the prophecy, nothing about magic."

"Of course she did," Gwyneth said, the stones clacking in her hand. "The more you think about a spirit such as Viola, the more you speak her name you feed her with magic, and the stronger she becomes. Then the better able she is to find you. Veronique never wanted to be taken by surprise again, so she sought out soothsayers in every century."

"Even if I get my body back, will Viola always be inside me?"

"Hard to know." There were little daisies in Gwyneth's matted hair. I'd never noticed before.

"Would she make me crazy if she was stuck inside my head?"

Gwyneth shrugged. "Maybe."

"That's the opposite of helpful," I said, annoyed. "If you feel so guilty about everything, *help* me." I shot to my feet, pacing the small confines of the cave. "Can you at least tell me why the crown freed her so completely?"

"Magic."

"I figured that out for myself, thanks." I kept pacing, avoiding the flickering shadow of Viola, snarling at me, dried blood on her chin.

"The crown is just a symbol. It worked as a talisman because Viola forced it to; there was no actual magic in it to begin with. It was just the magic already in her, finding a trigger."

I paced by Viola again, noticing the bats near the ceiling. I couldn't tell if they were real or not. Only her eyes and the pendant around her neck were in sharp focus, glittering. "What about the pendant?" I asked. "It's clearly magical. It activated Viola's spell, and it trapped you here. So if I destroy it, will Viola be destroyed too?"

"Finally, you ask the right question."

"Oh my God," I snapped. "What is it with witches and riddles? If you knew something, why didn't you just *tell* me?"

"That's not the way it works," Gwyneth said, unrepentant. "You needed to see what you saw and do what you did to have the strength to do what must be done."

I rolled my eyes. "Great."

She grinned. It was fleeting and rusty, as if she'd forgotten how. "Besides, I didn't know you, did I? Not *really*. I didn't know if you were strong enough. And every time one of her hosts fails, she goes on a rampage." She touched her scar again.

"Host? You make it sound like a dinner party," I muttered. "For the psychotic undead." I stopped pacing. "Why are you helping me now?" I still didn't know if she could actually be trusted. She'd been right when she said we didn't really know each other. But the enemy of my enemy is my friend and all that. It was one of Dad's favorite sayings.

"Penance, I suppose. And you've lasted this long. Maybe it's enough."

"Gee, thanks." I sighed. "I don't suppose you know where the stupid pendant is hidden?"

"It's not hidden at all. Viola wears it here at all times."

I paused, narrowing my eyes. "That's way too easy."

"It would be, yes. If that was the end of it. But you'll need to find a way to lure her out."

"And then?"

"And then you get the pendant from her and smash it." Gwyneth cast the stones she'd been holding, reading their pattern and trying to decipher the future. I'd seen Isabeau do something similar, and Lucy's mom read my tarot cards every year on my birthday. Well, she hadn't read them this year, for obvious reasons. One stupid, vague prophecy at a time.

"Can I win?" I asked, seeing nothing but painted lines like sticks. The smoke from the fire made my eyes burn.

"You can." I couldn't help but smile. She didn't smile back. "I say you *can*, not that you *will*."

"You really have to work on your pep talks."

She gathered up her painted stones, dropping them back into a leather pouch. "Do you think you can make her find you?"

"Yes." I smiled grimly as the phantom bats screeched in the corner. "I know exactly what to do."

I was barely at the gatehouse when another memory hit.

1199

The caves were dark and damp and smelled like iron. Water streamed down the walls, icy and uncomfortable. But she was safe. No one would think to look for her here. Only the bats dared enter, mostly because they'd been sleeping here by the hundreds long before she'd ever stumbled out of Bornebow Hall covered in blood. They caught in her hair and bit at her hands but she barely noticed. She tried to stay awake but couldn't. The day weighed heavily on her and she carried it in her breast like the hot coal they used in trials to prove innocence. It burned her because she was guilty.

It hardly mattered. The guilt didn't carry her through the sickness— only thoughts of Tristan could do that. He hadn't come for her. He didn't know she was here. He might never know if she couldn't find her way out. So she fed on deer and wolves and the thieves who hid in the woods until she was strong enough.

Vertigo slammed through me and I had to hold onto the stones for support. Luckily the gatehouse guard was holding his head and retching behind a barrel. I crept past him, wincing at the bloody bruise on his temple.

"Sorry," I whispered, ducking into the outer bailey. The moon made the long expanses of grass silvery and sharp. I stayed pressed against the inside of the wall, considering my options. I didn't need to get right inside the castle. I just needed a spot that I could defend from the knights until Viola was pissed off enough to seek me out.

Which shouldn't be a problem.

Since she already knew I was here.

Viola looked down at her gown, the fine silk wet with blood. She could still taste it on her tongue, sliding hotly down her parched throat. It should have made her sick.

Instead, it made her feel invincible.

She understood everything now. Her father's nighttime habits, her mother's illness. Her own impossible lineage.

She could barely see the bodies at her feet, drained dry. Everything was too sharp, too bright.

Too red.

I clenched my jaw, my fangs aching against the stabbing thirst. She was making me believe I was starving, that I was turning into a papery husk. I hadn't fed in nights and Viola was forcing me to relive the feast she had made of innocent bodies.

She wanted me to feel her madness, her confusion, her fear.

But I'd also felt something else from her.

Love.

I knew the key to luring her out.

Constantine.

Chapter 18

Isabeau

Wednesday night

Running through the woods with a pack of dogs at my heels usually made me happy.

It made me feel free and wild and part of the mysteries, a true handmaiden to the Hounds. It was invigorating and grounding. Necessary. But too slow. Frustrated, I pushed harder. Pine boughs slapped at me. Magda ran beside me, slapping back at them. Snow shivered in the air behind us. The dogs lowered their heads and flattened their ears, streaking between the trees. Even as fast as we were, we'd never make it in time.

"I hate your boyfriend," Magda snapped as more snow fell on her head.

"You didn't have to come," I reminded her, leaping over a fallen tree. Charlemagne sailed over it, tight at my side. His tongue lolled out in a happy canine smile. The pack on my back bounced against my shoulder blades, filled with ritual gear.

"Like I'm going to leave you alone with the Drakes," Magda shot back. The moonlight caught on the daggers at her belt and the chainmail sewn into my tunic over my heart. "After what happened last time."

And by that, she meant the time I'd brought one of them home with me. Logan had snuck under my defenses with his old-world courtesy and quick grin, and now he was an initiated member of our tribe. Something that never failed to infuriate Magda, on principle, if nothing else. She didn't share well. It was another ten minutes before we broke out of the forest and along a deserted road. Headlights flashed as a Jeep sped up behind us.

Logan.

Magda called him something rude under her breath before yanking the back door open. Charlemagne leaped in after her. "*Suivez*," I ordered the other dogs who had stopped running and were barking from the shadows.

Logan reached over to push my door open and I climbed in. His hair falling over his pale forehead and the lace at his cuffs did nothing to detract from his grim expression. His smile though, when he saw me, was gentle. I didn't have time to smile back; he'd already slammed his foot on the pedal. I held tightly onto the door handle as the vehicle sped down the road. I knew it was faster than running, and more efficient than the carriages I remembered, but I still preferred the carriages. They didn't make me feel trapped.

I held on tighter, my fangs poking out from under my top lip. Hounds didn't generally bother retracting their fangs since we lived in secrecy and had no need or desire to blend into society, even vampire society. They feared our extra set of teeth. I'd caught more than one vampire sniffing me back at the camp, to make sure I wasn't *Hel-Blar*.

Logan glanced at me out of the corner of his eye. They were grass green even in the dim glow from the lights on the dash. I still wasn't sure how he could read me so well but he didn't say anything, only pushed a button and the window slid open. Cold cedar-and-snow-scented air made the bone beads in my hair clatter. I could see the shadows of the dogs chasing us on either side. Charlemagne pushed his head out my window from the backseat.

"Are you sure about this?" Magda asked, as she'd asked me on the hour every hour since I'd made my offer. It didn't matter that Logan was sitting right next to me.

"*Oui*," I replied. "*Bien sur.*" I wasn't acting as the handmaiden to Kala, the Hounds' Shamanka in this; just as Magda wasn't acting as my guard or ritual sister, but as my friend.

"Thank you," Logan murmured. "We have to try."

I reached out, interlacing my fingers through his. "There was too much magic unleashed the day Solange took the crown, and that is no coincidence. Else it would have happened when your mother was crowned too."

We crested a hill and at the bottom another car was set off the road, the front dented around a fence post. The lights were still on and beyond them, Solange lay on the ground tied up with rope. Around her stood Kieran, Lucy, Quinn, and Connor. A tall man with black hair and a vicious smile broke out of the trees, flinging stakes. One of them narrowly avoided Lucy's cheek, and only because Quinn kicked her feet out from under her, dropping her like a stone. She pushed to her hands and knees, scrambling to grab a crossbow before it was crushed under various boots.

"Constantine," Logan spat, slamming on the brakes and screeching to a halt. I could hear the approach of the dogs on the other side of the hill.

"And *Hel-Blar*," Magda added. "On your left."

On the other side of the street, *Hel-Blar* shuffled in our direction, reeking of mushrooms and mildew. Charlemagne growled, despite his training. He knew danger and it made his hackles rise. "*Non*," I told him sharply. It was too risky for any of the dogs to attack the *Hel-Blar* and they were all carefully trained to avoid them, by their smell and the sound of their clacking jaws. I whistled to forbid them from attacking. They were on the other side of the hill, but they'd still be able to hear me.

"Shit," Logan swore. "Incoming!" he yelled to the others.

"Not again," Lucy said, whirling to face them. Her first cross-bow bolt caught the closest one in the chest, right through the heart. He crumbled into pieces and disintegrated. His companions scuttled through his ashes, snarling and undaunted. They smelled blood and battle and Solange's pheromones. They'd never stop coming.

"I need to dreamwalk," I said, despite the danger all around us.

"What, here?" Magda asked. "*Now?*" She whipped out one of her daggers. "Little busy."

"I still need to get into Solange's mind. And for that, I need to be touching her and she won't let me do that until we get the collar on her. But I never got Lucy's blood for immunity." I withdrew the copper collar Logan's brothers and Christabel had stolen from the *Hel-Blar*.

Made of beaten copper and glimmering like trapped firelight, it was smooth and simple and curved like a half-moon. The collar was powerful, and even after Kala and I had both examined it thoroughly, we still weren't entirely sure how it worked. I was taking a risk by using a magical item that might not be dependable, and judging by the foul look Magda shot me, she realized it too.

"You don't need my blood," Lucy piped up. "You've got me."

I grabbed her wrist. "Then let's go."

Magda gave a twisted, screeching kind of laugh and leaped at the *Hel-Blar*. Logan followed, distinctly less enthusiastic, but then I'd seen rabid dogs with less enthusiasm for violence than Magda. "Guys!" he shouted at his brothers. "A little help here?"

But they couldn't help him. They couldn't even help themselves.

Because Solange was awake now.

She lifted her head, pupils flaring, the whites of her eyes bleeding out in red rivers. The twins stumbled, cursing. "Let me go," she said softly.

"Don't!" Lucy shouted.

But it was too late for warnings and they wouldn't have done any good regardless.

"Let me go," Solange demanded again. "*Now.*"

Logan was safe from Solange's pheromones but he was also too busy fighting off *Hel-Blar*. I felt the pull of her power as well. Charlemagne moved across me, leaning his considerable weight across my knees to stop me from getting closer. Luckily, I was still far enough away to retain some sovereignty over myself.

"Take my nose plugs—" Lucy stopped. "Damn it, I gave them to Christabel."

They might have helped but they weren't a perfect shield. I swayed toward Solange but at least my feet stayed rooted. Between Charlemagne and my own magic, I could buy myself a few more moments. The twins weren't so lucky. Quinn was already slicing through the thick ropes that bound her. Sweat dampened his hair as he struggled uselessly to fight the compulsion. Connor kneeled next to him and snapped the handcuffs apart. Constantine was trying to get to her and Kieran was just as determined to stop him. The twins stood, hovering beside their sister, straining on invisible leashes.

The *Hel-Blar* continued to advance.

Solange rose to her feet, like something out of the fairy stories my nursemaid told me when I was a child. Her hair was black as coal, her lips red as blood. Even her dress floated around her as if compelled.

Constantine backhanded Kieran and sent him sailing over our heads. I ducked before his boot could graze my temple but kept running, dragging Lucy behind me. She made a small strangled sound of surprise. Quinn and Connor moved to block Solange. I'd have to get through them to get to her.

"Can you take them?" Lucy asked. "Without killing them?"

"*Oui.*"

"Without them killing you?"

"I am not so easy to kill." I handed her the copper collar, which she looped over her wrist like a large bracelet so that she could keep a grip on her crossbow. Her eyes widened suddenly and I knew Constantine must be behind me. Charlemagne was already leaping at him. Constantine dodged, but only barely. He had vampire speed, the kind that comes from being ancient. If he reached Solange before we did, we wouldn't be able to start the ritual. And Logan's brothers might die.

I spun on my heel to face him. My dogs raced down the street toward us, leaping the fences and skirting around trees. Constantine went low and I leaped high, avoiding his strike. I landed with a stake in each hand, braids and beads rattling like bones.

"We just want safe passage," Constantine said. His accent was vaguely British, clipped but charming.

Charming didn't work on me.

I didn't waste time with idle talk, only threw one of my stakes. He danced out of the way but not quickly enough to avoid it entirely. It sliced through his side, under his arm, as he turned. His blood stung the air, hot and metallic.

Solange shrieked at the twins.

"Kill the witch!"

CHAPTER 19

Lucy

Things weren't exactly going according to plan.

Big surprise.

Logan and Magda started to sprint toward Isabeau, *Hel-Blar* at their heels. "*Non!*" she told them even as Quinn and Connor did the same thing. Her tattoos looked very blue against the moonlight and snow. "*Dans un cercle!*" she ordered the dozen or so dogs milling through the snow. She pointed at Solange and they lunged for her. Quinn went down under the weight of a Rottweiler, knocking Connor down with him as he fell. The dogs paced a circle around Solange. Logan and Magda went back to fighting *Hel-Blar*.

Constantine snarled, wiping blood from his side. His violet eyes locked on me, snapping to the copper collar swinging around my arm. I stumbled back a step, trying to figure out how to reach

Solange without turning my back on him. I wanted to make a run for it but I knew I'd never make it.

"You," he said darkly, stalking toward me so quickly his hair flattened back away from his face. He was gorgeous, plain and simple. He downright smoldered. But that wasn't enough for Solange. There was something else going on here. "You get away from her." He seethed. Solange hissed behind me. The dogs barked and snapped at her knees.

I had nowhere to go. I was about to be skewered inside an undead vampire sandwich with a side of dog teeth. Karma for hitting Solange with a car. Not to mention Tasering her just last month.

The twins were currently trapped under dogs. Logan and Magda were trying not to get mushroom stench all over them, and Kieran was still on the ground, a hand pressed to a bloody gash on his head. Isabeau tossed handfuls of herbs on the ground, a dog-bone rattle in her other hand. She was chanting something under her breath.

Constantine reached for me. I tossed the collar toward Isabeau. Constantine veered toward it. Isabeau didn't even look up from her ritual preparations. She just swung around, slamming her boot into his chest. He grunted in pain, and I heard ribs crack as he flew away from me. Isabeau caught the collar, returning to her chanting before he'd landed. He crashed, skidding through the snow so deeply he left a groove in the grass underneath.

Constantine landed next to Kieran, who shot his arm out, releasing the Hypnos strapped under his cuff. "Stay down, you son of a bitch."

The white powder drifted over Constantine, and he stayed

sprawled on the ground, gnashing his teeth with fury. Isabeau snapped her fingers, and several dogs paced around him, snarling. Charlemagne's giant paws pressed into his wounded side. Constantine wheezed, blood staining the corner of his mouth.

I spun back to face Solange. Her face contorted, glaring at me, at the dogs, at Isabeau, who was burning some kind of incense in a long dish that looked like a hollowed-out dog femur. "Solange, if you can hear me, we're trying to help you."

Her lips lifted off her teeth. "I don't need help from a human."

"Get out of her, you bitch!" My dad would have said namecalling was a refuge for the weak and ignorant. I didn't care. I was about to do a lot worse.

"No." She smirked, even though her dress was stained with blood where the dogs were nipping at her legs. I couldn't quite reach her. Even with the dogs, she'd be able to knock the collar out of my hand before I got it around her neck. She might even bite my fingers right off my hand.

"Okay, next plan," I muttered. I tried not to give myself away with a wince before I aimed the crossbow at her and released the trigger. Constantine yelled but he seemed very far away. The world narrowed down to the arrow, to the stiff black fletchings, and the pointed arrowhead. My breath stuck in my throat. I could only hope my aim was as good as everyone claimed, including me.

Because I was taking a hell of a risk. Even if I hadn't aimed for her heart . . .

An inch too low or too high or too far to the left, and I'd turn my best friend into ashes.

The moment stretched and stretched, unbearable in its jagged tension. It finally shattered when the arrow slammed into Solange, throwing her back and pinning her to a tree with a violent bloody jolt. She hissed with pain. She jerked and flailed but wasn't able to get free. Blood bloomed along her collar and dripped down her useless arm. She was hurting, she was furious, and she hated me.

But at least she wasn't a pile of ash.

"Collar!" I stuck my arm out without looking, knowing Isabeau would kick it to me. I caught it, the cold copper edges digging into my palm. I darted forward, the dogs scattering. "I'm sorry, Sol. God, I'm so sorry," I babbled.

"Kill her," she shrieked, pheromones shooting off her like darts. They didn't affect me like the others but even I felt a little fuzzy. And I could smell dead roses and chocolate. Quinn was the first to get free and stagger to his feet. He ran at me, blurring, fangs elongating, hiss snaking out into the cold air.

Kieran threw a stake at him but it missed.

Quinn gathered speed.

And at the last moment, just as the cold air buffeted me, warning me of his imminent descent, Connor was suddenly there. He'd been far enough away from Solange, since the arrow had tossed her back several feet, that he wasn't affected by her pheromones anymore. He tackled his twin and they tumbled through the snow, dogs nipping at their heels.

I jerked back, physically unable to contain the sudden slap of not actually being dead.

Solange blinked, blood leaking from the corner of her eyes. "Lucy?" Her voice was small, tentative.

I froze. "Sol?"

She shifted, cringing when the movement yanked on the hole on her shoulder. "What's happening?" She glanced down at the arrow. "What did I do? What did I do?" she asked frantically.

"Solange." Kieran stumbled around Isabeau, hope making him look younger. I could almost imagine the Kieran who had apparently filled the school birdbaths with red Jell-o. "Finally."

She tried to smile at him over my shoulder. "So . . . sorry . . ." She looked at me, all three set of fangs wickedly long. Blue veins throbbed under her pale skin. She gritted her teeth. "I'm trying to hold her . . . Can't . . ."

"Fight!" I begged her. "You're a Drake. Drakes fight, damn it!"

"She's a Drake too." She had to spit out a mouthful of blood before she could speak again. "Viola."

"Her name is Viola?" Isabeau asked silkily. "*Bien*. I will try to contain her as I show you how to get back home." She dropped to sit cross-legged at the foot of the tree and clasped Solange's limp hand, the one dripping blood. She wound a ribbon around them, tightening the knot with her teeth. She closed her eyes and began to chant.

"Do it," Solange croaked. "Whatever it is, do it now!"

I jammed the collar around her neck, fumbling to hook it on tightly. She yelped in pain, eyelids flying open to reveal red irises. They burned and snapped like a line of gasoline catching fire. She strained against the arrow, pulling it with searing infinitesimal slowness through her ragged flesh. She tried to free her hand but it was lodged tightly against Isabeau's, the ribbon slick with blood.

Her fingers twitched as if they burned. Isabeau didn't move, already deep in a trance.

"I said, kill the witch!" She seethed, clearly back to being Viola. No one moved.

Isabeau was right there, bathed in pheromones, and she didn't so much as blink. Quinn and Connor limped into range. Still no reaction. Solange slumped, confused and exhausted.

"No!" Constantine struggled, his odd eyes gleaming as if he was holding back tears. "What have you done?"

Solange didn't need pheromones to punch me in the face.

So she clearly wasn't *that* exhausted.

She backhanded me with her free hand and the force of it knocked me off my feet. I flew sideways, head snapping back, jaw screaming with pain. I bit through the inside of my cheek. My neck spasmed. I tensed as the ground raced up to meet me, despite Jenna's lesson on how to fall and my parents' advice on going limp if arrested at a protest. It happened too fast. I didn't have time to shield myself with an arm to break my fall. The impact was going to shatter my teeth or my cheekbone; at the very least I was looking at a concussion.

I never landed.

Nicholas caught me.

My eyes were screwed up so tight it took me a moment to realize I wasn't broken. I was so close to the ground that the snow was cold on the back of my legs but a hand cradled my head gently. My heart stuttered. Nicholas leaned over me, one knee on the ground as he supported my weight. His hair fell over his forehead, his expression as beautiful and solemn as ever.

"I hit my head, didn't I?" I asked, wobbily. "You're not real."

His mouth quirked. "I'm real, Lucky."

He stood up slowly, drawing me back to my feet. I was a little light-headed and a lot confused. "Where did you even come from?" I asked, awed despite myself. I didn't give him a chance to answer, just stood on my tiptoes and pressed my mouth to his. I kissed him as if I wasn't covered in blood, with water freezing into icicles at the bottom of my jeans and a bruise forming on my face. He drew me up against his chest, his kisses dark and deep and sweet. I wanted them to last forever. We didn't have forever, though. We barely had right now.

"I followed Constantine," he finally explained when I pulled away long enough to let him talk. "I would have been here sooner but I got cornered by a Huntsman. He's now being chased by one of Isabeau's dogs."

His brothers converged on us with happy whoops, slapping his back and jostling me right out of the way so that I bumped into Kieran. He had to catch me so I wouldn't topple.

"I'm sure this is all very touching," Magda said acidly. "But we're kind of in the middle of something."

More *Hel-Blar* were closing in, drawn by the violence and the blood in the snow. It wouldn't be long before other vampires joined them, and then hunters. We had to get out of here and we didn't have time to fight them all individually. Not to mention that Isabeau was still deep in her magical trance.

"We need to buy some time," Connor said, frowning at the *Hel-Blar*. "And we're running out of stakes."

"We could blow up the car," I suggested. Kieran didn't even look surprised, though it was his car.

"What is it with you and blowing up shit?" Quinn asked as Magda leaped off the hood, stabbing down with two daggers and catching two *Hel-Blar* at the same time. She was like a feral cat in a rainstorm, all claws and teeth.

"Hey, I didn't blow up that ghost town. That was all Hunter."

Nicholas stood behind me close enough that I could lean back slightly and touch him. I still wasn't convinced he was real. "We could light the gasoline as well," he suggested. "In a perimeter around us. It would keep them back for a little while."

"Good idea," Logan approved. "We'll need rope or something for that. Too much snow otherwise."

"I've got rope in the trunk," Kieran said.

"I'll get the gas tank out." Nicholas took a step forward but Quinn stopped him. He just raised an eyebrow in reply.

"I'm older," Quinn insisted. "And you've already had a bad week."

Nicholas snorted. "Do you even known where the gas tank is?"

"Well, crap."

"Cover me," was all Nicholas said before leaping into the fray. Quinn and Connor fanned out behind him. Logan doubled back to protect Isabeau and Solange. Solange's eyes were rolled back in her head as she fought her own inner battle.

"Wait." I grabbed Kieran's coat before he could take off. "You're the hunter boy scout. Do you have matches or something?"

Kieran pulled a lighter out of one of his cargo pockets. "Standard issue, upper left pocket," he said with a grin. "We have to get you into a school uniform."

"Just as soon as I can paint vampire happy faces all over them."

Nicholas was already sliding under the back of the car. Quinn and Magda were both laughing like undead hyenas. Vampire battles were so fast they made my brain hurt. I was panting and exhausted even though I'd barely moved. Kieran took off to grab the rope from the trunk. The car rattled and shuddered. There was the sound of metal grinding against metal and then the sharp cloying fumes of gasoline pouring out, and mixing with the smell of rot. Nicholas crawled back out covered in snow and engine grease. The gas tank was ripped open but it still sloshed impressively.

"Got it!" he called out. "Fall back." Nicholas didn't usually give his brothers orders and they didn't usually listen. But this time Quinn and Connor both obeyed and even Magda fell back. Nicholas sacrificed a little of the gasoline, sloshing it over the car. The chemicals left in the engines would have to do the rest of the work. We took off at a dead run, crowding in a protective circle around the tree. Charlemagne leaped through the snow to land beside Isabeau.

"Go!" Magda ordered the rest of the dogs. "Home!"

They took off into the forest as Nicholas stuffed the rope into the tank to soak up the gasoline. "Let me go," Solange shrieked. She kept screaming until she was hoarse.

Quinn grabbed the end of the rope and stretched it out into a circle around us. When he was well out of the way, Kieran lit one end. The fire sputtered, smoked, and finally traveled slowly from end to end. Smoke and fumes seared the air.

Connor grabbed the lighter from Kieran. "Hey!" Quinn shouted. Whoever dashed out through the flames to set the car on fire would be vulnerable. And they might not make it back through the circle if it finally burned the way we wanted it to.

"You may be prettier." Connor grinned. "But I'm faster."

"You're both pretty and you're both idiots," I said. "Stay in the circle." I dipped the end of my last arrow into the tiny bit of gasoline left in the tank and armed the crossbow. "I got this one."

I lit the arrow, fire engulfing the steel tip. It would melt through the plastic of the bow and fry the mechanisms if I waited too long. I aimed carefully, holding my breath so I wouldn't choke. It was difficult to see through the fire and smoke. Luckily the car was one big-ass shiny target. I fired.

The arrow whizzed through the circle, catching more fire as it went.

I didn't breathe again until it thudded into the car with a rattle. The fire spread slowly at first, catching the sprinkled gasoline. The seat burned next, smoke pouring thickly out of the open window. "Nice shot," Nicholas murmured in my ear, lips brushing my hair.

The fire shot up, snapping whips of light and heat. The snow melted into water, shining on the pavement and trickling into the grass.

And then the car finally exploded.

The sound rattled the trees. Bits of burning metal shot out, slicing through a *Hel-Blar*'s arm, setting another one on fire. The smell of charred mushrooms made me gag. We clumped closer together, heat and smoke pressing against us.

Isabeau's eyes snapped open but they were red, blind. Solange lost consciousness and her head lolled forward.

The fire snapped and kept burning with a constant hiss, throwing light over the snow all around us.

Just enough light to see that Constantine was gone.

CHAPTER 20

Solange

I was hiding behind a mound of hay along the wall, the contents of the tapestry pouch scattered on the ground when Isabeau found me. I was nauseated and disoriented, trying to remember why there was a gaping, bloody hole in my shoulder. Was I pinned to a tree in Violet Hill? Did I smell fire? And how was I suddenly in the castle's outer wall, in the bailey, not Violet Hill anymore? Whatever Lucy and the others were doing, they'd have to do it fast.

Because here in the castle, someone was standing over me.

I was so surprised, I threw one of the boxes at Isabeau's head.

She ducked. I pushed up to my knees, waiting for the star-stung sky to whirl back into its proper place. "Isabeau?"

"*Oui.*" The blue fleur-de-lis tattoo on her neck seemed to glow, as did the chainmail pieces sewn into her leather tunic-dress. She frowned at me. "We have to go." She looked around distaste-fully. "This place is unpleasant," she added, even though the bailey was quiet and idyllic looking.

"I can't go."

"You must. *Maintenant*." She sounded agitated, which was defi-nitely not a good sign. Isabeau only ever sounded polite and French.

"I have to destroy her talisman first," I explained, gathering the boxes. "I have to make sure she can't ever do this to me again."

"Your cord is weak."

I blinked. "My what? Is that code for something?"

She gestured to my belly button, where I could just make out a faint glow if I squinted really hard. Not spending a lot of time look-ing at my navel, I'd never noticed it before. It was thin and frayed, like a braid fading to ragged gray here and there. It was stretched so thin I could barely see it in spots. In contrast, Isabeau's cord was like frozen moonlight and silver. It looked strong enough to hoist a truck.

"If that cord snaps you'll be trapped here forever," she told me, tones clipped and no-nonsense, like a nurse in an ER. "You need to follow it home to your body."

"I still need to call her out," I explained, even though her words had fear souring in my belly. I smashed the box with the lady and her knight painted on it. It sparked when the pieces came apart. I felt a twang go through the air, as if the castle was a tapestry and one of the warp threads had just snapped.

"That will take too long," Isabeau said. "But I can help, now that I know her name." She smiled and it reminded me of my mother. Sword blades were softer than that smile. "You under-stand that I cannot fight her?" she asked. "Only her guards and protectors."

I nodded once. "This fight's mine."

"*Bien.*" She glanced down at the broken box. A shard with half of Constantine's face had landed near her foot. "They are still dear to each other."

"Yes, it's all very romantic," I said drily.

"These are memories, I assume?" When I nodded, she looked pleased. "You've done well, Solange."

"I had help," I said so quietly I wasn't sure she heard me.

"Is there a place nearby that has some sentimental value?" She peered through the shadows. "Where they were together?"

I looked around as well, trying to remember which memories I'd seen that had taken place here. They'd mostly been at Borne-bow Hall. Except for the time she and Constantine had gone to the Drake castle to find Viola's mother chained to a post and Madame Veronique in the courtyard. There was the Christmas feast, the dance with the candles, and the kiss by the tree.

The tree.

"There." I nodded to the tree at the base of the hill leading up to the inner bailey. It hadn't been there in her memory, but she'd incorporated it into her psychic safe place. I grabbed the remaining boxes and dashed over the grass until we were under its shielding branches. It was a pale birch tree, the leaves glinting like emerald drops and tinkling musically.

Isabeau glanced at me, an ax suddenly appearing in her hand.

"Okay, that's cool," I said. "I didn't know I could do that."

"I've done this sort of thing before," she reminded me with a ghost of a smile. "You continue smashing the boxes and I'll see if I can't entice our little friend out farther."

I still had the rock in my hand. I cracked it over the boxes.

"It helps if you call her name," Isabeau suggested. "Especially as I'm now here and foreign to her dreamscape. She'll be looking this way." She brought the ax down swiftly, severing a branch. "Viola!"

"Viola!" I added, jumping up and down on all of the box pieces. I'd pulverize them into dust if I had to. Isabeau hacked at the tree. "Viola!" Stomp. "Viola!" Hack. "Viol—ew."

Thick blood oozed out of the broken branches and the gouges in the white trunk. Rivulets coursed down, filling the spaces between the roots like tiny, bloody wishing wells.

Suddenly, I felt weird. I grabbed at a branch for support. I could hear the thunder of horses riding out of the upper gate, the flash of swords and armor.

"Crap," I said thickly as my vision started to go black. "One more thing." I felt my body slumping but couldn't stop it. Viola's knights were still advancing, Isabeau was still chopping at the tree, and I was still falling. "I've been blacking out."

1199

Viola walked through the tournament camp, pennants snapping from pavilion spires and horses nickering in corrals. The sounds pierced her sensitive ears and she had to stop herself from wincing. Sunset had given way to evening, the sky was full of stars, and the fields full of torches. The lights stung her eyes. Knights, pages, and stable hands crowded around, tending to horses and armor. The smell of so many bodies pressed together made her mouth water. She knew they were staring at her, but she couldn't bring herself to care. They were beneath her notice, unimportant.

Not Tristan.

None of it mattered without him.

She kept walking, barefoot, in a tattered gown stained with blood. Whispers boiled in her wake, weapons dropped with a clatter. A man stepped into her path, frowning. "Lady, are you well?"

He stumbled back out of her way when she raised her eyes to his. He blanched, confused, but was able to get back to the safety of his tent. She searched the family crests, the rampant lions, the unicorns, and the bar sinister, which was the black stripe that proclaimed illegitimacy. She felt strangely fond of that black mark, despite the evidence that she wasn't a bastard after all. Her father was still begging for her mother's forgiveness. Viola, remembering decades of tears and blood, wanted no part of it.

She only wanted Tristan.

There. The coat-of-arms of the Constantine family. It was a small tent, part of the larger circle belonging to a baron. Tristan had had to pledge himself to a new lord when Phillip Vale was found murdered in his bed.

She stepped through the painted canvas opening, feeling as hopeful as she had the first time Tristan had told her he loved her. He'd pledged himself to her, and she'd tied a ribbon to his shield. That same shield was propped against a table, the ribbon faded and tattered. He sat on a curved wooden bench, his head in his hands. His black hair fell into his eyes, obscuring his vision. He looked pale and tired.

"Leave it," he said curtly. "I'm not hungry."

"But I am," she whispered.

He froze. "Viola?" His voice cracked. He clenched his hands in his hair. "No. Away with you, spirit."

She glided forward, closing the small distance that still lay between them. "I am no spirit, my love."

He looked up, eyes bloodshot and ringed with shadows. There was stubble on his jaw and his cheekbones looked more prominent. She smiled gently. "Won't you kiss me?"

"Vi?" Tears clogged his voice. "It's not possible. The massacre . . ." He blinked, finally looking hard at her. She knew her hair was tangled with leaves and that there were unmentionable stains on her best gown. And she knew it didn't matter, not when they were together. "You're hurt." He got up so fast the bench flew backward, hitting his pallet.

"No, I survived."

He gathered her up into his arms, tears turning to a wild choked laugh. "I thought you were dead with all the others. No one knew where you were. It's been weeks. Weeks." He kissed her desperately, lips moving from her mouth to her temple to her hair and back to her mouth again. She kissed him back, laughing with him. She could restrain herself. She'd fed on a group of outlaws who'd thought to surprise her in the woods. *And kissing him made her feel whole again, sane again. She could almost ignore the hot pulse of his blood under his skin, his scent making her head spin.*

He ran his hand over her hair, pulling out the knots. "What happened to you?"

She burrowed into the circle of his arms, her cheek against his chest. His heart echoed in his chest and reverberated through her head, like the bell in the churchyard. "Men with crosses and stakes." She shuddered. "They think I'm evil just because I survived."

He looked down at her. "You're Lady Viola Drake," he said darkly. "And they will not touch you."

"There are hunters still after me," she said. "My own family sent them. I am a Drake no longer."

His face hardened. "I won't let them hurt you. Any of them."

"I know," she whispered. "Nor I, you." Her fangs cut through her gums like knives, but Tristan was already turning away to take up his sword. He didn't see her face change, her eyes gleam. "We can be together forever now," she said.

I woke up in the damn stairwell again.

Which meant Isabeau was alone in the courtyard with the bleeding tree and Viola's knights. I flung myself down the steps even though I wasn't steady on my feet yet. I crashed into the wall and kept going, using the stones to hold me up. I tripped on my hem and nearly knocked my own fangs out. The hall was smoky and warm as I dashed through it. The dried flowers and rushes on the dirt floor were covered by half-eaten chicken bones and dog droppings. The veneer was starting to peel off Viola's inner sanctuary.

Grimly satisfied at that small triumph, I almost ran into a sword. The knight had his helmet's visor down so I couldn't see his face. He was just creaking armor and flashing weapons. I dodged, rolling low. I popped back onto my feet behind him. I didn't stay to fight, just kept running.

I broke through the top gate just in time to see the knights closing in on Isabeau. She swung her ax in a wide circle, keeping them at bay. The tree wept blood, the white wood scarred and ragged. Isabeau leaped over a sword strike and cut off the arm that was attached to it as she landed. She was holding her own. But she didn't see the little girl with long blond hair coming up behind her, weeping pathetically in her embroidered dress, looking lost. Looking innocent and sweet.

She wasn't.

But Isabeau might not know that. "Behind you!" I yelled, half running, half sliding down the hill. "Not a little girl! Not a little girl!"

I was sliding too fast.

"No!" I yelled, frustrated as everything spun. The stars smeared on the dark canvas of the sky. "Not again." I held on tight, digging my fingers into the grass, willing myself to stay where I was.

The guards crossed their lances together, preventing Viola from entering. She didn't even pause, just whipped both arms out so fast and hard the knights flew into the wall and slumped, unconscious. She marched into the chamber, the candlelight flickering in the draft she created.

Tristan lay in the bed, his chest bare except for a bloody bandage around his ribs. Cuts and bruises marked him from head to toe. Blood trickled slowly from a gash in the back of his head. She stifled a sob, flying to his side. He didn't stir.

"One of my guards found him," Veronique said, stepping out of the shadows. Her servant cowered in the corner like a trapped rabbit, eyes wide.

Viola crawled into the bed, touching his face, his arms, his chest. He had no heartbeat.

"Hunters did this," she wept. They'd burst into the tent before she could turn Tristan and the fight had gone on too long. Dawn crept over the horizon and she'd had to crawl into a chest and lock it. When she woke she was alone.

And now she was truly alone.

"And yet you're the one bringing shame to our family," Veronique snapped. "We can't keep cleaning up your mess. You have no discretion. Even animals dispose of their kill with more grace."

"I don't care about that." Her tears soaked into his bandages.

"That is apparent."

"Do you even have a heart?" she shouted bitterly, her lover's blood on her hands, and on her lips.

"Yes," Veronique replied coldly. "But it is not selfish."

Viola hissed at her. Veronique snarled back, power clinging to her like ice on a winter lake. "Don't push me, girl," she warned. "We have rules and secrets to keep. You're endangering us all."

"He's dead!" Viola shrieked, eyes bleeding red. "And you're next, old woman," she promised balefully. "You're next."

She knew she couldn't take her right then. So she'd wait. She'd get stronger, lethal. With one last hiss, she flung herself out of the window, landing on the stable roof and sliding down onto her horse. She was riding away when Tristan jerked violently in his bed, bolting into consciousness. Fangs cut through his lower lip as he fought the unknown war inside his body. His eyes were open, but unseeing. Veronique gestured for a servant to pass him a jug filled with blood.

Viola rode over the hills, a cold wind howling inside her body. Tristan was dead.

Dead.

The world was a lamb to be led to the slaughter.

The red veil descended again.

At least this time I woke up in the same place.

And with the same battle brewing at the bottom of the hill, but Isabeau had already dispatched the last three knights. Their horses bolted away. She turned to the little weeping girl. "Not a little girl," I repeated, leaping frantically over the fallen knights.

"I know," Isabeau said. She had the shard of a mirror in her other hand. She angled it toward the little girl and glanced down into it. The reflection of the little girl shimmered into Viola.

Then the actual little girl did the same thing.

Viola looked like a medieval maiden from a painting, with her gold hair adorned with flowers and the butterfly sleeves of her blue gown. The carved pendant swung on a long chain around her neck.

The knights stirred at her feet. They stood up, armor creaking, and placed themselves between us. I wrested the sword from the decapitated arm, never taking my gaze off Viola. I brandished it, getting a feel for the weight. It wasn't a rapier, like I preferred, but it would do.

I skewered the first knight, driving the tip of the sword in the crease between his arm and breastplate. I caught the dagger from his hand when he fell. I was suddenly grateful for all the studying I'd had to do on the twelfth century. I knew the weak points to plate armor, knew that it made them slow when they were off their horses. I waited until the next knight lumbered awkwardly to look at his companion, then flung the dagger. It pierced through the eye slat.

Viola's smile died when the second knight landed back at her feet.

"*Merde*," Isabeau swore as the ax faded out of her hand. She looked wispy. "I've been here too long." She faded for a moment, like a candle flame flickering out. She solidified again but I could see it cost her. Her tattoos and amulets were the brightest thing about her.

"You said I had to fight her anyway," I said. "So go! Go now!"

"Come with me, Solange!"

"I have to do this," I insisted, pointing my sword at Viola. Isabeau wavered again. "Go!" I yelled at her. "Go now!"

Isabeau kept fading but took the knights out with her, knocking them out with the last blast of her magic. Even the guards on the ramparts collapsed. Viola blanched. Isabeau had just time enough to shoot me one of her rare smiles before she exploded into light. The glow hovered there for a moment before channeling into my tattered silver cord.

I was alone with Viola.

Finally.

CHAPTER 21

Lucy

The fire died all too soon.

We were left choking on smoke with a burning vehicle and half a dozen screeching *Hel-Blar*. I was out of arrows and there were only a few stakes left between us all. Even Kieran's bottomless cargo pockets weren't turning up anything to help us right now.

"Kieran, can you make a run for it with Lucy?" Nicholas asked. "You can take one of the Jeeps," he added as Logan tossed Kieran his keys.

"I'm not leaving you guys," I sputtered. "When did you fall and hit your head?"

"Lucy, you're out of arrows and we're out of options." He darted a quick glance at Quinn, who was behind me.

I grabbed a fistful of Nicholas's shirt. "I'm not leaving you, you big dumb idiot." I whipped my head around and shot Quinn a glare. "Take one more step. I dare you." I knew full well he'd planned to sneak up on me and toss me over his shoulder. He paused, knowing equally well that I'd damage him if he tried.

He did it anyway.

I was suddenly airborne and then draped over his shoulder, which dug painfully under my ribs. "It's just faster this way," he said.

I shifted, cursing. "Put me down, you undead asshat."

"Just trying to save your ungrateful life," he shot back with grim cheer. I punched him right in the ass since I couldn't reach any other part of him. "Ready, Kieran?"

All I could see was the melted snow at his feet. The clacking of jaws got louder and the smell of burning metal and rubber was noxious. I coughed. Quinn dashed ahead, Kieran running all out to keep up. And then Quinn stumbled to such an abrupt halt that I swung uncomfortably, getting queasy. I held onto his belt as all the blood rushed to my head. "What's going on?" I tried to peer around. "Hello?"

"Mom," Quinn said, startled.

"Thank God," I said, feeling like we might have a chance for the first time that night. "Put me down." I pinched his butt this time instead of punching it.

He jerked. "Ow."

"Well, put me down."

"I thought I told you boys to keep that girl at home," Helena said.

"On second thought, it's safer up here," I muttered. Quinn released me so fast pain flared up my legs when I hit the ground. I turned around, gulping. "Hi."

Helena flicked us a warning glance that had Quinn and I stepping closer to each other for self-preservation. Liam was behind her, eyes glistening. "Solange? Nicholas?" Helena whirled and we were out of her crosshairs for the moment. "Isabeau found you," Liam said, his voice clogged with tears. "Thank God."

Aunt Hyacinth, Sebastian, and Marcus were fighting off the *Hel-Blar*. Kieran's car was still burning. Duncan slid behind the wheel of Logan's Jeep and hit the accelerator, aiming for them like Kieran had earlier. It was like watching a game of vampire Frogger. Uncle Geoffrey was already inspecting Solange's wound. He was about to pull the arrow out when Isabeau jerked violently. She'd been sitting so still, we all jumped in response.

She swallowed thickly. "I couldn't stay any longer."

Logan reached down and sliced the ribbon in half, helping her to her feet. She looked exhausted but energy crackled off her at the same time. "Don't," she warned Uncle Geoffrey. "She's still fighting for control."

"Is she . . . all right?" Helena asked, as if she was afraid of the answer. She touched Solange's hair. Liam had his arms around Nicholas as if he meant never to let go. I knew just how he felt.

"She is stronger than we thought," Isabeau answered wearily. "She has been fighting off this spirit since before the coronation."

"We had no idea," Helena said. Her fangs poked out from under her lip. "We thought she was just adjusting. Badly."

"I believe the spirit of Viola Drake has been trying to gain a foothold since Solange's birthday."

"Viola Drake?" Liam asked.

"Damn it, how could we not know that?" Helena snapped. "And who the hell is Viola Drake?"

"We can't stay here," Uncle Geoffrey interrupted.

"We won't know for certain until she wakes up tomorrow, but I am almost certain she will prevail." Isabeau straightened. Even though I could see she was so tired she wanted to slump against Logan, she wouldn't let herself. She dug her fingers into Charlemagne's fur. "I did what I could to help her."

"Thank you," Liam whispered.

"I'll have to sedate her, if you think she might still be dangerous," Uncle Geoffrey said. "But we have to get her home. The *Hel-Blar* aren't the only danger out tonight."

"We've got Huntsmen on our tail," Helena explained tersely.

"Good," Kieran broke in. "They can take care of the rest of these *Hel-Blar*."

"Good thinking." Helena nodded approvingly. She might not eviscerate him for not getting me back to school, after all.

Uncle Geoffrey took a wickedly long syringe out of his black leather case. It was stuffed with vials of blood, bottles of Hypnos, stakes, and restraints. Apparently they'd been prepared for just about anything with this exorcism. He injected Solange with the sedative and then pulled the arrow out in one quick tug. Blood pooled in the wound. She slumped forward bonelessly. Helena caught her, lifting her up as if she were a baby.

"We've got three Jeeps," Liam said. "Should be enough room for everyone."

"I'll go back to the caves," Magda said.

"It's not safe out there," Liam argued, but Magda had already swung up into a tree and was leaping from branch to branch.

"She'll be fine," Isabeau assured him. "But I'll go back with you, just in case I can help Solange more."

"And I'll take Lucy and Kieran back," Nicholas offered. Kieran tossed him Logan's keys.

Liam clasped his shoulder. "Hurry home."

A fire truck siren wailed in the distance. "That's our cue. Let's get out of here and let the Huntsmen do their job."

Uncle Geoffrey's nostrils flared. "They're nearly here."

Liam looked at his sons. "Ready?" They nodded. "Go!"

Helena had already taken off with Solange, who hung limply, blood dripping from her shoulder. The *Hel-Blar* howled, straining to get past the others to get to her. They went mad with pheromone poisoning and their natural feral hunger. The stink of rot mixed with toxic smoke. I covered my nose and mouth with the collar of my sweater and made a run for it, Nicholas and Kieran keeping pace.

On either side of us, the Drakes fought back. The sound of bones breaking was audible, even over the murmur and hiss of the fire. Duncan did a 360 with his vehicle, sliding into perfect position. Helena tossed Solange in the backseat, then flipped up onto the roof as the others piled in. She kicked viciously at any approaching *Hel-Blar*. Liam escorted the second carload with equal ferocity.

Nicholas loped ahead and by the time I reached the Jeep, the passenger door was open and he was sliding across the hood to the driver's seat. Kieran dove into the backseat behind me and I slammed my door shut. As Nicholas peeled away, I saw the first of a group of Huntsmen break out of the cover of the trees. They were armed to the teeth and more than capable of dispatching the remaining *Hel-Blar*. The other cars shot in the opposite direction, toward the farm.

Nicholas sped past Kieran's smoking car and turned off on the first side road, to avoid the approaching fire trucks. We were far enough away from town that it would take them at least another five minutes to get here. Kieran called in the location as we bumped along the dirt road. The Helios-Ra were equipped to deal with officials if the Huntsmen took off before they finished the job.

I rubbed my side. "I think Quinn broke my spleen."

"Which is nothing compared to what his mother will do to mine," Kieran said, tilting his head back.

"Don't worry," I assured. "She'll tire herself out kicking my ass first."

Nicholas rolled all the windows down until the cold wind created a little hurricane inside the car. I pushed hair off my face to glance his way. His jaw was clenched tight.

"You okay?" I murmured.

"Fine."

"Oh, cause that's convincing."

"Need my nose plugs?" Kieran asked casually, but I could see him reaching for his last stake.

Nicholas opened the skylight as well. He stopped grinding his teeth as the wind tunneled around him. "I'm good," he said, and this time we believed him. I shivered, turning up the heaters.

"You couldn't have sat in a car like this with both of us a few weeks ago," I pointed out.

"I've been through worse since," he replied quietly. I winced and reached for his hand. He held on tightly, weaving his fingers through mine.

"Anyone else think evil should take a vacation so we can catch a nap?" I asked lightly, trying to ease the tension. The lights of Violet Hill got closer and Nicholas slowed down to the speeding limit. He pulled up to the curb in front of Kieran's house.

"Hell of a night," Kieran said in way of a good-bye as he got out.

"Hey," I said, leaning out the window as he walked away, limping slightly. "Are you going to the farm tomorrow?"

He paused. "I don't know if that's a good idea." He turned his head. "Call me and tell me if she's okay."

We watched Kieran walk up to his front porch, covered in soot and mud.

"Think they'll work it out?" Nicholas asked.

"The emo twins?" I asked. "They love each other, so yes. Plus, I plan to smack their heads together."

We drove back out of town in silence, until Nicholas pulled over just before reaching the school. He switched off the lights but kept the car running so I wouldn't freeze with the open windows. I unbuckled my seatbelt so I could turn to face him. I felt weirdly shy. Now that he was safe, I could really see the changes in him. His smile was just as serious but it carried a certain darkness it hadn't before. He'd been pushed, the way soldiers at war are pushed. What if everything about him had changed, including the way he felt about me?

"Why is your heart racing like that?" he asked, rubbing his thumb over the pulse on the inside of my wrist.

I swallowed. "Adrenaline."

He tilted his head. "You know I can smell when you're lying."

"Hey." I scowled. "No vampire superpowers allowed."

"I never agreed to that." He smiled his endearingly crooked smile and it nearly batted away my doubts. "What's going on inside that busy little head of yours, Lucy?"

"Nothing." He just stared at me until I squirmed. "It's stupid," I mumbled. "Especially considering the night we just had."

"Tell me, anyway."

"You're different."

I felt him pull back slightly. "Different how?"

"Not in a bad way, you've just been through so much."

"And?" He prodded.

"I'm still just me. What if . . ." I shrugged, feeling even dumber now that I had to put it into words.

"You little idiot," he said, half laughing. "You're the only thing that saved me. Again. You keep saving me and you don't even know it."

His words melted the iceberg in my chest. We stared at each other for a long time. His gray eyes were like smoke. He still had scars on his neck and arms. But he was here. We were together. There was so much to say but no words to say it with.

We reached for each other instead, falling into a kiss so deep and necessary it made every awful thing we'd just been through bearable. His mouth was wicked, nearly desperate. I traced the muscles in his arms, over his chest. I couldn't get close enough. He dragged his lips slowly down my throat and I shivered down to my toes. I could barely catch my breath.

"You got rid of your glasses," he said softly, running his fingertip down my nose.

"You kept fogging them up," I teased, still kissing him. His lips curved under mine, and then the playfulness was gone and he leaned over, pressing me into the seat. He nipped at my mouth, teasing and tasting until my head spun, until my lips tingled, and my knees melted. Our tongues touched, his hand fisted in my hair. I pulled him closer. It wasn't close enough. I wiggled to make more room in the cramped seat and smacked my elbow on the console. The pins and needles in my arm distracted me. Nicholas pulled back slightly.

"Ouch," I said, ruefully. "I guess I should go before my detention turns to an expulsion."

There was a promise in his gray eyes. My cheeks went hot. His thumb traced my lower lip, his gaze dropping back to my mouth. He kissed me once more, a soft lingering kiss that stole every coherent thought right out of my head.

He eased away and it took a long moment before I felt I could remember how to work the door handle. "I'll get out here. You definitely can't be on campus right now with all the extra hunters and Huntsmen. On the plus side, I'll be perfectly safe."

"Text me anyway when you get inside."

"Okay. And I'll be at the farm at sunset for when Solange finally wakes up."

"Don't you have class?" he asked, his hair tousled from my touch. "And detention?"

I snorted. "Yeah, like that's going to stop me."

CHAPTER 22

Solange

"I was in love," Viola said, looking melancholy and defenseless. "Surely I have a right to be happy. Madame Veronique stole that from me." A single tear trembled on her lower lash before falling down her cheek. "I didn't even know what she'd done to my beloved Tristan until I was already dead, until there was no hope for us at all."

I'd feel a lot sorrier for her if she wasn't such a psychotic bitch.

"What about all those people at Bornebow Hall?" I asked.

"That was . . . an accident." Her regret seemed genuine, even if it weighed a lot less than her selfish need for Constantine. Her lower lip trembled. "I didn't know what I was. I woke up covered in blood."

That part I could almost forgive. If she'd had no idea she was changing, how would she know how to leash the hunger? I was still struggling and I'd had centuries of practice essentially encoded in my DNA. Mind you, I'd been dealing with both of our needs without even realizing it.

"I saw what you did," I replied steadily. "Even before Veronique was involved."

"We could be great together," she said. "We could be queen. Not even our grandmother could stop us."

"I have no intention of being stuck with you forever," I told her, the light flaring through my silver cord. It felt like tiny electrical shocks pinging through my belly, like someone was yanking it from the other end. "And how many times do I have to say it? I don't want to be freaking queen of the freaking vampires."

"Forget the crown then," she said, proving that it was secondary to her plans. We'd been right in thinking the crown was just a symbol, something that focused her will. That's all magic is, in the end. Focused will. I remember Isabeau telling me that once. "I only want Tristan. We deserve a chance to be together."

"Not more than Kieran and I deserve to be together. Not more than my family and my friends deserve their own happiness."

Her maiden-in-distress mask crumpled like poorly fired clay. "She took him from me," she hissed. Bats circled, squeaking. She flicked her fingers, sending them dive-bombing my way. I held up my palm and they stopped as if hitting an invisible wall. If I had to carry her sins, I'd damn well take my compensation with her other gifts. She snarled. "She killed me, did she tell you that?"

"Madame Veronique didn't tell me anything about you," I

murmured, watching blood pour out of the tree behind her. It trickled through the grass toward her feet, staining the hem of her kirtle. I remembered her walking through the tournament camp looking very similar. "She was ashamed of you and erased your name from our family tree."

I knew it would enrage her. I'd spent long enough walking through her memories and trapped in her head to know which buttons to push. And Dad always says, if you act in anger you lose the battle.

"I only did what she made me do."

"My dad has a whole responsibility speech you should hear," I said. "Only I really don't want to be here for a second longer."

"Agreed." Her hands curled like claws as she closed them around a sword hilt she plucked from one of her knights. The blade was starting to rust, shedding copper-colored flakes. She swung at me and I leaped back, easily avoiding the strike. She wasn't very good. I parried the next stab and spun around, elbowing her in the face. She howled and swung blindly.

And then I realized she wasn't trying to run me through.

She was trying to sever the silver cord that linked me to my body, to cut off my only way home.

I blocked another lunge and pushed at her arm so she was forced to continue the movement, angling away from me. I drove the sword hilt into the back of her neck and she stumbled, shrieking. The flowers in her hair were wilting and the fine embroidery was unraveling off her sleeves. Only the pendant stayed polished and perfect, the painted happy couple mocking me with every sway.

I waited for her to spin back around to face me and as it lifted in the air, I swung at it. The sharp blade sliced through the chain. Before the pendant landed, our swords clashed again, viciously and brutally. Bits of iron and rust exploded.

The pendant fell into the grass between us.

For a moment everything faded to shades of gray, as if the pendant had leeched all the color out of the world and kept them for itself. The painted dress, Constantine's violet eyes, Viola's red lips.

Her gaze shot to mine, showing real fear for the first time.

We both lunged for it simultaneously. She pulled up abruptly, clotheslining me even as I dove for the pendant. The force of her arm across my throat had me gagging and seeing stars. As I fell, I flipped in midair, slamming the soles of my feet into her chest. We crashed to the ground so hard it trembled under us. Stones toppled from the wall as moss and ivy began to grow between them, pulling apart the mortar. Viola bared her teeth at me as she tried to push up on her elbows, glancing around for help that wasn't coming. Isabeau had demolished her backup.

But we were still inside her head, and she'd been doing this a lot longer than I had.

"Tristan!"

I hadn't even pushed up to my knees before Constantine came racing around the other side of the hill, a dozen knights on horseback behind him. Swords and spears stabbed at the sky. Their battle yell reverberated all around.

I tried one last leap for the pendant before I was trampled under hooves. Viola couldn't get to her feet. She looked as broken as I felt. Instead she wriggled down and tried to kick me in the face. I dodged, but she caught my shoulder and pain shot sparks down my arm. Bats tangled in my hair.

She was really starting to get on my nerves.

My silver cord flared, going from starlight to sunlight and blinding her momentarily. That was something, at least. But not enough.

The knights surrounded us, horses pawing at the ground. Constantine lowered his lance, the wickedly pointed tip aimed at my already bruised throat. His eyes were the same violet color, but without the vampire intensity. His black hair curled over his chainmail and there were scars on his hands. This was Viola's Tristan. He wasn't a vampire yet, just a human knight.

I scrounged in the dirt for my sword hilt, shrinking back from the lance. The sound of blades leaving their scabbards hissed all around me, like poisonous serpents. Viola had her resurrected knights, and her true love. They'd die for her. And they'd cheerfully kill for her. They weren't even technically real, just figments of her past. Memories.

But in this place, memories could kill.

There was only one other person left whom she couldn't control, who was as real as I was.

Gwyneth.

She stood in the arch of the gate, the ivy and moss growing wildly behind her, pulling down stones and cracking the walls. Her bare muddy toes dug into the grass and the ground fractured like spiderweb cracks in a windshield.

"You!" Viola snapped, with equal fear and hatred. "It's not

possible. Get her!" she ordered, and half the knights charged Gwyneth, hooves flinging clumps of dirt all over me. In the momentary pause, I managed to grab hold of my sword and blocked Tristan's lance, shoving it aside. I rolled beyond its range and into the space abandoned by the knight behind me. I landed on the balls of my feet, springing up, sword at the ready. The nearest horse tried to bite me. Constantine's lance was still between me and the pendant.

"Call the dragon!" Gwyneth yelled to me, as the ground heaved and buckled around her. The knights reined in their horses, pacing side to side, trying to find a way through.

"How?" I yelled back. "This isn't *The Lord of the Rings*!"

"Blood to blood," she said. "Only you can end this now."

The dragon would serve me. It contained Viola's memory of Madame Veronique and the entire Drake clan and she feared it because she feared her family.

I didn't. It was the very source of my strength.

I needed Viola's blood but I couldn't get to her, not with Constantine and his knights protecting her. I needed some kind of diversion. I pointed at one of the bats and flicked my hand, directing it at Constantine. The bat dipped low at his head. He ducked, swearing. I sent three more, like a music conductor leading a symphony of bats. His horse shied nervously. I guided the other bats to the other knights, leaving the rest to hover over the pendant in a frantic black cloud when Viola crawled forward. She waved them away and they pinged between us, confused.

Time was running out. Already one of the bats was being skewered by a lance.

I ran to the tree, dragging my hand along the sword blade. Blood sprang to the surface as my cut sliced open. It hurt a lot more than it looked like it did in the movies. I slapped my palm over one of the bleeding gouges in the tree trunk and waited. Viola screamed and ran at me.

And then the dragon tore out of the sky as if it was made of nothing more than glittery indigo tissue paper.

It was just as huge as I remembered, all blue-and-silver scales and ridges on its spine as tall as standing stones. It circled over us, menacing and awe inspiring. Its tail whipped back and forth, creating a powerful wind that flattened the grass. Smoke and sparks streamed out of its nostrils.

Viola made a choking sound as she gave into fear and turned back to scramble up into the saddle behind Constantine. The pendant was still on the ground. The dragon opened its enormous jaws and shot out a ball of fire like a comet. It trailed enough sparks to singe the grass and blacken the stones. The horse reared, panicking.

The knights divided their attention, battling the dragon and Gwyneth, while still trying to protect Viola and keep me from the pendant. The dragon dipped low, tearing his talons over the battlements. One of the smaller towers fell in on itself, already weakened by fire and creeping ivy. The drag from its flapping wings nearly knocked a horse over. The knight went tumbling into the smoldering hay. Gwyneth stayed under the support of the gate archway. She was covered in soot and burns, but looked the happiest I'd ever seen her. She was actually smiling.

The dragon circled back, steam curling out of nostrils the size of caves as it took a deep breath to shoot more fire. This time when the horses bucked, Viola fell off. Constantine steadied his mount before sliding out of the saddle to reach for her.

This was my only chance.

Dragon's breath baked the air until my throat was as parched as the rest of me was soaked. My silver cord flared painfully. I felt sure Isabeau was on the other end, pulling it as hard as she could. It actually yanked me through the grass. I knew it was a warning, knew I was running out of time. Still, I pulled back, staggering the last few feet. The pendant was within reach. I was so close now.

I hacked at it with the sword. The blade pinged off, leaving a scratch but not much else. I tried again and the force nearly shot it right back to Viola. It was sturdier than I'd assumed. The wood didn't shatter to pieces like a cameo or a glass pendant would have and the decorative filigrees were made of iron. I scuffed the paint off, but the damage wasn't enough to free me from Viola's magical stronghold.

I scooped it up, searching frantically for another way to destroy it. There were little fires burning everywhere but none of them looked hot enough to consume the pendant quickly enough to prevent Viola from reaching it to put it out. Already, rain was starting to fall, hard as silver coins. Mud made everything slippery within seconds. Thunder rumbled, as if an angry dog crouched over us.

Dragon fire was the only thing that would burn hot enough, even in a deluge.

I slid through the wet grass, blinking the water out of my lashes and dodging panicked horses and flashing swords. The cut on my hand bled sluggishly, making the pendant slick. I had to get myself into a better position. I darted out of the protective shield of tree branches and ran as fast as I possibly could toward the dragon while everyone else was running away from it.

Everyone except Viola and Constantine, who were back in a saddle and so close behind me I could hear the horse snorting. The hooves were merciless, a constant hammer bearing down on me. Above us, the storm continued to crash.

Lightning tore through one of the dragon's leathery wings. It bellowed in pain, fire erupting in one giant cloud, tinged with the acrid odor of charred flesh and blood. It spiraled, losing control and clipping the roof. Shingles and slate shot in every direction. Constantine launched his spear at me but it went wide as he concentrated on controlling his fire-maddened horse.

The dragon roared again, spewing more fire. It was close enough to singe the tips of my hair and turn my cheeks red, as if I was sunburned. I tossed the pendant up high into the flames and leaped out of the way. The heat from the fire made steam lift off my wet clothes.

"No!" Viola shrieked. "No!"

I landed hard, sliding down a hillock to the gatehouse where Gwyneth was hiding. My silver cord went so bright, it was like a moonlight path through the dark woods.

Now or never.

"Go!" Gwyneth shouted. "Now!"

"Come with me!" I shouted back, trying to grab for her hand.

She just shook her head sadly. "I can't."

And then she shoved me.

This time, I didn't fall into one of Viola's stored memories, but into a flash of silver, like lightning.

CHAPTER 23

Lucy

Thursday

"You have *got* to stop writing in the library books," Tyson said.

"I will if you stop looking at me like I just kicked a kitten," I replied, sliding the offending book away from him. "I couldn't help it. Someone needs to edit these things."

He sat back in the library chair. "Yeah, they're called editors and they already did that."

I snorted. "Please. I could drive a truck through the holes in your education."

"We're here about your education, not mine." He actually lowered his forehead to bang it on the table. The librarian sent me a stern glance.

"What?" I said. "I'm not the one giving myself a lobotomy." Concentrating was even harder than usual. We wouldn't know how Solange was doing until sunset and that was still hours away. I was relegated to tutoring to keep from going insane. Teasing Tyson was more fun. I nudged his shoe. "Come on, you love it. You're into learning shit just for the sake of learning. And vampires don't eat raw hearts."

"What about Lady Natasha?"

"Please, she was batshit crazy. You can't judge all vampires by her. That would be like judging all Helios-Ra by Hope." Which, I had to admit, I'd done myself at first. "And hello, you've never met a crazy human?"

"I'm talking to one right now," he shot back, his voice muffled.

I patted his shoulder encouragingly. "Don't worry, I'll make it up to you by telling Jenna how smart and hot you are."

"What?" He lifted his head, half-horrified, half-intrigued. "Why? What?"

I chuckled, flipping through the next history book on the pile between us. "Hey, get out! My grandma's in here." I goggled. "I had no idea she'd staked that many *Hel-Blar* in her seventies."

"What do you mean about Jenna?" Tyson asked, lowering his voice so we wouldn't be overheard.

"Aren't we supposed to be studying?" I asked him primly.

"Lucy."

I burst out laughing. "Oh, Tyson, you really are adorable."

"Great," he muttered. "I'm puppies and kittens."

"I'm sure Jenna doesn't think that." I gave my most dazzling grin over his shoulder. "And here she comes now."

"No." He swallowed, his Adam's apple bobbing. "What have you done?"

"I just told her to meet me here," I said, blinking innocently. "But I forgot I have to meet Hunter."

"No, you don't."

"Hi, Jenna," I said brightly, hooking my foot around Tyson's ankle under the table so he wouldn't bolt. I felt bad for nearly getting him and Jenna killed at that field party and I wanted to make it up to them. I wasn't sure if Jenna returned his feelings, but I knew they'd never find out if he didn't talk to her alone for more than three minutes.

"Hey," she said. The wide bandage was gone, replaced by two neat stitches. She wore a Helios-Ra Academy T-shirt with the rising sun logo and yoga pants. "I heard you guys had quite a night."

"Yeah, between the *Hel-Blar* and the Huntsmen, life is never dull," I agreed. "But they have nothing on Tyson. He's way tougher to outsmart." I showed her the essay he'd marked. It was practically dipped in red ink.

Jenna made a sympathetic face, then took a closer look. She rolled her eyes. "Well, no wonder. Helios-Ra don't wear spandex tights and capes. We're not superheroes."

"But you kind of think you are." I winked. "I just wrote that to see if he was paying attention."

"You wrote it because you're a brat," he muttered.

I beamed at him. "Now you sound like one of the Drake

brothers." I shoved my new crop of books into my knapsack. "But despite your sweet talk, I have to go. I was supposed to pass on a message to Hunter from Quinn," I lied. I didn't go far. I just hid in the next aisle, peeping at them between the books.

"How's your head?" I heard Tyson ask her.

"I'm cleared for class again." She rubbed her hands together gleefully. "I'm going to go watch the sparring match in the gym and then run a few laps." It was saying a lot when my vampire friends weren't my weirdest friends. Hunter and Jenna just loved running laps way too much. And Jenna, apparently, loved it more than Tyson. I mentally apologized to him. I'd been so sure they'd at least make really good friends.

Then Jenna paused, her red ponytails swinging. "Are you coming?" she asked him over her shoulder.

He practically concussed himself with his own bag in his hurry to follow her. I popped my hand out for a high five as he passed my aisle. He obliged, trying not to grin, and took off. I snuck out the back door, also grinning. I decided to go visit Hunter anyway since we had an hour to kill before the next round of classes. I knocked on the door.

"Go away," Chloe yelled.

"It's me," I yelled back. She was notorious for scaring all the ninth-grade students who came to talk to Hunter, since she was their floor monitor. Half of them had memorized Chloe's schedule so they wouldn't run into her.

"Oh. Come in, Lucy." She was sitting on the edge of her bed eating chocolate. Hunter stood by the window, staring out at the pond with a weird look on her face. She forced a smile before going back to brooding. Since she wasn't usually a brooder, I felt instant trepidation. Solange hadn't been a brooder either.

"Please tell me you're not possessed too," I said. Hunter half smiled in response. Her eyes were a little red. "What's wrong?"

"Her grandfather just hung up on her again," Chloe explained.

"That sucks," I said. Her grandfather was an old-school vampire hunter and as long as Hunter was dating Quinn, he refused to acknowledge her.

"It's fine. I'm used to it."

"Still sucks," I said.

She nodded. "Really does."

"Shouldn't you be eating chocolate?" I asked. "Guaranteed cure-all." I motioned at Chloe. "Give her some."

"She didn't want it," Chloe said. "And you can't have it." She stuffed the rest into her mouth, nearly choking.

Hunter chuckled. "I swear she's going to choke to death on chocolate one day," she said. "I feel sorry for whoever has to write her epitaph."

Chloe swallowed. "Please, if I had a boyfriend as hot as Quinn, I wouldn't need so much chocolate," she said. "Making out would be my new preferred therapy for everything all the time. Stress, bad marks, splinters. Basically, why aren't you kissing him right now?"

Hunter smiled, looking more like herself. "Because I'm in the sparring match in ten minutes." She grabbed her gym bag. "So I should go."

Chloe looked disappointed, as if Hunter had personally betrayed her. "You are wasting a perfectly hot Drake brother."

She smiled wickedly. "I'm seeing him tonight."

Chloe sighed. "Take pictures."

Hunter glanced at me. "Does this happen to you?"

I thought of my friend Nathan and his crush on Nicholas. "All the time," I confirmed. "You get used to it."

"I guess I should go to the match and cheer her on," Chloe said reluctantly.

"Careful, all that enthusiasm will wear you right out."

She grimaced. "Since Dailey and her weird-ass drugs are gone, and Mom's weird-ass steroids are out of my system, I just don't care as much. I'd rather break through Bellwood's personal firewalls and encryption codes. There are secret e-mails flying around the League," she said. "And I want in." She grabbed her laptop. "What about you? Want to watch Hunter wipe the floor with some guy twice her size?"

"Actually, that does sounds like fun," I agreed as we headed to the front door. "But I'm going to the Drake farm."

"What, all the detention we already have isn't enough for you?"

"I have permission this time," I said.

"It's still daylight," she pointed out.

I glanced at the sky. The sun wasn't anywhere near enough to the horizon. "I know. I'll just study over there."

"Say hi to Connor. And don't drink any coffee," Chloe advised turning off onto the path toward the gym. "Your entire nervous system might explode."

Since it wasn't raining I drove my own car to the farm. Duncan had done a temporary fix on the engine so it only worked in dry, clear weather but it was better than nothing. My face hurt from my wide grin that I just couldn't help. I was driving to the farm again. I could almost remember what it felt like to drop by for an ordinary visit or a sleepover. I was pulling into the driveway when my mom called.

"Hi, Mom."

"Hi, Lucky. I haven't heard you this happy in a long time."

"I know." If I sounded any happier sunshine and lollipops would come out of my butt. "I'm at the farm."

"I figured. That's what I wanted to talk to you about."

"What's up?" I asked, grabbing my bag and getting out of the car.

"I'm so glad Nicholas is back. I know you two missed each other a lot." She paused.

I groaned. I knew where this was going. "Mom."

"I just want you to be careful."

I rolled my eyes even though she couldn't see me. "No more safe sex lectures," I said. "I get it. I'm still finding all the condoms you snuck into my stuff before I moved into the dorms."

"I don't just mean that," she said quietly, sounding uncomfortable.

Since repeatedly talking about sex didn't make her uncomfortable I leaned against the hood of my car, frowning nervously. "Okay, then what?"

"It's easy to get carried away when you're so happy, when you're celebrating. But you're still too young to make decisions that will affect your entire future."

"Are you sure this isn't the sex talk?"

"People talk about being together forever," she explained. "But in your case, it's not just talk."

"Oh." This wasn't the sex talk. It was worse. It was the vampire talk.

"You're too young to risk your life to live forever," she continued. "Please don't do anything rash."

"Mom, are you asking me if I'm going to let Nicholas turn me into a vampire?"

"I'm asking you to think long and carefully."

It's not like I hadn't thought about it. Of course, I had. But it was always something to think about for *later*.

"It's dangerous," she continued. "It could kill you."

"Mom," I interrupted her because she sounded like she was about to panic. "You can relax. I don't want to be sixteen forever."

"You say that now."

"And I mean it. Being carded for eternity doesn't appeal." I bit my lip. "I can't promise I won't ever make that decision, Mom," I added. "But I can promise I'm not making it right now."

She exhaled so forcefully it sounded like there was a hurricane trapped in my phone. "Okay," she said. "Okay. Thank you." She laughed, sounding both relieved and anxious. "Oh honey, talking about condoms is so much easier."

I snorted. "Maybe for you."

I hung up and went up the pathway to the farmhouse, shaking my head. It was so familiar to see Bruno standing on the front porch with his bald head, tattoos, and dangerous weapons, that I just had to hug him.

"Lass," he said in his Scottish accent. "Shouldn't you be in school?"

"I brought homework," I said. "Can I just sit in the living room until Solange wakes up?"

"Sure," he said, running his big hand over my hair. He pushed the door open and when the dogs came barreling at us, I crouched down for another hug. This one was considerably furrier. "Guard," he ordered them, pointing at me. Boudicca and Byron followed me to the library end of the living room and lay down around my chair. They followed me into the kitchen when I went to make tea and even insisted on coming into the bathroom with me.

For a while I just sat there looking out the window at the fields and the line of trees beyond. My tea grew cold and Byron started to snore. I went back to my books, trying to find references to "Dawn." Not much to go on. Most anti-vampire zealots associated themselves with a sun motif. Even the Helios-Ra used the sun in their crests and logos. I checked the Drake collection but they had even less information and it was just as boring. I fell asleep and didn't wake up until Bruno touched my shoulder.

"Lucy," he said gently.

"Mmfwl?" I blinked blearily, wondering why it was so dark in the living room. Bruno grinned and leaned over to switch on one of the Tiffany lamps. The light had a purplish hue as it glowed through the blue-and-red glass.

"Solange is awake," Bruno said.

CHAPTER 24

Solange

Thursday evening

I woke up to most of my family staring at me intently. Thank God Aunt Ruby wasn't there or I might have had a heart attack. I shifted, wondering what felt different. Another shift in my bed and I realized two things: I was in my own bedroom and I didn't feel the usual searing hunger threatening to break me open.

"Easy," Uncle Geoffrey said when I tried to sit up. I was hooked up to an IV full of blood, which explained my curious lack of homicidal bloodthirst. He was giving me a transfusion, the way he still did for Christabel.

Only I was chained up.

The chains rattled as I sat up against my rose-embroidered pillows.

"How do you feel?" Uncle Geoffrey asked, sounding clinical and detached. No one else had even spoken yet, they were all too busy staring at me. Mom's eyes were suspiciously bright. Dad stepped forward with a small key.

"No, don't," I said. "Not until I'm sure."

"That's the Solange I know," Mom said softly.

Then she burst into tears.

To say we were stunned is an understatement. Frankly, rabid badgers could have crawled through the window in matching tutus and performed ballet pirouettes and we would have been less surprised. "It's really you."

"I'm fine, Mom." It was the same thing I'd been saying for weeks leading up to my birthday, back when I *was* still myself. She must have recognized the litany because she lowered herself onto the edge of my bed and squeezed my hand.

"I'm so sorry," she said, lips trembling as she tried to regain her composure. "We should have known."

Dad leaned down to kiss my forehead. "Welcome back, Sol."

I swallowed hard so I wouldn't cry too. "I'm sorry too," I said, my voice much smaller than I would have liked. "For everything."

"We're just glad you're back," Logan told me. Quinn winked. Connor, Duncan, and Sebastian all smiled, though carefully, as if I was about to leap off the bed and attack them. Nicholas was there too, leaning against the wall.

"You're okay too?" I asked, scratching under the edge of the copper collar. My skin felt raw. "What happened?"

"Dawn, hunters, psychotic doctors. It's a long story," he replied.

I bit down hard on my lip to stifle a sob. Between Mom's weeping and my teary eyes, all of my brothers had taken a step backward, as if we might detonate. Only Marcus was brave enough to stay close, but that was only because he was unhooking the blood bag from the tube in my arm. He watched me as closely as if I were a specimen under his microscope. I hesitated, scrutinizing every feeling and twinge that went through me.

My fangs were extended. There were still three pairs of them; exorcising Viola hadn't changed that. The blue of my veins was slightly faded, like old ink. The thirst that prowled through me like a hungry jungle cat was lazy now, rolling belly-up in the sunshine. Settling back into my own body was a strange, uncomfortable experience. I felt as if I'd been gone on a long journey and was coming home to a dusty, empty house.

I probed my memories of Constantine but there was no alien voice in my head, no rush of emotions that weren't my own guilt and anger. I was alone.

"It's safe," I said finally, smiling brightly. "I don't feel her anymore."

"I knew you were stronger than that," Aunt Hyacinth said and I noticed for the first time that she wasn't wearing her veil. Her cheek was lightly scarred up to her temple. Marcus slid the needle out of my arm when Uncle Geoffrey gave him the nod. He pressed a cotton ball to the small pinprick but it was already healing. Dad unlocked the cuffs on my wrists and ankles. I wanted to laugh and cry and hug everyone really hard, from silent Sebastian to tattooed Isabeau in the corner.

"Viola?" I asked.

"She is gone," Isabeau confirmed. "There is no trace of magic on you or anything unusual in your aura."

Dad ran a hand along his jaw. "Anyone mind explaining to us what exactly is going on?"

"Viola was in my head for weeks before I realized it," I said. "And when she put the crown on, she switched places with me." Mom reached for one of the slender silver daggers in her boot but I don't even think she realized she was doing it. "She was the first Drake daughter, that's how she was able to possess me. And Madame Veronique knew." I explained the rest of the story as best I could. When I got to the part about Madame Veronique's handmaidens, I had to share my terrible news. "London died protecting me from her handmaids," I added, tears burning in the back of my throat. "She's really gone."

Mom swore. Dad's eyes glistened. "Damn," he said softly.

"We have to have a memorial of some kind," I insisted.

"Of course," Dad agreed. My brothers nodded, looking shocked.

"She shouldn't have died for me." Guilt sent needles of pain through me. I tried to push it back. Ending these battles and political games would avenge her, not hand-wringing and wailing. But it was a struggle to stay calm. My gums ached around my fangs.

"I'll have to call London's father," he added. I understood now why London had always been so distant and wary of us. Our fathers were cousins of a sort and hers was descended from the Christophe Drake branch of the family tree, while ours descended from his twin Arnaud Drake. Madame Veronique had always treated them,

London included, differently and now I knew why. Until I came along, she'd been waiting for them to give birth to the next Viola.

Lucy's arrival was a welcome interruption to the bleak silence. She burst into the room with a shout of "Bruno said it was okay!" She elbowed Logan out of the way and launched onto my bed, heedless of the tubes and the audience. The wolfhound puppy nipped at her heels, ecstatic with the new game. She wasn't wearing her glasses but otherwise she looked just the same. She still smelled like cherries and pepper and the incense off the sweater her mother must have made for her. I was sated enough that I could smell her scent and the blood under her skin without turning predatory. I had twinges but they were easily ignored. I hugged her so tightly her back cracked. I let go abruptly. "Sorry! God, sorry!"

She just laughed and hugged me again. Her crystal beads dug into me and her hair tickled my nose. I was finally, truly home.

"I missed you," we said at the same time, then grinned at each other like lunatics.

"It's about time," she added.

"I'll go check on Christabel," Uncle Geoffrey said, easing out of the crowded room.

"Say hi for me," Lucy called after him, since it was still too near sunset for her to visit.

"Good to have you back, kid," Sebastian said, following him.

"What about your pheromones?" Marcus asked thoughtfully, as he gathered the last of the blood transfusion supplies into a bag. "Were they partly Viola's as well?"

"I don't know," I replied. "I can't tell."

"We should try an experiment."

"Make Duncan bark like a dog," Quinn suggested, jerking his head toward Duncan.

"Or you could try something more difficult, like making Quinn shut up," Duncan returned.

"Something simple would be best," Dad suggested drily. "And less likely to start a century-long feud."

I swung my feet over the side of the bed. The collar felt itchy around my neck. I shifted, trying to get comfortable. I looked at Quinn.

"Quinn, sit down."

Cursing, he slid down the wall until he was sitting.

His swearing was nothing to mine. The annoying itch of the collar against my skin had turned into a searing burn, as if I was wearing fire. I clawed at it, screaming. Dad grabbed me before I kicked Lucy clear across the room. Mom plucked her off the bed.

"What's happening?" Dad yelled, fumbling to unlock the collar. The more he pulled at the clasp, the worse it became. I whimpered, trying to crawl away.

"Stop." Isabeau pushed through my brothers. "It's the magic of the collar," she said. "Don't touch it. Only magic can open it now that the lock has been activated."

She kneeled on the bed behind me, trying to hold me still, her hands on my shoulders and nowhere near my throat. Charlemagne crawled up beside us. I dug my fingers into his fur, still whimpering. I'd already scratched myself bloody, and my veins felt as if they were full of lightning. Pain made me grind my teeth. Sweat trickled into the raw skin over my collarbone.

I tried to concentrate on pulling my pheromones back, drawing them in as if I was pulling a shawl tightly around myself. It helped a little.

Isabeau murmured something, and the heat increased. I flinched. She sat back. "Saga had this made, yes?"

Connor nodded. "Her and Aidan."

"And Aidan changed Christabel?" She pursed her lips. "I need a little of Christabel's blood." Connor eased out of the room and came back with a test tube Uncle Geoffrey must have given him. He handed it to Isabeau, who opened it and put a drop on the lock. Cold seeped from Isabeau's palm, went through the blood and turned to ice. The collar popped off.

I rubbed my raw, scratched neck gratefully. "Thank you," I croaked. I'd hurt my throat screaming. "Let me try one thing," I panted, looking at Quinn.

He nodded jerkily. "Make it fast."

"Fight me this time." I swallowed, still imagining the pheromones as a shawl pulled close. "Quinn, sit down," I said again, since he'd leaped to his feet when I'd started screaming.

His jaw clenched as he struggled to stay standing. I pulled my pheromones in tighter. He finally staggered back, eyes wide.

"What did you do different?" Dad asked.

"I tried to leash in the pheromones," I explained, wiping sweat off my face. "I need more practice."

"It's a good start." He kissed my temple. "Don't push too hard tonight, Sol. We already have to go to the camp soon," he said. "I know you must be tired but the tribes are restless and the peace is fragile."

"I have cleanup to do," I replied quietly. The thought of what Viola might have done but attributed to me made me sick to my stomach. "I know."

"We'll leave you a few minutes to catch up," he said before he and Mom went to make preparations.

Lucy pulled a jar of ointment out of my dresser. Her mom had made it for me last year when we both got poison ivy. "Here," she said, scooping the thick white cream into her hand. "This'll help." It was cold and soothing on my scratches. She eyed me carefully. "You're not going to go all emo now, are you?"

"Maybe later. I don't have time right now."

"Finally!" She grinned. "You're really back! We should have an unbirthday party to celebrate."

"You can be the Mad Hatter," I told her. She nudged me and I forced the nervous, morose look off my face.

"What's wrong with your brothers?" she whispered loudly, recapping the jar.

"The usual," I returned, sliding back into our comforting routine. "Drake white-knight complex."

"Quit standing around being creepy," she told them, as she'd been telling them for months before my birthday. "Go away now."

They filed out and Nicholas was the last to leave, pushing off from the wall where he'd been leaning the whole time, his ankles crossed. Lucy winked at him before he shut the door behind him.

She wriggled into the bed with me, sharing my pillow. "Okay, so seriously, are you all right?"

"I feel a little weird, but mostly okay." I paused. "I didn't do anything to you, did I?"

"*You* didn't," she pointed out. "And I'll get over Viola. The bitch."

"Maybe I'll just hang a sign around my neck that says 'I'm sorry.'"

She snorted as her phone vibrated. To my sensitive hearing it sounded like she had a grasshopper in her pocket. She checked her texts and slid me a sidelong glance. "Want to talk to Kieran?"

An embarrassed flush crawled up my cheeks. "No."

"He's sent seven texts in the last half hour." She clicked a quick message. "I'm going to at least tell him you're okay, and then you're going to tell me why you don't want to talk to your boyfriend."

"He's not my boyfriend anymore."

"Oh, please." She rolled her eyes. "Sell that line to someone who doesn't know you both better. He's freaking out, just like you." She put her phone away. "But since we've all nearly died horribly several times in the past few days, I'll give you a free pass just for tonight. But you might, oh, I don't know, *talk* to him."

"And say what?" I asked, scrambling out of the bed. I pulled my favorite jeans out of my closet and rummaged for a T-shirt. "Sorry I nearly chewed through your jugular? They don't exactly make a card for that."

"I could draw one for you."

"Ew."

We fell into giggling, just because we could. If my laughter edged toward hysterical, Lucy didn't comment. I was pulling on my Converse sneakers when shots rang out in the woods surrounding the house. We leaped to our feet. I pulled the window open and stuck my head out through the decorative iron bars. Snowflakes landed on my eyelashes. Sebastian was already a shadow streaking across the snow. I couldn't see anything else.

I ducked back into the room and turned around. "I don't know," I said in answer to Lucy's questioning glance. I heard the faint whistle of an arrow and instinct had me leaping aside before my brain had fully catalogued the sound. I kicked Lucy lightly as my feet left the floor, knocking her back onto the bed and out of harm's way. The arrow thudded into the wall, cracking the plaster.

"Shit," I said, staring at Lucy.

She stared back, equally wide-eyed. "God, you'll do anything to get out of talking to Kieran." She sat up, rubbing her hip where I'd kicked her. "Nice moves, by the way." She shook her head as my phone rang in the pocket of the dress I'd just taken off. "Who could get through your defenses like that?"

I glanced at the screen, my belly going cold. It was like I'd swallowed icicles.

"Constantine."

"Have I mentioned lately how much I do *not* like him?"

"*Viola, wait for me. I'm coming,*" I read aloud. And then I added a combination of words so foul Lucy choked.

Constantine was outside.

Worse yet, he wasn't alone.

Because the fletchings of the arrow were the distinctive red the Chandramaa favored. And none of them knew I was the real Solange again, they only knew their queen had been captured by her banished family in a time when civil war loomed from every corner.

I did the only thing I could think of.

"Mom!"

CHAPTER 25

Lucy

Solange was already down in the front hall by the time I was thundering down the stairs after her. Nicholas slipped wordlessly around the banister to stand next to me.

"It's Constantine," Solange told her parents tightly. "And the Chandramaa," she added, showing them the arrow she'd yanked out of the wall. "He doesn't know I'm not Viola anymore."

Helena started snapping orders into her cell phone to guards posted around the farm. Bruno must have already left with Sebastian because I didn't see him anywhere. Logan was pulling a chest full of stakes out of the closet and Isabeau helped him hand them out. Marcus and Duncan went downstairs for more weapons and Hypnos. I checked the vial in my sleeve and automatically counted my other weapons out of habit: four stakes of various sizes,

Hypnos, two pepper eggs, a hand crossbow, a can of mace, and a Taser.

"Here, put these on." Liam slid a basket across the floor. It was filled with what looked like miniature shields. He wore one on a strap across his chest and it covered his heart in front with a second shield fitted to his back. It was only about the size of his palm. "Bruno's been working on these for the last week," he explained as I pulled one out and helped buckle it onto Nicholas.

Another shot rang out, shivering across the quiet winter night.

"I'm not letting anyone else die for me," Solange said. She'd said it a hundred times since the summer, only this time she didn't sound frantic, just determined and eerily calm.

There was a strange whistling sound and then something fiery crashed through the living room window. A second missile hit upstairs. The smell of smoke and winter rushed through the broken glass. Duncan dashed upstairs and Quinn and Connor grabbed a blanket from the couch to put the fire out before it reached the rug and traveled. I had to extricate myself from between the wall and Nicholas, where he'd pressed against me to protect me. It probably never occurred to him that he was flammable too.

Helena went to the glass. "Bastard's trying to burn us out." She checked her phone. "They're in the back as well."

A huge stone crashed outside. The front door shook. "That one hit the porch," Quinn said. He blinked at the next rock that came through. "Does he have a trebuchet?"

"He's laying siege," Solange said. "So he might. At heart he's still a knight. He'll wait us out or burn us out."

"We have supplies," Connor pointed out. "And come sunrise he has to give up his ground."

"Only if he doesn't have humans fighting for him," Duncan added as he and Marcus came back up the stairs.

"We could take *them*," Quinn scoffed. "Hell, Lucy could take them."

I grabbed a bow from Marcus and a quiver of arrows. "Can I start now?"

"Stay away from the windows, Lucy," Helena said, automatically. Another Chandramaa arrow came through the broken glass, skimming the bottom of the chandelier and slamming into the stair railing. There was a note wrapped around the painted shaft. Liam reached up to snap it loose.

"Give us the queen," he read out just as the phone rang.

Helena plucked it out of the cradle. I could see the deadly glint in her eye reflected in the mirror hanging over the table. I reached back to hold Nicholas's hand. That look never boded well. "We don't deal with cowards and terrorists," she spat in the phone. "So you can take your—"

Liam grabbed the phone. Helena hissed at him and they had a mini tug-of-war over the receiver. Liam finally wrested it free but only after she broke his little finger. He set it with a crack and a telling glance that had her shrugging sheepishly.

"I can stop this," Solange said as her dad spoke evenly and calmly into the phone. When no one answered her, she stepped toward the front door. Suddenly everyone leaped forward, crowding in front of her. She sighed. "This is ridiculous."

"What else do you suggest, young lady?" Helena asked. "That we just let you waltz out there unprotected?"

"Just let me go out there and call off the Chandramaa and revoke your banishment. They have to listen to me, I'm their freaking queen, remember?" She grimaced slightly when she said the word 'queen' as if she couldn't help herself. I wondered if she remembered lounging in the tent wearing a crown on her head.

"Constantine has other men," Isabeau interjected. "It would be a mistake to assume it is only Chandramaa out there."

"It doesn't matter," Solange argued. "They don't want to hurt me."

"No," Helena said, but she was frowning thoughtfully.

"At least listen to me," Solange retorted quietly. I could tell by the way she curled her fingers that she was trying not to nervously wipe her palms on her jeans. She occupied herself with fitting the dark-painted shield over her heart. "I know Viola well enough by now that I should be able to fool Constantine just long enough to get back inside the camp, especially if you put up a token fight so he doesn't suspect anything."

"It's a good plan," Liam agreed slowly, after hanging up. "There's only one problem with it."

"Which is?"

"Sending my baby girl out alone to that bloody lot of degenerates," he replied acidly.

"Daddy, it's the best way and you know it. I'm as safe with them as I am with you. They're the only other ones left who don't want to kill me, apparently."

"Not precisely a winning argument," Liam said, but he was half smiling. It made him look younger and just like Nicholas.

"You can follow us. That way, as soon as I get in there to call off the banishment, you'll be right there already."

"I hate every part of this plan," Helena said darkly as I coughed on the smoke lingering in the hall. "Especially the part where you might just be right."

"London died because of this stupid prophecy and these stupid politics," Solange said. "If I can stop it but instead I sit here and let everyone else risk their lives then she died for nothing. And one of you might be next. What would that make me?"

I blinked. "London died?" I might not have liked her, but she didn't deserve to be really *dead*.

Something that sounded like a small bomb went off somewhere at the end of the driveway.

"And the longer we wait here, the more danger Sebastian and Bruno are in," Solange added as Byron hid under the library table. Boudicca went to the solarium and growled viciously through the glass. Helena swore.

"Okay," she said finally, after she and Liam looked at each other. "We'll go out first and clear a path. Solange, you go next. Quinn, Connor, Duncan, you take the rear guard in case anyone breaks through. Logan, Marcus, go around back. Isabeau?"

"I will fight," she said.

"Thank you. Geoffrey and Hyacinth will stay with Christabel. Nicholas, you take Lucy home. Take the secret tunnel." It was the one reserved for family emergencies. I wasn't even sure my mom knew how to get to it.

"I can go alone," I said. "They're not after me."

"No." It was a Drake chorus, each voice with the same sharp tone. Even Isabeau chimed in.

"We are having a hell of a slumber party when this is over," I said, hugging Solange hard.

"Chocolate death," she agreed, hugging me back.

"You'll kick ass," I whispered. "And kick his once for me too. And call me when you can."

She added a few more stakes to her belt and then added her leather jacket. She watched her parents cross the porch, staying low. An arrow hit one of the cars in the driveway.

"Goddamn it," Duncan said.

"Ready?" Solange yelled over her shoulder. "Don't kill them if you don't have to, they think they're doing their job," she reminded them before kicking the door open and stalking outside. "Tristan!" she shouted, her voice sounding wobbly and delicate. "I'm here."

She ran across the snow as if being chased. There was an eerie silence, broken only by the sound of swords clashing in the distance. I grabbed the bow and darted upstairs as the others slipped out the back door. Nicholas frowned at me from the bottom step. "Where are you going? Tunnels are generally underground, Hamilton."

I snorted from the landing. "I'm not running away."

He dashed up the staircase, groaning. "Don't do this to me again."

"I can help," I insisted. "And I promise you can rescue me in a minute. Just let me clear the way a little first." I went into Aunt Hyacinth's room because it had the best vantage point from the window. Her pug, Mrs. Brown, tried to bite my ankle before she remembered she knew me. I slipped outside onto the widow's walk and notched an arrow, smiling grimly. Nicholas tried to edge into the space with me but he banged into my elbow.

"Nicky, there's not enough room for the overprotective boy-friend thing right now," I said, elbowing him back. "But I could use your eyes," I added. The moonlight and the snow made it easier but it was still too dark for me to see very well and I didn't have night-vision goggles on me. I hadn't even thought to pack them. Tonight was supposed to be the long-awaited family reconciliation party, not another ambush.

You'd think I'd learn.

Nicholas climbed up on the overhang, straddling the shingles. With his eyes gleaming and fangs out he looked like a particularly creepy gargoyle on a gothic mansion. "Ready?"

I lifted the bow again, sinking into my breath, finding that quiet center where nothing mattered except my fingers around the bow-string, the arrow and the path it needed to take. I shut out my boy-friend crouched above me, the cold wind, the howl of coyotes in the wood. I was the bow. I was the arrow.

"On your right, two o'clock," Nicholas said.

I squinted, catching the shadow. I loosed an arrow, aiming it slightly to the right. I didn't want to kill the vampire, as Solange said, just take him out of commission for the night. He flew off his feet, clutching the arrow in his shoulder.

"Nine o'clock, by the cedar hedge. Watch out for Quinn!"

Very faintly I heard: "Lucy!"

I winced. "Oops."

"He's fine. Eleven o'clock, go low."

Another arrow.

Solange was still running, crossing the field like a deer in hunting season.

"In the oak tree right of the driveway, up on a top branch," he said. "Can you see?"

If I squinted, I could just make out a faint pale blur, and only because I knew exactly where to look. I took aim again and fired.

This target fired back.

The arrow slid with a violent twang into the very peak of the balcony's overhang. An inch higher and it would have gotten Nicholas in the face, an inch lower and it would have scalped me. The fletching were red, like the arrow in Solange's room. Chandramaa.

It was a warning shot. No one could have hit that target without being really, really good. Certainly good enough to take either one of us out. I exhaled sharply, my breath clouding in the cold.

"Okay, no more helping," Nicholas said, sliding back down to the ground and shoving me back inside all in one fluid motion. "Let's go."

We raced around Aunt Hyacinth's overdecorated tables full of knickknacks, Nicholas dragging me behind him like a kite. If he went any faster I might even get airtime. We went down two flights of stairs and passed the weapons room and the blood storage room before he slowed down. I was panting and jittery. Adrenaline, my old friend.

We went through the door to the regular tunnels, and down the damp corridor lit with blue emergency lights. The stone floor was slick with moisture. Nicholas was counting his steps. At eighty-three, he stopped abruptly and turned to the left. He ran his hand along the wall, dislodging dirt and spiders until he found a tiny nick a foot or so off the ground. He crouched and dug his thumb into it, turning hard. Instead of a regular door opening, there was a soft snick from the ceiling.

I blinked at the trapdoor. "Cool. I'm surprised you don't have retina scans down here."

"Technology breaks," he replied, straightening. He pushed the door open and stale cold air drifted over us. "Usually at the worst possible time."

I could just guess what Connor would have to say to that. Nicholas interlaced his fingers and made a step out of his hands. I settled my foot into it and he launched me up. I grabbed hold of the edge of the opening and struggled to pull myself up. I was inching across on my stomach, red-faced and gasping when he practically floated up beside me. I rolled over, covered in dust and spiderwebs.

There were no lights at all in this tunnel. It was so dark that once Nicholas closed the trapdoor behind us, I was disoriented. I couldn't even see my own hands as I tried to sit up. If I'd been smart, I would have worn my regulation cargos with all their pockets. I was sure there were light sticks in most of them as part of standard procedure, not to mention a flashlight. I really needed to remember I was supposed to be a vampire hunter now. At least, part of the time.

Nicholas helped me up and I gripped his arm tightly as he led me down the corridor. I had no idea where we were or where we were going. I stumbled, tripping over a bit of uneven ground. It was so quiet I could hear the blood rushing in my ears, my uneven breath amplified and raspy. I scraped the back of my hand on the wall. We walked for at least ten minutes but I couldn't really be sure. It was so strange to be in such complete blackness. Even time was too dark to see. We could have been here an hour.

Eventually, Nicholas stopped. The tunnel didn't feel any different to me, it was still damp and rough and smelled like iron, but now there was the sound of a lock opening. A narrow door opened and we went through. Something swung, grazing my shoulder. I jumped, yelping.

"Rope ladder," Nicholas told me. I could hear the smile in his voice. "I'll go up first and open the door and make sure it's secure. Wait until I give you the all clear."

In less than a minute the door creaked open. Leaves and moonlight drifted down. The air was cold and cleansing, chasing away the clinging mildew. "Another rope ladder," I muttered. At least this one had actually rope steps, not just knots like the one I'd climbed in the treetops.

"Okay, Lucy," Nicholas called down. "Come on up."

"He makes it sound so easy." It helped to mutter and mumble. It distracted me from the slick twine, the dizzying spinning that made me nauseated. My arm muscles muttered and mumbled too, finally giving in to out-and-out screaming. I was sweating by the time Nicholas grabbed my wrists and pulled me out.

The forest was beautiful and still all around us, like a painting. Snow clung to the bare branches and stars peeked through when the wind shifted. Ice glinted on the mossy trunks.

"We'll have to walk from here," Nicholas said. We started the long walk back to the school, moving quietly between the trees, holding hands. It was a stolen moment, sweet and swift. When we reached the road that led to the academy, I paused.

"School's overrun with hunters," I murmured. "And Huntsmen. So I'll go from here on my own."

The moment might have been sweet but the kiss scalded, like chili peppers in hot chocolate. By rights, the snow should have melted into puddles at our feet. I turned away reluctantly, toward the school buildings and the security lights; from one family to another.

I knew he was at the edge of the wintry woods, watching me. I couldn't see him, but I could feel his presence, just as I felt him lope away when I texted him that I was safely on campus.

Chapter 26

Solange

My every instinct screamed at me to run in the opposite direction.

Not only did I have to run straight into Constantine's arms instead, but I had to do it without snarling. I was picking up speed when Sebastian grabbed my arm and spun me around the other side of a tree. "What the hell, Sol?"

"All part of the plan," I told him quickly. "Talk to Mom." His hold didn't slacken. "Check your phone."

When he read the warning text I was sure Mom had Connor send to everyone, he dropped his hand. "When exactly did Mom and Dad lose their minds?"

"Viola!" Constantine shouted. I could see the glint of his sword as he raced between the trees toward us.

"We need to make this look good," I whispered urgently. Sebastian sighed and lifted his chin.

I punched him.

I didn't even break his nose, which would disappoint Lucy on principle, but he still flew through the air as if a giant had tossed him. He landed in the snow, exactly where Constantine could see him. He even groaned, clutching a fake wound. I had no idea my quiet brother had such a theatrical side. "Sorry," I murmured, jumping over him to cut off Constantine before he reached us and decided to finish what I'd started. He shot me a boyish grin so unlike his usually solemn silences that I stumbled.

The moonlight made Constantine's violet eyes even brighter. Three men followed behind him, swords also drawn. I leaped a fallen log, scattering snow and icicles.

"Viola." The relief in his smile was sincere. He gathered me up in his arms, looking even more knightly.

"Tristan," I murmured. Viola had never called him Constantine and he'd never divulged his first name to Solange. When he bent his head to kiss me, I nearly panicked. The last time he'd done that it had called Viola to the surface. He knew that his presence had strengthened her hold on me. I threw a fearful glance over my shoulder and his mouth grazed my ear. "They're coming," I said. "Don't let them take me again."

He straightened. "I only left you with them in the first place because they'd never hurt Solange and I needed to marshal my defenses."

I made my lower lip quiver. The Viola I knew, and the Viola Constantine had known before her bloodchange, were vastly different. I couldn't quite understand why he'd let everything go so badly since she returned. He had to see there was something off about her, didn't he? Was he blind? "Can we just go home now?" I asked.

"Of course." He ran his hand down my back. I looked up at him with what I hoped could be construed as love and gratitude. The worst part of it was that I'd genuinely liked him. He'd listened to me. He'd even understood me and pushed me to accept myself. Even if he'd done it to free Viola, I couldn't help but think we'd been friends.

"Chandramaa with us, but you stay here and make sure the Drakes don't follow," Constantine ordered his men.

"Don't hurt them!" I burst out.

"Such a soft heart, love," he said, smiling down at me.

Yeah, right. Clearly, he didn't know Viola as well as he thought he did.

"We might need them later," I added hastily. Since we had home advantage and knew the terrain intimately, I had to believe my family could take Constantine's men. Plus, we had Mom. Still, I wasn't going to take any chances.

Luckily, there was no need to speak as we made our way through the forest to the encampment. Every so often we would pause in a clearing so Constantine could map our location using the position of the stars. I couldn't see or hear the Chandramaa guard around us, but I knew they were there. Eventually the snow gave way to tramped-down dirt trails, all snaking to the same center. We passed a guard, then the field where Duncan had kept his motorcycles, then between two trees into the outskirts of the camp. I could hear faint drumming and see the warm flicker of torches and bonfires.

Guards divested us of all our weapons, right down to the slender toothpick stake strapped to my ankle under my pants.

I waited until we'd entered the main field, the wind snapping the pennants and banners on the painted pavilions. Lanterns swung between the tents. Vampires turned toward us slowly.

"Chandramaa!" I called out. Constantine paused curiously. I met his eyes. "I am formally calling off the banishment on the House of Drake. Do you hear me?" I added, just as loudly.

"We hear you," someone answered from the treetops. "Consider it done."

"We hear you as well," a hard voice said from behind us.

"What are you doing?" Constantine asked me at the same time. We turned to face the speaker. He was huge, with ropes of muscles and braided blond hair. He didn't look impressed.

And he wasn't alone.

Vampires circled around us, pressing closer. They muttered unhappily, menacingly. "The little queen finally makes an appearance," the blond vampire said disdainfully. "Been too busy breaking all of our covenants and terrorizing the town to sit council?"

I swallowed. "I'm sorry."

"What do we care about the town, Lars?" someone else shouted. "Do the humans care about the cattle they eat?"

"She's turning too many eyes our way," Lars snapped. "And if we're going to have a figurehead queen, she should at least be benign."

"What, like Natasha was? You weren't here in the eighties."

They were starting to shove one another to get closer to me. Constantine angled himself to shield me. They didn't have weapons of course, but the press of their anger was sharp and unyielding. "Don't hurt her." A woman cuffed Lars on the back of the head. "Do you want a red arrow through your head?"

"Alva, quit it," he grumbled.

"You have every right to be angry," I tried to shout above the harsh words and hissing. Constantine shoved at someone who came too close. "I was possessed," I said, trying not to give away the fear choking my throat like smoke. I knew they'd be able to smell it. "Please, listen." I tried to force my pheromones out over the crowd, but there were too many of them.

"A likely story," a girl scoffed.

"It's true," I insisted, stumbling when an elbow hit me in the spine.

Constantine caught me, turned me to face him as if we were alone under the moon. "What are you saying?"

"I'm not Viola," I told him coldly. "We cast her out. She's not coming back."

He staggered as if in physical pain. "That's not possible."

The mob shifted and I could suddenly see down the path to a circle of torches. The light glinted off metal chain and a tall heavy tree, cut down to become a post. People were tied to it at various lengths, huddled around small fires. I froze. "What is that?"

"The post you ordered," Lars barked. "As if you didn't know."

Viola had set up the same kind of post her own mother had been chained to. It wasn't just cruelty, it was madness too. "Take it down!" I shouted, ill at the sight of it. I could remember only too well Lady Venetia covered in bite marks. "Let them go!"

Someone had me by the hair. I was dragged toward the post, the angry mob moving with us. I couldn't get away. I caught a glimpse of a trio of laughing girls all wearing white brocade gowns with dyed white hair. The Furies.

"Too little too late, princess," Lars said, deliberately not referring to me as the queen. I couldn't care less about that, except it meant I was losing what little ground I still had.

And I really didn't want to have my head chopped off or whatever it was they were planning to do.

"The Chandramaa," I croaked. Constantine was just standing on the deserted path, broken. He swayed, looking worse than I felt, and I was the one about to be torn apart by an angry mob.

"Vampire tradition allows us a royal execution if all the tribes agree."

"But I was possessed! Can't I abdicate? Name a regent or something?" I was really starting to hate vampire traditions. There was no fairness to them, no second chances. Just a stake in the heart if you made a mistake, like medieval law. I'd seen the Middle Ages firsthand and it wasn't all pretty dresses.

"That seems fair," a girl pointed out, the pink daisy in her hair incongruous against all the fangs and bloodshot eyes.

"Not good enough," Lars argued fiercely. The Furies shouted their agreement. "She nearly exposed us all. My own son fell to a Huntsman just last night because of her recklessness."

"Murdering a sixteen-year-old girl won't bring him back," his wife said wearily.

He growled like a wounded bear. "If they won't grant me an

execution, then I demand blood debt. Her life for my son's life." He smiled then, and it made me take a step back. "Trial by combat."

"Are you kidding?" I blurted out. He was more than twice my size. All I had were bats. A few circled over us, squeaking.

"If you insist on that antiquated tradition," my father suddenly interjected loudly from the edge of the crowd, his eyes flashing, "then my daughter has the right to name a champion to fight in her place."

"Fine. Who will it be? You?" He chuckled condescendingly. "The peacemaker?"

"No," my mother corrected, stepping out from behind my dad, her smile cold and dreadful. "Me."

Lars blanched.

If I'd been five years old still, I would have added a "nah-nah-nah-boo-boo."

The crowd fell silent. He let go of my hair and I scrambled out of his reach, rubbing my tingling scalp.

"You can still withdraw with honor," Dad said gently. "And we can reconvene the council and continue with the real work of the hour." Lars spat on the ground. "Guess not," Dad added mildly. "Before you begin, know that my daughter was the victim of possession and has been exorcised. The Hounds' handmaiden will attest to it."

"The one allied to your family?" someone scoffed loudly. "With your own son initiated? What do you take us for?"

"Are you maligning Kala?" Finn asked quietly. He was tall and blond and usually so silent it was creepy. He could have given

Sebastian lessons. He was also thousands of years old and I hadn't seen him since Isabeau had first arrived at the courts. Those months felt like years.

Whoever had spoken lost herself in the crowd.

"Choose your own shaman," Dad suggested. "And have my daughter tested."

"No, we'll decide now," Lars insisted.

A Chandramaa guard stepped forward, holding two quarter-staves with pointed tips. She was tall, with short black hair and the red insignia stitched onto her sleeveless tunic. She gave Mom the black-tipped staff and Lars took the white one. They each had a red feather attached, like the one the guard wore in her hair.

Someone I didn't know placed the crown on the ground between Mom and Lars. More Moon guards stood in a circle, defining the battling ground. Lars's clan stood behind his wife, fists over their hearts in solidarity. "Dad," I said, holding his hand tightly, as if I was still a little girl. "Has anyone realized this is the twenty-first century? This isn't justice."

"I know," he squeezed my fingers. "Don't worry," he added, but I could see the way his jaw clenched. Mom was the only one who didn't seem bothered. She actually looked pleased.

"To the death, I presume?" she asked lightly, swinging her staff experimentally to get the feel of it.

"Yes," Lars replied.

"No," his wife broke in hotly. "I've lost my son; I won't lose my husband too."

Lars raised his eyebrows. "Alva, she's tiny."

Alva looked disgusted. I had the distinct impression that if she'd had an iron skillet nearby she'd have clobbered him over the head with it. "Don't be an ass." She pointed at the guard, fangs extended. "First blood." Lars grumbled but didn't say anything else when his wife shot him the kind of look I thought only Mom could wield.

Mom inclined her head. "First blood is acceptable."

They both held out their left hands, palm up. The Chandramaa guard scored them lightly with the tip of a ruby-handled blade until blood welled to the surface. They flung the drops over the crown and stepped back; the fight had automatically begun.

Lars attacked first, his staff missing Mom so narrowly I yelped. The pointed tip slammed into the dirt with such force it sounded like a horse's hoof hitting the ground. It stuck slightly when he went to swing it again. Snow and earth flung in every direction. Mom ducked and used her own staff for leverage. She swung around, using her locked legs as a battering ram. Her boots smashed into his chest. Lars staggered backward, knocking down several bystanders.

He swung low, hoping to catch more across the knees. She leaped up nimbly, slamming the butt of her staff into his shoulder. He howled, bones cracking. But she hadn't cut through his skin and there was no blood. The fight continued.

Their staffs cracked against each other, like bones breaking and skulls shattering. Mom deflected a downward blow by reaching up with the staff in a horizontal position. Lars parried her next attack by smashing it aside. She danced backward and then extended, flipping the staff in both hands as if it were a sword. She thrust forward, hitting his sternum. She feinted low and when he went to block she caught him in the throat. He gagged, his muscles contracting viciously. He slammed his staff down into her upper thigh, catching her at such a brutal angle that her leg gave out. She fell to one knee.

"Helena," Dad breathed.

Mom shifted her hold on the staff and instead of using it to get back on her feet, she jabbed up, hitting Lars under the chin. The staff kept going, hitting his mouth and nose. Blood splattered into the ground.

"First blood!" the Chandramaa guard announced. "Surrender your weapons." Her compatriots rushed in to disarm Lars and my mother. Mom limped over to where he was sprawled in the dirt, blood oozing from his split lip and cracked nose.

"I'm sorry your son died," she said bluntly. "But my daughter was a victim of the same person. She's gone now. I hope you find some comfort in that."

"Enough," Alva said, when Lars swore, fists clenched. There were tears mingling with the blood on his face.

The guard used the end of one of the staffs to hook the crown and toss it at me. "It is done." She bowed in my direction. "Hail the queen."

I cringed, holding the bloody crown clutched in my hands.

CHAPTER 27

Lucy

Thursday night/Friday morning, past curfew

After Nicholas walked me to school, I still had two classes left. I went to each of them, taking conscientious notes and doing drills until sweat soaked the back of my shirt to make up for skipping so much this past week. Connor snuck me a text to let me know that everyone was okay so I was even able to concentrate.

I was washing my face in the deserted girls' bathroom minutes before curfew when I heard a *"psst."* I splashed more water on my face, thinking one of the taps must be leaking.

"I said, *psst.*"

I turned off the water. "Um, hello?" I looked over my shoulder. Chloe's head poked out of one of the stalls, her wild hair ruthlessly scraped into a tight ponytail. She wore a black T-shirt and black leggings. I blinked at her. "Are you a cat burglar now?"

She eased out, casting a suspicious glance under the other stall doors. "We're breaking into Bellwood's office," she whispered so low it was barely audible.

"What, *now?*"

She nodded. "I hacked an e-mail that said all the teachers are in a meeting with Hart right now and most of the other hunters are out patroling. It's now or never."

"Is there any particular reason we're breaking into the principal's office?" I asked curiously.

"I can't break her encryption," Chloe answered crankily. "But there's definitely something going on. And the last time something was going on I nearly grew a mustache and students died." She paused in the hallway. "So are you in?"

"Of course, I'm in," I replied. "What a question."

"What about . . ." She nodded to my dorm room door, where my roommate lay in her perfectly made bed.

I glanced at my watch. "Lights out," I said drily. "Sarita is nothing if not punctual."

"Won't she tattle?"

"I still have my permission slip for tonight," I told her.

We snuck down the back stairwell where Hunter and her friend Jason waited. He had a kind, gentle smile. I'd met him a few times in the cafeteria during meals. Hunter shook her head. "How much backup do you think we need?" she asked Chloe. "It's like sneaking a herd of elephants."

"Jason's the best at locks," Chloe reminded her.

"And I'm just here because I'm nosy," I added helpfully.

"Just don't get caught," Hunter said.

"I already have enough detention, thanks."

"I'm not worried about your detention." She snorted. "I'm worried about mine. We're looking at expulsion if this goes wrong."

I beamed at her, smiling wide. "What could go wrong?"

"Exactly." She checked her watch. "Jenna is already up a tree on lookout. I'm going to take the back door to the building. Lucy, you keep a lookout inside the building, outside the office door when Jason and Chloe go in. Everyone's got their phone on silent mode?"

"Sir, yes sir!" I gave her a mock salute. She just stuck out her tongue at me. "If Sarita could see you now, she'd be crushed," I added with pretend-sorrow.

"Let's go," Hunter suggested, rolling her eyes at me. "And be careful. Most of the agents are out on patrol but you just never know."

I stopped teasing once we were outside because she was right, we could get in a lot of trouble for this. The moon was bright over the snow, which made it all that much harder to sneak about. We darted from tree to tree, giving the infirmary with its bright lights a wide berth. Hunter was already ahead of us, picking through the gardens. I saw the bushes shiver when she did a weird acrobatic back bend. "What is she doing?"

"Avoiding the cameras," Chloe explained. "I temporarily deactivated the ones in the office but if I tampered with too many of them it would be a red flag."

"I'm a little scared of how efficient you guys are."

"This coming from the girl who regularly punches vampires in the nose and lives to tell about it."

The building was quiet with all the classrooms dark and empty. Classes had ended over a couple of hours ago and as promised, Bellwood's office was also deserted. We picked our way past the lockers, our shoes scuffing on the polished wooden floors. Jason led the way down the hall and Chloe and I pressed our backs to the wall, waiting for him to deactivate the lock. He had a bag filled with old-fashioned lock picks, complicated listening devices, rings of keys, and plastic cards. After about ten minutes of patient fiddling, which would have had me screaming with frustration, the door swung open on oiled hinges.

Chloe kissed his cheeks with a louder squeak than the hinges. "You are brilliant."

"The windows have the serious security," he said modestly. "No one's dumb enough to try this from inside."

"Except us," she said proudly. "I want those passwords." She rubbed her hands together like a villain in a bad movie.

"If you hear anything, flash a light at us," Jason whispered, handing me his flashlight. "The office might be bugged."

It was both boring and surprisingly nerve-racking to be lookout. I was used to being thrown into events without warning, but all this careful listening and excruciating waiting was making my palms sweat. I jumped twice at the sound of my own heartbeat, mistaking it for footsteps. A half hour later, when my back teeth hurt from clenching them so tightly, Chloe practically skipped out of the office. She waved a data stick at me. Her smile was huge and smug as a cat's. "Got 'em." She beamed.

The return trip to the dorms wasn't nearly as smooth.

For one thing, a van of hunters returned just as we were stepping out of the building. Jason didn't speak, only shoved us back inside. We stumbled against one another just as the spear of headlights swept across the pathway. The van rumbled across the lawn, straight to the infirmary.

Hunter popped out of the bushes beside us, frowning. "That's not good."

Chloe yelped and elbowed me in the boob. "Shit, Chloe!" I yelped back.

"Shh," Hunter added. "Hello? Stealthy, remember?"

"Tell that to my left boob."

We eased around the building, trying to find a safe spot to hide to get a better look at the van. Jenna dropped out of a tree and Jason clamped a hand over Chloe's mouth so her startled scream wouldn't give us away. The van stopped and the headlights went out. Hunter motioned us to the pond but didn't follow. Instead, she went low, and headed to the van. We dashed away, then crouched in the darkness to watch and wait. We lay in the long grass, our feet tucked against the bank of dark water. The snow seeped into my pants, making me shiver.

Hunter crept along the edge of the gardens, as close to the front door as she could. She stopped halfway up the path, hiding behind a juniper. She tossed something into the bushes and then ran to join us as the van's front doors opened. She slid into the grass as if she were playing baseball. The swan gave a loud indignant honk. "I hate that bird," she muttered.

Two hunters stepped out onto the path, wearing their full gear under the cover of winter coats. When Hunter fished a small black surveillance gadget out of her pocket, we could hear the sound of their footsteps as they went around to the back of the van.

"Wireless surveillance amplifier," she explained with a smile equally as smug as Chloe's when she'd danced out of Bellwood's office. "There's only one bug left inside the infirmary. They keep doing sweeps."

"Where do you get this stuff?" I asked. "Seriously, do you stockpile it?"

"Kieran stole this for me last week from his uncle's basement. It's last year's model so no one will miss it."

"I had no idea the boy scout was such a delinquent," I said, impressed. "He keeps surprising me." We tucked ourselves deeper into the frostbitten grass as the hunters began to talk. Chloe couldn't help but inspect the surveillance gadget.

"Another body," the man said wearily when Theo came out of the infirmary. "She died on the way here."

Theo shook his head. "Damn it, I feel as if I'm running a morgue instead of an infirmary."

"Keep her under surveillance," the female hunter said as she slid the gurney out of the van. "If she doesn't turn we'll put her back where we found her and call the authorities."

"And if she turns?" Theo asked, even though I could tell by the look on his face that he already knew the answer.

"We stake her."

"She's not instantly evil," I whispered furiously. "She'd just be a vampire." In my indignation, I must have been louder than I'd thought because the hunters reached for their stakes.

"Shit." Hunter started to scuttle backward. "Into the pond," she added, sliding under the cold water. We followed as quickly and quietly as we could. The hunter stalked our way as the icy water stole my breath. Even though I wanted to scream at the shock of it, there was no air left in my lungs. It wasn't as cold here as in the mountains and the snow was still merely decorative, but it was still too damn cold for a swim. Chloe's head popped up beside mine and we curled into the weeds. Jason's lips were already blue.

The hunters were getting closer.

Too close.

The woman had a gun at her belt and looked like she was in the mood to shoot first and ask questions later. My fingers cramped with cold as I held onto the bank, trying not to move my legs and create any ripples.

Just as they were crossing into the longer grass, Hunter dove under the water and yanked on the swan's leg. It squawked and hurled itself into the air, flying so erratically in its surprise that it clipped one of the hunters in the ear. They stumbled, cursing and ducking.

We crawled out of the pond as quickly as we could. The water made my sweater three times as heavy as it had been and filled my boots. My teeth chattered. Even my bones were cold.

"That damn bird still lives here?" the guy muttered as they

turned away from the pond and went to push the sheet-covered body up to the double doors. The fluorescent lights were cruel and uncompromising, falling brightly over bloodstains. Theo peered under the sheet and frowned as we huddled close to one another, trying not to die from exposure. Hunter, being Hunter, had the foresight to leave the transmitter in the grass, so we would still hear them talking. She'd even knocked Chloe's data stick out of her hand, since she was still clutching it like a little girl at her first carnival with her first cotton candy.

"She was alive when you found her?" Theo asked.

"Barely, but yes."

"Those bite marks are too perfect for all the blood she lost. And those cuts on her wrists are older, as if she was chained up." Theo shook his head. "These damn disappearances and attacks are getting stranger and stranger." The door shut behind them and we couldn't hear what else he had to say.

"Solange didn't do that," I whispered, my knees creaking as I pushed off the snow. "She's herself again. Plus she's been at the camp." My jeans felt like they were frozen right onto my skin.

"I can't help but wonder if this Dawn chick would get better results," the female hunter muttered, as she and her partner left the infirmary. "'Cause we're shit useless these days."

Dawn again.

I had to physically stop myself from hissing at her name. Hunter reached for a stake out of habit before she realized it was just me and not a vampire. The hunters climbed into the van, cutting off their conversation. They drove to the smallest barn, which had been converted into sleeping quarters for families from out of town and traveling Helios-Ra hunters. Apparently it was full to capacity, which had never happened before. That was all very interesting except for the fact that I was frozen through and my fingers were numb.

"Let's go," Hunter croaked, sounding equally miserable.

We ran back to the dorms with considerably less stealth and grace. It was only sheer luck that had us back in the building and taking hot showers without getting caught. Feeling returned to my fingertips in hot sparks, burning under my skin and up my arms. I was still shivering slightly, even bundled in my flannel pajamas and Sarita's bathrobe, which I borrowed off its hook. I snuck downstairs to Hunter's room where everyone was waiting, also freshly showered and wearing every sweater they could find. Jason was pouring hot water from a plug-in kettle into cups filled with hot chocolate mix. I seriously considered kissing him for that. With tongue.

Chloe was already at the computer, her hair up in a towel, her eyes squinting at the computer screen. "I hope it was worth it," I said, curling my fingers around the mug Jason passed me.

"Definitely worth it," Hunter said. "We already know more than we did an hour ago."

"Yeah, like the pond is freaking cold," I said.

"Better that than being caught and expelled."

"Better hypothermia than expulsion?" I asked through another violent shiver that trembled up my spine out of nowhere.

She waved that aside with a tired grin. "It wasn't cold enough for that and we weren't in long enough."

I groaned, curling into a ball on her bed, still clutching my mug. "I feel like all of my bones turned into soggy noodles."

Hunter crawled under the blanket next to me. Jenna rolled herself up in Chloe's bed, moving over to make space for Jason. He slid in beside her after taking off the extra blanket and draping it over Chloe's shoulders. "Now what?" I yawned.

"Now we wait for Chloe to be brilliant," Jenna yawned back.

"Wake me up when the genius hits," I murmured. My eyes were closing when my phone vibrated in the pocket of the bathrobe. There was a text from Solange. "*Are you awake?*"

It was so great to get a text from her, just like regular best friends, that I smiled at it goofily for a moment. "Oh God," Chloe muttered. "You got something from Nicholas. I know a dorky Drake grin when I see one."

"No, not Nicholas," I said. "*Talk soon*," I texted Solange back at the same time.

"Lend me your phone?" Hunter murmured. "Mine's all the way over there on my desk." It did look like miles away. I passed her my phone. She dialed slowly, as if her fingers tingled as painfully as mine did. Defrosting hurt more than the actual freezing. "Kieran, did I wake you up?" She yawned so widely she had to repeat herself. "Know anything about this Dawn person? Besides what Nicholas told Lucy?" She shook her head when we all looked at her, waiting for an answer. "Chloe's doing her mojo. If she breaks the code can you crack some of your uncle's files? Thanks."

I took the phone back from her before she could hang up. "Call Solange, dumbass."

Kieran groaned. "One crisis not enough for you, Hamilton?"

"Call her," I repeated before hanging up.

"Dawn must be a Huntsman," Jenna said, her eyes closed. "Or really old-school League."

"And it sounds like she's recruiting," Hunter agreed.

"Is that a bad thing?" Chloe asked, still hunched at her desk. She'd broken out a bag of jelly beans and was munching through them mechanically. "I mean, don't we need the extra help?"

"I guess it depends what she's recruiting them for," Hunter said.

"Evil," I replied promptly.

"You can't know that."

"You didn't see what she did to Nicholas," I returned darkly. My tone was hard enough to crack stones. I remembered every scar, every bruise and every tear in his shirt. Most of all, I remembered that stark wild look in his eyes when he'd stumbled into the clearing where Solange had me pinned.

Chloe winced. "Sorry, I forgot about that part."

"She's torturing vampires and humans," I reminded her. "And she hurt my boyfriend. So she gets a big, fat, karmic, steel-toe boot up the ass."

"Agreed," Hunter said quietly. I knew she was thinking about Quinn. It could just as easily have been him who'd been abducted and tortured.

Even as angry as I was, the toll of the last few nights and the warmth finally spreading through my body again lulled me to sleep before I'd finished uttering death threats. I wasn't sure how long I was out before Chloe slapped her keyboard loudly. "Stupid thing!"

I jumped, startled awake. Hunter and I were snuggled up together and Jenna was sprawled comfortably on Chloe's bed. Jason had somehow ended up on the floor, but judging by his snoring it didn't seem to bother him. Until Chloe rolled away from her desk, and her chair yanked out his hair. He jerked up but his hair was caught and he was stuck there, swearing. "Damn it, Chloe. Are you trying to crack a code or my head?"

She winced down at him. "Sorry." She rolled her chair carefully away.

He sat up rubbing his head. She handed him a bag of chocolate macaroons from her desk drawer as a peace offering. He ate a handful, still bleary-eyed and rubbing his temple.

Hunter poked her head up. "Chloe, go to bed. It's almost four in the morning. You can try again later."

Chloe just reached for another energy drink.

Jason groaned. "Great. Like you need more caffeine." He pushed to his feet. "I'm going to my own room before you run over something I might actually need one day."

Chloe was already chugging the drink and trying to eye her computer balefully at the same time when it beeped at her. She hit a few keys and then lowered the empty can, wincing.

"The *Gazette* is running another headline about the Dracula Killer," she said. "A college guy was found dead and drained of blood outside the library."

"Another one?" I frowned. "But Solange is okay now," I repeated. "She didn't do this."

"Not to mention that vampires generally clean up after

themselves," Hunter pointed out. "Something doesn't add up with all these missing people, just like Theo said. It can't just be vampires feeding."

"It has to be Dawn," I told her. "She's obviously framing vampires."

"That's a pretty brutal way to do it. If she's pro-human, then why kill so many of us?"

"Vampires make a convenient scapegoat. But why frame Solange at a high school field party of all places?" I wondered.

"Everyone's after Solange, you know that. She's an even more convenient scapegoat."

"This sucks." I scowled.

Hunter scowled back. "And who the hell is this Dawn anyway?"

"Can you guys grumble somewhere else?" Chloe muttered. "It's distracting."

Hunter burrowed back under the blankets, frowning thoughtfully. Jenna was still asleep somewhere under a pile of Chloe's pillows. Jason and I parted ways on the landing to the second floor. Instead of going back to my room, I went to the bathroom and hid in one of the stalls to call Solange back. She answered on the first ring. "I think I'll be successfully cured of any martyr tendencies by the end of the week," she said drily.

"That well, huh?"

"Mom beat up a warrior with muscles the size of my head and it's been politics and condescension ever since."

"Yawn."

"Yeah, it alternates between boring and terrifying. I spend most of my time apologizing and then not being allowed to talk as every vampire within a ten-mile radius gives a long speech about honor and traditions and basically hacking people up."

"Fun."

"You should have seen Dad's face when the one guy went on about reintroducing human hunts and feeding zoos."

"Dude."

"I know, right?"

"Did you take down that stupid post?" I asked, remembering the feel of the iron chains on my wrists. "'Cause I gotta tell you, that thing's not helping our cause." I could just imagine what Jody would do if she ever found out.

"It was the first thing I did," she promised. "Once they stopped trying to kill me. What about you?"

"I went for a swim."

"In November?"

"Wasn't my idea." I shut the lid on the toilet and sat down, leaning against the stall. "We're looking into League secrets and trying to find out more about this Dawn person."

The silence on the other end of the line was colder than the pond water. "Yeah," Solange finally said. "I want a piece of her."

"We'll share," I returned. "And give the rest to your mom. Kinda like the remaining pieces of Constantine. What happened to him anyway? Did your mom tie his entrails into a pretty bow?"

"He took off during the trial by combat," she replied quietly. "Even his guards don't know where he is. They're just milling about all nervous and confused."

"Pardon me if I don't exactly feel sorry for them."

"I really thought he was my friend," she said in a small voice.

"He should be so lucky," I said.

"Tomorrow I have to be tested by Kala in front of everyone to prove I'm me again."

"You should be grateful it's not my mom. She'd make you chant naked out in the backyard under the full moon."

"I'd deserve it. Not that most of them believe I was possessed in the first place. Especially since Constantine's gone and can't admit to anything."

"He'd just lie anyway."

"Not if *my* mom was there."

We both thought about that for a moment then shivered. "I should warn you," I added. "The papers are still printing stories about the murders and disappearances. There were two more tonight."

"You know I had nothing to do with those, right?" I could tell she was pacing at vampire speed from the soft whooshing sound in the background. "Damn it, everyone's going to think it was me. I have to find out who's doing this."

"We will," I assured her. "Somehow."

"Do you think . . ." She trailed off uncertainly.

"What?" I pressed.

"Never mind."

"Like that's going to happen." Especially since I had a feeling I knew what this was about. "Spit it out, Sol."

"Well," she continued reluctantly. "Do you think Kieran thinks I did it?"

"No, of course not. But speaking of which, has he called you yet?" I demanded.

"No."

"Have you called him?"

"No."

"Are you both doing this on purpose to make me nuts?"

"Oh right, like that's our fault," she scoffed. "You were born that way. Too much tofu."

I smiled. "I missed you, fangface."

"Me too."

"Enough to call Kieran?"

"You're obsessed."

"I also happen to be right," I pointed out. "You can't just leave it like this."

"Let me just get through tomorrow night." She paused. "Lucy, I'm going to try to formally abdicate."

"Can you do that?"

"I don't know," she admitted. "I don't think anyone ever has. But I'm going to change a few things first."

"Like what?" I asked. "And, cool."

"I want to set up some sort of council so there's no need for kings or queens."

"Dismantling the monarchy." I grinned. "You little rebel. It's always the quiet ones."

"I just don't think one person should represent all these different tribes, especially not with new ones like the Na-Foir coming out of hiding. And I definitely don't think that someone should be me."

She sounded disgusted. "I mean, I'm sixteen. Why does no one seem to notice that? Especially since they're all like three hundred or whatever. This whole system is stupid."

"You really mean it," I realized. I hadn't heard her sound so animated since she'd gotten a new kiln.

"I've had a lot of time to think," she said drily. Her voice changed. "And London died because everyone's first reaction is to get all stabby."

"Preaching to the converted," I agreed. "I mean, that sedative that your uncle used to knock you out? Why the hell aren't we using that? Maybe not on *Hel-Blar*," I amended. "But at least when we don't know anything about the person we're fighting."

"Exactly!" she nearly shouted. "God, I wish you could come with me to this council."

"You'll be great," I said firmly. "You'll kick vampire ass, I'll kick Helios-Ra ass and then we'll celebrate with hot fudge sundaes."

"Deal."

CHAPTER 28

Solange

Friday night

Kala's ritual testing wasn't as awful as I'd thought it would be.

All I had to do was stand in the center of nearly a hundred vampires while Kala circled around me with her dog-tooth rattle and her clinking amulets. Isabeau followed behind her, carrying an abalone shell and a hawk feather, wafting sage smoke over us. Four other Hounds stood in each direction, each with a dog at their feet, and each playing a drum.

The other vampires shifted restlessly. They were fascinated by the reclusive Hounds but they didn't trust them enough to truly enjoy the spectacle of a rare magical ritual. Mom and Dad, my uncle, my aunt, and all of my brothers stood together in a half-moon shape. Lucy's cousin Christabel stood uncertainly with Saga and Aidan, who had *Hel-Blar* on leashes, their mushroom stench adding to the miasma of anger and fright. Connor stood with our family, but his eyes never left Christabel. I'd even invited Madame Veronique and her handmaidens so she could stop trying to kill me, assuming I was Viola. I knew Viola had crossed into cruelty and evil, had trapped me and used me, but part of me couldn't help feel a little sorry for her. How different would her life had been if she'd known who she was? If she'd had my family instead of Madame Veronique?

The representatives of the Raktapa Council sat at a long table. The other vampires who still supported Viola, without even knowing it was her they supported, had taken to leading their humans on leashes like pets after I had the post demolished. Constantine's men stayed close to them, eyeing me hatefully. Chandramaa stood inside the circle and were stationed on the path. In the center, to my left was a small table holding the royal crown.

There was a nefarious kind of tension clinging to everyone and everything. It hadn't been here at the start of the Blood Moon but now fear hung in the air, sour and fetid. Too many had lost loved ones to hunters, and too many eyes were searching for blood-drinking murderers. The secure haven of the encampment didn't feel particularly secure anymore.

Still, the ritual itself was easier than the one in the caves where Kala had shown me the prophecy being spoken.

Until she came at me with a sharpened dog bone, like a cross between a giant knitting needle and a stake.

I had to force myself to stand utterly still, even as my every nerve ending screeched for me to fight back, to run, to dodge, *anything*. Since she wasn't instantly turned to dust on the tip of a Chandramaa arrow, the ritual obviously had been approved beforehand. I'd ordered them to let Kala do what she had to, but that was when I'd thought the worst thing I might have to do was chant in my underwear. Mom took a step forward.

Kala jabbed the pointed tip into each of my wrists, and once over my heart. The cuts were shallow but they bled quickly and swiftly. The *Hel-Blar* clacked their jaws together and howled so viciously, Aidan had to struggle to keep them contained. Kala ignored them all, the screeching, the muttering, the hissing. She only cared about the blood currently dripping into the snow.

She touched her fingertip to the rivulet trickling from my heart and smeared the blood over her forehead, then mine. Isabeau held a small bowl carved from stone under my wrists until my blood gathered there like wine. She passed it to Kala who drank from it, taking a small ritual sip. There was no hunger to it, her fangs were always extended but they didn't look any sharper or longer than usual. She was deep in her magical trance, seeing things the rest of us couldn't see. The drumming got louder, faster, like a thousand humming bees. It made me feel slightly disoriented.

When Kala lifted her head from the bowl, the whites of her eyes were red. The drumming stopped abruptly, as one. No one moved, no one spoke. Even the wind seemed to be holding its breath. Kala didn't move but it was obvious she was somewhere else. Less obvious to the others perhaps, that she was prowling through my inner landscape. I could feel her prying open doors and rusted locks, peering under the bed for monsters. It was the strangest feeling and not altogether pleasant. My teeth chattered.

"Spirit," Kala whispered in a creepy singsong voice. It was all wrong, like a doll in a frilly pink dress holding a butcher knife. "Spirit."

Wounds that still ached, throbbed inside my head. I was being scraped raw.

"*Viola*," Kala snapped. "Show yourself."

I shivered all over, knees buckling. I landed in the bloody snow. But there was no voice, no sense of vertigo or disconnection.

"The last test," Kala announced.

I looked up at the sound of weeping.

Constantine.

I blinked, confused. It took a moment to realize the weeping wasn't inside my head. A pack of the Hounds's dogs milled about his ankles, snapping and growling to get him moving. There were bloody bite marks on his calves. His hair stood on end and his eyes were bloodshot and red. He was weeping loudly, brokenly. He looked nothing like the charming, witty vampire who had saved my life from the Furies and kissed me in the Bower. He looked, quite frankly, insane.

He stumbled, distracted by the sight of Madame Veronique. "You." He seethed, fury and pain contorting his usually handsome features. His fangs gleamed. "You did this," he shouted, tripping over the dogs as he tried to get to her.

Madame Veronique didn't react, she didn't even blink. She sat like a medieval ice statue in a velvet dress. Her handmaidens stepped protectively in front of her, but it was Isabeau who knocked him off his feet before he reached her and before the Chandramaa could attack.

"You may die on your own time," she said briskly, her accent sharp. "*After* the testing." She yanked him to his feet by the back of his collar and the dogs raced back in, hackles rising. Their teeth looked every bit as dangerous as a vampire's fangs.

I shrank back as the dogs brought him closer to me, remembering that it was his presence that had called Viola out, had tethered her inside my body. Constantine fell to his knees in front of me, grabbing at my arms. "Viola?" he asked with such fractured hope in his violet eyes that it was painful to look at him. "Viola, come back to me."

And then he kissed me.

A kiss to tell the truth from a lie.

I tensed, listening so intently for Viola's whisper that I could hear the scuttling of moles in the earth beneath us. But nothing else. I sagged with relief even as Constantine shook me frantically. "No!" He sobbed. "No!"

"He's no threat." Kala dismissed him. "He's broken inside."

I pulled sharply out of his hold and rose slowly to my feet. He knelt, weeping and gnashing his teeth. I'd never seen an ancient vampire having a breakdown before. It wasn't pretty. Blood seeped from his eyes and his chewed lips. I just stared at him, unable to feel anything but pity. I couldn't even muster enough hatred to hit him again, as I'd done that day under the tree bridges, even as he tried to hold on to my feet so I wouldn't move away.

The same couldn't be said for my family. My mom snarled, but it was my dad who hauled off and punched Constantine in the throat. "Come near my daughter again and I'll kill you," he said calmly, almost politely, as he loomed over him. "Slowly."

Kala stepped back, blinking blood from her eyes. "The spirit has been banished, all because this girl," she pointed at me, "was strong enough to hold her ground when all around her were blind to the battle. This other spirit can do you no harm," she told the council and the others. Her voice didn't get louder but it seemed to reach everywhere, snaking between bodies to the very furthest corners of the camp. "The prophecy has been fulfilled," she added. "And is no longer any concern of yours."

My dad seemed to deflate briefly with relief. Madame Veronique's posture got stiffer. Voices slammed into one another. Kala walked out of the circle to sit on a pile of pelts, dogs curled at her feet. Isabeau stood next to her, at attention. Constantine crawled away. I couldn't even look at him.

Everyone else started to talk at once. My family surrounded me but they were all shouting between themselves as well. The delegates from visiting tribes were demanding council.

"I have something to say." I tried to be heard over the cacophony but it was next to impossible. I went on my tiptoes and tried to catch the eye of one of the Raktapa representatives but they were too busy talking among themselves.

"I have something to say!" I tried again but with no greater success. Mom would have been confident and terrifying; it was just her way. Dad's way would be to find some sort of common ground to negotiate with. I only had my own way, whatever that might be. I'd have to rely on logic and common sense, and appeal to our united goal, which was, essentially, the desire to be left alone. That was something I understood on a level my parents didn't truly appreciate.

But if they were going to listen to me, I'd have to make them hear me first.

My voice was just one of many, no matter how loudly I shouted. So I'd stop shouting.

I was the quiet one anyway, as Lucy had teased me on the phone. So I'd use it to my advantage. I surreptitiously reached over and took the crown. Between Viola and the prophecy, it was a symbol everyone seemed to be obsessed with. And again, this time I'd make it work *for* me instead of against me.

I slipped through the jostling crowd, easing between arguments and apologies, bloodslaves and brothers. I stopped at the foot of the chopped down tree post. There were still chains curled at its base, still bloodstains in the dirt. I scaled the post, splinters breaking off under my boots. When I reached the top, I pulled myself up so I was standing. I didn't do anything else, I just stood there, waiting silently and patiently, with bats circling over me.

It was several minutes before anyone noticed me. Sebastian was first, then the vampires around the post, then Nicholas, then Duncan. Slowly the conversations around me faltered, the silence spreading. The bats dipped down between the few still arguing, startling them apart.

Faces looked up at me and I had to swallow on a dry throat. "I have a proposition to make." My voice trembled slightly. I straightened my shoulders to compensate.

"I'm not wise enough to be your queen," I said. "But I'm wise enough to know it. I'm also wise enough to know that this system is hopelessly outdated and only sets us against one another. We can't keep killing one another as if it's the only way to sort out our differences. My cousin died for me, for this stupid prophecy, and the war over the crown. And I won't let her death be in vain. Humans have trials and laws and jails, so why can't we?" Dad looked so proud I thought he was going to start weeping right then and there. "If we're going to gather from all over the world and sit at a council table, then we need to make changes. We all need to make treaties with the Helios-Ra, not just the local Violet Hill families." Someone spat in the snow. I eyed her calmly. "The League is changing, just like we are. This isn't the twelfth century." I looked coldly at Madame Veronique. "And we need to stop acting as if it is."

I held up the crown. "This is just an object," I insisted. "It's not worth dying for. But if you all really want it so desperately, then take it." I snapped off one of the rubies. Someone gasped. I jumped off the post and walked toward Kala. "The Hounds answer to themselves." I handed her the ruby. The whispers swelled angrily. I snapped off another one and turned to Saga. "The Na-Foir answer to themselves." She grinned cockily, snatching the ruby out of the air. The last ruby I placed on the table in front of the Raktapa Council. "The ancient families answer to themselves." I tossed the seed pearls that dangled on what was left of the crown, scattering them like tiny white mistletoe berries.

"And we all answer to one another." My father had said those words enough times that they came naturally. "I want to abdicate the throne." The hissing and shouting was so loud I flinched. Dad caught my eye and leaned his head ever so subtly in Mom's direction. "But for the time being, I name Helena Drake as my Regent." I smiled at Dad. "And Liam Drake as co-Regent." Mom would be able to keep order in the chaos but Dad was the one who'd be able to make this plan work. He could settle disputes and soothe tempers. If he could handle Mom, he could handle vengeful vampires.

"And the rest of us?" a man in a plaid jacket asked. "Who represents us?"

I hadn't considered that. I nibbled on my lower lip, fangs stinging as they poked through my skin. I wasn't strictly Raktapa, because I wasn't like the other Drakes. I wasn't Hound or Na-Foir. I thought of Marigold and the others of the Bower. I was outside the circle, just like the solitary vampires who chose not to ally themselves. "I will," I offered. "Until you choose your own representative, I'll stand for the tribeless. If you'll have me." Dad really did cry then, just one tear, which he brushed hastily away before anyone could see him.

"Nicely done," Nicholas said hours later to me as I stepped out of the main pavilion. Apparently when you took down the monarchy, you then had to sit and listen to speeches for hours, until your butt went numb.

"I just couldn't let London die for nothing, and then have it happen all over again the next time some old woman gets stoned on weird mushroom tea." I rubbed my face wearily. "But do you think it will work?" I asked, doubtfully. "We're not exactly known for our laid-back nature. I mean, Aunt Hyacinth is still holding a grudge against that boy who waved a pistol at Queen Victoria's carriage. And that was in 1872."

"It's worth a try," he replied. "Some of the vampires have already packed up and left in a snit. But just as many are making toasts to a new era."

"I can see that." I watched one vampire lean drunkenly on another. While we'd been talking and talking and talking, everyone else had been drinking. We turned and wandered down the path. A group of vampires gathered outside one of the tents, whispering and staring.

"One thing hasn't changed," I muttered. "I'm going to start my own circus and be the main attraction." I glanced at Nicholas. "Want to get out of here for a while?" I'd never been comfortable in crowds and whatever Nicholas had been through on Dawn's orders had made him nearly as solitary as Duncan. I wanted to kill her all over again. My fangs poked into my lower lip drawing blood. One of the vampires by the tent pointed at me.

Nicholas just raised his eyebrows. "You're so hungry you're trying to eat your own face?"

I elbowed him. "Some people are scared of me, you know. Like that guy over there." The guy in question paled when I looked his way and tried to hide behind a banner half his size.

Nicholas snorted. "Ten points if you can make him hide behind that creepy little girl over there." It was such normal banter, tears sprung to my eyes. Nicholas was instantly horrified. "What? What'd I do?"

"You should hate me." I sniffled. "I made you drink from Lucy. I'm so sorry, Nic."

"Lucy called me a drama queen when I was sorry about that too."

I choked out a laugh. "Seriously?"

"Yeah." He quirked a smile. "So stop being so soggy."

I swallowed. "Brothers are so sentimental." My smile was watery. And actually, they totally were. They just thought no one knew it.

"So where are we going?" he asked as the snow began to fall very softly around us, so softly it was barely there at all.

"I don't know," I admitted as we passed between the trees and cut through the field of dirt bikes. "Just random hunting, I guess. No speech in the world is going to avert hunter-vampire war if we don't stop these killings. So you know, clear my name, stop some murders, avenge my brother. The usual."

Nicholas stopped me with a hand on my arm. His face was serious, gray eyes so pale they were like frozen moonlight. "Don't go avenging me, Sol. I'm not dead."

"They *tortured* you."

"I mean it, Sol. This has to stop somewhere. You said so yourself."

I shrugged out of his grasp. "You could have died. You nearly did."

"So did you," he reminded me lightly. "Quinn would say the

reason everyone's always trying to kill us Drakes is because we're so pretty." He passed me a stake. "Now are we going to hunt, or what?"

I refused the stake, showing him the tranquilizer gun I'd gotten off Uncle Geoffrey before leaving the farm. "Let's try something new."

"Okay, but I'm not having a chat with a rabid *Hel-Blar*."

"Agreed."

Walking through the quiet forest was soothing. The silhouettes of the trees gleamed with ice, the leaves and twigs underfoot bristled with frost. There were rabbit prints and gouges on a tree from where a deer had rubbed its antlers. When we crossed the river, it looked as if it were filled with bits of broken mirrors. We found traces of old blood and footprints, but nothing terribly useful. We wandered aimlessly until I led us to the place I felt safe, without even realizing it. The tree where Kieran and I had slipped underground into the tunnels to escape Hope's rogue Helios-Ra unit. We'd spent the day in a safe house and he'd stayed with me, watching over me when I was at my weakest.

The tree was just as mossy, spreading out its branches in a wide circle, dripping delicate and deadly icicles. The points looked as sharp as stakes. The roots made a complicated nest, like the Celtic knot work patterns on some of Bruno's tattoos. Nicholas searched the path for strange scents or any other kind of clues, just as we'd been doing all night. I couldn't help myself, I crouched down to slide my hands in the tiny caves the roots created. I felt around for some kind of note or letter, just as he'd mentioned that night on his front porch. It felt like a lifetime ago.

I reached deeper into the roots. The wind rattled the frosted branches overhead, icicles tinkling like wind chimes. I smelled snow and pine and cold. I touched dirt, stones, a startled beetle. Nothing else.

It was empty.

Disappointment was a palpable burn in my belly. I sat back on my heels and chided myself for being an idiot. What had I been expecting? A love letter? Of course Kieran hadn't left me a message. I'd bitten him on the neck and drunk his blood. I'd kissed Constantine. I'd generally behaved like an ass.

And Lucy wondered why I was too embarrassed to phone him.

I pushed to my feet, swallowing hard against the lump growing in my throat. Ex-vampire queens probably shouldn't cry over their ex-boyfriend's perfectly reasonable decision to have nothing to do with them. A tear slipped through anyway, scalding hot on my cold cheek. I hurried to wipe it off before Nicholas could see me. The crack of a twig underfoot and the familiar mixture of mint and cedar had me spinning around. I knew that scent.

Kieran.

He was standing right there behind me, on the edge of the roots. I had no idea how long he'd been there. The wind had covered his scent and my own misery had muffled the sound of his heartbeat. He was perfectly still, wearing a dark gray fisherman's sweater and his usual black cargos. His dark hair was ruffled by the wind and there was the faintest scrape of stubble on his jaw. I couldn't look away, even as scared as I was to see what might be reflected in his black eyes. I expected anger, disgust, even fear. But he only looked as startled as I felt, as if he wasn't even sure I was real.

Nicholas came around the tree and we still hadn't moved.

"Kieran." He was the first to speak, breaking the silence that was starting to feel like a spell, weaving around us. Kieran and I might have stood there staring at each other for the rest of the night otherwise. If he didn't speak, I couldn't hear the recrimination in his voice. I straightened my spine, wanting to hear whatever he had to say. I owed him that much, at least.

"Hey, man," Nicholas continued, as if he wasn't surrounded by frozen mimes. "It's good to see you."

Kieran tore his gaze from mine as if it was physically painful. "Nicholas." They didn't shake hands but clasped forearms as usual, like fellow warriors.

"Well, I guess it's safe to leave you here for a bit," Nicholas said. He eyed Kieran's friends, who were equally frozen behind him. "I'm going to go for a walk." He tossed me a grin before loping away and becoming just another shadow in the forest.

What exactly did you say to the boy you'd kissed senseless and then nearly killed?

I licked my lips. "Hi."

Oh my god, I really *was* an idiot.

Kieran blinked. A ghost of a smile nearly tugged at the side of his mouth. "Hi."

We stared at each other for another interminable moment, longer than any history exam Aunt Hyacinth had ever set me. I squirmed. He slipped on a pair of nose plugs.

"I'm learning to control the pheromones," I said quietly. He didn't take them off.

But he also didn't look away, even as he spoke to his friends. "Go away, guys."

I could hear them leaving, one of them whispering, "That's her? She's so tiny."

And then it was just Kieran and me alone in the woods.

I'd literally never felt so awkward in my entire life.

"Are you okay?" we both blurted out at the same time.

"I didn't kill those people," I added miserably. "The ones in the paper. I promise. Though I don't know why you'd believe me."

"I believe you," he said quietly. "You're as much of a victim of Viola as the rest of us. More so."

"But I . . ." I motioned vaguely to his neck. There was a scar from where my incisors had ripped through his skin, just barely visible above the neck of his sweater and the collar of his coat. "I'm so sorry."

"It's okay," he said. I could tell he meant it and it nearly undid me.

"I could have killed you. You should hate me."

"I could never hate you," he said quietly. "And I know what it feels like. After my dad died and I was on a vendetta, I did some things I'm not proud of."

"Did you throw your own brother into a tent post and threaten to snap your best friend's neck?"

"Who'd you throw?"

"Duncan."

He whistled, looking briefly impressed. "Bet he loved that."

I wrinkled my nose. "He still looks at me like I might do it again."

"He'll get over it."

"I'm bad luck, Kieran. Without me and that stupid prophecy, so many people would be better off. London would still be alive."

"Without you," Kieran pointed out, "Logan wouldn't have met Isabeau, Hunter wouldn't have met Quinn, and Connor wouldn't have met Christabel. Did you ever think of that?" He paused. "And we wouldn't have met either."

"But I drank from you. And you've been attacked too many times because of me." I wasn't sure why I was arguing. But I had to make him understand.

"It was worth it."

"How can you say that?" I gaped at him even as he stepped closer, bridging the distance between us.

"Because it's the truth," he replied hoarsely, his thumb trailing softly over my jawline. "You're worth it, Solange. All of it."

I bit down on the inside of my cheek to stop my lower lip from wobbling embarrassingly. Of all the things I'd ever imagined him saying to me, that had never even made the list. The sob trapped in my chest morphed into a laugh. But I couldn't let it out. Not quite yet. "How can you still be so nice to me?" This was the part I'd been dreading, the reason I'd avoided him. Hearing him say that final good-bye. I clenched my fists. "Your friends and family, the entire League; they'll hate me even more now—and you if . . . if we . . . if we stay together."

"To hell with them," he said roughly.

"I know why I want to be with you," I said. "You're strong and honest and forgiving. But how can you still want to be with me?" I whispered. "When I'm like this?" I lifted my wrists showing him the blue veins under pale skin, knowing my triple set of fangs were extended, my irises ringed with red.

He touched my wrists, lightly stroking the veins, moving up my arms to dig his fingers in my hair and tilt my head back so I'd look at him directly instead of at my feet. "You were brave and beautiful when I first met you as a human. You're still brave and beautiful, Solange. That hasn't changed." He tugged me a little closer. "Besides, Hart is still negotiating with your dad. They still want peace and if anyone can pull it off, especially now, it's those two. And we'll help," he added. "All of us."

I desperately wanted him to be right, already feeling the ice that had clawed at my insides melting away. "Kieran, you've already lost your dad. I can't ask you to lose everyone else that you love."

"Then don't ask me to lose you too, Solange."

CHAPTER 29

Hunter

Saturday night

"Grandpa!" I knocked on the door. "I know you're in there!"

I tried to peer through the peephole even though I knew it was equipped with several layers of safety mechanisms. I also knew the house and lawns were sprayed down with holy water on a daily basis. Grandpa had a barrel of it out in the backyard, attached to a garden hose. He'd made me wash my hair with it until I left for the academy.

I kept pounding on the door. The UV bulbs in the security lights over the porch were so intense I could get a tan standing here, even though it was just past twilight. I gave up before my nose could get sunburned and shoved my key into the lock.

It didn't fit.

My own grandfather had changed the locks on me.

My stomach dropped as if I were suddenly hollow inside. I knew he was still angry but we were the only family left to each other. He'd always been there for me. He'd been the one to show me how to use my first crossbow. He'd given me my own stake, which he'd whittled himself. He'd even learned to braid my hair, when I was seven years old and pitched a fit when he suggested I cut it short.

And now he'd locked me out.

I could feel dismal about it and stand here trying not to cry, or I could feel dismal about it and pick the damn lock on principle.

No contest.

"This isn't over, old man," I said to the security camera fitted into the eaves of the porch roof. I was glad I'd brought my full hunter's kit with me, just in case. I'd never be able to break the door down since it was outfitted with so many locks, bars, and booby traps. I'd wondered if he might arm them out of spite, but I didn't think he'd go so far as to call a locksmith.

From the outside, the house looked like any other bungalow on the street, set back against the edge of the woods. The driveway was interlocking brick, the hedges were trimmed neatly, and the garbage was taken out every Wednesday morning at 7:00 a.m. exactly. No one saw the cameras or the sensors, and no one realized the decorative bars on the windows were actually sturdy military-strength steel.

The biggest problem was making sure the neighbors didn't call the police before recognizing me—especially Mrs. Gormley, who had a crush on Grandpa and spied on him through her blinds. She wore sweaters that looked like doilies, hung curtains that looked like doilies, and brought over casseroles draped in doilies. Grandpa had actually incorporated her into his security plans. So much so, that the side and back doors had way more locking mechanisms since they weren't being guarded by the Doily Dragon.

It took me a few minutes to defeat the first lock—only three more to go. By the time I was done, my fingers were cramping and my ears hurt from straining to listen to the soft snick of the tumblers. I straightened and stepped inside.

I hadn't been home since the school year started, since Grandpa had caught me with Quinn, to be precise. He'd filed formal complaints against the academy and Bellwood in particular, for letting vampires onto campus grounds. And he'd refused to speak to me ever since I called him from the hospital after being poisoned by Ms. Dailey—a *teacher*, not a vampire, something that I pointed out to him repeatedly.

And yet he claimed *I* was the one who was as stubborn as six mules.

"Grandpa!" He wasn't in the living room, watching me on the security screens. As I went down the hall, premonition crawled on trembling mouse feet over the back of my neck. The house looked the same. I hadn't expected it to change; it was just that everything else in my life had undergone such a drastic transformation, it was almost shocking to see the same rugs, the same photos on the wall, the same lumpy clay dinosaur I'd made Grandpa for Christmas one year. The plants in the window were still thriving—I was the one they curled up and died around. Grandpa had a green thumb and grew his own tomatoes every year. They were so big the neighborhood kids liked to climb over the fence to steal them for food fights.

I froze in the doorway to the kitchen. "Grandpa?"

He was slumped at the pine table beside a half-empty bottle of whiskey. The fumes hung on the air. There was gray stubble on his cheeks and his eyes were bleary and bloodshot when he blinked at me. "Kitten?"

I'd never seen him like this before—not after my parents died, not when the League forced him to retire him because of his arthritis, not even when he'd caught me kissing a vampire. I swallowed, feeling all of six years old. I didn't know what to do. He was supposed to be shouting at me and smashing things, not looking old and uncharacteristically frail. I crouched beside him.

"Grandpa, what are you doing?"

He touched my hair with a massive, trembling hand. I could see the scars on his arms from his numerous battles. "Such a pretty girl," he mumbled. "And always so smart. I miss you."

"I miss you too, Grandpa." I stood up to steady him when he started to list to the side, like a giant snowman melting on the first warm day. "I'm going to make you some coffee, okay?"

"Not thirsty."

"Too bad," I said, crossing over to fill the coffee pot with water. I doubled back to snatch the bottle out of his hand when he reached for it. "How long have you been like this?"

He shrugged one shoulder petulantly. "A while."

"Why?"

"'Cause." He rubbed his face so thoroughly he nearly pulled his lip up over his nose. "My granddaughter is defiling the Wild family name."

I turned to spear him with a look, even though he probably wouldn't remember I'd even been here. "Oh, but being drunk and pouty is an honor?"

"Don't be smart."

"Then don't be stupid." He cared about blood as much as any vampire I'd ever met. Family lineage was as vital to him as feeding was to Quinn. They were more alike than they knew or would have liked. I took a deep breath. "Grandpa, did something else happen? Quinn and I have been together for nearly two months now, it's not exactly breaking news."

"Don't say his name in this house," he snapped. "He's a monster."

"He's not," I said evenly, scooping the coffee grounds into the filter with more force than was strictly necessary.

"Then let me see your neck, little girl."

I stalked over to him, my temper fraying. I showed him my neck and my wrists for good measure. "Happy now?" I snapped. "Give me a little credit, Grandpa."

"How'm I supposed to do that? Whole world's turned upside down. Kieran dropped out to avenge his father and ended up dating a vampire princess, for Christ's sake. One who killed a girl at a field party, just last week."

I shook my head. "You don't know that. Her family says she was framed." In fact, Lucy had been the one to find both the victim and the royal medallion that pointed to Solange.

"Well, of course they do," he huffed. "What's the matter with you, girl? You're supposed to be my little hunter. Now look at you. Have you been reading those vampire romance books?"

"I'm still a hunter," I reminded him, choosing to ignore that last bit. "And I know things are changing, Grandpa. But isn't that a good thing? Isn't it better that we don't have to fight our battles on so many fronts now?"

"No," he slurred. "It's not."

"Why not?" I was dangerously close to yelling and I'd never yelled at him in my whole life.

"Don't you see?" he choked out. "If I accept all vampires aren't monsters, then I have to admit I might have killed innocent folk. Some of them barely older than you. What does that make *me*?" his voice broke. "I'll tell you. One of the monsters." He drained the whiskey out of the bottom of his glass—I'd forgotten to remove it with the bottle. "All I ever wanted was to keep you safe."

I stared at him, stunned. The last thing I'd expected out of my grandfather was existential angst and an identity crisis. "Oh, Grandpa."

He just rested his head on his arm and started to snore.

I don't know how long I stood there, feeling sad and sorry. I couldn't pity him when he was awake, drunk or sober. I could only pity him now, when it wouldn't hurt what was left of his pride. I got a blanket from the couch and tucked it around his shoulders and when I'd made him as comfortable as I could, I sat at his desk and called Chloe. "I'm in."

It was probably wrong to take advantage of my grandfather's drunken stupor, but he was exactly the kind of disenchanted Helios-Ra hunter I would target if I was Dawn. I didn't think for one second that he'd know about her side deal with the human victims but he wouldn't have to. All that would matter to him was that the objective was simple and familiar: kill vampires. All of them. And someone like Dawn would know that.

Feeling slightly ill, I sat in front of his computer and tried to concentrate on what Chloe was telling me to do. It was simple enough to crack his codes, they were all related either to my birthday or my grade point average. He never bothered with computer security the way he did with physical safety. Any seriously tricky embedded codes and encryption inside the information I stole, Chloe could deal with. I slipped the data stick she'd given me into the port and downloaded most of Grandpa's in-box and files.

When I was finished, I went back to the kitchen to check on him. If he stayed in that uncomfortable position much longer his back would seize up completely. I set a cup of strong black coffee on the table by his nose, waiting for the scent to wake him up. It never failed.

He opened one eye grumpily. "Did you stake that damn vampire yet?"

"It's considered bad taste to kill your boyfriend, Grandpa," I replied as mildly as I could.

"Bah." He glowered up at me. "He came to the door."

I blinked, shocked. "Quinn came *here?*"

"Wanted me to call you," he grumbled. "As if I don't know what's best for my own granddaughter."

Quinn was clearly crazy. And sweet. It amazed me how sweet he was beneath the smirk. "What did you do?" I asked, half-afraid of the answer.

"I didn't stake him," he replied.

"But did you try?"

"Well, of course I did. I'm a hunter, he's a vampire. One of us has to remember the rules."

Since Quinn had texted me just before dawn, I knew he was safe. He'd conveniently managed to forget to tell me about his little excursion into insanity. "Just drink your coffee," I said, my mind whirling. "I don't want to leave you until I know you won't fall over and break a hip."

Just as I'd planned, he sat straight up, insulted. "I'm strong as an ox, missy."

"And you kind of smell like one," I retorted briskly. "How long have you been sitting here feeling sorry for yourself? Since Quinn dropped by?" I knew if I showed the slightest trace of concern or worry now that he wasn't quite so drunk, he'd act like a wounded bear with a thorn in his paw.

He scowled. "What are you doing here, anyway?"

"I live here," I reminded him. "Despite your little trick with the lock."

He had the grace to redden slightly. "I was mad," he said defensively. "I still am."

"I know." I bent to kiss his cheek. "But you're wrong so you're going to have to get over it."

"You're not welcome here until you come to your senses."

"I know that too," I said, hoisting my knapsack over my shoulder and heading to the front door.

"Where are you going?" he demanded, even though he'd basically just told me to get out.

"I have class," I answered, hiding a smile. "And I'm not cleaning up your mess," I added. "So you'd better get to it before Mrs. Gormley comes over and does it for you."

"That woman will cover the place in doilies," he grumbled.

"Exactly," I said. "And I'll encourage her."

"Hunter," he said as I reached for the handle. He sounded more like himself, gruff and battle-scarred. "You're a good girl," he added quietly. "But you're on the wrong side of this war."

"I'm not fighting a war, Grandpa," I returned, just as quietly. "I'm just trying to survive high school." I glanced over my shoulder. "I'll check the perimeter," I added, hoping to remind him that I was still the same girl he'd raised. I'd been checking the perimeter before leaving the house since I was twelve.

I had to stop on the front stoop and take a deep breath. I waved at Mrs. Gormley when I saw her silhouette cross the window. Her blinds twitched in response. I crossed the lawn to the property line and walked the fence. It was made of whitethorn, like all traditional stakes, and soaked in holy water. There were stakes and daggers set into the post at regular intervals for easy access. He'd added pouches of Hypnos powder since I'd left. I circled around to the back.

There was enough glow cast by the outside sensor lights to see the pale shadow on the edge of the woods. I shot my crossbow without hesitation. Grandpa had made enough enemies among vampires that we never took chances.

Turned out there wasn't quite enough light to notice, until it was too late, that I was shooting my own boyfriend.

And I had really good aim.

Luckily, he had equally good reflexes, not to mention vampire speed.

As my arrow sliced through the cold air toward his heart, he stepped neatly and swiftly out of the way. He turned to the side completely, making himself a smaller target. After the arrow landed harmlessly in the woods, he ran toward me with that mad, charming grin that always made me feel like I should be blushing.

He was about to jump the fence when I reached him.

"Don't touch it," I said, moving to block him from view in case my grandfather happened to glance out the window. Even half-drunk, he'd come out roaring. "It's soaked in holy water."

Quinn's hands recoiled from the fence and he let me nudge him into the privacy of the woods once I'd hopped over it.

"You came to see my grandfather?" I smacked him in the arm. "Do you have a death wish?"

His expression turned serious. "Hunter, do you think I don't see how it kills you that he's shut you out?"

"And you thought getting yourself dusted by my grandpa would help?" I asked incredulously.

"He's an old man," he drawled. "Not exactly a threat."

"He's a decorated vampire hunter. Do you have any idea how many medals he has?"

Quinn looked briefly distracted. "There are Helios-Ra medals?"

"Yes." I poked him in the chest. "So be careful."

His hand closed over mine, cool fingers wrapping around my wrist. I know he could feel my pulse flutter in reaction. He grinned wolfishly.

"What are you doing here?" I asked.

"Solange overthrew the monarchy," he said, sounding as if he couldn't quite believe it. "So we get a few nights off to patrol while they talk treaties and blood debts." He shook his head, longish hair falling into eyes as blue as a summer lake. "Not quite how I'd want to spend my night off, especially since I can think of better ways to pass the time."

He crowded me against a tree, a wicked gleam in his eye. "Chloe told me you were ditching class when I called your room. Hot."

I laughed despite myself, even as he bent his head and stole my breath with a slow, deep kiss. I kissed him back, clutching his shirt and raising up on my tiptoes. His hand splayed across my lower back as the kiss went open-mouthed and desperate. It was always like this between us, like two stars colliding. We were all heat and light.

And then he pulled back abruptly. I immediately reached for the crossbow, now propped against the tree by my leg. "What?" I mouthed silently.

The cloak of the predator settled over him, or else the human-ness he wore like a costume peeled away. I could never quite be sure.

He turned his head but his body stayed right where it was, pressed against mine. I shifted, knowing exactly what he was doing. It was biologically impossible for a Drake not to make themselves into a shield. It didn't matter, I could shoot over his shoulder if I had to.

His pupils dilated, the black edging out that icy mysterious blue. His cheekbones looked like they might cut right through his skin. "*Hel-Blar* coming this way," he murmured. "They're after something." His nostrils flared. His lips lifted off his fangs, now poking out of his gums. "This way," he said sharply, taking me by the hand and pulling me behind him.

We scaled the neighbor's fence instead of my grandfather's and cut between the houses to the road. "He's fine," Quinn said when I paused under one of the windows. "He's in the shower."

Relieved, I followed him to the sidewalk. The streetlights glowed with amber light. A car passed us. I squinted, trying to see what it was Quinn had smelled, besides rotting mushrooms. I had to jog to keep up with him. Several houses down, near the corner, I finally saw what he saw.

A body sprawled at the edge of someone's garden, half-tucked behind a parked car.

My jog turned into a sprint. Quinn got there first, then recoiled. A woman lay half-conscious, blood pouring from her throat. There were raw scrapes and bruises on her wrists. I pulled a bandanna out of my pocket and pressed it against her wound. She swallowed, eyelids fluttering weakly.

"Vamp . . . ire . . . ," she moaned.

"A vampire didn't do that," Quinn disagreed immediately. "There are way too many scents on her."

"She was left on the street of a well-known vampire hunter," I pointed out, thinking of what my grandfather would have done if he'd found her. "That's not a coincidence." I tucked us deeper into the shadows of the hedge. The last thing we needed was for someone to look out their window and call the cops. Or turn vigilante. Thank God, we were out of the range of Mrs. Gormley's binoculars.

"You wait for your unit," he said darkly as I reached for my cell phone. "And I'll go deal with the *Hel-Blar* before they join the party."

When I glanced up, he was already gone.

"Help is coming." I pressed as hard as I could on her neck. "Try to stay with me. Can you tell me what happened?" Her hands twitched. "Did you say a vampire did this to you?"

She moved her head, as if trying to shake it. "Vampires. Humans too," she wheezed, pale as the snow around her. She shivered as shock set in. "Caves." She shivered more violently. I tried to staunch the blood seeping faster through the bandanna. "Sun tattoo."

Sun tattoo.

Helios-Ra agents had sun tattoos.

I felt hot and cold all over, that icy feeling of dread tingling under my skin again.

"Was it Dawn?" I asked. "Someone named Dawn?"

The woman didn't answer me. She'd already passed out. I didn't have time to try to revive her and press her for more details before a dark minivan with a Baby on Board sticker pulled up to the curb. That sticker worked better as subterfuge than anything else the League had previously implemented. No one looked twice as they drove by. The agents left the front door open to block us.

"Status," the man asked, his bald head gleaming under the streetlights.

"Neck wound," I said, getting out of the way. "Not *Hel-Blar*." I couldn't smell anything on her and more importantly, neither had Quinn.

I didn't mention the sun tattoo.

I didn't know who else to trust anymore.

The other agent pulled on hospital gloves before looking at the messy wound under the blood-soaked bandanna. "We need to hurry," she said. They lifted her into the van and made a U-turn without another word.

I watched them drive away and didn't move until Quinn's wild laugh echoed from the woods, startling me out of my thoughts. I darted between the houses, back to the woods, and followed the sounds of fighting. I broke out of a thick clump of trees to the edge of the river, calculating escape routes and trajectory angles. Someone had to. Quinn had clearly never heard of procedure. He was fighting like he always did; all instinct and mayhem.

There were two *Hel-Blar* closing in, with a third on the crest of a hill behind him, the steady hum of the narrow waterfall masking his movements. He was the easiest to take out from my current position. A single arrow turned him into ashes. I only had two left, having wasted one shooting at Quinn. I also had half a dozen stakes, several daggers, and Hypnos secured in my cuff.

Quinn had led them into the river, the frigid water splashing around his knees. I knew why he did it: to cover the scents of battle so we wouldn't attract any more undead visitors. I braced my back against a tree where I couldn't be surprised from behind and lifted my crossbow, another arrow at the ready.

Quinn kicked a *Hel-Blar* so hard in the stomach she flew backward into the waterfall. The other clawed at him, saliva dripping from his sharpened fangs. The female scrambled back to her feet and I took aim but it was impossible to get a clear shot. Quinn and the other *Hel-Blar* were fighting too quickly and unpredictably. I'd have to get in closer.

"Don't you dare!" Quinn shouted when I pushed away from the tree.

I ignored him, of course. It was the only way to deal with outright crazy Drake martyrdom. Lucy taught me that. I crept closer, keeping my footing steady in the icy snow. "Quit hogging the monsters," I shouted back. "I'm ready!"

He pivoted sharply, swearing, and elbowed the *Hel-Blar* nearest to me in the jugular, then the forehead, and lastly, the sternum. He did it in such quick succession there was no defense. The *Hel-Blar* sailed backward, landing with an icy splash at my feet. I staked him quickly, not wanting to waste an arrow. I used my heel to drive the stake through his rib cage and into his heart. He crumbled to ashes, drifting away on the sluggish current. Quinn dispatched the last vampire with an antique stake I was sure he'd stolen off a Helios-Ra agent somewhere along the way.

Silence returned to the snow-dusted forest. Quinn rinsed his hands in the river, running his wet fingers through his hair. "Well, that was fun," he said, flipping his now-damp hair off his face. Adrenaline made his smile even more dangerous than usual. I actually felt seared by it, even several feet away. He caught my eye.

"Wanna make out again?"

CHAPTER 30

Lucy

Sunday night

When I'd told Solange I was going to kick Helios-Ra ass, scrubbing toilets wasn't exactly what I had in mind.

Hunter didn't look any more thrilled than I did, kneeling on the cold tiles with sponges and spray cleaner. Only Chloe looked cheerful, but that was mostly because she was perched on the counter, tapping away on her laptop.

"Hey, this is your detention too," Hunter grumbled. She was wearing bright yellow rubber gloves and a disgruntled expression.

"I'm working." Chloe snapped her bubble gum. "I'm cracking codes so you can crack heads."

"This detention is archaic," I muttered from the back shower stall where I was scrubbing mildew out of the grout. It was just past midnight and we had half an hour to finish this last bathroom before curfew and lights out. We'd finally reached the top floor, after an hour of inhaling bleach fumes. "Not to mention disgusting."

"Hunters tend to hit each other a lot without creative and powerful deterrents," Hunter said, pushing her hair off her face with her elbows.

"All we did was sneak out."

"Yeah, but she was pissed. This is her favorite weapon. And Bellwood says it's as much about teaching us not to kill each other as it is about teaching us how to kill vampires."

"I don't know," I said, moving to the next stall. "This kinda puts me in a murdering mood. Speaking of which," I added when the door swung open and Jody came in for the third time that night. There were several pounds of dirt and melting snow on her boots. She smirked.

"You can't possibly have to pee again," Chloe said. "And this isn't even your floor."

"So?" She shrugged. "Anyway, I'm looking for an earring I dropped."

"You are not," I grumbled.

She opened all the stall doors, making sure to knock as much muddy water off her treads as she went into each one, pretending to look. "I guess it's not here," she said, just before knocking over the bucket. "Oops," she said with a cold, insincere smile as dirty water seeped over the floor.

"All right, that's it," Hunter snapped, jumping up so she wouldn't get soaked. "I've had it. Jody, I'm the floor monitor for this section and you're not allowed up here anymore." She narrowed her eyes while I grinned behind her. Chloe caught my eye and also grinned. It was so rare that Hunter lost her temper. I kind of wished we had popcorn for the show. "You're being childish and a bully, two things I know Bellwood disapproves of."

"And you're a traitor, Wild."

"I'm getting tired of that accusation," she said mildly. "Especially from a cheater."

Jody scowled. "What are you talking about?"

"I know you cheated on your kickboxing demonstration last week."

Jody paled, before blustering. "You can't prove it."

"I don't have to," Hunter said. "I just have to suggest you show the class that move again so we can learn from you. Only this time you won't get a chance to bully your opponent beforehand, because I'll volunteer. And I promise I won't fold at the exact right moment."

Jody muttered something under her breath but since she did it while fleeing, none of us cared.

"You totally blackmailed her." I beamed at Hunter.

"She's getting on my nerves. She needs to learn how to save her bullying for *Hel-Blar* instead of everyone around here." She jammed the wooden doorstop under the door to keep it closed.

"That was just beautiful," I insisted, reaching for the mop. "I'll wash the floor, since she was only doing it to get to me anyway."

Hunter leaned against the counter. "We shouldn't be fighting among ourselves," she said as I pushed the mop through the gritty puddle.

"Never mind, we can—" Chloe stopped swinging her feet, her

expression turning as serious as Hunter doing drills. "Got something."

We both froze, then hurried over to huddle next to her, trying to read her computer screen. "What did you figure out?" Hunter asked.

"That I am as awesome as we always suspected," she replied, cracking her knuckles. "I've finally cracked the encryption code. I should be able to download and read all those e-mails now." She scrolled, reading quickly. "Bellwood had a few sent to her," Chloe whistled. "Her reply was . . . scary. I didn't even know she knew *how* to swear." She read for a few more minutes, frowning when it didn't load quickly enough for her. "I think we're going to need the Black Lodge," she said quietly.

"Why?" Hunter asked.

"Because I think I just found a list of targets."

"Targets?" I repeated. "What, like for assassination?" Chloe nodded. "Let me guess, Drakes?"

"Worse."

Hunter and I blinked at her. "*Worse?*"

"They're at least used to it . . . This list is for human targets."

Hunter looked vaguely nauseated. "A hit list?"

"Dawn placed bounties on a lot of important people," Chloe said. "Hart. Kieran."

Hunter instantly reached for her phone and started to text.

Chloe bit her lower lip. "Oh."

"*What?*" Hunter and I cried at the same time.

"Your grandfather," Chloe explained, wincing.

"He's on a hit list?" Hunter gaped. "I have to warn him—"

"No," Chloe interrupted softly. "Hunter, you don't understand. He's the one who *sent* the e-mail."

Hunter stared at her. "That's not possible."

"It's his IP address," Chloe said miserably.

"Check again."

"I already—"

"*Check again.*"

Chloe checked three more times. "I'm sorry, Hunter."

"You can't possibly think he's Dawn," she said, starkly. "That doesn't even make sense. And he would never hurt Kieran."

"He didn't write the e-mail," Chloe agreed. "He just passed it on. There's one IP that pops up way more frequently but it's bouncing off a bunch of other places. That has to be Dawn. It'll take me a while to pin her down, even with Connor's help." She clenched her jaw. "We'll figure it out. I promise."

The lights blinked off suddenly and then flicked back on with such intensity it was like a physical slap. Spots exploded behind my lids every time I blinked, as if I'd been staring into the flash of a camera. The lights went out again. Each of our cell phones rang and steel bars clamped down over the window. "Now what?" I asked as a red emergency light blinked over the door.

Hunter and Chloe exchanged a grim glance. "Lockdown," Hunter said.

"What the hell is lockdown?" I asked.

"Usually we get speed drills, to test our response times for escape. Red light means this is something else," Hunter explained, going to the small window and peering out. "All I can see is the roof from here," she said, sounding just as formal and stern as Kieran had sounded the first time I'd met him. School training was taking over. "But the UV lights aren't on, so this isn't a vampire attack."

Chloe's keyboard tapping became violent. "Signal's down too."

Hunter kicked the doorstop out of the way and yanked the door open. I felt my way along the counter, less sure of myself in the shadows. Chloe snapped her laptop shut and slung the case over the shoulder.

"Bathroom duty and creepy fascist midnight drills," I muttered, following them down the hall. Red lights blinked at all the windows and along the walls. "As if regular high school isn't bad enough."

Doors opened, ninth grade students peering out fearfully. Hunter paused. "You know what to do," she called out. "Get your kits and meet at your assigned exits."

"I don't think this is a test," Chloe whispered.

"I know," Hunter whispered back. "But they'll only panic if we tell them that."

A girl our age came out of her room, wrapped in a purple bathrobe. "Not another drill." She sighed.

"Not quite," Hunter replied between her teeth. "Keep an eye on them while I find out what's going on, Courtney."

"Hey, I'm the floor monitor here, you're just my assistant."

We just kept walking. Her door slammed shut. A girl squeaked and scrambled back into her own room, also slamming the door. The rest of us just naturally followed Hunter's lead, even when she kept repeating that she didn't know what was going on either.

"Keep it together," Jason told his group. His flashlight beam swung over the faces of very young, nervous-looking boys.

Students milled about in every common room as we made our way downstairs.

"I thought Chloe had all the drills mapped out," Jenna asked as she fell in beside us.

"This isn't on the official list," Chloe explained in undertones. Jenna immediately reached for a stake.

"What do we do now?" I asked.

"Speed drills lead us out the side, through an obstacle course in the basement. Fire drills just lead right out to the front lawn," Jenna replied. "This one appears to be leading us nowhere."

"Can I have your attention, please." It wasn't a request. A man's voice cut through the chatter. He stood by the front doors, wearing vampire fangs tipped in gold on a chain. Huntsman.

"That's weird," Jenna whispered. "They're way out of their jurisdiction."

"We have entered lockdown for your own protection," he continued. "Please return to your rooms immediately and await further instructions."

"Where's York?" Hunter asked, confused. "He's always in charge of drills and evacuations."

"He's busy, Miss Wild," someone else replied, coming down the hall from the common room. Since she wore the standard Helios-Ra field gear, Hunter backed down. I could tell she was still desperately trying to figure out what was going on though.

"Back to your rooms," the agent repeated sharply. "Now!"

"Couldn't have announced *that* in the first place?" Jason muttered as he tried to corral his students back up the crowded staircase. We all moved quickly and with a surprising lack of conversation. Even Jody couldn't be bothered to hiss a snide remark at me when she bumped into me.

Sarita was already in our room, of course, and sitting on the edge of her neatly made bed. Her hands were clenched tightly around a stake and she jumped nervously when I came in. The movement was jerky enough to see, even under the very faint red light from above the door. I flicked the regular light switch but nothing happened. I sighed and dropped onto the edge of my own, considerably more rumpled bed. I dragged my hunter kit out from underneath.

"This is still more fun than detention," I said.

Sarita just sat there looking tense.

"I'm sure everything's okay," I offered awkwardly, trying to reassure her. On the scale of scary-ass things that had happened to me this past week alone, this ranked pretty low.

"I hate drills," Sarita admitted softly. "They give me panic attacks. I'm much better with regular exams."

"You'll do fine," I assured her, choosing not to share Hunter and Chloe's opinion that this was no ordinary drill. She might sink into a full-blown anxiety attack. Better to smile encouragingly. "Just breathe deeply."

After about five minutes of sitting in the dark, a knock sounded at the door, startling us both. It seemed excessively loud in the silence. Sarita squeaked. It swung open to reveal the agent from downstairs. Sarita visibly relaxed when she saw the regulation cargo pants.

"Lucy Hamilton."

I stood up slowly. "Yes?"

"Come with me."

I frowned. "Where?" I was trying to remember what I could possibly have done this time to be singled out like this. It seemed an excessive reaction to sneaking out past curfew.

"Just come with me, please."

"Go." Sarita pushed me gently. "She's an agent."

I wasn't raised a Helios-Ra hunter, so I didn't find the sight of black cargos particularly reassuring.

"Is something wrong?" I asked when we were out in the empty hallway.

"It's your friend Solange," she answered. When she went down the back stairwell, I followed at a dead run.

"What happened? Is she okay?" I stumbled outside to the deserted campus. The Huntsman stationed out front nodded to us as we crossed to the van idling on the lawn. Two more agents and another Huntsman slid the door open. I frowned at his trophy necklace, feeling a trickle of unease beneath the instinctual panic at the thought of Solange being in trouble.

"Hang on," I said. Because Hunter was right. Something was seriously off.

For one thing, why would a bunch of hunters care one way or another about Solange?

Too late.

The Huntsman yanked me inside. I heard a distant yell through the window and saw Mr. York sprinting across the snow. I struggled and tried to yell back. I managed to kick one of the hunters in the kidney but the Huntsman was stronger than me and didn't loosen his hold even for a second. A cloth soaked in some kind of sickly sweet liquid covered my mouth and nose. I held my breath for as long as I could, which wasn't nearly long enough. Eventually, I had to inhale.

The inside of the van spun and went black.

When I opened my eyes again, I had no idea how long I'd been unconscious. I only knew it was still dark out and I was in the forest with my hands tied together. My vision was blurry and I was disoriented, trying to get my thoughts to make sense. I could see Helios-Ra hunters, Huntsmen, even a vampire in the brown leather tunic of Montmartre's Host. I shrunk back, making myself smaller. And then the camp lantern above my head swung in a sudden gust of wind, casting a wider pool of light.

"But—" I blurted out. "You're supposed to be dead."

Chapter 31

Solange

As it turned out, being a revolutionary was actually quite boring.

Until the assassin returned, that was.

Before that, I mostly had to sit quietly and restrain myself from rolling my eyes when vampires ten times my age acted like toddlers in need of a nap. There was a lot of shouting and slamming of fists on the council table. Dad said the pressure had built up so long it needed a healthy outlet before we got down to the real work. If they didn't start being more productive by the end of the night, I felt sure everyone was going to be treated to one of the famous Liam lectures.

In the meantime, I just had to survive.

I'd been wandering through the field of dirt bikes and motor-cycles, now covered in a thin dusting of snow. Duncan was puttering with one of the antique Triumphs, mostly to get away from the crowds. Marcus sat on a bench with a pile of books. The immunity powers of my blood, the magic in the copper collars, and the way Viola survived, had all posed more questions than they'd answered. And there was nothing he loved so much as a riddle.

I was on the edge of the field, wondering if I'd finally have a chance to spend an hour at my pottery wheel when we got home, when the first body dropped from the treetop.

The girl landed in front of me with a thud that scattered icicles and dead leaves. Three slender silver spikes stuck out of her chest, all surrounding her heart and the Chandramaa crest stitched in her vest. She wheezed, blood spattering her lips. I crouched down to pull the stakes out and her eyes tracked me, wide and terrified.

Whatever could scare the Blood Moon guard was not something I wanted to tangle with. She rolled over, coughing more blood into the snow. The next body turned to ash before it hit the ground. A quiver of red-tipped arrows and a set of leather armor caught in the tree branches. I leaped back, after snagging one of the bloody-tipped stakes I'd pulled from the first guard. No arrows rained down to stop me. They were clearly too busy.

The silver spike that whistled toward me wasn't Chandramaa. It bit into my hand before I could dodge, pain making me yelp. I'd seen a spike like it before, had plucked one out of my own arm. I knew who was taking out the Chandramaa.

Seki.

And I knew why she was doing it.

I'd managed to forget about her in all of the chaos, assuming she'd forgotten about me too since I wasn't Viola anymore. I briefly considered running from the camp, to draw her away from my family but Duncan and Marcus were already dashing toward me. So I did the next best thing.

"Mom!"

Someone else screamed from the treetops. Duncan and Marcus grabbed the other two spikes and stood beside me as a cloud of bats swarmed in, called by my fear. They flung themselves about, screeching and being generally unhelpful. I tried to marshal them into fanged, winged missiles but I didn't even know where Seki was. She could be behind us, above us, anywhere.

"What the hell?" Duncan asked, scanning the branches.

"It's Seki," I replied. It wasn't technically her name but close enough. "Vampire assassin."

Marcus frowned. "I thought they were a myth."

"Not so much," I replied as another guard toppled from one of the tree bridges.

Mom and Dad broke through the trees behind us. "What's going on?" Mom demanded. She stared at the silver spikes. "Where did you get those?"

Seki dropped down in a cloud of ashes before I could answer. She wore the same white leather, with the same white braids and eyes like abalone shells.

"Get Madame Veronique," Dad said. Marcus was fastest, gone before Duncan and I had time to react, leaving Mom his spike.

That was all the time we had before silver spikes flung through the air like birds. A bat flying too low caught one in the wing and spiraled to the ground. Mom kicked the second one out of its trajectory as Dad knocked me to the ground. He caught the spike Mom had knocked aside before it slammed into a tree behind us. He and Duncan stood over me, side to side. They wouldn't let me back up. I crawled away between their feet.

Mom attacked Seki, heedless of the danger. If the Chandramaa were no match for Seki, I wasn't sure my mother would fare much better. Seki wasn't like the rest of us. Even with the nose plugs blocking my pheromones, she could track my location. I had to do something. Fast. More bats were falling, dropping like black rain.

I may as well make it easy for her.

"I'm over here!" I called out after Seki's spike pierced Mom's shoulder. I jumped to my feet, waving my arms even though I knew she couldn't see me in the usual sense.

"Solange, no," Mom said between clenched teeth as she yanked the spike out of her flesh. Blood oozed. She flung the spike back, grazing Seki's hand as she lifted it to stab my father. Dad dodged during that brief moment of distraction and slammed his foot into her knees, knocking her back. She fell backward, still flinging spikes. One of them sliced a long gouge in Duncan's cheek.

We'd barely begun and already we couldn't hold her off much longer.

"Cease," Madame Veronique said calmly, as if her family weren't being beaten to a bloody pulp around her. She used a tiny pearl-encrusted dagger to cut her finger, and flung her own blood into the snow as she approached us.

Seki stopped, standing preternaturally still. She only moved her head, turning it to pin Madame Veronique with her ghostly moonlight eyes.

"You did this!" Mom spat at Madame Veronique.

"Yes, and only my blood will call her off," Madame Veronique said. She flicked a cold glance at my dad. "Really, Liam, you might try to control your wife."

"Hey," I snapped, fully aware of the lengths to which Madame Veronique went to restrain the wife of one of her twin sons. "You leave my mother out of this."

"Solange," Dad said quietly.

"She's the reason London died!" I exclaimed. "And she knew about the prophecy from the beginning."

"Hush," he murmured. Marcus put a restraining hand on my arm. Duncan's eye was already mottled and bruised. One of the tree bridges above us appeared to be on fire, throwing flickering light and embers. Dad helped Mom to her feet as Madame Veronique gestured at me imperiously. I just narrowed my eyes at her.

"If you wish this assassin to leave you and yours alone, you will come here, little girl."

Walking calmly toward her was harder than dodging Seki's spikes. Still, I gave her a wide berth as well. Madame Veronique's handmaidens stood in a half-circle behind her, expressions unreadable. She pinched her finger so that more blood welled to the surface and then smeared it on my forehead. What was it with everyone painting their blood all over me? Even for a vampire it was getting kind of gross.

Seki bowed in our direction and then stalked away, her white leather blending into the snow.

Relief had me exhaling even though I hadn't taken a breath. Madame Veronique sheathed her dagger on her jeweled belt.

"Thank you," Dad said, as bits of fiery rope smoldered and drifted down around us. "And I don't think," he continued in a silky, menacing voice I'd never heard before, "that we'll be taking orders from you anymore."

She sniffed. "I am the eldest of your lineage, boy."

"Consider our branch of the family tree severed," he said calmly.

"And if you come near our daughter again, it won't be all that's severed," Mom promised.

They stared at each other for a long deadly moment before I flicked my hand, casually bringing a curtain of bats between them.

"We'll discuss this later," Madame Veronique said before moving away.

"Remember when the most exciting thing you did was make lopsided pots at your wheel?" Duncan asked, wiping blood off his face. "Good times."

I smiled slightly. "I promise to make you a dozen lopsided pots for Christmas."

He just groaned and moved his shoulder until it cracked back into place.

"Some sweet sixteen," Mom said, sliding her silver spike into her boot, as the Chandramaa were too busy to stop her. "I don't remember sixteen being quite so treacherous."

"I was there," Dad reminded her drily. "I'd say it's a family trait."

She just laughed, winding her arm through his. It was her first true laugh since my bloodchange. Duncan, Marcus, and I grinned sloppily at one another. Then Dad kissed her and we looked hastily away, grimacing.

"Haven't we suffered enough?" Duncan muttered as we left them, still kissing. It didn't seem to bother them that Chandramaa guards were now racing up and down rope ladders with buckets of water and refusing to let any other vampires out of the camp until they'd gotten the fire under control.

I followed Seki's barely-there footsteps, just to reassure myself that she was truly gone. I felt better when her footsteps disappeared and no one tried to kill me for five whole minutes. The soft, quiet beauty of the woods in winter helped. They were cleansing, hopeful. I could finally hear myself think again.

And in that soft quiet moment, I couldn't help but think of Kieran.

I wanted to call him but I was still out of signal range. I wrote a text and then decided to take a walk to the Bower to find a signal strong enough to send it. I wondered what he was doing right now. Had he thought of me at all, since our conversation at the tree? There'd been no mention of getting back together, no reunion kiss. But he'd told me I was worth it. Surely that meant something? Was it too soon to ask him on a date? Would we ever even be able to reclaim such a normal pastime after all we'd been through?

I wouldn't find out by being a coward.

I hit "send" on my text before I'd even reached the Bower. The connection was weak, but it eventually went through. Now I could go back to concentrating on history, politics, and the traditions of tribeless vampires around the world.

I was turning around to head back when I spotted Nicholas moving furtively between the trees. He was holding the back of his neck.

"Nic," I called out, hurrying to catch up to him. He didn't hear me. He was stumbling, as if in pain.

"Nicholas!" I was running alongside him now and he still couldn't hear me. He kept scratching at his neck, but there was nothing here. There were no wounds on him, no blood. But he was acting as if he didn't even know I was there. "Hey," I said. "Stop."

Even my pheromones didn't work. He kept staggering along, but he was also now clutching at his head, moaning. I dropped back, not wanting to cause him more pain.

Frowning, I hung back out of sight, tracking my brother as he went deeper and deeper into the forest.

CHAPTER 32

Lucy

"I thought she was dead too."

I shifted awkwardly toward the familiar voice, the rope chafing my wrists. "Kieran? What are you doing here?" I frowned. "And what am *I* doing here? And, by the way? Where *is* here?"

We were inside the entrance to a damp series of caves lit with camping lanterns. I could see gleaming steel tables, manacles, and strange instruments whose purpose I had no desire to learn. A man in a stained leather apron was investigating the contents of a steel pan with a smile that made me shiver. There were stockpiles of weapons and opposite us, several barred openings in a row. Pale, fanged faces flitted briefly into view, then crawled back into the darkness. Humans were curled up behind the nearest gate, dirty and frightened. The sight of them soured my belly. Between us and them, and between us and the forest outside, were Huntsmen, agents in Helios-Ra gear, and Host vampires.

None of it made sense.

"We're hostages," Kieran explained, keeping his voice low. There were bruises on his face and jagged tears in his jacket. "They just brought me in. I was on my way to the Helios-Ra headquarters after my uncle sent a distress signal when they got me. I thought they were there to help."

"We thought so too," I said, thinking of the lockdown at the school. "And speaking of distress signals . . ."

"Don't scream," he interrupted hurriedly when I opened my mouth to do just that. "They'll just chloroform you again."

"Is that what that stuff was?" I asked, snapping my teeth together. "It was nasty." I could still taste it in the back of my throat. I was so thirsty, it hurt to swallow. It made it hard to concentrate. I leaned my cheek against the damp stone for a moment. The cold helped clear the fogginess from my head.

"I don't understand," I said finally. "Is that really Hope?"

Because there she was, standing at a table, her blond hair swinging cheerfully behind her. She was just as tiny, just as cute . . . just as alive. "Hunter told me she killed herself last month while in League custody."

"I guess she got better," Kieran said darkly. Rage sent a dark red flush creeping up his neck. Hope was the one who'd murdered his father, after all.

"Kieran, don't freak out yet," I said, my teeth chattering from cold and adrenaline. "If you freak out, I'll have to freak out too."

His lip curled but he managed to get the homicidal gleam out of his eye. I felt only marginally better. Escape seemed impossible, not escaping, even worse.

"Get out of here," someone moaned from a dark corner. "They'll kill you." The warning ended in a broken-sounding cough. Chains rattled somewhere down the line of caves. Kieran and I stared at each other helplessly. How long before someone missed us? Would Sarita tell someone I'd been taken away? Had she realized yet that the lockdown wasn't school-sanctioned? Would York know what to do? And could they even find us? My head swam as I watched Hope speak into a walkie-talkie, then order two vampires out of the cave.

She'd thought Kieran's father was too liberal and murdered him.

She'd tried to kill Solange.

She'd allied herself with Lady Natasha in order to take over the League completely.

She didn't approve of treaties with vampires.

"She's Dawn," I said slowly. "She has to be."

Which meant she was also the one who'd kidnapped Nicholas and had him tortured.

Now *I* was the one feeling the homicidal rage.

"And that's Ms. Dailey beside her," Kieran said, glaring at the woman next to her. They both looked our way. "I should have known."

"The teacher who dosed Hunter with poison?"

"Yes."

"I thought she was awaiting trial," I said out of the corner of my mouth as they strode toward us.

"Apparently there are serious gaps in the Helios-Ra security system."

"Apparently." No wonder her alias worked so well. She'd been clear off any of our radars. "Hope has to be the one behind all of the disappearances too."

"Clever girl," Hope said, suddenly standing over me. She was thinner than she'd been before. "I'd hoped you'd join the League and our cause."

"I didn't join your cause," I said. "You're killing people."

"Collateral damage." She waved that aside. "We had to make everyone see the truth. A vampire gathering right here and the League looks the other way." She shook her head sadly. "It's not right. And I'm not the only one who thinks so."

"You murdered people," I repeated. "You're keeping people locked up! And you framed Solange, didn't you?"

"I had to show the League the worm in the rose."

"You're the worm in the rose," I shot back.

She slapped me across the face. Kieran surged to his feet, getting in front of me as I staggered back against the stones. Hope looked down her nose at him. "Little Kieran Black," she said. "You've always been more trouble than you're worth. Better hope your uncle doesn't think so."

"Why?" he asked as I wiped blood from my lip.

"Because if he tries to break out of headquarters, you die. I couldn't have him or his deluded agents interfering, now could I? Not tonight, not after all this careful planning."

"What happens tonight?" I asked.

Hope and Ms. Dailey exchanged a significant glance. "I suppose we can tell you," Hope conceded, pride lacing her words. "After all, it's too late for you to get in my way." The man in the apron started to slice long, fleshy lengths out of what looked like a half-calcified heart. Parts of it turned to ashes under his fingertips. I gagged and tried not to look. "Tonight, we finally take down the Blood Moon."

Kieran and I gaped at her. "I don't know how to get back there," I said.

Hope just laughed, reading my sudden pause. "I don't need you, silly girl. I finally have accurate GPS."

"Where the hell did you get that?" Kieran asked.

"From him," Hope replied, smiling, as two Huntsmen dragged a vampire between them. "He's clean of weapons," one of them said. The vampire flashed his fangs, hissing weakly. His gray eyes were practically all pupil. He was so pale he was the color of old ashes.

Nicholas.

"Get off him!" I yelled, struggling wildly against the ropes. I barely felt the burn of the twine leaving raw sores on my wrists. They knocked him down so that he landed on his knees, forcing his head forward. The back of his neck was bare and vulnerable and laced with bloody scratches. "Stop it," I begged, still trying to squirm free of my restraints as the man in the leather apron approached. "What are you doing to him?"

"Retrieving my GPS coordinates," Hope replied smugly. "Go on, doctor."

Kieran was trying to hold me back, and he was clenching his teeth so hard I could hear them grinding together.

The light flashed off the hook in the doctor's hand. I made a sound like an animal in pain because Nicholas wouldn't. He was too still, too silent. I'd have tried to chew through my ropes if I'd thought there was any chance of success. Nicholas stayed on his knees on the dirty floor, water and blood trickling past him in deep grooves. A Huntsman kept his head down in a vicious grip.

"Nicholas, fight," I pleaded.

He struggled weakly but it was halfhearted at best. He was twitching as if there was something screeching in his ear. The doctor stood over him.

This couldn't be happening.

The smallest details seemed curiously important: the smell of wet stone, the mud on my sleeve, the snow drifting in from outside. Nicholas's dark gray shirt, torn at the collar. The scuff of Kieran's boot as he shifted. And then the slide of my own boots on the slippery mud when I launched forward.

A Huntsman grabbed me by the hair from behind as the doctor slowly inserted the tip of the hook into Nicholas's neck. He dug around, widening the wound until he found a tiny metal square, the kind I imagined filled the insides of computers and machinery. Connor would have known exactly what it was called.

"It seems your failsafe worked," Hope approved.

"Yes, I'd heard the signal satellites were blocked," the doctor said, examining the bloody chip. "This way, when the coordinates were finally locked in and there was still no way to send the information to us, the pain led him here. It forced him to find us. If he went in the wrong direction it just got worse."

Nicholas's fists clenched on the dirty floor. "You bastard."

"Secure him with the others for now," Hope said. "And get the units mobilized," she added to Ms. Dailey. "We're ready."

They snapped metal cuffs around Nicholas's wrists, knowing he could have snapped through the ropes eventually. They shoved him hard enough that he crashed into the wall. He fell at my feet, blinking. "Lucy? I thought you were a hallucination."

I dropped down beside him, smiling through my tears. "I thought they were going to kill you." When I leaned against him, my hands came away bloody.

"Not yet," he said, sitting up properly. "Dr. Frankenstein over there likes to have his fun first." He noticed Kieran finally. "Shit, Black. Not you too."

"Afraid so."

"And was that really Hope?"

"Yeah," I grumbled. "I thought we kicked her ass already too."

"She's ambushing the camp," Kieran explained.

"Where all vampires, my family included, are weaponless," Nicholas finished grimly. I tried to hold his hand but between the ropes and the cuffs, it was more of a tangle of fingertips.

"Those Blood Moon guards can protect them, can't they?" I asked.

"Depends how outnumbered they are," Nicholas pointed out as dozens of armed vampire hunters filed past us and out of the caves. Several Host vampires remained, stationed at the gates. They eyed

Nicholas with particular distaste, seeing as his mother and baby sister had killed their leader Montmartre. With a tiara. He totally deserved it.

"How could *they* be working with Hope of all people?" I asked.

"Same deal she made with Lady Natasha, I expect," Kieran said thoughtfully. "They deal only with Hope, she deals only with them, everyone else scrambles. Not to mention, if things go the way Hope wants them too, the Host might be the very few left standing. Instant power."

"How long before someone realizes you're missing?" I asked Nicholas.

He shook his head. "Could be hours. Depends how paranoid Mom's feeling."

"Hunter might catch on that I'm not there," I added, "but only if Sarita happens to tell her I was taken away. It looked pretty official. Mind you, one of the teachers might be on to them. I think he was yelling, but it's hard to tell." The moments before the chloroform were fuzzy. "Chloe was cracking secret e-mails. She already found the hit list." I slid Kieran a glance. "Which you're on."

"I figured," Kieran said. "Hart knows there's a coup in the works. Especially if Hope is using me to buy his silence."

"Will he stay quiet?" Nicholas asked.

"I sure as hell hope not." He crouched down beside us, keeping his back to the cave wall. "We need a plan," he said quietly. He glanced at Nicholas. "What can you tell us about this place? How did you get out of here the first time?"

"They *let* me get out," Nicholas reminded him bitterly. "So I could lead them right to the encampment like an idiot."

"Tell me anyway," he insisted, his inner boy scout turning military. "Access points, weapons, weaknesses. Everything."

Nicholas rested his head against the wall behind him, his legs stretched out. He made his posture slump, made it as unthreatening as possible. I followed suit, adding the occasional shiver to make myself appear even more unthreatening. It wasn't exactly difficult, since I was cold and still felt a little funny from the chloroform.

"I had help," Nicholas said softly. I shifted to cover the sound of his voice, in case the other vampires were listening. "A good man died helping me get out. All for nothing."

"Not for nothing," I said sharply. "Not yet."

He nodded, swallowing. "Lee created a diversion but it cost him his life. I tried to come back for the others, but I couldn't find the caves, even with all the markings I left behind. I've been out every night, searching. But there was just too much snow." He rubbed at his face with his bound hands. After a beat of stark, charged silence, he continued. "There's a pond of holy water past the guards there. Each cell is barred and locked, a few have crevices between the two." The muscles in his already clenched jaw tightened. "You've figured out by now that they're keeping the humans to dump their bodies in town and blame vampires?" We both nodded. "And they're taking vampires for the same reason, to frame humans."

"Outright war." Kieran exhaled sharply. "Damn." I glanced around surreptitiously. "I count five vampires, three hunters."

"Two more vampires in the back," Nicholas added. "And one

outside with two more hunters. And Dr. Frankenstein there." He barely glanced at the man in the leather apron. Fear and fury made his eyes gleam like broken pearls. "He just likes torture. He thinks he's a scientist." He ground his back teeth. "But he's just an ordinary zealot."

"That's enough chatter," one of the Host barked at us. "This isn't a party, children."

We stopped talking, waiting for them to get bored and turn their attention elsewhere.

"Weapons?" Kieran asked under his breath, his lips barely moving.

I shook my head. "They took my stakes," I said. I reached casually down to adjust my pants. "Shit. My phone too."

They both shifted to check their own pockets, then nodded. "So we're down to the element of surprise to get us out," Kieran murmured. "Great."

"And my teeth," Nicholas murmured back. Kieran's eyes widened. He moved over, shielding us. I lifted my wrists and Nicholas's fangs elongated. He sliced through my ropes. I kept my hands held together so it wouldn't be obvious.

"It's not just us," Nicholas said. "Them too." He glanced at the dirty faces surreptitiously watching us from the cells. "They'll fight if we can get them free. Regardless, once we get Lucy out, we get everyone else out too. Before or after the fight."

"Agreed."

I eyed them both. "I'm going to pretend you didn't just say that," I stated as calmly as I could. "We will *all* get out of this together."

"Lucy."

"Nicholas." I raised my eyebrows. "You know you need me. We're already hopelessly outnumbered. And I'm a better shot than you. So be reasonable."

"You first."

"Oh God," Kieran groaned. "We're doomed."

CHAPTER 33

Solange

I was too far away to stop the Huntsmen from grabbing Nicholas, and then I had to hide from the Host vampire who was trailing them, taking up the rear guard. I followed him as quietly as I could. I'd never been this far into the mountains before so I wasn't sure of the terrain. I finally caught the distinct glow of lantern lights and fire from the mouth of a cave a few yards up into the rock.

I heard the stomp of boots, then the unmistakable sound of running and panting. Flashlights bobbed between the trees. I scaled a shaggy pine tree, narrowly avoiding being spotlighted. I stayed where I was, peering down as dozens of hunters marched past me. I caught glimpses of military cargos, guns, stakes. Walkie-talkies burbled. I heard *"Base secure"* and *"Operation Dawn underway,"* followed by *"wait for the signal."* I stayed still until I was sure they'd all passed by.

"Okay, that was weird," I muttered.

I climbed higher until I could lean out and get a better look at the cave. The smell of pine resin was interrupted by blood, iron, sweat. My fangs hurt in my gums. I couldn't see inside, but there were Huntsmen on guard detail, and human hunters as well. And when the wind died down, I could hear just fine.

Kieran.

I gripped the branch so hard, bits of the moss and bark broke off. I forced myself not to jump down and attack, to instead listen carefully until I knew what was going on. He didn't sound as if he was in pain, only angry.

And not alone.

Nicholas answered him, and then Lucy.

I had to get them out.

I waited for what felt like a hundred years, as useless as Snow White after her bite of the apple. I strained to hear more but someone barked at them to be quiet and they fell silent after that. I could only hear the scrape of metal on metal, and someone weeping.

I didn't have time to go for help so I was going to have to do this on my own.

I had Mom's training, Dad's creative thinking, my own pheromones.

And I had more than the Drake name.

I had *me*.

I smiled for the first time. Because there was one thing the Host wanted more than to kill Hounds and avenge Montmartre.

Me.

And if everyone insisted on seeing me as a helpless little girl, then that's exactly what I'd be.

First I had to lure some of the hunters away, to even the odds as much as possible. I climbed down the branches and scouted the area, choosing a patch of cedar surrounded by boulders from some long-ago avalanche. I hid myself carefully and then broke a twig between my fingers. It snapped like a gunshot.

"What was that?" one of the hunters asked his companion.

"Mountain lion maybe?" he replied, sourly. "What do we care? We're missing all the action."

"Then we may as well do our job right," the first hunter shot back. I cracked another twig. "I'm going," he said. "Cover me."

"I'm telling you there's nothing out there."

I waited until he climbed down far enough to be out of sight of the others before I reached out and punched him. He staggered. Lucy would be proud. I caught him before he crashed through the branches. His lip was split and he was unconscious.

After a long moment, his companion came to the edge of the overhang. "Hey, Jordan, you okay?"

A short pause.

"You taking a leak, man?" He sounded nervous now. I could smell the sweat on him and hear the sudden increase in his heartbeat. "Jordan?"

Jordan groaned. I leaned down. "Shh," I said. His eyes fluttered back in his head. I crouched, waiting for Jordan's friend. The tip of his rifle preceded him, sliding through the pine boughs, practically grazing my cheek. I waited, willing my muscles not to move. He stepped farther into the undergrowth, tripped on Jordan's boot. When he stumbled, I brought the heel of my hand down on the back of his neck. He toppled like a tree. I turned him over, dragging him to lie next to his friend.

"Stay here and be quiet," I ordered them, concentrating on my pheromones wrapping around them. "And don't fight unless you're in mortal danger."

I turned back, watching the Host vampire stationed just inside the mouth of the cave move slightly. I reached for a rock, smashing it on the boulder until it split. I dragged the jagged edge over my forearm so that blood trickled down my arm. It was hot and thick and fragrant. I scattered the drops over the ground, and smeared it on the trees.

"What are you two doing?" the vampire finally called out, stepping out of the mouth of the cave. I hid myself under the overhang. I heard him sniff before dirt dislodged by his boots rained down on me. "Roman, get out here," he barked. I could hear the bloodlust in his voice. So could the others, judging by how many of them crowded behind him. I counted four, maybe five.

"I smell a Drake," one of them said. "Not the boy?"

"Not just a Drake," the first vampire corrected. "Solange Drake."

The hatred in the hissing that accompanied that statement rose the fine hairs on the back of my neck, like hackles. The sound of a long serrated sword leaving its scabbard didn't help.

I pushed away from the protective overhang and dragged myself through the snow, making sure to leave a tantalizing trail of blood behind me. I stopped on the trail where they could see me and pretended to sag weakly.

"She's mine," one of them said, leaping down off the overhang. He landed a little too close for comfort. I scuttled back.

Another vampire landed next to the first.

"She belongs to all the Host," he said.

"Kill her."

I moved weakly, sluggishly. I wondered if adding a moan would be too much.

"No, keep her and drain her slowly."

"For Montmartre!"

I finally allowed myself to scramble to my feet while they argued.

"Boys, boys, there's no need to fight over me," I called out with false confidence. They stopped, staring at me. "Want me?" I taunted, flicking blood at them. "Come and get me!"

And then I ran like hell.

CHAPTER 34

Lucy

Nicholas shot to his feet so quickly my hair flattened off my forehead.

"Solange is here," he said.

Kieran leaped up too. "*What?*"

Nicholas smiled slowly, surprising us both. "She's not a hostage." He sliced through Kieran's bonds. "Yet."

I tripped one of the Host as he shot past us. He was remarkably ungraceful as he stumbled. I tucked my legs back in before he could reach out and snap one of them in half as retaliation. He was one of the few still left in the cave. Dr. Frankenstein frowned. "What on earth is going on out there? Can't you see I'm working?"

"He's got the keys," Nicholas said, jangling his handcuffs.

Kieran used the edge of one of the tables for leverage, jumping and landing on a Host while using his locked elbow as a weapon. The table shot away, rolling on squeaky wheels, until it collided with

Dr. Frankenstein. He spilled a beaker of green liquid over himself, then it fell to the ground and shattered. He collapsed groaning, but still conscious. I leaped on him, fumbling through the strange implements in his apron pockets, trying to find the keys.

"Stay down," Nicholas warned me, grabbing one of the iron bars set over the dungeons. He jumped, using his entire body as a battering ram, knocking one Host into another.

Kieran managed to get a hold of a long, rusty spike and used it to stake the Host he'd just knocked down. Ashes coated the already slippery ground. One down, three more to go. Now if only I could find the damn keys. My fingers still tingled from being restrained so tightly and felt as agile as frozen sausages. I pulled out three vials, a corkscrew, a gold coin, a tangle of fish hooks, a Helios-Ra medallion, two stakes, and something squishy that made me want to throw up. I flung it at the wall with a shudder. Dr. Frankenstein's eyes opened. "Not that," he moaned. "It's important."

"You hurt my boyfriend," I said, right before knocking his head back into the floor.

And finally, finally, my fingers closed over a key ring. "Got it!"

Nicholas flung himself free of the bar, his hands outstretched when he landed in front of me. I jammed key after key into the tiny lock. He kicked back once, catching a Host who got too close. More of them were rushing back in from outside. The handcuffs finally unlocked and Nicholas snapped them apart. "Go," he yelled at Kieran. "Help Solange."

Kieran took off, grabbing weapons as he went. There was a box of stakes and daggers on hooks on the wall, crossbows and staves and various other things.

Nicholas spun back around, facing the others, half smiling. "I think I'm going to enjoy this."

He became a blur of pale skin and fangs. Three Host circled around him. He had no weapons, no means of escape.

But he had me.

I filled my hands with stakes and then crouched under the shelter of one of the tables, waiting. The first blow that knocked Nicholas down had him landing hard. I rolled a stake toward him. He grabbed it and flipped back to his feet. One of the Host crumbled into thick dust.

Nicholas went low, into a rolling somersault, his palm out. I threw another stake. His fingers curled around it as he leaped back up. He'd managed to break out of the circle and with every stake he threw, I passed him another.

One of the prisoners stuck her arm out, clotheslining a passing Huntsman. Nicholas was right, we had an army behind the bars. I grinned at her. She cradled her now-broken arm, grinning back through the pain.

Since Nicholas seemed to be channeling a vampire ninja and I was out of stakes, I hurried to the nearest iron gate. I went through the key rings again, until I found the one that fit the padlocks. The first prisoner stumbled out, squinting in the artificial light. Sores and frostbite scars coverered his bare arms. He must have been here for weeks. I swung open gate after gate and humans and vampires emerged blinking like half-blind moles.

The vampires went straight to a fridge powered by a humming generator, ripping into blood bags. A woman tore through a camping bag full of protein bars and beef jerky.

When more vampires and Huntsmen came out of a passage on the other side of the small murky underground pond, the prisoners swarmed them. They weren't particularly strong, having been starved and shackled for so long, but they were enraged. The ones doing most of the biting weren't even vampires. There was a kind of frenzy in the air that made my mouth go dry.

Nicholas kicked a Host, breaking his thighbone, and I shoved him as he fell, sending him into one of the dank cells. I slammed the gate shut, locking it. "We can't stay here," I said to Nicholas. "Let's lock them all in and stop Hope." I thought, before this turns into a bloodbath. I had to shove an old man off a Huntsman before things got really ugly and the Huntsman choked on his own fang necklace.

Nicholas stood over Dr. Frankenstein, his boot pressing lightly on the other man's throat. The doctor gagged, his eyes bulging with fear. "Nic, stop." I grabbed his arm.

"You don't know the things he's done. He's a monster." He pressed down just a little harder. Veins bulged in the doctor's forehead. He clawed at Nicholas's ankle.

"Don't let turning you into a murderer be another one of his crimes." I tightened my grip on his arm, holding on as tight as I could. "Don't let him break you, Nicky." I shook him. "Lock him up so we can go save the rest of your family."

He moved his boot just as I was wondering where my Nicholas had gone. He leaned against the wall, wiping his face with a trembling hand. "Shit," he said. "Shit, Lucy."

"Let's just get out of here," I said gently. "Take my hand."

Everything was getting too ugly, too fast. Nicholas wasn't the only one who'd reacted to the miasma of fear and the memory of torture. The vampires who had fed were now prowling the perimeter of the cave, snarling. Hunters lay in pools of blood. Violence had a coppery smell, like burning pennies. "I need a tranq gun," I muttered. There was a box of them next to the other crates of weapons but the way was blocked.

"I'll get it," Nicholas said, staking between a Host vampire and a Huntsman, and tossing them both apart as if they were toy soldiers. He plucked one of the guns out of the pile, checked that it was loaded, and then tossed it to me. It looked like a pistol and fit easily in my hand. My first shot went wide as I got used to the new weapon. Unfortunately, it didn't go so wide as to hit the wall; instead a dart hit one of the prisoners in the butt. She fell over, curses slurring as she fell asleep. "Oops." I stared at Nicholas, wincing. He just shook his head at me.

My next shot was much more accurate, felling a Host vampire after two darts. "I need the vamp stuff," I called when the vampire stirred after just a few seconds of unconsciousness.

Nicholas crouched over Dr. Frankenstein. "Where's the vampire sedatives?" he asked darkly. "I know you have some." Dr. Frankenstein started to babble, trying to protect his neck with his arm. Nicholas leaned in closer, pupils dilated. "Tell me."

"In the small fridge," he finally said as the pheromones slipped under his defenses. "The bottle with the blue labels."

"And?"

He gulped. "And there's a box of preloaded darts t-there . . . under m-my work table . . ."

Nicholas didn't look away as he grabbed the box and slid it to me. Then he pulled the whole table down, dumping beakers and test tubes and microscopes onto the floor. Broken glass and dented equipment skidded in all directions. "Oops," he said, echoing me.

One of the more recent prisoners, judging by her lack of cuts and bruises, hauled the now-weeping Dr. Frankenstein into a cell. She broke his wrist doing it, but none of us much cared, especially when he kept wailing about his "work."

"He used to be one of us," she said, disgusted. There was a Helios-Ra sun tattoo on her arm. I reloaded the gun just as one of the prisoners sailed past me. Nicholas caught her before she landed in the broken glass.

I shot three more vampires. They sank to the ground as if they were suddenly made of water. When there were finally only three Huntsmen left, I grabbed one of the emergency foghorns from a metal shelf piled with signaling devices. I pressed the button and the sound bounced off the stones. Everyone stopped, grabbing at their ears. One vampire tried to hide her head under her sweater, gnashing her fangs. Nicholas swung his head to stare at me. I added another blast for good measure.

"Lock them up!" I snapped in that military-school tone Hunter was so good at. "Now."

There was some grumbling and someone called me a rather uncomplimentary name but the majority looked relieved to shake the violence off and have some kind of direction. We dragged the limp bodies into the cramped dungeons. Nicholas punched one of the Huntsmen who refused to move, even with a vampire sedative aimed at his head.

"We have to go," I said to the Helios-Ra woman before the echo of the clanging gates had faded. She seemed the most capable and definitely the most stable. The old man was laughing to himself and peeing along the line of gates. I shuddered.

"Can you keep them calm until morning?" I asked her as Nicholas sorted through the crates of weapons.

"We'll build a fire out on the edge," she said. "And keep warm. That'll stop most of them from freaking out further."

"I just want to go home," a college student muttered.

"If you go now you'll just get lost in the forest and be even worse off," I told him.

"She's right," the agent agreed. "We'll keep guard, call for help on one of the machines and wait until first light."

"League headquarters are under siege," I warned her, hanging a miniature crossbow off my belt. "You might not get an answer right away." I slung a regular bow over one shoulder and added two quivers of arrows. They were much faster to reload than a crossbow. I took three more tranquilizer guns as Nicholas dumped the stash of vampire sedatives into a pack. I added at least a dozen stakes all over myself, from pocket to pant cuff. If I tripped and fell I was in very great danger of puncturing a vital organ.

Nicholas and I were finally ready to leave the caves. Nicholas shoved the last Huntsman on the ledge right off the side. He swore all the way down, even though it was only a drop of a few feet. Huntsmen really were drama queens. Nicholas leaped down and then turned to steady me as I climbed after him, with far less grace. I clung to weeds and rock.

"Did you just cop a feel?" I asked when he let me drag down the length of his body. His smile was so quick I nearly missed it.

We ran down the trail, passing two prone hunters, a pile of ashes, and several broken saplings. We found Solange and Kieran back to back, fighting off Host vampires. Just this summer, he'd been threatening to kill her, and now he was trying to protect her and her whole family. If Solange could ignite change in vampire society, maybe Kieran could do the same for the League.

Solange disarmed one of the Host and claimed his sword. She was mostly blocking savage blows. She kept leaning in to whisper softly.

"What's she saying?" I asked Nicholas.

"She's telling them to get lost."

The vampires, taking the order literally while under the influence of her pheromones, wandered away dazed. When Kieran was knocked over by a particularly vicious jab and nearly eviscerated himself falling onto a tree, Solange kicked back. She was fierce and confident; the Solange I knew so well but few ever had a chance to glimpse.

She extended her arm, cracking the vampire across the jaw, then spun on her foot and smashed the hilt of her sword into his face. Buffeted by blows, he staggered. She finished him off with a pheromone-soaked suggestion that he give up a life of crime and survive off rats.

"We've reclaimed the caves," I called out. "And stuffed the evil asshats into the dungeons."

She ordered the next vampire to give himself up and peacefully allow himself to be locked up. The last two vampires decided it was more prudent to abandon the fight and tear off into the dark forest.

Solange pushed her long black hair off her face. "Everyone okay?"

I hugged her tightly. "You saved us. All of us." I pulled away, wrinkling my nose. "Did Kieran catch you up?"

"Fate of the world," she said. "Betrayal, battles, blah, blah, blah."

"Just like old times."

CHAPTER 35

Solange

We ran for a long time.

Lucy and Kieran were slowing down, pressing their sides. Not so long ago I would have felt the same painful stitch under my ribs, the same burn in my lungs and legs. Now I could run all night. Well, until dawn anyway.

"I'm out," Kieran panted at his uncle, having called him on my cell phone. "Whatever you're going to do, do it now." He paused, snorting incredulously. "I'll tell her but you're nuts if you think she'll listen." He hung up and glanced at us. "He's going to call the cops on Hope's unit," he explained even though I'd heard every word as if it had been spoken right into my ear. Lucy probably couldn't hear over her own heartbeat right now. It was loud enough to sound as if she'd smuggled a rapid-fire shotgun under her shirt.

"The cops," Lucy echoed. "Can we do that?"

"The other alternative is to fight through the siege at the head-quarters, and then people will die. They can't even sneak out through the secret passageway since all the Helios-Ra agents there already know about them. "But," he said, smiling darkly, "hanging around a house filled with highly suspect weapons is still totally illegal. And downright crazy if you start talking vampires." He dialed the phone again as Lucy leaned weakly against the nearest tree.

"Go on ahead," she said, taking slow, deep breaths.

"No," Nicholas and I both said.

"We'll catch up."

"No," Nicholas repeated calmly, handing her a bottle of water from the huge pack he'd taken out of the caves. It was stocked with supplies for the average hiker and vampire killer.

"Hunter," Kieran said into the phone. She started bombarding him with questions, orders, and threats almost before he'd finished saying her name. "I'm with Lucy," he cut her off. "We're fine. Hart's fine too. He says that under no circumstances are high school students allowed to fight this battle." He rolled his eyes, looking younger than the blood on his sleeve and the bruises on his face might suggest. "I already told him that. Where are you now?" He checked the GPS on my phone quickly. "We're not far. See you soon."

"You know, one day we'll go on a double date without swords or stakes of any kind," Lucy said cheerfully, slinging her arm through mine.

"Oh, right, just as soon as my boyfriend and I stop having to save each other's lives."

My voice carried farther than I'd planned.

Kieran's head turned sharply in my direction. Lucy grinned at me sympathetically as I realized just how loudly I'd spoken.

My words hung in the air like giant neon balloons. I swallowed, feeling a flush creep up my cheeks. "I mean . . ." I looked away, mortified. "We should go."

I ran so fast they had no chance of catching up with me. I stopped and waited for them, once I'd stopped feeling like I might choke on my own stupid embarrassment. Luckily, by the time they did, we had more pressing problems. Nothing like a little war to distract you.

I couldn't even look at Kieran as we waited for Hunter and the others. When they showed up there was a small group of them, including Quinn. Hunter rattled off her friends' names: Chloe, Jason, Jenna, Drew, Griffin, Kelly, Regan, and Tyson, among others. They exchanged wary glances, sticking close together. Other than Hunter, only Chloe and Jason didn't seem particularly fazed.

"Is it true you overthrew the monarchy?" Chloe asked me. She looked disappointed when I nodded.

Despite not being able to look at Kieran, I also couldn't quite stop myself from sneaking little glances at him. He was standing close enough that his sleeve brushed mine when he shifted.

I forced myself to stop being an idiot.

"Between Chloe and Connor, we intercepted and tracked the call to ambush the camp," Hunter was explaining. "All landlines to headquarters are down. I managed to get a hold of Spencer and he's going to mobilize whatever Bower vampires are willing to go in with us."

"Sebastian, Marcus, and Duncan are still inside the camp with our parents and aunt and uncle," Quinn added. "Logan's gone to see if he and Isabeau can rally any of the Hounds to help us, and Connor's with Christabel trying to get the Na-Foir to fight too. Not convinced on that end, I gotta say."

"Well, Saga likes a good fight," Lucy put in. "So that might help."

"So we have a secret Black Lodge of students, a handful of vampires, and some weapons?" Hunter asked. "I'm not loving the odds yet."

"And some tranq guns," Lucy said. "I stole three."

"And I hid a bunch of them up a tree near the Bower," I added.

"You did?" Quinn asked. "When? Why?"

"Lucy and I were talking and it gave me some ideas. I got some of Uncle Geoffrey's sedative and loaded a bunch of dart guns, just in case."

"Because of London," Nicholas guessed quietly.

"Partly."

"There's the Chandramaa too," Quinn added before the moment stretched from awkward to sad. "They've got Mom's ferocity and Lucy's aim."

"Aw, thanks." Lucy beamed at him.

"But they were decimated earlier tonight," I broke in. "Their numbers are definitely depleted." When they stared at me I just waved it away. "Vampire assassin. Long story."

"So maybe we need a new enemy," Kieran suggested slowly. "One both sides have to stop fighting each other to defeat."

"Like who?" Hunter asked.

"Saga's *Hel-Blar*."

Nicholas gaped at him. "Why not just throw a live grenade and blow everyone up instead? Be quicker."

"Those *Hel-Blar* aren't quite as feral as the others," I pointed out, agreeing with Kieran. "At least not while they're wearing the collars." I rubbed my neck. "It suppressed my pheromones. It does the same for them in some weird way."

"Do we still not know how those work?" Hunter asked.

"Magic," I said. "At least partly. So basically, no. No idea."

We spread out between the trees, moving as quietly as we could. The students all had compasses with the coordinates Connor had sent Chloe. My brothers and I just followed the scent of the night, which was already tainted. It was faint but wrong, and very hard to describe, something between burning petals and wet, rusty iron.

I hung back, keeping pace with Kieran. "Can I talk to you?"

He stopped, turning to face me. His eyes were so dark, like a moonlit night. I tried not to stare at the faint scar on his throat. "I was hoping . . ." I trailed off, biting my lower lip. "That is, I know you're going to the college in Scotland. But I wondered . . ."

"Solange, what are you trying to say?"

I drank in the sight of him, standing so tall and patient with the snow and the bare black trees all around him. "I'm saying I still love you," I replied, forcing myself to be brave. If I could face the kind of fight we were about to walk into, I could face this. He deserved better than my shy, awkward fear. Especially now. I wanted him to remember *me*, not Viola. "And I know I hurt you but I'm hoping maybe you could give me a chance to make it up to you."

"You fought your way back to me," he replied, just as quietly; but his smile was like an ember, catching fire to all the cold inside my chest. "That's all I care about."

And then he finally kissed me.

It was like a first kiss, tentative, gentle, searching. I could remember who we used to be, could follow the trail of all the nights we'd spend talking, walking on the beach, driving around. I could follow them like fireflies, like shooting stars, like sparks.

Everything melted away for one brief, beautiful moment. The kiss seared through me as he slanted his mouth over mine. Our tongues met, our fingers tangled, our bodies touched. I could have kept kissing him for hours, if we'd had the time.

We parted reluctantly and kept walking through the snow silent and smiling.

The others were silhouettes all around us, but I could still hear them. I caught the occasional glint of light off a metal zipper, the rasp of a stake being passed anxiously from hand to hand. "So you've changed your mind about Solange?" Lucy was asking the girl with the red hair.

"No way." She snorted. "I'll do this for the League and for you and Hunter because you're sisters-at-arms, but she's a vampire."

"She's a *girl*."

"Who drinks blood."

"Please," Lucy scoffed. "I've seen you eat marzipan. On purpose. That stuff's just gross." She paused. I could hear her smirking. "So did Tyson ask you out?"

"Tell you what," Jenna shot back. "If I don't die horribly tonight, I'll worry about my love life. It can wait."

"Take it from me," Lucy said drily. "If you're waiting for all this drama to be over before making your move, you'll be waiting forever."

And then the nervous chatter, the sidelong glances, the checking of weapons all fell away.

There wasn't room for anything but what we were about to do.

CHAPTER 36

Lucy

It was one thing to train in the gym, to practice kickboxing and archery, to read about wars and tactical strategy and listen to Helena threaten to pull organs out of various people's noses.

It was quite another thing to walk right into a war.

Objectively speaking, we knew the vampires at the Blood Moon were inside the circle, with a ring of Hope's followers around them, and the rest of us on the outside ring. On paper, this would have looked great—if the vampires in the center were armed. Because even super speed and strength could only go so far against stakes and arrows. And Hope wasn't about to give them that chance anyway. She was waiting for sunrise when they'd be at their weakest.

So we'd take away their element of surprise.

Jenna was already climbing up a soot-covered chain ladder to get a better vantage point. She didn't have just one hand crossbow, she had three. Chloe followed behind her but Hunter stayed on the ground with Quinn since she was better at hand-to-hand. Kieran went off with Solange and the rest of the Black Lodge dispersed around the perimeter. Nicholas was right at my side, or I was at his, it hardly mattered. Where one of us went, the other followed.

We hadn't even reached the Chandramaa yet, we were still technically on the outskirts of the official camp. And we still had no idea if or when the *Hel-Blar* would be released. And if they would make things better or considerably worse.

I already felt like I was moving in slow motion but everything around me was sped up. Even the brightness of the snow looked different. The reality of a sound attack wasn't just about the logic behind the plan, it was also the thrum of my blood in my veins, my heart stuttering, my mouth going dry.

Hunter looked perfectly calm but when Spencer came up beside her, she nearly staked him. He ducked even as Quinn grabbed her elbow to stop her follow-through.

"You have got to stop sneaking up on me," she grumbled at him.

"Sorry," he said. "My unit's pretty small but I set up a few spells to compensate. And no, before you ask, no one will smell like cheese." He gave her a friendly nudge with his shoulder. Neither of them were quite used to his vampire strength yet so Quinn had to catch her when she nearly plowed into him. "Don't die," Spencer ordered. "One of us is enough."

"I'll take care of her," Quinn promised.

"And I'll stake you both right now if you two don't cut it out," Hunter added drily.

In the trees above us, Jenna shot arrows into the camp, the shafts wrapped with notes addressed to Helena Drake and Liam Drake. I shot a few more from my position. We hoped at least one of the arrows made it through the compromised Chandramaa ranks.

Which officially made this our last chance to talk our way out of this.

"Are you sure about this?" Quinn bent his head to whisper in Hunter's ear. She leaned into him briefly but her answer didn't change.

"I have to try." When he tried to follow her, fierce and charming as only a Drake brother could be, she stopped him. "I have to do this alone."

"It's not safe."

"Nowhere's safe anymore," she reminded him. "But they won't listen to me if my vampire boyfriend is standing next to me. They're seriously old school." A muscle in his jaw leaped. "Jenna's got me covered from up there." She kissed him quickly, despite her earlier contention that she couldn't be seen standing with him right now, never mind kissing him. When she moved away he pulled her sharply back, lengthening the kiss until it looked as though it could have easily burned through all of our fears.

"Kick some ass, Buffy," he murmured.

"I'm going with you," I said, catching up to Hunter. "I'm technically one of you and one of them. Maybe it'll help."

Nicholas didn't look thrilled. "Maybe you should stay here."

I just looked at him.

He sighed. "Then I'm coming with you."

"No way. Didn't you hear what Hunter just told Quinn. And anyway, remember our last date? When Helios-Ra students and Huntsmen tried to kill you? How is that going to help me?" I went on my tiptoes and kissed him quickly. "I'll be fine."

Hunter and I followed the trail to where it ended, knowing full well that both Quinn and Nicholas were tailing us. We'd have done the same thing. There were dozens of other eyes watching as we stepped into the narrow clearing, the snow crunching under my school-issued boots. Hunter stood straight-backed and proud as any new recruit. I just nocked an arrow, feeling trapped.

"The vampires know you're here," Hunter called out. She didn't even call them names. I totally would have. "You've lost the element of surprise and the weapon of dawn." I knew she specifically used "dawn" instead of sunrise. "Any minute now they'll be coming out to defend themselves. We can end this before it starts."

"Why would we want to?" someone said with a snort. "Now get out of the way, vampire lover."

"Yeah, we're not the monsters here," another hunter broke in. "Or have you forgotten which side you're on?"

"Oh, I haven't forgotten," she answered grimly, nudging me when I opened my mouth to fire back a retort. "This isn't defending an innocent from a vampire feeding or even a *Hel-Blar*. And I'm not suggesting some vampires shouldn't be taken out for everyone's safety. I think we can agree Lady Natasha and Montmartre aren't going to be missed."

There was a soft, menacing hiss from somewhere behind me. I tensed but refused to give in to fear. Hunter didn't betray even a flutter of nerves. "Jenna has our back," she murmured to me. And the vampire, no doubt once one of Montmartre's Host, wouldn't have bothered wasting his time hissing if he'd really wanted to kill us where we stood.

"We have a right to protect our town," someone said.

"But that's not what this is," Kieran argued, stepping up beside us. He and Hunter stood shoulder to shoulder, as I imagined they had since they were little. It was the same way I would have stood with Solange or any of her brothers. "This is genocide and murder. It's not who we are. We deserve better than what Dawn is making us into."

"They're vampires and we're vampire hunters. Do the math. They've been killing in Violet Hill, leaving bodies behind every night. That queen of theirs is insane, worse than the last two."

"Most of that was Dawn," I argued, searching the undergrowth, hoping to see a hunter I recognized, someone who might actually listen. "She murdered humans to manipulate you all into this attack. She manipulated the vampires too. She framed Solange." I thought about the vampires we'd found in Kieran's house that night. "And she hired vampires to kill Kieran, to set Solange off, to set us all off." I was sure of it. "She's playing you."

"Son of a bitch," Kieran muttered, realizing I was right.

"We don't care," a hunter barked, though I still couldn't see his face.

"You have to listen!" Hunter insisted.

"We're doing right. Who the hell are you to tell us differently?"

"She's my best student," Bellwood barked back, suddenly emerging out of the shadows. I'd never seen her in her field gear outside of the old yearbooks in the library. "If I don't expel her for this, of course."

"Um . . ."

I wasn't sure I'd ever seen Hunter that flustered. Of course, what else can you say to the headmistress of your school while standing in the middle of the forest at night during a covert op, surrounded by hostile hunters and vampires?

She slanted us a look. "You didn't really think you could do this alone and undetected, did you?" Her stern gaze shifted, raking the faces now peering out of the bushes and trees. I'd be willing to bet over half the hunters around us had studied at the academy under Bellwood.

"And Ms. Dailey is in on it too," Kieran called out. "I saw her at the caves. She tried to poison Hunter, one of our own. How is that honorable?"

Bellwood nodded her approval. "I've taught you better than this."

"School's been out for a long time, lady," a Huntsman sneered. "Now move!"

He wasn't the only one yelling at us.

"Hunter Wild, you go back to school right now."

Hunter spun around. "Grandpa?"

He barreled out of a thicket, wearing leather straps across his chest, studded with stakes, Hypnos, nose plugs, and wild fear in his blue eyes. "Get out of here," he said. "That is an order, young lady."

"Nothing like being scolded by your grandfather to really make you look like a force to be reckoned with," Hunter muttered. "You know I can't do that," she added louder, even though the vein in his temple was pulsing alarmingly. "Grandpa, this is wrong. And it's going to be a massacre."

"This ambush was a perfectly good tactical move you just shot to hell," he growled. He glared at Kieran. "I expected better from you."

Kieran's eyes flashed, his rare temper sparking. "That woman you're working with killed my father. And her accomplice tried to kill Hunter. Of the two of us, you're the one who should be ashamed."

"What the bloody hell are you talking about?" Grandpa frowned. "Dawn didn't kill your father."

"Dawn is Hope," Kieran told him. He made sure his voice carried. "The same Hope who murdered my father, the leader of the Helios-Ra, and made it look like vampires. Sound familiar?"

"And she's working with the Host," I added. "Just like she worked with Lady Natasha."

"Not true." Grandpa looked shocked. "You have pheromone poisoning. You're just kids. It hits you harder."

"Grandpa, I saw the hit list," Hunter said, disgusted. "How could you?"

He went gray under the red flush of his temper. "Hard choices, kitten."

"Kieran was on that list," she snapped. "Did you even look at it?"

He shook his head. "I was just a messenger," he said, sounding old.

A Huntsman strode out of his hiding place, furious. "I don't give a damn about your politics. All I care about is taking out that nest of monsters over there." He leaned into Hunter aggressively. "Now shut the hell up or I will do it for you."

Hunter's grandpa rounded on him, shoving him hard. "Don't you threaten her."

And then there was no more time for talking.

There was no warning.

The clearing went from a field of snow to a battlefield. Arrows and stakes cut the night into cold, dangerous pieces. Vampires rushed out of the camp and hunters swarmed forward.

And we were caught in the middle, because we didn't want to kill either side.

This wasn't going to end well.

The sound boiled the air. It made me nauseated, and light-headed as it vibrated in my eardrums. The silky, sinister speed of angry vampires was like a hundred snakes slithering around me. I was in the fight before my brain caught up, my reflexes recognizing what my body needed to do.

Hunter used a hammer fist strike to knock a Huntsman off her feet as she shot past me. We both spent a good five minutes tripping and shoving hunters as they tried to join the battle. I felt like I was back on the playground. I grabbed a long branch, using it like a staff and jamming it at a Host vampire's knees to knock him off course as well. Nicholas was back at my side, silent and serious.

It was already taking all of our combined strength to stay together. The world was a confusing mass of weapons, hisses, limbs flailing. I couldn't even see Quinn in the melee, but I knew he had to be nearby since I could just make out the gleam of Hunter's blond hair.

I whipped a stake at the vampire who darted at me, snarling. It wasn't enough to dust her. She howled, plucking the wooden stake from her flesh. I'd hit the right target, but it hadn't gone through her rib cage with enough force to pierce her heart. It snagged her shirt and she pulled it completely free before flinging it back at me. I ducked even as Nicholas slammed the stake out of its trajectory with the side of his hand. I still only narrowly avoided losing an eye.

The vampire hissed, bloodlust making her eyes red. She turned to the nearest human.

Hunter.

"Hunter, watch out!" I yelled, even as the vampire turned on her. Hunter kicked out, slamming her boot into the vampire's stomach. It would have bought her a few seconds if Hunter hadn't slipped on a patch of ice and crashed onto her tailbone. When the vampire laughed, Hunter staked her foot to the ground, pinning her there long enough for Jody, of all people, to stake her. I blinked at her, nonplussed. Had the whole school come down for extracurricular credit? She took off before we could thank her. Or wonder what side she was fighting for.

Quinn's mad laugh cut off with a strangled growl. He was tossed off his feet, landing on his back and skidding in the snow beside Hunter. Judging by the bruises and bleeding cuts all over his chest and arms, he'd been trying to fight his way to her. Hunter rolled over, shooting the Host in the chest before he could lean down and snap Quinn's neck. He crumbled to ash.

Quinn grinned at Hunter, his blue eyes burning. They kept their gazes locked as they both jumped up, weapons raised. Another vampire was on her, dagger in his hand. Quinn pushed her out of the way.

"Not her, Elijah," Spencer added, knocking the dagger out of his hand at the same time. He caught it before it skewered her. "She's on our side." He helped Hunter up. "I thought I said don't die."

"This friendly fire's a bitch," Quinn added, flipping his hair off his face before jumping back into the fray.

"We need to get high up," I said to Nicholas.

He nodded tersely. "Quinn, cover us."

Hunter came with us, using a small crossbow she plucked out of a pile of ashes and medieval chainmail armor. A hunter fell across our path, gurgling blood. A red-tipped arrow stuck out of his stomach. I had no idea who was winning or if there would even be a winner. It was hard to think, hard to do anything but survive. If we didn't get this sorted by sunrise, I couldn't imagine the resulting massacre. There was already blood in the snow and fires burning up in the treetops. A tent on the other side of the tree line billowed thick gray smoke, choking us. I needed to get up onto a platform where I could use my bow.

A Huntsman dropped, eyes rolling back in her head. The vampire beside her also staggered, a dart in the side of her neck. I couldn't see Kieran anymore, or even Solange. There was too much happening, too many grunts of pain, too many snapping bones and swords clashing. A vertical deadly rain of stakes threatened everyone, no matter who or what we were defending.

Three hunters lay defenseless in the snow. Tyson crawled forward, keeping his head out of the line of fire, and dragged them into a copse of cedars to protect them. Tranquilizers were a good idea in theory, but they had their own pitfalls. Chloe and Jason rushed out to help them. I saw Duncan and Marcus doing the same with fallen vampires, bringing them to the same shelter. Sebastian helped Jason with a particularly large hunter.

While Quinn and Nicholas took on three Host between us and the platforms, I turned just in time to see a Huntsman, flung by an angry vampire, crash right into Hunter behind me. She fell hard on her knee, gasping in pain. She grabbed for her crossbow, which had skittered just out of reach. I didn't have the space to nock an arrow. I leaped forward, kicking the crossbow back to her.

When she tried to stand up, her leg buckled. She nearly pitched forward. I tried to get to her but there was a vampire and a Huntsman in my path, each trying to tear the other's throat out. I tried to go around them and got knocked off my feet.

Hunter propped herself up by holding onto a low branch to steady herself. She lifted her reclaimed crossbow, resting it on the branch and taking aim, but there was no hope for a clear shot. I scuttled toward her, staying on my back where I had enough clearance to use my own crossbow. I took out two Host vampires with regular bolts, turning them to ashes.

"You again." Ms. Dailey, who I recognized from the caves, picked her way over clumps of ashes and the bodies of her fellow hunters. She looked so furious that she'd tipped over into a creepy calm.

And she was pointing a gun at Hunter.

Hunter froze. I fumbled to load my crossbow with another arrow. A boot clomped down beside me, nearly snapping it out of my hand.

"This is your fault," Ms. Dailey spat. "If you'd just died like you were supposed to, Hope and I could have taken care of this under the radar. You had me put away."

"You slipped me vampire roofies," Hunter returned, her voice shaking slightly.

"You really could have been someone." She shook her head. Her gun aim was steady. "You chose the wrong side, Hunter."

I tried to creep closer and get proper aim but there were too many fists and stakes between us. The clouds of ashes didn't help either. Quinn swore, trying to fight his way to Hunter, but he and Nicholas were surrounded by more Host.

Ms. Dailey pulled the trigger.

Hunter fell backward before I realized the bullet hadn't touched her. It hit her grandfather instead.

"Grandpa!" She crawled to where he'd landed, sprawled on his back. "You're okay!" she said. "You're okay." She pressed a wadded-up bandanna to the wound in his chest. Blood soaked through it within seconds. "No," she pleaded. "Grandpa, don't go."

He coughed. "Don't fuss, kitten."

And then he shot Ms. Dailey over Hunter's shoulder before she could fire again. She slammed into a tree, and fell into a spindly hazel thicket.

"I'll get help," I babbled, even though I had no idea how I was supposed to do that. There was no way I'd be able to find Uncle Geoffrey in this chaos. Hunter kept applying pressure to her grandpa's chest. Her ponytail slipped over one shoulder, the tip dragging in his blood.

"No need for that." He tried to smile, blood foaming at the corner of his mouth. "You're a good girl, Hunter."

And then he died, smiling and patting her hand.

Quinn slid to her side in the snow.

That's when the first wave of *Hel-Blar* hit.

CHAPTER 37

Solange

I was floating over the battle, pale and transparent as mist.

For a long, sickening, horrifying moment, I thought I was back in Viola's spirit castle.

"No," I said, frantically. "Absolutely not."

I had to get out of here. I couldn't be trapped like this again, not now, while I could see my family below fighting for their lives. They glowed faintly blue. I shook my head, as if that would make everything normal again.

"I really can't be crazy right now," I moaned out loud.

"*Merde*, Solange, what are you doing here?"

Isabeau's voice startled me so thoroughly I hollered, and jerked back violently, spinning like cotton candy at a carnival booth. I came to a dizzying stop while Isabeau floated next to me, frowning delicately.

I flapped my hands at her. "Help me!"

Her eyes were fierce as wolf's eyes. "Where is your body, Solange?"

"Kieran and I were on one of the platforms," I said, trying to remember. I squinted at the strange, black-and-white, overexposed photograph of the camp below us. People and vampires glowed like superimposed colorful fireflies. "There!" I pointed, trying to see through the leaves. I could just make out the gold flare of Kieran's aura outlining his body as he stood over me, where I was sprawled unconscious at his feet.

"I have got to stop doing that," I muttered.

"*Bien*." Isabeau looked relieved. "But this is still most unusual. The energy I put into your spirit cord when you were trapped in the castle must still be linking us." She looked briefly curious. "You and Logan are both naturals at dreamwalking."

"That's great," I said evenly, trying not to panic. "What the hell is dreamwalking? And how do I stop?"

"Just recline into your body as if it were a bed."

I couldn't quite get the hang of it. I drifted up a few more feet before Isabeau told me to stare at my body and think of heavy things like ship anchors and mountains. Then she shoved me. The feel of her ghostly hand touching my ghostly shoulder was cold and unpleasant and strangely jelly-like.

I reached the top branches of the tree when she yanked me back up. I shivered, cold to my bones.

"*Non*," she said sharply, changing her mind. "I am sensing too much strange magic around us. Stay close." She lifted one of the amulets around her neck. It was round and metallic, the kind people keep perfume in. The same kind I'd kept Madame Veronique's blood in on a chain around my neck before my birthday. She pulled a long thin thread of white glittering light out of it and looped it around our wrists, where she'd tied the ribbon while she exorcised me. "I cannot wait. The spell must be done now. You will have to come with me."

"Are you calling up that mystical fog you used the night Mom killed Montmartre and Magda killed Greyhaven?"

She shook her head. "It would only put your humans at a disadvantage."

Molten silver dripped from tree branches around us, gathering in puddles in the snow. "What is that?" I asked.

"Blood," Isabeau replied.

Suddenly it was easy to feel the violence below seep into the air, making my spirit vision murky. I shuddered.

"Isabeau."

I heard Logan's voice clearly, even though he was whispering in Isabeau's ear. "Hope is hiding in a pile of boulders southwest of the camp entrance."

We drifted farther away from the safety of my body, searching through the auras. The boulders glowed with a yellowish-green light.

"Hope," Isabeau said, sounding satisfied. There were six or seven guards around her position but they couldn't see us.

Someone else did.

Something magical focused onto Isabeau. The feel of it bled off her onto me, like poisoned molasses, sticky and toxic.

"The Host," she said darkly, clenching her jaw as she worked to repel it. The magic she was fighting prickled uncomfortably through me, but it wasn't having the same effect on me as it clearly had on her. She went particularly pale, as if she were made entirely of silver and shadows. She was in pain.

Montmartre used magic against me in the past, and apparently his men were still using it. They hated me for helping to kill Montmartre. And they hated the Hounds, almost as much as the Hounds hated them. They hated Isabeau most of all, particularly for helping to defeat both Montmartre and his first lieutenant Greyhaven.

They'd known she would be here.

Because this spell clearly had only one target.

And it wasn't my family.

It wasn't even me.

It was Isabeau.

CHAPTER 38

Lucy

"Nicholas!" Connor grabbed his arm and nearly got decapitated before Nicholas realized who it was. "We need backup. Now. Because if this works, we won't be safe anywhere." He paused, frowning at Quinn, who looked up at his twin with his fangs extended. Hunter crouched over her grandfather, in shock.

Connor took a step forward, but Quinn shook his head. "Go," he mouthed.

"Wait for me!" I scrambled after Nicholas and Connor and they turned as one. Nicholas didn't even look back, he just put his arm out behind him so I could grab his hand. He towed me around bloody skirmishes, his firm grip a comforting anchor. I tried not to notice the smell of blood, the moans of pain, the red staining the snow.

We raced between the trees, circling around to the edge of the camp and then up into the mountains. By the time Connor had taken us to one of the caves, my lungs burned and my calf muscles were tight as bowstrings. Inside the damp cave, Christabel was arguing with Saga and Aidan.

And clearly getting nowhere.

"We don't owe you," Saga fumed. "Aidan saved you, you ungrateful wretch."

"If he hadn't kidnapped me, he wouldn't have had to save me!" Christabel yelled back.

Saga didn't even look our way, but the dagger she threw would have caught me right in the stomach if Connor hadn't reached out to grab it, even as Nicholas tackled me to the cold ground. I landed hard, my breath knocked right out of my already strained lungs. Nicholas turned his head to glare, his eyes a deadly silver.

"That's my cousin!" Christabel shouted.

I coughed painfully as Nicholas eased off me.

"Oh, Lucy, I'm so sorry," she said, reaching down to help me up. Her grip nearly broke my fingers. When I squeaked, she winced. "Sorry! I keep forgetting I'm like the Incredible Hulk."

Nicholas stayed between me and Saga. She didn't looked particularly sorry, mostly amused. Aidan just looked tired.

"You brought a human to our home uninvited?" Saga asked, her red hair like fire down her back. "You ought to know the consequences."

"My family," Christabel snapped.

"We're your family now." Saga shrugged.

"Then act like it," she shot back smugly.

"I thought we'd been through this already," Aidan interjected, trying to sound reasonable. They both bared their fangs at him.

"If you want to be part of vampire society so badly," Connor said, "then be a part of it. Especially now that it needs your help."

"And where were the lot of you when we needed help?" Saga scoffed.

Now that daggers weren't being thrown at me, I couldn't help but glance around curiously. The cave was full of pelts and weapons and the usual coolers of blood bags. Saga and Aidan were both so pale, even more than Christabel. They were nearly translucent, the blue of their veins like gasoline trails. Saga wore rolled-up jeans and a silvery breastplate. Aidan had a bear-tooth amulet around his neck that my father would love. His hair was straight and black, and he was distractingly handsome. My heart must have sped up because Nicholas nudged me with his elbow. I tried to look innocent.

Christabel narrowed her eyes. "Fine," she said smoothly. "Then let me quote your precious Ann Bonny." Saga was nothing if not a pirate at heart. "If you would have fought like a man you needn't die like a dog."

"Nice," Connor approved quietly.

"I looked it up," she admitted. That was pure Christabel. She'd be speaking in rhyming couplets any second now.

"I'm not dying for your precious camp," Saga said. "We have too much left to accomplish when this is over. But I like your sister well enough."

"You do?" Connor looked startled. Frankly, so was I. After Viola, Solange wasn't exactly winning any popularity contests.

"She broke the crown into pieces and gave us our due," Saga explained, as if we were dumb. "Of course I like her. So for that reason, we'll give you a few of our pets," she offered finally. "And the wild ones will find you soon enough, if they haven't already" She shook her head at us. "You're barking mad, you are."

Aidan slipped away to give the order to release some of the *Hel-Blar*. They screeched and howled, sending shivers up my spine. There was something deeply unsettling about watching them scurry and scuttle down the mountainside.

"Now what?" Christabel asked. "I'm not exactly trained for battle."

"Got a poem for this?" Connor teased her. "*Not* 'The Highwayman,'" he added. "I finally read it to the end. She kills herself to warn her lover off a trap."

She wrinkled her nose. "It's romantic."

He laughed. She poked him but she was smiling too. No one saw the soft girl under her tough girl quite like Connor did. And no one saw the tough guy under the geek like she did. I was happy for them both, despite the circumstances.

"I hate that I'm a liability to you guys," she said. "I should stay up here, shouldn't I? I'll only hold you back."

"To be honest, I'd feel better if you were safely up here," he admitted. "But between my mom and Lucy I'd have been terrified to suggest it."

"Hey," I said. Then I glanced at Nicholas. "And don't get any ideas."

Christabel sighed. "I can't see how I can help down there." She slid him a glance. "You could stay with me."

"How about I find us one of the better hidden satellites," he suggested. "We can all go together and if we're lucky, no one will even notice us."

Do I even have to say it?

We were totally noticed.

CHAPTER 39

Solange

Isabeau's shields glowed brightly, deflecting the sinister ooze of tainted magic as it tried to slip around us like ropes.

"Isabeau!" Logan shouted. Back on the ground our bodies must be reacting just as our spirits were.

Isabeau closed her eyes and I imagined her pulling energy from the earth and the trees and even the snow drifting slowly down. She used it to form a sword, sharper and more lethal than any forged in the physical world. It glowed like fire. She hacked at the muddy ropes as they tried to drain us. They were insidious and clever. I was exhausted before I'd even realized what they were doing. Everything looked dimmer.

As Isabeau I sliced through them, they fell apart into black smoke, and reformed in the shape of Greyhaven's face. He smiled at her. I hissed at him, knowing he'd been the one to turn Isabeau into a vampire, leaving her buried in a coffin for hundreds of years.

"*Non*," she said as the magic slipped through our barriers. For a moment I saw what she saw and felt what she felt: the weight of the earth over her head, pale roots easing slowly down through the wooden slats of the coffin. The footsteps of mourners passing the graveyard. The smell of the flowers they left to rot under the headstones. The struggle to stave off the madness that licked at her, the hunger burning her into a hollow, papery husk. The blackness when she'd passed out inside the coffin, blessedly cool and numb.

Her spirit body flickered like a candle in a gust of wind.

"Isabeau," Logan called again, more frantically.

"*Non*," she moaned again. The sword in her hand flared.

I knew she wouldn't break the spell, not yet. Despite the fact that I felt as haggard and gray as she looked, she still needed to do the spell. She wouldn't let the Host win.

And she certainly wouldn't let Greyhaven win.

She pushed back, until light shot out of her tattoos, out of her amulets, and finally, out of her aura.

It touched me like rain, washing away the dark magic as if it were mud sticking to my skin.

"Logan once told me to survive Greyhaven," she said, suddenly sounding like my mother, fierce and deadly. She brought her sword down through Greyhaven's face and the smoke dissipated, hissing as if it felt pain. The last of the muddy tendrils fell away completely. My spirit cord flared briefly, painfully.

Isabeau lifted the leg bone of what must have been a truly huge dog. It was painted with runes and swirls and hung with crystals. It was an echo of a real talisman, one reserved for Shamankas and their handmaidens; I'd seen something similar when Kala had used magic to help me see the prophecy. It was so deeply imbued with magic that the moment Isabeau snapped it in half, the dried marrow exploded into a cloud of glitter.

"*Vérité*," she whispered in her native French tongue. "*Vérité*," she said again, shaking the magic off the bone over Hope's head until it covered her like dandelion pollen. "*Vérité*," she repeated for the last time.

Hope frowned suddenly, shaking her head as if an insect had crawled into her ear.

"*C'est fini*." Isabeau smiled and drifted away, taking me with her.

"Okay, what just happened?" I asked. "I assume you didn't do all that just to make her itchy?"

Isabeau didn't answer. She was too busy scowling down at the *Hel-Blar* scurrying through the camp, clacking their jaws. One of them stopped to lick the dried blood off the splintered ruins of the post and the chains coiled like dead snakes. I could also see the outcropping jutting over the long feast table where Logan stood over Isabeau's body with his sword, looking pale. Charlemagne sat behind her head.

"It's time," she said, snapping the ribbon of light that bound our wrists. "You must return to your body. Do not linger."

I shivered, feeling odd. "Don't worry." The pull of the silver cord was making me nauseated as it tugged my spirit back home. I followed the trail, passing through pine boughs and branches, to the platform where Kieran was crouched by my side, looking frantic. I reclined into my body, the way Isabeau told me. My eyes snapped open.

Kieran jerked back, slipped, and fell on his butt. I blinked again, feeling the cold boards under my back, the snow seeping into my clothes, the warmth emanating off Kieran's body.

"You scared the hell out of me," he said hoarsely, as he got to his feet. "Again." He offered me his hand to help me up and I shot up so quickly I ended up pressed against his chest. The sounds of the bloody battle beneath us receded for one moment. And then one of Lucy's classmates darted past, jostling us.

"What the hell happened?" Kieran asked, stepping back but not letting go of me completely.

"Magic," I replied. "Isabeau this time, so I'm okay. And she worked a spell on Hope, so it was worth it." I finally stepped away from him, feeling the cold wind snake between us. His scent of cedar and mint clung to me. "But there are *Hel-Blar* down there now. So I should go."

"We should go," he corrected me.

CHAPTER 40

Lucy

We ran over the rocky terrain, heading around to the far end of the Blood Moon camp into a grove of red pine. There was nothing but dead needles and snow on the ground, no bushes or undergrowth to hide us as we raced against the wind and right into a clutch of *Hel-Blar*. What was the plural for *Hel-Blar* anyway? Pack? Nest? Murder.

Definitely murder.

These weren't even the ones Aidan had just released. They wore no collars, no leashes. They'd been drawn by the smell of spilled blood.

"Climb up that tree." Connor tossed Christabel up onto a low branch and spun back around, a stake in each hand. The *Hel-Blar* clacked their jaws, saliva dripping off their fangs. "When you reach the satellite give a holler."

"I'll give a holler when I crash out of this tree and onto your head from fifty feet up," she muttered. I knew why she was muttering, I was doing the same thing as I climbed up after her to distract myself from the height, the adrenaline swimming through me, the sounds of jaws clacking at Nicholas and Connor, and people dying in the near distance.

"Being a vampire seemed like a lot more fun in those books you used to read," she said to me as I pulled myself up onto a wide, sturdy branch below her. "And it's probably not a good sign that all I can think about it is Tennyson's 'Charge of the Light Brigade': 'Theirs was not to question why, theirs was but to do and die.'"

I shook my head. "Connor's right, your taste in poetry has gotten downright depressing."

On the ground, Connor dodged a clawing grab, swinging up onto a branch just long enough to swing back down, stomping hard. His boot crushed a *Hel-Blar*'s shoulder, cracking his bones. He howled, stumbling. Connor kicked him onto the stake he'd left sticking out of the ground.

"Who could have guessed smart geeky boys were so hot?" Christabel flashed me a conspiratorial grin. She wrinkled her nose. "Being a vampire and hanging out with you again is clearly a bad influence. I'm thinking how hot Connor is when we might all die horribly before the sun comes up."

"Keep calm and carry on," I said cheerfully.

"Isn't that from World War II London when the bombs were falling?"

"I stand by the comparison."

I glanced at the feral blue monsters currently attacking our boyfriends. "Good point." She climbed faster, until she reached the small satellite. "Got it," she yelled down.

"Okay, flick on the switches behind the dish, on the left," Connor called up, then grunted when he tried to avoid a bite and hit the tree hard enough that we nearly lost our perches.

We clung to the trunk, swearing. "Are you okay?" Christa asked.

"Fine," he replied, sounding pissed. The *Hel-Blar* went to dust at his feet. "It'll take a few minutes to boot up before we can recalibrate it. Just hang on."

Once the satellite had little red lights popping up, he had me connect his laptop, which was in my backpack. Considering he'd had to fix my laptop one of the first times I'd met him because I'd accidentally pressed a button I didn't even know existed, I thought he was being rather optimistic. He gave me a bunch of letters and backslashes to type in. The screen garbled at me, but when I read him what I saw he seemed satisfied. Until I got the blue screen of death. Even I knew what that meant.

"It's frozen," I called down.

"Turn it off and on again."

"I tried that already."

He climbed up to my branch. "Keep watch," he said to me as we attached nose plugs over our nostrils. I started to climb back down, to be closer to Nicholas. He couldn't fight off all those *Hel-Blar* by himself, no matter how kick-ass he was lately.

Connor opened his laptop and slipped straight into computer geek mode. He muttered words that made no sense to me, the same way Christabel muttered nineteenth-century poetry.

From my vantage point I could see a fresh wave of *Hel-Blar* arriving. Even on a purely moonless, starless night, I would have seen them. That many *Hel-Blar* were hard to miss. "Incoming!"

They swarmed around us, running to the battle. A few passed right underneath us and I had a fleeting hope that they'd all keep running by and Nicholas could scurry up the tree to safety. The last few found the ashes of their brothers coating the roots and screeched in fury. Half a dozen surrounded our tree and began to climb up. Nicholas did his best to stop them, grabbing their clothing and yanking them off even as he defended himself from fangs and fetid breath.

Christabel frowned down at me when I started to move. "Where are you going?"

"I have to help Nicholas."

She pulled out of her bag a handful of the Hypnos-pepper eggs that Uncle Geoffrey duplicated from a mixture I'd stolen from school. Stakes and swords weren't much use to her, but she could throw these like rotten eggs on Halloween night, if she had to.

She had to.

She lowered her backpack with the rest of her stash to me. I put my arms through the straps, wearing it over my chest for easy access. "Nic, heads up!" I tossed an extra pair at him when he looked up. "Connor," I said, throwing my first egg. I was glad I was only halfway up the tree. Any higher and I would have been dizzy with vertigo by now. "You might want to hurry up."

He glanced down, swore, and started to type faster. "I just have to wait for this to bounce to Chloe and her files. Chloe's trying to activate Hope's cell phone's GPS tag. Now we just have to combine the codes and IPs with the GPS system."

I wasn't really listening, I was too busy trying to toss eggs at the *Hel-Blar* without also tossing myself. I wrapped my ankle around a branch and leaned as far forward as I could. Cayenne pepper and Hypnos exploded. Above me, Christabel did the same.

"Go to sleep!" I shouted as the powder sank into their pores and drifted up their nostrils and down their throats. Two *Hel-Blar* tumbled out of the tree, arms and legs still curled as if they were climbing. Branches splintered as they fell. I kept throwing, as hard as I could. I kept them off Nicholas as he kicked them into the bushes.

By the time Connor gave a triumphant hoot, *Hel-Blar* littered the ground like dead cockroaches, hands and feet sticking up.

"Gotcha," Connor said, grimly satisfied. He reached for his phone, dialing quickly as he clambered down to mid-tree level, behind Christabel. "Bruno," he said. "Phase Two is complete, and Logan sent word that Phase Three is also done." I couldn't hear Bruno's exact words but the smug triumph was clearly audible. Connor was equally smug when he added, "And now I have Hope's exact location."

CHAPTER 41

Solange

I couldn't find my brothers.

There were too many bodies and too many battles and too much blood. I couldn't even hear Quinn's mad battle laugh over the noise. The *Hel-Blar* had finally found us. And though we'd been right about them forcing the hunters and the vampires to split their focus, the results were chaotic.

Somehow Mom spotted Kieran and me the moment we stepped off the ladders leading down from the platforms. There was a gash on her arm where something sharp had sliced through her sleeve and then her skin. Her eyes flared so pale, they were like frozen water. I didn't know where the rest of my family was, except for Aunt Ruby, who was hunched over one of the dead hunters, collecting treasures from his pockets. She considered anything shiny a treasure; coin, knife, safety pin. She moved on to rifle through the discarded clothing of a dusted vampire.

Mom kissed my forehead and then pivoted, dragging her dagger across the throat of a *Hel-Blar*. He gurgled as she finished him off with the stake in her other hand. "Take cover," she ordered me, spinning away again, her braid lifting behind her.

She left a trail of ashes ending in an unconscious Huntsman. He'd tried to stake her and she'd backhanded him into a tree. The Huntsmen had figured out that we were trying not to kill them. They had no such qualms.

And then the Host caught sight of my mother and me fighting together and they went as mad with bloodlust as any *Hel-Blar* I'd ever seen.

The sight of so many familiar brown tunics, all painted with Montmartre's crest, made me freeze for a moment.

A moment too long.

I knew better. I'd trained for hours the way most girls spent hours reading books or shopping at the mall or learning to play the piano. I knew how to riposte and parry with a fencing foil, how to throw daggers and axes, how to execute a proper roundhouse kick. But in that second, all I could see was Montmartre as he'd grabbed me and the feel of the tiara as I'd shoved it through his chest.

The rest of his warriors, still loyal to his memory and the torch of blood vengeance, closed around us like a fist. They moved with military precision.

Luckily, so did Kieran.

CHAPTER 42

Lucy

We ran all the way to the platforms, trailing jaw-clacking *Hel-Blar*.

There was so much adrenaline coursing through me, I felt sick. "This was a better idea in theory." I panted, even though between Nicholas on one side and Christabel on the other, my feet barely touched the ground.

Nicholas managed to find an actual rope ladder, not just a rope with knots for handholds. Connor went up first so he could hang down and lift us up when we got within reach. I followed Christabel. Nicholas stayed on the ground, a long dagger in one hand and a stake in the other. He broke into a run when we were too far up the tree to stop him, drawing the *Hel-Blar* off our scent.

"Damn it," Connor said, practically tossing me up on the platform. "Why does he keep doing that?"

I raced across the platforms, keeping my eye on Nicholas, willing him to stop running so I could cover him properly with my bow. Connor dropped back down to the ground, darting after his brother. Christabel and I kept going, leaping over the broken boards and skirting small fires. I choked on smoke, eyes tearing.

It wasn't long before we were back on the edge of the battle and the *Hel-Blar* abandoned us in favor of the fallen wounded, who were bleeding in the snow. Nicholas and Connor went for the nearest ladder, pulling it up behind them once they'd reached a platform. We ran until we found Chloe sitting on the rough planks, rubbing the back of her neck. She was hunched over her laptop. Jenna had lashed herself to a branch by her waist. She straddled it, feet dangling on either side. I had to duck under her boots. These platforms must have been used by the Moon Guard because there were rails and makeshift roofs, baskets of food, and a jug of water. I took a long drink, only now realizing how thirsty I was.

"How's it going?" I asked.

Jenna just grunted and loosed another arrow. Chloe was slightly wild-eyed. "I much prefer computer hacking to actual hacking," she said. "I'm sending Hope's coordinates to Hart," she added to Connor.

"And Hunter?" I asked, peering over the side.

Hunter still hadn't moved away from her grandfather's body. She was defending it with grim precision, her blond ponytail swinging behind her. Quinn stayed at her side, dispatching a *Hel-Blar* and knocking aside a hunter with the same blow. Jenna shot another arrow, taking out a *Hel-Blar* who strayed too close to them. I reached for my own arrows, nocking one to the bowstring even as I widened my stance for better balance.

I searched for Solange, finally spotting her at the edge of the clearing with Kieran and Helena, all surrounded by Host vampires. Nicholas saw them too.

"Stay here," he ordered as I shot an arrow through two Host, turning them both to dust. "Please," he added desperately. Since I was better able to help from up here, I didn't argue. He kissed me quickly, fiercely, and then he was gone over the railing. He landed nimbly and I covered him as he crossed the battlefield toward Solange.

Having a Drake for a boyfriend and one for a best friend was a full-time job.

CHAPTER 43

Solange

Kieran stepped in front of both Mom and me and shot one of the guns off his belt. It didn't fire bullets or holy water. Instead, flares exploded with fiery trails, blinding the Host who were coming for us. Red flashes seared the darkness for a blinding, eye-stabbing moment.

Mom was already flipping over Kieran's head, landing in front of him once the flares had burned out. Trails of light burned into my eyelids like comets every time I blinked. The Host closest to us shouted, covering their faces. There was a pause in the fighting as everyone was silhouetted in impossible red light.

I snapped out of my momentary panic and balanced my mother's flip by sliding low through the snow, stake in hand. I went left as she went right and we made our own fist, closing deadly fingers around the Host. They didn't notice right away, assuming they had the upper hand because there were more of them.

You'd think they'd have figured out not to underestimate my mother by now.

As for me, I was happy to be underestimated. I'd finally realized being underestimated could be a powerful weapon. I stood still, pretending to be frozen with fear again.

They turned toward me, eyes flaring and fangs flashing.

Mom's sword turned hilt over tip above their heads and I reached up to grab it out of the air. The familiar weight of a sword in my hand made me smile. I used it to knock a stake out of a vampire's hand, flipping it to Kieran. He caught it, immediately going into a fight stance. The world narrowed to my sword, the crunch of snow under the boots of approaching Host, the hiss of anger as they got closer to me, and the sound of bat wings.

And then Kieran went down.

He vanished from sight as Host closed around him. An arrow flew out of the trees behind us. It hit one of the Host and she stumbled back, clutching at the shaft embedded in her stomach. Blood welled between her fingers. *Hel-Blar* howled at the edge of the circle, trying to join the fray when they smelled her fresh blood.

I still couldn't see what had happened to Kieran.

I leaped forward, decapitating the *Hel-Blar* and stabbing the nearest Host. When he doubled over in pain, I kicked him out of the way. The next Host crumbled to ashes when I slid the tip of my blade into his chest. I was yanking the sword free when a blow caught me on the back of the neck. I stumbled and fell hard to my knees. Bats lowered like a curtain. Shielded, I crawled forward in the boot-churned snow.

Kieran was bleeding from a cut over his eyebrow and there was a gash on his knee through a tear in his cargo pants, but he was alive. Relief made my eyes water. We scrambled to our feet, standing back to back against the rest of the Host. Nicholas was suddenly there too. Bats and arrows shot between us, as if the very air wanted us to fight back.

But there was one weapon left in Hope's arsenal and it was far more dangerous than rogue units, stakes, and Hypnos powder. None of us could defeat it, not even my mother.

Actual dawn.

CHAPTER 44

Lucy

There were bodies everywhere.

Jenna and I had run out of arrows and we were leaning against the tree, shaking out our exhausted arms when the sun shot its first rays between the bare trees. Fires belched smoke and heat. The bats had finally flown away to some nearby cave. The snow was red with blood.

I searched the bodies for familiar faces. Unconscious hunters lay next to sedated vampires. Hunter still refused to let anyone near the body of her grandfather. Bellwood's leg was broken. Jenna made a strange sound. I glanced at her. "What?"

She shoved past me, sliding down the rope so fast her hands must have chafed raw. I ran to the other side of the bridge and saw her grab Tyson and try to lift him up. He didn't respond. When she looked up at Chloe, Nicholas and me, she shook her head, tears running down the soot and dirt on her face. I felt my own eyes burn hotly in response.

Night faded slowly, lightening from black to gray until finally a warm glow seeped between the trees.

Solange was the first to fall.

Kieran caught her up in his arms and dashed over bodies and ashes to get her to the safety of the bunker under the Drake tent. Helena followed behind, pulling a hood up over her head to shield herself. Her footsteps dragged and I knew it was strictly force of will that made her able to run that fast. She'd be fine under the cover of the tent, but the bright sunlight reflecting off the snow was too much for her. It was too much for most of the vampires. Liam and Uncle Geoffrey searched for the brothers, finding Quinn, Logan, and Isabeau. Connor stumbled out of the woods, carrying a passed-out Christabel before he fell over himself. Marcus and Duncan were helping each other, stumbling like drunken college students as I shimmied down the rope.

I didn't even know how to feel until Nicholas collapsed.

Logically, I knew he wasn't hurt. It was just the dawn, taking him away. But I reacted as if he was Tyson or Hunter's grandfather or any of the piles of unidentified ashes blowing over the churned-up snow.

I leaped over bodies to land crouched beside him, bow in hand, snarling protectively. Aunt Hyacinth was the one who came to take him away, being the eldest and the most able to withstand the sun. There were gashes in her corset and her bustle had long since deflated.

She put Nicholas over her shoulder and stalked away as I watched, panic receding slightly.

Jason stood next to Sebastian, looking worried. Sebastian was slurring his words, trying to stay upright. Aunt Hyacinth stopped momentarily and frowned at Jason. "Well? Bring him, boy!"

Jason hurried to comply, putting an arm under Sebastian's shoulder and supporting his weight. Chloe joined Kieran, who now had his arm around Hunter. Her eyes were red but dry, like embers. "Bruno found Spencer," Hunter told us. "He's all right. They took him to the Drake tent." Numbly, we watched new hunters arrive down the path. Jenna stood next to us, in shock.

Hart was in the lead, snapping his gaze immediately onto Kieran who had just returned from the tents. "Are you all right?"

Kieran just nodded, exhausted. Hart took stock of the area, swearing wearily. He sent the Helios-Ra agents who'd come from town with him to help the others. There were the sounds of struggles and swearing behind us. The hunters who hadn't been sedated and had started coming out of the woods to finish off any vulnerable vampires were being blocked by Hart's unit. I felt sure anyone attempting to storm the Drake tent would get a fangful of Helena.

Paramedics picked their way through the mess. Theo was already stabilizing Bellwood's leg. Ms. Dailey hadn't survived the gunshot to her belly. More teachers came to help. Mr. York arrived to relieve the rest of the Black Lodge, still guarding the drugged hunters, some of whom were stirring awake.

I took notice of everything, but nothing made sense. I was running on the last sour dregs of adrenaline and shock. There was blood on my jeans and I didn't even know whose it was.

Liam doubled back to join us, covered in a thick coat with a hood. Blood trickled from various wounds and the sleeve of his coat was ripped, but from fang or knife, I couldn't tell. He was pale as glass but perfectly upright and coherent. "Everyone's accounted for," he said, after kissing the top of my head. "You're grounded," he said as an afterthought, before turning to Hart.

"Is it done?" Hart asked.

Liam nodded. "We're ready for you."

"Are you sure it'll work?"

"Sure enough," he replied.

"And how long will it last?"

"Until the new moon," Liam said. "That should give the authorities plenty of time."

"Anyone know what's going on?" I asked Hunter, Kieran, and Chloe. They all shook their heads, as confused as I was. When Liam and Hart walked away, we followed. They led us to a pile of boulders on the edge of the battleground. Bruno and his men had Hope handcuffed and her guards tied up on the ground. Hart motioned to a woman with a small camera. She switched it on to record and aimed it at Hope.

"Okay, that's weird," I whispered. "I mean weirder than usual. Right?"

"Hope," Liam said, his pupils dilating dangerously. Hope shrank back from the compulsion cast by his pheromones but she had nowhere to go. Bruno held her in place. "Do you have anything to confess?"

She opened her mouth, then snapped it shut. It opened again, as if she couldn't help herself. Her eyes rolled in her head like a wild, panicked horse. "I, Hope MacAllister, confess to killing Roarke Black. I also organized the kidnapping of Kieran Black and Lucy Hamilton. I confess to other kidnappings and forcible confinement and the draining of blood from several victims taken from Violet Hill, attributed to the Dracula Killer." Sweat beaded on her upper lip. She shook her head desperately. "No," she moaned.

The woman switched the camera off. Liam approached Hope, pulling paper and a pen out of the inside pocket of his coat. We blinked at him. I, for one, had expected a sword or at the very least a Taser. I'd lend him mine. "Sign here." He pointed at the document.

She struggled, sweat now rolling off the side of her neck. "What is that?"

"Signed confession."

"No," she moaned again. "What did you do to me?"

Liam leaned in very close. I didn't see the change in his expression but I saw the fear suddenly shooting off Hope. "Sign here or I will remember in very great detail how it felt to know that you had my son kidnapped and tortured while trying to frame my daughter. Not to mention the innocent humans you've killed, and your treatment of Lucy Hamilton, who is under our protection."

"You won't kill me." Hope swallowed. "Not the peaceful Liam Drake."

"No," he admitted with a sudden smile that made her flinch. "But I will turn you into a vampire."

She went gray, then green. She grabbed for the pen, awkwardly signing the confession with bound hands.

"Remember what I said, Hope," Liam added silkily, before

stepping away. "You'll be tagged, just like my son was. I will always be able to find you. You'll only be safe in prison. Am I clear?"

Fear made her gag on whatever else she'd been about to say.

Hart gestured for his men to take her away.

"Isabeau worked a truth spell on her," Liam told us with a brief smile. "Now go home, all of you. Hart has a van waiting on the road, if you think you can walk that far. Or we can find a tent for you for a few hours."

"I just want to go home." Chloe shivered.

I glanced at the torn-up field and the burning ropes swinging from the trees.

"Me too."

CHAPTER 45

Solange

Monday evening

The snow all around the decimated camp was clogged with ashes and blood. I barely had time to register the aftermath of broken tent poles, scorched trees, and discarded vampire clothing before my brothers and I were hurried away. Some of the surviving vampires were wandering out of the tents over the underground bunkers and the rest followed the tunnels out to safer ground. The caves would be full with the overflow tonight.

The stunned silence had a texture, like lace curtains muffling all sound. Hart had managed to keep the League occupied over the course of the day, but only barely. We had a couple of hours, at most, to abandon the Blood Moon before other Huntsmen and hunters came to finish the job. Not to mention the *Hel-Blar*, who'd return for the carrion feast.

It was two days before I had a chance to leave the farm. I spent the first night listening to my parents planning around the kitchen table as the dogs snored at their feet, only waking long enough to bark at the vampires Mom trusted enough to allow on the farm. Hart would drop by later when he'd dealt with his own League fallout. Dad suggested biannual council meetings until we figured out the best way to run the new political system. Even after Hope's infiltration, most of us wanted to try to make the council work. Or maybe, *because* of her attack. It had reminded even solitary vampires that they couldn't stand alone anymore. Not all the time.

The Raktapa Council families and a few others temporarily pitched their tents over one of the tunnel entrances at the edge of the property, under the shadow of the mountains. The Host were locked up in the dungeons Hope had created. Nicholas removed all the torture devices himself the very first night after the battle. He incinerated them and then refused to speak of it again. Hart was going to have the hunters who'd worked with Hope on the kidnappings brought up on aiding and abetting charges.

I called Lucy again, but her roommate said she was still sleeping. I wandered into the living room. The moon was waning, pouring faint light over the snow and glittering on the frost nibbling at the windows. Lalita, one of the many Amrita daughters, was curled up on the velvet couch while our parents talked. She looked up from fiddling with her phone and smiled at me, her fangs dimpling her lower lip. Her eyes were the green of the mint tea Aunt Hyacinth told me she drank once in Marrakesh.

"Hi," I said politely. I'd been relegated to hostess duties, which I considered penance. And vaguely ironic, since people were still too scared to be rude to me in my parents' house. "Can I get you anything?" I couldn't remember if the Amrita family drank human blood or animal blood.

"I'm just hiding out from my little sisters. They giggle." She tilted her head. "Where are all your famous brothers?"

"Around."

She rolled her eyes. "Are they as insufferable as mine?"

I rolled my eyes back. "Worse."

She looked unconvinced. "I only have the one," she pointed out. "My family has daughters the way yours has sons. His rarity has made Haridas's head roughly the size of a hot-air balloon."

I had to grin. "I have seven of those."

"Seven what?" Quinn interrupted, leaning in the doorway. "Seven heroically patient big brothers of which I am the obvious favorite?"

"Something like that," I allowed. "You know, if you replace 'brother' with 'baboon'?"

It felt so wonderful to banter normally with Quinn that my eyes burned. The forest was stained with blood, the smell of charred wood and smoke lingered on the wind, and too many were still unaccounted for, but these small simple moments were healing.

They were precious, emblematic of what we'd been protecting: family.

And talking to Lalita, even so briefly, was also emblematic of how sheltered I'd always been. Because of our exile, Madame

Veronique's secrets, and the prophecy, we'd kept to ourselves. There was so much about the vampire world outside of Violet Hill that I didn't know about. An hour at the Blood Moon camp had been enough to show me that.

Others might still say I was barely sixteen years old, but there was no denying I wasn't like other girls. I knew how to use a sword *and* a pottery kiln, how to plan for a war *and* a medieval siege. And I knew that my family loved me.

Now I needed to know so much more.

I needed to know everything, see everything, understand the world for myself, not just through the prism of prophecy or fear.

"I don't like the look on your face," Quinn groaned.

"I've just had an idea."

He groaned louder. "I'll get protective headgear for everyone."

Lalita laughed, winking at me sympathetically. "You're right, seven brothers must be worse," she said as she uncurled from the sofa. "But this one's much cuter than mine."

Quinn grinned. "I am the prettiest," he agreed modestly.

I went to the shed to figure how to get my parents to agree to my plan. The shed was messier then it had ever been. I barely even remembered the temper tantrum I must have pitched to have left so much broken crockery behind. I reached for the broom and swept out the floor and tidied the shelves. It was soothing, rhythmic work, the kind Lucy's mom would have called meditative.

I couldn't pretend I hadn't experienced the last few months. I couldn't go back to being the girl fighting the weight of a prophecy, a spirit, and her own self.

I had a lot of planning to do.

First things first.

I texted Kieran, feeling butterflies in my belly. Then I went up to Connor's room, and cornered Sebastian afterward in the library, as the last of the council members filed out of the house. I'd have to talk to my parents now, before they left for another round of talks at a secret location. The bloody end to the camp councils had cut short too many important and tricky discussions.

"I'd like to meet Kieran," I said quietly. "I've already activated the GPS in my phone, sent Connor the coordinates, and asked Sebastian to come with me. And I'll take Boudicca." She lifted her head at the sound of her name and trotted over to stick her cold wet nose in my palm. "I'm only going as far as the tree by the bunker on the other side of the creek."

My parents looked at me for a long squirming moment. Mom finally stood up and hugged me. "Thank you," she said simply. "Don't forget your sword."

Another mother might have said, "Don't forget your mittens."

It didn't take long to reach the tree with its mossy roots under the snow. Sebastian melted politely into the night, quiet as just another shadow. Boudicca went to investigate interesting smells. The night was crisp and clean, the snow broken only by the footprints from the last time I'd met Kieran here. I had to force myself not to remember Viola and Constantine's special tree, the one that bled like a flesh wound. They'd loved each other and they'd let it turn tragic and terrifying. Well, Viola more than Constantine.

I wasn't going to let that happen to Kieran and me.

Even though he hadn't arrived yet. And even if he'd changed his mind.

Boudicca's ears perked up just as I heard the soft tread of boots approaching. The wind tossed the bare branches overhead, showing a thousand stars. Kieran stood under a pine tree, wearing jeans instead of cargos and a regular pea coat. He waited patiently, half smiling. I swallowed and walked toward him, feeling as nervous as if this was a first date.

"You came," I said softly, stopping awkwardly in front of him. He reached out and took my hand, our cold fingers tangling. Snow fell lightly, catching in my eyelashes. I smelled the cedar-and-mint scent of him.

"Of course," he said, as if it was a given. "Sorry, I'm late. I had to sneak out. League's a mess."

"How's Hunter?"

"Rough," he answered. "As expected. I made her move in with me for a few days. Mom will feed her tea and Quinn can visit. Campus is far from safe," he added. "In case you or Nicholas are planning to see Lucy."

"She's still asleep."

"I'm not surprised."

He was close enough that I had to tilt my chin up to meet his eyes. There were butterfly stiches over his left eyebrow and bruises on his cheekbone. "Who would have thought, the day I snuck into your front yard to claim the bounty that we'd end up here," he murmured.

"Do you regret it?"

He shook his head, tugging me closer. "Do you?"

"No," I replied. "Only that I hurt you."

"That was a hundred years ago."

I quirked a smile. "It wasn't even a week ago. I've made a decision," I blurted out before I could lose myself in his nearness. He waited patiently for me to elaborate. "I'm going to convince my parents to let me travel."

He lifted the eyebrow without the bandage. "Think they'll let you?"

"If I plan it carefully enough. Maybe one of my brothers can come, or Aunt Hyacinth. Besides, it can't be any less safe out there than it is here. We're not exactly hidden away and reclusive anymore." I lifted up on my tiptoes a little, then back down. I was filled with energy, with a sense of excitement I couldn't contain. "It feels right. Part of the reason the battle went as far as it did is because none of us really know each other."

He traced his thumb over the corner of my mouth, which was curved in a hopeful smile. "I think it's brilliant."

"I'll be the first vampire anthropologist," I said lightly.

"When will you leave?" he asked, tugging me closer to him.

"Not for a couple of months at least," I replied. "My parents will take some convincing. You?"

"Same." He brushed the snow off my cheek. "Classes start at the college in January."

"So we have a little time," I said, standing on the tip of my toes to kiss him. His arms went around me and he lifted me right off my feet, kissing me back. "If you're still willing to give me another chance."

"It's just distance," he murmured in my ear. "It doesn't mean anything."

I kissed him again, lingering and swimming in the stolen moment. It turned dark and sweet and I pulled back slightly. I blinked, feeling my eyes going red. I ducked my head.

"Don't hide from me, Solange," he said hoarsely. "Not now."

It took courage to lift my chin and meet his calm gaze. I tried not to imagine how the veins must be blue as ink under my skin, how all three sets of my fangs were poking out of my gums.

He smiled. "Where are you going to go first?"

I smiled back at him, slowly. "I hear Scotland is lovely this time of year."

Chapter 46

Lucy

Tuesday night

I slept for twenty-seven hours straight.

And then the only reason I woke up was because my parents couldn't wait a second longer. My dad and mom had met me at the school after Hart had us brought to the infirmary to be checked out after the battle. I was too tired to even get to the car, so they let me collapse into my dorm bed and then they just stood there, teary eyed and staring creepily until I mumbled at them to go away. Mom called three times Monday, and Dad just drove over first thing Tuesday morning and waited in the parking lot. They weren't pulling me out of school, mostly because I wouldn't let them, but they wanted me home for recuperation. Bellwood had called off classes for the week anyway, while extra counselors were brought in for students and the extra agents were encouraged to leave campus as quickly as possible. There would be a memorial for the fallen, including Tyson, and a traditional Helios-Ra funeral for Hunter's grandfather.

In the meantime, Dad was plying me with chamomile tea and mom kept baking me whole-wheat honey cookies. It was kind of nice to spend the day in bed with Gandhi and Van Helsing, even if they did have doggy breath. Just before midnight, after my parents had gone to sleep, Solange showed up at my bedroom window.

She grinned, pulling up the glass. "Hey, wanna have a sleepover?"

"Can we still do that? Since you don't sleep at night?" I asked as she climbed inside.

"Then we'll have a wake-over."

I grabbed the knapsack she'd tossed onto my bed. "Please tell me you brought chocolate."

"And licorice, sour gummy worms, and those gross marshmallow cookies you love so much."

"And I don't even have to share," I teased, rifling through her stuff until I found the chocolate bars and sugar-coated worms. "There are definite perks to your being a vampire."

We wiggled under my blanket, trying to squeeze into what little space the dogs had left us. I turned on music and we lay back and stared at the ceiling, the way we'd been doing since we were little.

"So." I slid her a sidelong glance. "You've been kissing Kieran."

She turned, blinking at me. Even with her pale eyes with their blood-ringed pupils and sharp fangs, she was still just Solange to me. "How did you know that?" she asked.

"I'm your best friend," I returned, biting the head off a gummy worm. "I know these things." I chewed the sticky candy and then swallowed. "Besides, you get this dreamy, goofy look on your face whenever you've been with Kieran."

"You mean, like the one you get around Nicholas?"

"I do not look dreamy!"

She just grinned. "Sure you don't, Hamilton."

I smacked her in the face with my pillow. She returned the favor until I was gasping for breath and we were both laughing hysterically. The dogs lumbered off the bed with canine sighs. We laughed harder. I was flushed and exhausted by the time we collapsed, still giggling.

"I have another surprise for you," Solange said, after glancing at the clock. "It's in the back garden, where your mom grows all that mint."

I sat up. "You left me a present out in the snow?"

"Yup. Go see."

Bewildered, I stuffed my feet into moccasins and pulled a sweater over my flannel pajamas. I went out the back door instead of wriggling out of my window. I still hurt all over, covered in bruises, scratches, and aching muscles. And now my stomach was sore from all that laughing.

Standing in the snow, with his hands in his pockets, was Nicholas. His eyes were like starlight, his smile crooked and quiet. "You two kind of sounded like hyenas."

I just launched myself at him. He wrapped his arms around me and let himself fall back into the snow, shielding me from the force of the landing.

"Hi," I said, grinning.

"Hi," he returned. "I missed you."

And then words were just a useless exercise, a waste of two perfectly good mouths. His kiss was dangerous and slow, building heat through my body until the snow felt like it was melting around us. It was everything we'd been fighting for, necessary and silent.

Perfect.

EPILOGUE

Solange

December 21

Every year Lucy's parents held a bonfire a few days before Christmas, on the winter solstice. It burned through the night, meant to encourage the sun to return after the longest night of the year. Once my mom started having babies who would one day turn into vampires, Lucy's mom turned part of the celebration into a Longest Night party for us. She'd been trying to find the joy in the things we might find scary, to find the beauty in the night we'd eventually have to claim almost exclusively. Just as she was doing again tonight, with the biggest bonfire I'd ever seen. My entire family was here and so were Lucy's friends from school. Bruno fell asleep on the couch after dinner and none of us had the heart to wake him.

We sat on the garden wall, swinging our feet over a pumpkin patch. Lucy handed me a bottle of something alarmingly frothy and pink. "What is that?" I asked dubiously.

"Some raspberry thing Aunt Hyacinth told my mom would be festive. Mom added healing herbs." She wrinkled her nose. "Looks nasty."

"You have no idea. Aunt Hyacinth's been so domestic since the battle."

"That never ends well," Lucy sympathized. "Personally, I'm sticking to chocolate as my therapy." She dipped her hand into the giant bag of macaroons in her lap. "That and the twice-weekly mandatory school counselor visits." They *were* helping. Her heartbeat was back to normal, without that stress-induced rapidity.

"Do you still have to check in every two hours when you're not home?" I asked her.

"Yes, not to mention I have to meditate with Mom every Sunday morning and show her some kind of artistic expression every week. But the counselor says if they're still making me check in during the new term, she'll recommend a psychologist for them too. So ha!" Lucy ate a few more macaroons. "The academy gave me a new tutor."

"And?" I knew that look.

"I don't like her."

"Why not?"

"Mostly because she's not Tyson," she admitted, watching Isabeau and Logan throw sticks for the dogs to retrieve. "I miss him."

"I miss London too," I said. "Even though we didn't even get along." We looked out over the crowd of people around the fire, the light warm and cheerful on their faces. Warm apple cider and hot chocolate circulated in the new hand-thrown clay mugs I'd made for Lucy's parents.

"Your mom's right," I said. "We needed this."

Lucy tilted her head. "Are Jason and Sebastian flirting?"

I followed her gaze, my eyebrows easing into my hairline. "Even more shocking, is Sebastian actually being chatty?"

"I had no idea." Lucy grinned. "Nathan's going to be pissed, but they're so cute."

"We really are," Quinn drawled, having only caught our last comment. Connor, standing next to him, rolled his eyes.

"How did you fit that big head of yours in the car on the drive over here?" Lucy teased.

"He had to stick it out the window like a dog," Nicholas added with a smirk as he came up behind Lucy. He sat beside her as Quinn pretended to look insulted.

"It's not my fault I'm so much prettier than the rest of you," he said with mock sorrow. "It's a burden. Now I'm going to be a hero and save my girlfriend." Quinn winked at Lucy before drifting over to where Hunter and Chloe were politely listening to Lucy's dad's explanations of how an ancient stone monument in Ireland was built to align with the rising sun on the day of the winter solstice. Connor went to join Christabel under a blanket, letting her read some long rhyming poem to him. He didn't seem to mind in the least.

"How's Hunter?" I asked quietly as Lucy leaned against Nicholas.

"Better. Kieran drops by school every few days to hang out with her," Lucy said. He'd be leaving soon for college in Scotland. I tried not to think about it. We had finally found each other again. Lucy frowned, fiddling with a macaroon but not eating it. "I still can't believe you're leaving," she said, as if she'd read my mind.

"Me neither." I'd finally convinced Mom and Dad to let me travel. I wanted to visit other vampire communities, learn new traditions, and forge new connections to make up for all those I'd accidentally severed. I needed to find someone to help me further control my pheromones and my hunger. And I wanted to make amends. My parents had only agreed when Aunt Hyacinth offered to come with me. My brothers would take turns joining us. Marcus was the first to volunteer, ever eager to gather new knowledge. He'd already helped me turn the copper collar into a bracelet cuff. I could wear it if I felt like my pheromones were too much.

"You have to e-mail me every day," Lucy demanded. She threw a macaroon at my head to illustrate the seriousness of her request.

I ducked it easily. "You too." I tossed one back at her, missed, and hit Nicholas in the temple.

"Ow," he said mildly. He wore a strand of wooden beads with a red tassel around his neck. Kieran was beside him, wearing the same kind of necklace.

Lucy chuckled. "Mom gave you prayer beads."

"Yes," Nicholas replied, sitting on the wall next to Lucy. His hair was tousled, which meant Lucy's mom had also hugged him and ruffled his hair, as she always did.

"And you're wearing them because you're awesome," Lucy said approvingly.

"That too."

"Anyone got a camera?" she asked as Kieran came to stand next to me, leaning against the wall. My knee pressed against his arm. "Because she made a set for everyone I want a photo of Bruno wearing his."

We sat for a long time, the four of us on the wall, silently enjoying the party. "This is the best Longest Night yet," Lucy said happily, snuggling against Nicholas and watching everyone revolving around the fire, laughing and eating homemade cake.

"Let's make a pact," I suggested, wanting to hold the moment in my hand like a little bird. I wasn't ready to let it fly away yet. "No matter where we are or what we're doing, every year we all meet up for a Longest Night celebration."

Kieran held up my hand, our fingers entwined. He kissed my knuckles. "Deal."

"Deal," Nicholas echoed.

Lucy held up her little finger, crooking it. "Pinky swear?"

I looped my finger through hers. "Pinky swear."

Because that's what best friends did—they stood by each other.

And because no one mentioned what happened to Snow White, Sleeping Beauty, or all of those other princesses sleeping through their lives. Eventually, the Longest Night gave way to morning.

Eventually, they woke up.

Author's Note

It is wonderfully strange to write the last book in a series. When I wrote *Hearts at Stake/My Love Lies Bleeding* I thought I was writing a standalone novel. I wanted to have fun with Snow White and with vampires, even though everyone kept saying vampires were dead (ha-ha). I wanted to tell my story regardless. I could never have imagined it would become a six-book series, and additional e-novellas and short stories. And that is what the Drake Chronicles taught me again and again: Tell Your Own Story.

I hope it's brought you a few hours of escape, a few thrills, and a few sighs over those Drake brothers.

I already miss them.

But there's always more to the story . . . so look for new Drake Chronicles e-novellas coming your way.

AUTHOR'S DISCLAIMERS

This is a work of fiction. Exchanging blood is NEVER safe. Do not attempt the blood oath in this book EVER. The risk of acquiring deadly diseases is very real.

The witchcraft in this book is purely literary. It is not intended to represent modern or ancient belief systems.

Sky has had her eye on Duncan Drake throughout the Blood Moon gathering. So when they find themselves isolated in the woods and attacked by the three Furies, she's in danger of losing more than her life – her heart is at stake . . .

Sound and Fury

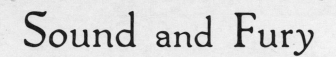

ALYXANDRA HARVEY

SKY

Vampires are a pain in the ass.

I should know. You'd be hard-pressed to find a more arrogant and proud race, and harder-pressed to find a family more proud of that than mine. The Shakespeares considered themselves just as important as any family on the Raktapa Council; we just happened to be stealthier. We weren't as old as they are, just old enough to be annoying about it. And with a pretentious assumed last name like Shakespeare, you just know we're really good at being annoying.

We weren't a normal family, of course, just a collection of vampires under the guidance of our patriarch, Oliver Shakespeare. He was made in 1847 and spent most of the Victorian period saving orphans, pickpockets, and runaways by changing them into vampires. He never got out of the habit, not even now, when such things were considerably harder to hide.

Exhibit A: Me.

He was still vaguely Dickensian, always dressed in a three-piece suit with pinstriped pants and a gold watch he wouldn't let anyone touch. He was so proud of our little raggedy tribe, it was almost nauseating. He just couldn't understand why I'd rather paint than roam the world learning about vampire customs and politics.

Yawn.

Also, painting landscapes and fairy tales was less likely to get me killed.

Don't get me wrong, I'm grateful he changed me, and I didn't even mind being one of the bloodsucking undead most of the time. The Blood Moon was cool; I'd learned more in the past week than I would have in any museum. I'd seen antique Russian gilded triptychs and painstakingly embroidered tapestries and painted leather scabbards for ancient swords—but there was no denying there were disadvantages. And I don't even mean trading chocolate for blood.

Take, for example, the fact that I was just literally knocked on my ass by some unseen force that slapped the camp the moment Solange Drake put the crown on her head.

I have to say it: being a vampire queen doesn't seem like a terribly viable career path. No longevity for one thing, if history was any indication. I would have let my mom keep the title if I were Solange. No accounting for tastes, I supposed.

The coronation ceremony began well enough, with drums and

parades of ancient vampires in ancient and beautiful clothing: hand-decorated saris, medieval leather tunics, pearl-encrusted Renaissance gowns, and beaded flapper dresses. The Shakespeares were the most ragtag, but Oliver insisted we congregate right up front, at the foot of the royal dais next to the council families. Someone made a boring speech about vampire pride, someone else rang a bell for some obscure reason I couldn't figure out. Helena stood with her husband, Liam, and their seven sons.

The Drake brothers were notoriously handsome, and vampires and humans alike hovered around them like moths around a flame. They wanted to singe their wings on all that dark, burning beauty. I just wanted the coronation to be over and done with so I could get back to my painting.

The moon was a perfect yellow harvest moon and I wanted to capture that honey light before it faded away. That was one thing I missed: daylight. It just made art easier. Still, the awesomely sharp vampire eyesight was pretty good compensation. I planned to use it to make a name for myself in the art world by painting mysterious nightscapes. Turn your weaknesses into strengths, that's what Oliver was always telling us.

Currently, my weakness was a rock digging into my backside.

Vampires pushed to their feet all around me, whispering and murmuring until the sound was like rain, or hail tearing through leaves, both soft and violent. I grabbed for Miranda. "Mir!"

She sat up, pushing her petticoats out of the way. Like most vampires, Oliver insisted we dress from his time period for special events. Usually that meant we looked like ragamuffins out of an

Oliver Twist remake. In fact, I secretly thought that was the only reason Oliver went by the name Oliver.

"Ow." Miranda sulked. There were pine needles in her braids. "That hurt."

I rubbed my tailbone. "I know."

We got to our feet. I didn't rise like dangerous smoke or deer in a field—I just stood up. I'd been a vampire for nearly two years now, but I still didn't have that undeadly grace. I just clomped around in my paint-stained overalls. Well, not tonight. Tonight I wore a bright blue jacket and layered skirts in burgundy and gray.

"I hope Duncan's okay," Miranda whispered. She'd been nurturing a crush on Duncan Drake since we'd arrived. She'd been bugging me to paint a portrait of him since the first time she saw him. Miranda moved closer to me. She'd never admit she was freaked out. She was fourteen and human and constantly trying to prove herself to everyone about every little thing. She was the only one of us who wore long skirts and half-gloves on a regular basis. I loved Oliver—he'd rescued me from unmentionable things—but I didn't worship him. Not like Miranda did.

It went against Oliver's rules to keep a human among us, especially one who was underage. But he was the one who took in Miranda when she was a baby, long before I ever came along. He'd found her abandoned at a bus depot on Christmas eve. She'd been coddled and spoiled ever since.

"I ripped my skirt," she complained as Oliver and the others made a protective circle around her. "What just happened?"

"I don't know," I replied. I felt odd, as if I were glittering inside.

I felt fuchsia and cerulean and lime green. I wiped my damp palms. I couldn't remember the last time I'd had damp palms; certainly not since turning vampire.

"Sky, take a turn, won't you?" Oliver asked in his smooth, sophisticated voice. "While we escort Miranda back to the tent."

"I want to go with Sky!" she protested. "She gets to have all the fun."

"Now," Oliver insisted, drilling a finger into her lower back to propel her forward.

I knew why he was sending me out to gather information. I spent so much time painting, and deliberately staying out of politics, that no one really knew who I was. Not that the Shakespeares were exactly well known, despite what Oliver might choose to think.

The encampment was buzzing with gossip. Dogs raced between the bodies, mostly toward the mountain where the Hounds were currently living. They barely left the privacy of the caves; I'd only seen two girls in the shadows once, tattooed and scarred. And I'd been looking. I heard there were ancient cave paintings drawn with actual red ochre and I was desperate to see them. So far, no luck.

The whispering was thick and annoying, like flies. Everyone had something to say about the surprise coronation. Councils would start the next night, now that the formal ceremony was finished. Solange would rule us all, and we were notoriously difficult to rule. Vampires tended to follow their maker and no one else. Even that wasn't easy sometimes, but centuries of hiding out in order to survive had bred a healthy respect for hierarchy into our bones, whatever our intellectual preferences.

Chandramaa guards marched from one end of the camp to the other. It was a show of power and control, in case anyone got any ideas. I avoided them. A cluster of women with dyed white hair and white beaded dresses wailed and wept. I avoided them too.

I crept as close to the Raktapa family areas as I dared, but I didn't hear anything useful. Music played in every tent, drowning out the sounds of conversations from even the best vampire hearing. Right now I knew what everyone else knew: Solange was queen through some kind of family coup involving bats.

And magic. I couldn't think of another explanation for why the crown had flared so bright, like a comet, and then ripped through the gathering with its power. I could still feel it inside me, like frost and fire. I refused to give in to the nervous energy sparking through the camp. One wrong word, one sudden movement, and it would tear through us like fire in a dry field. I already felt as if I were walking on sword tips, gingerly and acutely aware of the possibility for dismemberment. It would make a good painting, but it made for a bad night.

DUNCAN

Usually being on a bike, any bike, cleared my head. It was just me and the wind in my ears, and the blur of the world around me. Nothing else mattered. I could go as fast and far as I wanted. I could keep riding until I was clear out of the country.

But tonight I could ride until I hit the ocean and my head still wouldn't be clear.

Solange was going darkside, as Connor put it. Nicholas was still missing. And we were all in exile. Actually, that last part wasn't so bad. We were used to it and I preferred it over all the acolytes and assassins. I didn't much like people, vampire or otherwise, so not having to show my face at the courts was a bonus. But the fact that I might get staked for it just pissed me off. Suddenly, prancing through the courts seemed like a fine idea.

Contrary, that's a Drake for you.

I rode between the trails, going fast enough that my teeth rattled. It would have hurt back when I was a human but now I barely noticed. It used to be dangerous too; one wrong turn, one root under the wheel, and I could have snapped my neck. I kind of missed the thrill of it. The terrain was rough and rocky, and tree branches slapped at me, but none of it could hurt me.

I was glad I'd hidden my motorcycle. The rough trails were murder on the engine, the wires, not to mention the shocks. For serious riding, I needed a dirt bike in the forest. It wasn't the same but it was better than nothing. I rode over the roots and twigs, kicking up dead pine needles behind me as I made my way to the rendezvous point. Dad had established several of them, fanning out in all directions from the Blood Moon camp. The one near the broken willow was the closest one leading away from the farmhouse, since anyone would assume we'd take the shortest route back home. Dad was as good at misdirection as Mom was at kicking ass.

I came up behind Quinn, Connor, and Christabel on the way. It hadn't even been a full month since she'd died and turned vampire. Before that she'd been a city girl, until a visit to Violet Hill had changed her forever.

"Hell of a night," Quinn muttered.

"Yeah, we put the fun in dysfunctional family," Connor agreed as I swung off my bike to pace along beside them. The smell of exhaust clung to me. Hardly stealthy. With a curse, I stashed the bike in a scraggly bush. I'd already made my rounds around the camp to make sure all the Drakes and Bruno's team were accounted for. It had gotten me as far as I'd needed it to.

A few minutes later, Mom stepped out of the shadows under the willow, her blue eyes glinting like broken lapis lazuli; the kind ancient queens in ancient deserts would have worn. Probably to decapitate traitors. Mom had as much use for jewelry as I did for crowds.

She looked weary in a way that made my brothers and me exchange sidelong glances. Still, she was Helena Drake, which meant that despite being knocked down by Solange's coup, she'd orchestrated her family's escape and managed to arm herself to the teeth within minutes.

"We're clear," I told her.

"Thank you. Any sign of Madame Veronique?" When I shook my head she clenched her teeth. "Damn. Well, your father's gone on ahead with the others," she said as Aunt Hyacinth joined us. Her veils had been trampled in the chaos after the magic inside the crown had knocked us all down. Her scarred cheeks were flushed with annoyance.

"I taught that girl better manners than this," she snapped, positively dripping Victorian displeasure.

"Regroup to fight again," Mom said tightly. Her fangs were so far extended they dimpled her lower lip. She hated retreating more than anything. Her face was still grim but she tried to gentle her voice. "Come with me, Christabel. You'll be safe."

Christabel, being Lucy's cousin and clearly every bit as insane, didn't look particularly scared. But she seemed to have already realized Mom had a pathological need to protect and she let herself be led away. Connor and Quinn followed, stakes in hand.

"Coming?" Aunt Hyacinth asked when I paused.

I flared my nostrils, sorting through the myriad of scents: pine, exhaust, wind off the mountain, blood.

Warm blood.

The stake was in my hand before I'd even thought about it.

There. A heartbeat, just under the sounds of owls and badgers and thunder far off in the distance. I pivoted slowly, trying to place the scent of strawberry lip gloss. I sighed suddenly.

"Miranda, get out here."

A red-haired girl eased out of the bushes where she'd been sneaking up on us. She wasn't bad for a human, and a kid at that.

"I just wanted to say good-bye," she said softly, uncertainly.

I lowered my stake. "Not a good time to sneak around, kid." I glanced at Aunt Hyacinth. "I'll take her back. I can double back to make sure our tracks are covered too." And add a few misleading prints while I was at it.

"I'll wait for you."

She still bore the scars of Helios-Ra holy water from the last time she'd waited for one of us. "I'll be fine," I said, trying not to sound as though I thought she needed protecting. It made Drake women rabid. "Tell Mom I'll catch up so she doesn't send the cavalry after me for being late."

She looked uncertain, but the thought of Mom's reaction must have convinced her. "Hurry."

Miranda didn't say much as I walked her back down the ragged trail. She kept biting her lip. She used to hang around my maintenance tent, before Solange had us all kicked out. She reminded me a little of Lucy, having grown up around vampires all her life. She tripped over a tree root in the dark and I grabbed the back of her jacket before she could fall on her face. She blushed to the roots of her hair.

"Why did your sister do that?" she asked. "Exile you like that?"

"Wish to hell I knew, kid," I muttered. "She—" I broke off with a curse. "Up that tree," I ordered, practically tossing her up into the nearest branch that would hold her weight. "Stay put," I added. I thought I heard her sigh, the same way Lucy used to sigh over Spike in the later *Buffy* episodes. I didn't care if she sang show tunes in her head, as long as she climbed.

I eased into the cover of a clump of cedar and pine, waiting patiently. Whoever was coming this way was moving carefully and quickly. Too quickly for a human and as if they had somewhere very particular to be. The only place around here was our secret rendezvous point.

Like hell.

I shut out the wandering of the winter wind off the mountains, Miranda trying to catch her breath as she scurried up another branch, some small creature burrowing under my boots. I continued to wait, still as the bad-tempered alley cat I'd been accused of emulating more than once. Mom's training kept my head clear and the adrenaline a quiet river instead of a poisonous waterfall. I cataloged my weapons: a stake in each boot, one on my belt, more in the pack on my bike which was too far, broken branches, speed, and fighting dirty.

I saw the toe of a boot, a swish of burgundy wool.

When I moved it was with the lethal grace of Mom's kata drills and the savagery of having six brothers.

I grabbed an arm and swung the intruder around, the cedar boughs lowering to cover us.

SKY

I was going to kill Miranda.

If she wasn't already dead.

Fear and fury made everything ochre and lime green, like a Van Gogh painting. And it had me hurrying, and trying not to panic instead of paying closer attention to my surroundings. I knew better.

Too late.

The hand that hauled me off my feet was uncompromising iron. The forest was shades of black, smears of green and snow white, and then my back slammed into a tree and I was pinned. I reached up to pull on the arm across my throat. My hand was dark on his pale arm, muscles tensed under my fingertips. I usually had the advantage around pale vampires. I was dark enough to blend when they gleamed like old bones sticking out of the earth.

Except no amount of blending could give me an advantage over a Drake brother.

Especially Duncan.

His eyes blazed into mine. They were a light shade of green. I couldn't help but wonder how I'd mix a color like that. Maybe hunter green with loads of white. And a touch of gray? or silver? He was close enough that I could smell the engine oil on his jeans, wood smoke and snow in his dark hair. There was a stake in his hand, violence in the set of his poet's mouth.

He blinked once. "Sky?"

And just like that he released me. But he was still close enough that if I moved even slightly, we'd be touching. I wished I'd been fast enough to kick him at least once, but I was better with a paintbrush. And fighting always meant the risk of damaging my hands. I'd heal from almost anything, but having to wait even a single night without the ability to draw made me feel sick inside.

I could always paint Duncan's portrait with him sprawled under my multicolored boots, weeping for mercy. Except he'd still make it look good. His jaw was clenched tightly enough that even the faint stubble on his cheek looked sharp as needles. He was rugged in that outdoorsy, I-can-fix-anything-with-gum-and-a-pocket-knife kind of way. Except for his mouth, which was pure poetry.

I was getting as bad as Miranda.

She'd spent most of the week sitting on a tree stump watching him tinker with engines and battery cables. He'd taught her how to ride up and down the field. She'd sat on the back and clutched at his shoulders. It was all she talked about for two full days until Oliver threatened to send her back home. When Duncan admitted he read poetry for fun, I thought Miranda's heart was going to explode right in the middle of her chest. Hungry vampires paced the perimeters of our tent, scenting the hot blood rushing through her until Oliver posted guards.

"It's not safe out here," Duncan said.

"No kidding," I returned drily, rubbing my throat.

"Sorry," he said. "Not a good night for the Drakes."

"I know. I'm sorry. . . ." A twig cracking in the undergrowth made us both pause. The wind shifted and I smelled something else: warm skin, bubble gum, lip gloss.

"Miranda Shakespeare," I snapped at the shadow sulking in the tree. "Do you have any idea how much trouble you're in? Oliver is going to kill you."

Miranda, being clever enough to know exactly how much trouble she was in, stayed up the tree. She did crawl down to a branch where she could see us properly. "I had to come."

"Now? *Tonight?*"

"I just . . ." She bit her lip. "Are you going away forever, Duncan?" She looked miserable, her red hair shining like firelight. I turned my head slightly, shooting him a warning look. If he broke her heart, I'd break his face. Never mind that I hadn't punched anyone since the summer I ran away from home and ended up sharing an alley with a crazy bag lady who thought vampires were real. Oh, the irony.

"I'll be around," he promised Miranda, without even acknowledging my warning.

"Promise?"

"Yeah," he replied. "I promise."

"Where's your motorcycle?" she asked. "The blue one? You said you never walked when you could ride."

"You know better than to trust vampires," he said. He grinned and all of a sudden he wasn't just one of the many Drake brothers anymore. We'd talked before, he'd even helped me get one of the bikes going, but now I could understand a little bit better how Miranda could mope about all night talking about him. It wasn't just that he was ridiculously gorgeous, it was all that silent confidence. And the killer smile didn't hurt. "I hid her in that cave; remember the one I showed you?" He took a set of keys out of his pocket and tossed it up to her. "Look after her?"

"Okay." Miranda pocketed the keys proudly.

"I wouldn't trust my girl to just anyone, you know that, right?"

"I'll take care of it."

"I know you will." He tilted his head, his green gaze sliding off mine to fix on the trees behind me for just a moment.

I paused when those eyes slammed into me again, nodding once to show him I understood. I grabbed a handful of mud, snow, and the humus of the forest floor before scaling the tree and rubbing it all over Miranda's face and neck, even though she squirmed, grimacing. She was accustomed to having her human scent covered in all manner of disgusting ways. This one was relatively insignificant. Coupled with the height of her perch, it should be enough to convince a passing vampire that she was a raccoon or a small bear or whatever the hell it was that climbed trees out here in the middle of nowhere.

I stepped from branch to branch, putting as much distance as I could between me and my fragile adopted sister. Duncan mirrored my movements on the other side, until we reached a willow split by rot or lightning bolt. I caught a glimpse of pale cheek, and then nothing more. The ground below us was a carpet of red fallen leaves and frost.

And then it may as well have been a marble floor in a castle lit with beeswax candles. Three women glided over the dirt, wearing silk dresses with panniers and hoop skirts. Crystal beads and pearls were sewn onto every available surface and each of them had long straight hair, bleached to the color of bone. It was the weeping, pale-haired, white-clad women from the camp. I'd heard them called the Furies. They'd been loyal to the last queen, Lady Natasha, before Helena Drake killed her.

Apparently when you were a court vampire, loyalty and revenge made you bleach your hair and dress like Marie Antoinette. I might have dismissed them as bad performance art if it wasn't for the cold, sinister bloodthirst that emanated off them.

"We need to get to Helena *now*."

"But what about her whelps? The whole damn tribe of them will be together now."

"This is our chance," the third woman insisted. "We take as many down as we can. But since we can't get to Solange right now, Helena is our goal. Kill the usurper before they get to the farmhouse. Once they're on their own land, we'll never get through their defenses. Not since they've started working with that Hound bitch."

"I smell something," the girl insisted, her bloodshot eyes glowing. She was as young as Miranda. I shivered. "The Drakes came this way."

"Track her while we wait for the others." The girl slipped off into the shadows, her bead-encrusted gown glimmering like moonlight on water. She should have looked ridiculous in her elaborate ball gown. She just looked creepy as hell. And she was either going to find Duncan or his mother.

I saw a flash of white when Duncan's lips lifted off his fangs. It was the only warning he gave. He dropped down, pale as a shooting star.

The girl hissed as he sent her flying off her feet. She landed hard at the feet of her sisters, snow crunching under her body. Clearly, Duncan had no intention of letting them track his mother. And clearly, they were harder than their pretty white dresses made them seem.

The one nearest to him lifted her hand, as if he should be kissing the back of her pale fingers. Instead, a puff of powder like confectioners' sugar exploded from a cartridge hidden under her sleeve.

Hypnos.

"Stay." She smiled with exaggerated courtesy. Her eyes glowed like amber. "And let us kill you, traitor's son."

Duncan struggled against invisible chains. Hypnos was devious and deadly; it stole your willpower until there was nothing you could do but obey commands. I'd never actually seen it in action before. I felt nauseated, watching his eyes roll and his jaw clench. He couldn't move, even with a white stake descended toward his heart.

I did the only thing I could think to do.

I jumped.

I landed on the Fury's outstretched arm, snapping it with a sickening crunch. The stake flew into the snow. She howled. Her sisters hissed, reaching for me. I didn't evade, just stepped into the grab, squeezing her other wrist as hard as I could. She had Hypnos under that sleeve as well, and the cartridge broke under my fingers. The drug hung in the air like mist.

"Duncan," I snapped, bending backward out of its reach. "Fight."

My command undid the previous order and he was suddenly everywhere at once. He moved so quickly he blurred around the edges. I'd never seen anyone fight like that. It wasn't the formal training of martial arts, or fencing, or any of the disciplines older vampires tended to study. It was simple bar-brawl fighting.

He spun the woman with the broken arm and she crashed into a tree with her face. She slumped gracefully into the snow. The other jumped him from behind, howling. Her stake tore his T-shirt and grazed the underside of his ribs. His blood was a burning rose, smelling as sweet as any flower. He twisted and the blunt end of the stake was between them, driving into the Fury's chest. When it pierced her heart, she crumbled to pale ashes.

The girl began to hiss like a rabid cat. Duncan barely noticed. He drove his elbow back and she doubled over, clutching her sternum. He knocked her out with an uppercut.

And then he turned toward me.

Fight.

I hadn't been specific enough.

He continued to stalk me, fangs extended, green eyes burning as hot and dangerous as fireworks. The surviving Furies were unconscious and I was the only one left to fight.

"Duncan, it's me. Sky," I said soothingly, even though nerves had my lips trembling. "Remember? You fixed a bike up for me."

He blinked.

"Remember?" I asked.

But he was back to prowling, smiling slightly so that his fangs gleamed.

"You don't have to fight me," I said, creeping backward slowly. If I ran, all of his instincts would force him to hunt me down. I aimed myself away from where Miranda was perched. "Duncan, please."

I tripped over a root and the sudden movement was enough to set him off. Suddenly I was falling or he was pushing, it didn't matter. I was pressed to a tree and he was pressed against me.

"This is getting to be a bad habit." I tried to keep my tone light, unconcerned. I knew he could smell the fear and the adrenaline in my system, just like we could both smell the heat of his blood dripping from his wound.

He was so close his lips brushed my cheek when he spoke. "I remember your scent."

Something shivered through me. It was too complicated and primal to explore. His fangs scraped along my throat.

I shoved my fingers into the raw cut under his ribs.

He jerked back, cursing darkly, hands tightening on my shoulders.

"Your family's in danger."

The last of the Hypnos burned out of him like a fever. His eyes were painfully bright, and then he slumped, disoriented.

"Sky?" He blinked, confused. He released me so abruptly, I nearly fell over. "Shit. What did I do? Are you okay?"

I nodded. "I'm fine."

"Shit," he said again. "I'm sorry." He touched my cheek so lightly I might have imagined it. "Really."

I swallowed, my mouth suddenly dry. I forced a smile because for some reason there was a hysterical giggle bubbling in the back of my throat.

He stepped back. He groaned, running a hand through his hair. "Hypnos hangover is worse than a real hangover," he said with disgust.

"What do we do with them?" I asked, looking down at the two unconscious vampires. Because it was safer than looking at him.

"We need to tie them up while I figure it out," he said. He pressed a hand to his wound as he bent to unlatch the girl's Hypnos cartridge. "Let's not go through that again."

I frowned. "You need to wrap your ribs."

"It's fine."

"You're bleeding all over your boots."

He glanced down. "I guess they'll match yours," he said lightly. My boots were covered in splotches of paint. I hadn't thought he'd notice something like that.

I cleared my throat. "I don't suppose you have rope conveniently stashed nearby?"

"No." He raised one eyebrow. "But I've got chains in my bike pack."

"You always carry chain?" I asked dubiously.

"It helps with bikes and cars stuck in snow. Plus, I'm a Drake," he said as if that explained it all. His grin was brief and did interesting things to my insides. I felt Miranda flutter beside me. Damn, those Drake pheromones were strong. The brothers should come with a warning label.

His bike wasn't far and he came back with a leather satchel over his shoulder and a length of chain in his opposite hand. He locked the Furies' wrists together. There was no telling how long they'd be out for. Vampires tended to be resilient.

"I can't call my mom," he muttered, stabbing at the numbers on his phone. "If her phone rings, they'll track her that much faster. Connor," he spoke into the phone. "I need the coordinates for the nearest safe house. I'm texting you mine now." He explained what had happened while I darted back to where Miranda was hiding.

She climbed down quickly, her eyes wide. "Are you okay? I heard noises."

"I'm fine."

"Duncan too?"

"Duncan too."

DUNCAN

Shit, way to go, Drake, I thought to myself. *Scare the crap out of the girl who saved your ass.*

So far, today was not improving.

I had to school my expression into something more civilized when I heard Miranda crashing through the trees. I stopped her before she tripped right over one of the vampires. "Stay back." She froze. "Got 'em, thanks," I added into the phone. "Don't let Mom go nuclear if you see her before I do." I squinted down at the tiny screen. "I hate these stupid things," I muttered.

"I can do it," Miranda offered. "I'm good with the tech stuff."

I shrugged, passing her the phone. "Knock yourself out. We're looking for the red dot on the GPS screen."

Sky met my eyes over Miranda's head. Her gaze was quietly assessing. When I didn't vamp out, she relaxed. I felt even guiltier. I was used to seeing her in overalls and an easy smile. Her coronation dress made her look Victorian, but not the way Aunt Hyacinth looked Victorian. For one thing, there was a big pink daisy in her Afro.

"Here," Miranda announced proudly from a few meters away. She looked around, frowning. "What's supposed to be here?" she asked, when there was nothing but more trees and more snow.

I looked from tree to tree, knowing exactly what I was looking for. It didn't take long. I crouched down and shoved aside leaves and dirt until a black iron door handle emerged. I yanked it open. The smell of damp unused cellar wafted up.

"Is that a crypt?" Miranda asked eagerly.

"No." I laughed despite myself. "And shouldn't you know better? Vampires don't really sleep in crypts."

"She's just naturally morbid," Sky explained.

"Are we going to bury them down there?" Miranda pressed.

"We're just going to . . . store them," I said. She looked disappointed.

Sky and I dragged the two vampires toward the opening and then dropped them down inside. I shut the door and kicked leaves and snow back over it. "Connor will lock that down remotely so they can't get out," I told them. "We'll unlock it tomorrow night. If we feel like it."

Miranda grinned. "That's so cool."

"Glad you think so, kid," I muttered, rubbing my face. The Hypnos hangover was still making me feel like shit. "I have no idea how many more of them might be coming. You two better clear out."

"We can't just leave you alone!" she exclaimed. "You need our help."

"She's right," Sky said. "You can't take on a bunch of Furies by yourself."

"And you can't let Miranda go back to the camp alone right now," I pointed out. "It's not safe anywhere." Unfortunately, I was right too. I could see it in Sky's face.

"But I can help!" Miranda protested.

"But I can't be rescued by a fourteen-year-old girl." I winked at her. "It's not very macho."

She giggled.

Sky frowned. "So what do we do now?"

"I need to lure them off my mom's scent," I said. "Luckily, I know exactly where to send them." I took my phone back from Miranda, pretending not to notice that she'd already programmed her number into it. I called the only number I ever called on a regular basis. "Bryn," I said when she answered. "Incoming."

Bryn and I shared a love of motorcycles and vintage cars, and an antisocial nature. We'd once spent twelve hours tinkering with a

'68 Mustang and never said a word the entire time. Plus, her family was as batshit crazy as mine. Possibly more so, and that was saying something. I hung up and the phone started to vibrate instantly. "And right on cue." I watched it go to voice mail, then texted Mom back, assuming that if she was secure enough to phone me, a text wouldn't compromise her safety.

"We can't just leave you." Sky was biting her lower lip. It was cute as hell.

"I'll be fine," I said, already running through options and tactics in the back of my head. I had no idea how many Furies were on my ass.

Sky just snorted. "You're right about Miranda, anyway. I don't have time to get her back."

"I don't need a babysitter." She huffed. "I can take care of myself."

"No, you can't," Sky and I both replied together. I'd been saying the same thing to Solange and Lucy since they were barely old enough to talk. She glowered at us both and folded her arms. Lucy once poured honey all over my favorite bike; a little glower didn't faze me.

"Bryn's family went survivalist in the mountains," I said. If they were determined to stick with me, we needed to move fast. And I could use the extra help. "And when they found out there were more than bears out there, they set traps. They also have safe houses, like we do. There's a crow's nest of sorts, made of whitethorn soaked in holy water. She'll be safe up there."

Sky nodded. "Okay."

I flipped open my pocketknife and jabbed it into my wound,

hissing in pain. Miranda squeaked. I let my blood drip into the snow. "We have to leave a trail even a psychotic groupie can follow," I said.

We were jogging slowly; Miranda was out and out running, sweat dampening her hair. I could smell her shampoo and her blood, warm and fresh. "Shit, kid," I barked, trying to hide my fangs. "What the hell are you doing?"

"You said we needed to leave a trail," she said calmly, dragging an opened pin from her jacket across her arm. It was an "I heart Damon" button and the tip of the pin was dripping with her blood. "Drake blood and human blood will be too much for them to resist, right?"

"Right," I said darkly. "But it will be too much for *any* vampire to resist."

That was the exact moment the *Hel-Blar* came leaping out of the bushes. He crashed into my side, opening my wound again. I used the momentum of my fall to roll, flipping the *Hel-Blar* off me before he could sink his diseased fangs into my neck. I landed hard, bruising my shoulder, and jumped up into a crouch. I balanced on the balls of my feet, pulling a stake from my jacket. The *Hel-Blar* had a stake as well but I was more concerned about the way he was clacking his teeth at me. One bite and I was done for. The smell of rot and mushrooms was nearly palpable.

The hell I was going to be turned into a *Hel-Blar*.

Tonight had already sucked enough.

He leaped at me, snarling. His hands were curled into claws, jaws wide open. I threw the stake, whipping it like a dart at a board in a pub. The whittled end flew true, bit through clothes and flesh. He came apart into ashes that stank of stagnant pond water.

I got to my feet, eyeing Miranda. "Don't help anymore, kid."

She winced, peeking out from behind Sky, who had moved to shield her. "Sorry."

I just shook my head and we kept running until I pointed to a tree, the top of which was shrouded in evergreen branches. "Up there."

Miranda wrapped her arms around Sky's shoulder and Sky scaled the tree, depositing her on the fenced wooden platform.

"Will she stay put?" I asked when Sky dropped back down to the ground, her skirts fluttering around her paint-smeared boots.

"She can be pretty stealthy," she replied. "She followed *you*, didn't she?"

"Yeah, how exactly did she manage that?"

"She's a fourteen-year-old girl with a crush. She could take down an entire army if it was standing between her and a cute boy."

I cringed. "Not cute."

"Rugged, then." She patted my arm teasingly. The touch made me pause. We both went silent, gazes tangling. Her eyes were a light blue gray, like water. She smelled like paint and vanilla and she was surprisingly easy company, even in this situation. She didn't chatter or cry or sigh when I looked in her direction. The perfect woman, clearly.

And where the hell had *that* come from?

Get your head in the game, idiot.

I stepped back. "We don't have much time."

"I should warn you," she said. "I'm not much of a fighter."

"How are you at running?"

"Pretty damn good when something scary-ass is chasing me."

I grinned. "Good." I grabbed her hand when she moved. "Careful. You'll end up in a snare trap."

She froze. "A what?"

"Bryn's parents are serious about their privacy and their safety. The snares and traps all around here are made with industrial-grade airplane cables and wires and they're big enough to hold an ancient vampire. They've even caught a few *Hel-Blar*. It wasn't pretty."

She made a face.

"Stay up in the trees," I suggested. "When you see a mark like this one, it means there's a snare below." I pointed to a barely perceptible silver line on the underside of a branch. "Green ones mean the trap is the next tree or clearing to the north." I turned my head quickly, pinpointing a scent. "Here they come."

Swearing, Sky scrambled up a tree. "How are you going to get them to this spot exactly?"

I grinned, wiping my own blood on the leaves. Then I pressed play on my latest voice mail message and set it on speaker. The sound quality was tinny but to a vampire on the hunt it may as well have been playing through a bullhorn. My mother's irate voice flooded the frozen forest. Mice scattered.

"Duncan Drake, you get your ass back here. I have told you a hundred times to stop protecting me."

I slipped on the nose plugs I'd taken from my bike satchel and waited. I felt like a garden spider about to feast on a flock of moths.

"Toss the phone up here," Sky whispered, and I obliged.

The Furies the others had been waiting for found us. The first of them ran at me so fast she may as well have been flying. Her white dress and white hair and white fangs blended into the snow. Her stake caught me in my already-raw wound.

"Son of a bitch." I grunted, kicking down hard along her shinbone. She tumbled, crying out in pain. Her leg gave out and I shoved her. She tumbled right into a deadfall trap. The hole was eight feet deep in the ground and narrow as a vertical tunnel. The walls were soaked with holy water. Climbing out was near impossible. She howled with rage.

The next Fury followed Sky, my mother's voice taunting them from her pocket. She was caught in an intricately hidden snare, the cable tightening around her ankle and flinging her up through the trees as though she'd been tossed from a trebuchet. She dangled uselessly, upside down, her fine silk dress around her ears.

A stake caught me to the left of my spine, pain searing through me like jagged teeth. I reached behind to pluck it loose, even as I pivoted to put a tree behind us. I leaped over a fallen trunk, which was actually another weight for a snare. The Fury followed until she tripped the wire and ended up hanging upside down next to her sister, shrieking. Sky led one into another snare, until it was starting to look like undead wind chimes dangling from the branches. My mother's voice continued to berate me. It was comforting. The Furies clearly didn't agree.

By the time we were done, there were seven would-be assassins trapped and snared. I waited for a while, straining to hear over the sounds of their hisses and curses. When I was certain there were no more of them sneaking up on us, I gave Sky the all-clear. She climbed back down, her eyes wide. "Is it always like this with your family?"

I grinned. "Yup."

I felt good, despite being poked by stakes. Adrenaline and the after-battle high was a potent combination. Add a pretty girl . . .

I probably shouldn't do it.

Hell with it.

SKY

He kissed me then, quick and hard.

It was all colors, cobalt blue, hunter green, red. His mouth slanted over mine, tasting and teasing. Our tongues tangled slowly, as if we had all the time in the world. And then he pulled away, green irises glowing around ink-black pupils. He ran his thumb along my lower lip.

"Well now," he said quietly, in that honest, direct way of his. "Isn't that interesting?"

I had to agree.

Or I would, once I figured out how to use words again. Everything was still a kaleidoscope inside my head.

And Miranda was scrambling down a rope ladder attached to the crow's nest. I put some distance between us. She'd have a temper tantrum right here in the forest surrounded with the psychotic undead if she caught us kissing. My lips were still tingling. I hoped I didn't have a goofy look on my face. I cleared my throat. Duncan's smoldering gaze wouldn't help. It set fire to all of the adrenaline still flooding through me.

Miranda landed clumsily and then turned on her heel, staring at the Furies. "Holy crap," she said. "Could that be any creepier?"

I eased her back so they couldn't see her through the pine needles and cedars to recognize her later. She resisted.

"Out of sight, kid," Duncan ordered, crowding us both into the shelter of a weeping cedar. She stepped back to my side meekly. She never obeyed orders like that for anyone else, not even Oliver.

"Are you just going to leave them here?" she whispered.

"Afraid so," Duncan replied. "It wouldn't be honorable to kill them."

"But they'd kill *you*."

"My point exactly." Though it looked like it rankled. "For now, it's enough to buy my family some time to get to safe territory. One of them will get free eventually and get the others out." He slipped a stake from his boot and tucked it into the scarred leather of his belt. "Let's get you back home."

"I can find the way," I said, even though I was hardly used to navigating in thick forest. Even if I could see the stars, I wouldn't know which direction was north. "You should find your family."

He just slid me a mild look. "I'll walk you back."

It was a quiet walk, our footsteps crunching through snowy layers of dead leaves. He reclaimed his bike from the bushes and escorted us to the edge of Chandramaa territory. He stayed well back from an arrow's reach.

"Watch your back," he said softly, his eyes saying the other things he couldn't say out loud. His scent was still on me, engine grease and pine.

I nodded. "Be careful."

"Sky?"

I glanced over my shoulder. "Yes?"

"I'll see you around." He flashed a quick grin before kicking his bike into high gear, tearing off through the ice-encrusted weeds. I turned back to Miranda, glad once again that I wasn't able to blush. I dragged her across the field, into the camp. She scowled at me, struggling to keep up. The growl of Duncan's bike faded.

"Did he kiss you?" she asked.

"What?"

"I think he did," Miranda said, dangerously close to pouting. "He was my friend first," she insisted. Her cheeks were red. She knew she was being absurd.

"Miranda, you're fourteen."

"So?" She was jogging to keep pace with me.

"He's twenty."

"So?"

"So, it's illegal and gross and we have enough to worry about."

"Like what?"

"Like the fact that you snuck out," Oliver interrupted smoothly as we headed straight for our tent, which was on the edge, by the crossroads. Torchlight gilded his pocket watch, the silver-gray streaks in his hair, the cold glitter of his smile. "I'm very disappointed in you, young lady."

Miranda slumped. "Sorry, Oliver."

"It's dangerous tonight," he continued ruthlessly. "And I'd hoped I could trust you to act as a woman, not a child. You know better than this."

"Sorry," she said again. "I just . . ."

He pointed to the tent. "I don't want to hear it," he said. "Inside. Now."

She slunk through the opening. I ducked inside behind her and dropped down to sit on a threadbare footstool, already wondering how I would capture Duncan on paper. Charcoal, maybe. Lots of shadows. Miranda curled up by the coal heater we'd put in to keep her warm. Her arms were crossed over her chest.

"Is Duncan Drake worth getting grounded over?" I asked.

All the chastised repentance bled out of her. Her smile was brief, dreamy. She sighed. "Totally."

I had to agree.

Read the Drake Chronicles
from the beginning . . .

Seven handsome brothers. Two best friends.
One captivating story.

Loved the Drakes? Thirsty for more vampire action?

Then sink your teeth into this breathtaking bind-up of novellas

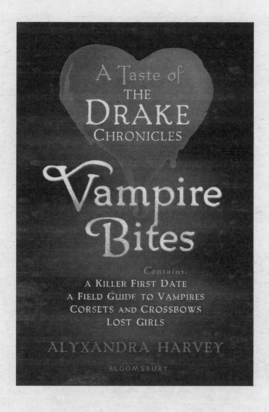

Three deliciously dark, romantic adventures, featuring some of your favourite characters from the series. Plus the ultimate guide to Violet Hill's vampires – to help you catch a handsome Drake brother of your own!

Prepare to be transported to Faery,
where nothing is as it seems ...

Catch up with the latest news and giveaways
from Alyxandra Harvey at
AlyxandraHarveyAuthor and
www.alyxandraharvey.com

MEET

ALYXANDRA HARVEY

Alyxandra Harvey was born in Montreal, Canada, during an ice storm, the day after Christmas. Before becoming a writer, Alyx worked as a volunteer for an archaeologist, cleaning and cataloguing bits of pottery and bones in a dark basement in Toronto, and as a jewellery designer. She even owned her own bead shop. But writing has always been Alyx's first love. She is now the author of *Haunting Violet*, *Stolen Away* and the Drake Chronicles series. Alyx likes medieval dresses and tattoos and has been accused of being born in the wrong century – except that she really likes running water, women's rights and ice cream. She lives in an old Victorian farmhouse in Ontario, Canada, with her husband, her dogs and a few resident ghosts. To find out more, read on . . .

What are your three favourite books, and why?
Pride and Prejudice, Jane Austen. Mr Darcy! Need I say more? Also, Elizabeth Bennet is my hero. She's smart and sassy and gets to wear a pelisse. I could do without the bonnet though.

The Wood Wife, Terri Windling. Beautiful, magical, poetic.
The Shadowy Horses, Susanna Kearsley. Historical, atmospheric, lovely.

What was your favourite book when you were a child?
Jane Eyre, Charlotte Brontë (I have a dog named Brontë)
Mists of Avalon, Marion Zimmer Bradley
Memory and Dream, Charles de Lint (in uni)

What book do you wish you had written?
The Wood Wife by Terri Windling.

When did you start writing?
Family legend says I started to write seriously around age 9 on a vacation where a friend of the family suggested I write a short story because I was very very bored and in need of distracting. I suspect I was also being very very annoying.

Who or what was your biggest influence in deciding to become a writer?
I don't remember ever not wanting to be a writer. I've been influenced by Jane Austen, the Brontë Sisters, the Romantic Poets, the Pre-Raphaelites, mythology and ancient history.

What inspired you to write the Drake Chronicles?
The story popped into my head as I was thinking of a way to retell the Snow White fairy tale. I wanted it to be fun and slightly snarky,

not to take itself too seriously, but to have layers to the story at the same time. And I like playing with vampires. I can indulge in a little historical fiction, some corsets, some magic and some girls who can kick serious butt.

Solange, Lucy, Isabeau and the other girls in your books are totally kick-butt characters. Are you?
Oooh good question! I'm not a violent person and though I do like to play with swords, I'd be more likely to stab myself in the foot. But when I draw a line, I'm pretty fierce. (cue ominous music)

If you could live in any time period, what would it be and why?
I would especially like to visit Regency England, circa 1815. I'd like to run around in a pelisse and flirt with handsome men wearing cravats. Don't worry, my husband is perfectly aware of this rather odd quirk in my character. :)

I'd also like to drop in to Iron Age Celtic Britain, England late 1100's, Ancient Egypt, Victorian London (and Yorkshire to meet the Brontës), Quebec around 1630 (to see my ancestors!) . . . I'd also kind of like to kick Henry VIII in the shins and then vanish back home safely before he could cut off my head. Is that so wrong?

If someone wanted to be a writer what would be your number one tip for them?
Read, read, read. Write, write, write. Carry a notebook. Don't give up! That last one. Don't give up! Two years after my first novel was

published, I received a delayed rejection for it from a different publisher.

Is there any particular routine involved in your writing process (favourite pen, lucky charm, special jumper)?
I try and write every day, even if it's just one page. It's easier to keep the flow going than to pick it up again after a week off.

I tend to read over what I've written during the day that night and then think about the next scene as I fall asleep. If I'm stuck I'll take a nap – or at least lie down. This either indicates that my muses like dark and quiet or that I'm naturally lazy.

Sometimes atmosphere is required: candles, incense, music (often Baroque. Lyrics are too distracting). Mostly I try not to get too precious about it. I love little rituals and amulets but I'd hate to think I'd be lost if I accidentally set my favourite pen on fire.

Do you want to know more? Then catch up with Alyx
on her blog at **www.alyxandraharvey.com**